Destined

Also by Patricia Haley

Destined

PATRICIA HALEY

G

GALLERY BOOKS

NEW YORK   LONDON   TORONTO   SYDNEY

G

GALLERY BOOKS
A Division of Simon & Schuster, Inc.
1230 Avenue of the Americas
New York, NY 10020

First Gallery Books trade paperback edition June 2010

GALLERY BOOKS and colophon are registered trademarks of
Simon & Schuster, Inc.

For information about special discounts for bulk purchases,
please contact Simon & Schuster Special Sales at 1-866-506-1949
or business@simonandschuster.com.

The Simon & Schuster Speakers Bureau can bring authors to your live
event. For more information or to book an event contact the
Simon & Schuster Speakers Bureau at 1-866-248-3049
or visit our website at www.simonspeakers.com.

Designed by Carla Jayne Little

Manufactured in the United States of America

10 9 8 7 6 5 4 3 2 1

Library of Congress Cataloging-in-Publication Data is available.

ISBN 978-1-4165-8063-8
ISBN 978-1-4165-8351-6 (ebook)

Destined is dedicated to special family members who've gone on to glory in the past year, but whose zest for life and love for family will always be remembered as an inspiration.

Uncle Willie David Haley
Aunt Hilda Mae Haley Handford
Demetri "Meechie" Miller, Sr.
and
Treva Ann Tenner

When anxiety was great within me,
your consolation brought joy to my soul.

—Psalm 94:19

Prologue

Heartache and disappointment were his constant companions. Once the recommendation was handed down from his so-called father, the almighty Dave Mitchell, his baby brother, Joel, was running the company. Twenty-three years old and barely out of diapers and teething rings. Don sat quietly with no retort, unlike his mother, Madeline. He slowly packed his belongings, avoiding eye contact with the board members as they scattered from the room with his mother nipping at their heels.

The decision was one of many rips in the veil of affection he'd worked so hard to mend. This time he wasn't four years old, crying himself to sleep for a father who now had a different home. He was a thirty-one-year-old man seeking only respect, since his father's love continued to elude him.

His mother came back into the room after chasing everyone else away. "Mother, it's done," he said while fumbling with the stack of papers in his portfolio. "Dave Mitchell made his choice and it wasn't me." He braced both hands against the mahogany table and let his head bow with eyes closed. "What did I expect?"

"Don't you worry," she consoled. "I'm not going to stand for this. You are the rightful heir to your father's ministry. Now that

DMI is worth more than a billion dollars, your father's little con-
niving, gold-digging wife wants it, too. I don't know what your father was thinking, but when I'm through, you'll be in charge.
That's a promise, if it's the last thing I do. I will not lose to her, not
again, not without a fight. I mean a real war this time." Her voice
faded for a second but Don knew she was putting on a brave face,
guarded by a tough disposition. Others saw his mother as a
shrewd businesswoman, but his image of her was padded by the
countless childhood memories he had of her crying when she
thought no one was looking. Loss after loss spread over two decades was bound to wear her down.

"Don, don't you worry. I'll take care of this. Your father has to
answer to me," she said, pausing for a moment, regaining strength
in her voice. "He has to do right by at least one of my children.
There's no way I'm going to stand by and let that woman and your
father destroy you. It won't happen."

Steering clear of the conversation surrounding his siblings was
the best approach to take with his mother, given the fresh layer of
defeat she was experiencing yet again at the hands of Dave and
Sherry Mitchell. "Mother, don't bother." Every time there was
peace and a chance for his mother to consider releasing the anger
she harbored about the divorce, something new came up to nurse
her bitterness—years of fresh cuts on an old scab.

Don's heart sank deeper, which he didn't think possible. Madeline was a committed and nurturing mother. He wanted her, at
sixty-two, to begin living her life outside the clutches of bitterness,
but he didn't know how to help her make the transition when he
couldn't help himself.

She squeezed his shoulder tight and pushed her cheek next to
his.

Don blew out a deep breath as he watched his mother leave the
boardroom. He wanted someone to do something, but in the end
he knew no one could. No sense fretting any longer. Don packed
up and left the room, semidazed. He clashed into Joel upon entering the hallway.

"Good, you're still here." Joel extended his hand to Don. "I know this is awkward but I look forward to us working together and maybe getting to know each other better," he said. "I can learn a lot from you," he said jovially.

Don didn't extend his hand. There wasn't much to say.

The enthusiasm in Joel's eyes fizzled. Maybe he was shocked and remorseful or maybe he really was that selfish, spoiled-rotten kid who was good at pretending to be sincere when it benefited him. Either way, Don would maintain a semblance of dignity. He planted his feet solidly, pleading with his soul not to let an inkling of his disappointment be exposed, not running the risk of giving Joel extra gratification.

"I had nothing to do with this decision. This came from our father," Joel said with his back stiffening. "For whatever reason, he feels that this is the way to go. Apparently he's prayed about it and feels like this is what God wants him to do. I didn't ask for the role. As a matter of fact, I asked Dad to reconsider and let you take the lead."

"Why would he do that? You're the new man in charge," Don said, and let the realization sink in. "Although I'm the oldest and the most legitimate."

Joel took a step back.

Don felt good letting the wind out of the chosen one's sails. The controversy surrounding their father leaving his wife to marry the much younger secretary wasn't easily forgotten. Twenty-five years had passed and the fallout remained raw. The innuendos about Joel's legitimacy must have stirred a hornet's nest, judging by the cutting look he was giving Don. It seemed best to calm the brooding waters before the awkward conversation got out of hand.

Conscious of escalating the tension, Don quickly acted to diffuse it. "If our father and Sherry deem you the most suited to run DMI, then that's the way it is."

"Leave my mother out of this."

"How can I?" Her reign as the other Mrs. Dave Mitchell had led to the perpetual and merciless annihilation of Don's family. Rehashing the past with his father's other son was a waste of time.

Before Joel became too defensive, Don shifted the focus back to the business. "Regardless, I'm willing to be a team player." He heard the words squeak through his teeth and wondered from where they'd come. If only they were true. Don was a half-smashed bug under Joel's feet, hoping the crushing weight would leave enough ego intact for him to crawl away, balancing a load of dejection on his back. This wasn't his brother. Joel was no more than an unwanted relative wedged into his world. Don conjured up as much gratitude as his pride would allow and slung it at his father's son.

"Don," Joel raised his voice and spewed, "I came to you with open arms and this is what I get from you?" He scowled. "You were welcome to stay, so long as you left my mother out of this, but that doesn't seem to be the case."

"What do you mean?" Don said, taking a step back this time. His father and Abigail, the consummate and faithful assistant, were gingerly moving toward them.

"I don't think you need to be around here."

"What?" He chuckled. "You have to be joking."

"I'm not," Joel said, staring into Don's eyes.

"Who do you think you are? My mother built this ministry. Your mother just stepped in." Abigail and Dad were coming close.

"Come on, is that the best you can do?" Joel said.

The passive approach wasn't working. Don had to demand that his disapproval remain harnessed. His glaring eyes clashed with Joel's in the center of the hallway before he began walking away, praying every step of the way that his burning distress would never graze the surface. What was the point? Hating his half brother for always getting the best couldn't come close to alleviating his rage.

He burst down the hallway seeking an exit, without speaking a single word to his father. Everything had been said.

Dad called out for Don, as he stood on his cane, letting his gaze limp around the room. Abigail went after Don. Joel didn't budge.

"What happened?" Dad asked, clearly shaken by the outrage of his sons.

"I had to fire him. I didn't want to, but what could I do?"

"He's your brother," Dad said, barely audible, as Don hustled down the corridor.

"And Sherry is my mother. I have to protect her. Let's face it, Don hates me and Mom. Dad, I know this isn't what you wanted to happen, but he had to go. If this company is going to succeed under my leadership, I have to cut out anything and anyone who wants to undermine me and your vision," he said, hesitating. "That includes family."

"Son, my heart is heavy. Don't give the enemy an opportunity to destroy our family or the ministry any further."

Don stood outside, looking but not seeing beyond his dilemma. He peered into the early evening autumn sky, watching the sun dip behind the tiny clouds, appearing unable to maintain its rightful position in the forefront. Abigail was gone. She'd followed him in a gracious attempt to comfort him. Generally her presence was sufficient to turn his cloudy days into sunny ones. The blow he'd sustained from his father and Joel were too powerful even for Abigail's healing touch. The sun's rays finally succumbed to the resistance and faded behind the baby clouds, offering no warmth for his chilled heart. The reality of his darkness set in. He dashed to his car determined to get away, as far away as possible.

chapter

1

"We don't have anyone else to turn to," Abigail said. "I shouldn't ask, but I truly need you to come home."

Her plea sailed across the miles, resonating with him. Don fed on the tranquil ambiance of Cape Town, peering from his office window into the majestic rich blue sky carpeted by the bay, which was generally still warm this early into the year. Solitude had suited him well. His small leadership training company was thriving. After fleeing from Detroit, Don poured his energy and wit into LTI, determined to make it a success without David Mitchell or DMI influence. His company didn't offer extravagant accommodations, but the breathtaking view of Table Mountain from any window seemed to keep morale soaring.

Two years and eleven months since he'd set foot in South Africa, and not a day wasted. Sanity was slow coming and forgiveness even slower, but he'd managed somehow to reach this place of peace, a place that seemed unattainable at the onset of his escape from Detroit, from the pit of his hell, the place he used to call home. Keeping a safe distance from the Mitchell drama was wise, but Abigail's plea was difficult to discount. Don recalled telling her that no matter where he was in the world, they would only be a phone call apart. He intended to honor his promise, especially since she hadn't asked him for anything before now. He wanted to say yes without hesitation, but the power of tranquility wouldn't let him hastily commit. "Why do I need to come back to Detroit? Can I help you from here?"

Abigail paused and he could sense the distress in her words. "I don't think so. We need you here, me and your mother. We're in big trouble with the company. I really believe Joel has gone too far with this merger and has driven DMI into serious financial instability."

"Is it that bad?"

"Worse. I'm not even doing it justice. We're in serious trouble and you're the only one who can help. You have to take over the CEO position, that's the only way we will have a shot at salvaging DMI." There was a time when no challenge, number of miles, or situation was large enough to keep him from getting to Abigail. But the time was a while ago. Life, Joel, and circumstances had eroded the pull but hadn't completely dissolved his affection for her.

"Your mother is calling an emergency board meeting in two days. I'm counting on a miracle. If you can get your sister's stock shares, your mother and I will give you ours. Combined, you'll have the majority."

"An easy ride into the CEO position?" A role he once earnestly sought, a dream that had been stomped out. The automatic elation wasn't there. He was smart enough not to get lured into the CEO illusion.

"You got it. Are you up for the challenge? Can we count on you to help us?"

"It's a huge request."

"But you're the only one that I can ask for help."

He wanted to say no flat out, but he couldn't do that to Abigail, not easily. "I don't know. I'll have to seriously think about it."

"Don't take too long. You'll need to leave soon if you plan to be here in time. I'm praying that you say yes."

"We'll see. I'll think about it and give you a call back later today," he said, closing out the conversation and clicking off the speakerphone button. He let his jumbled thoughts wander. The excruciating ache deep in his heart had subsided to a dull manageable pain. There wasn't an urgency to dig into the closed wound by hopping a plane to Detroit without absolute certainty that there was no other way to help.

The melodious voice interrupted him, breaking his gaze across the ocean. Naledi graced the room with the blended hue of her skin capturing the essence of Africa, India, and Europe. Even her accent was perfectly blended with a heavy dose of the local dialect and a distinctive sprinkling of French. After twenty-three months together, he was as equally mesmerized by her today as he was when they'd met. He looked up to catch a quick glimpse of her standing at his office door and was comforted. She renewed his faith in the possibility of long-lasting commitment. Disappointment and heartache would no longer hold him captive. Don beckoned for her to come in.

"We must make a visit to Unilever in their Paris office. Have a look at your diary and let me know what dates are good." Naledi said.

Images of Detroit and his deceased father's struggling ministry, DMI, whisked in like a tsunami, hindering his ability to concentrate on what Naledi was saying. He beckoned for her to take a seat. "You might have to take the trip to Paris for me." That part was easy, asking her to fill in for him. He'd grown to rely heavily on her loyalty and aptitude, a certainty that had long passed from his old friend in Detroit. Abigail belonged to DMI and to his brother, the core of his ache. *Shake it off,* he thought. Naledi looked puzzled. "I might have to go home," he told her.

"I see; it has been a time since your last visit. Will you be there one week?"

"I'm not sure, maybe a day, maybe a week, maybe a month," he said, rearing back in the chair, tapping his fingers together. "If I go, and that's a big if, I'll be there as long as it takes, I guess," he said, not interested in conveying false confidence. He felt compelled but not fully devoted to saving his father's company from the peril his brother had created. The peace he languished so freely was a direct result of cutting the ties with Detroit and building his own world. Jumping back into the fray wasn't generating a warm sensation. Yet, the only two people he cared about in Detroit were seeking his help. His head, which was responsible for rational thinking, wasn't aligned with his heart, which was pushing him toward shark-infested waters to save a drowning company.

"I do hope that all is well with your family."

Don chuckled. "My family is never completely well. There's always something wrong with somebody." He chuckled more. "It's the Mitchell way." The translation into terms Naledi could understand would be too much, so he didn't bother. Not because she was South African, more so because she was from a close family and couldn't possibly understand his.

"My friend Abigail pleaded with me to return to the States to fix a problem with DMI. Against my better judgment, I might have to go."

"If you're not comfortable going, why should you go?"

"I've asked myself the same question a thousand times and keep getting the same answer—*maybe*. Abigail wouldn't ask unless it was critical. I can't tell her no. On the other hand, I can't say yes," he said clasping his hands behind his neck and rearing back in the chair, then realizing no position would minimize his discomfort. "I'm not sure what I have to do there or how long it will take but I have to make a decision. I'd have to leave tonight or early tomorrow morning." If he waited a single day, he'd probably not get involved at all.

Naledi kept silent initially, then said, "Go for as long as you must. I will take care of matters here. Don't worry; you can rely on me."

He already knew that. Don stood to give her a hug. At least in one corner of the world, life was stable for him, finally.

Naledi left and Don reclaimed the seat at his desk. No sense putting off the inevitable. The bridge to Michigan had to be mended if there was to be any chance at success. Abigail was hoping for a miracle. Maybe he could pull one off without having to board a plane. He flipped through his phone directory, reaching the letter *M*. It had been so long since he and Joel had spoken that the number had long left his memory. In thinking about it, the number may not have ever been in his long-term mental database. Joel was his brother by blood, at least the Mitchell portion, and that was the extent of the connection. Neither had tried to make the forced fit more than it was. But today he dialed the phone, recognizing that working together was the most ideal path to saving a company that Joel had driven to the brink of bankruptcy, according to Abigail.

Several rings and Joel was on the line. Words didn't immediately spring forward. Finally Don was able to string a thought together, void of substantial resentment. "This is Don." Silence hovered, neither taking the next step until Don reflected on his mission. If he could get Joel to accept outside help with managing the company, Don could be spared the dilemma of going to Detroit. "It's been a long time, little brother."

"It has been," Joel said, offering no more.

"Look, I'm not calling to make small talk. Let me get right to business. I understand that DMI is going through a financial crisis with your merger and there might be a way for me to help."

"DMI is fine and has been since I've been CEO. I don't know what your mother has told you," Joel said, letting the words roll off with a sharp bite, "but this company has done better under my leadership than it ever did with my father."

"Our father," Don interjected.

"Wow, that's interesting coming from you, someone who wanted nothing to do with our father or our company when you left. I'm curious as to why it is that all of a sudden you care one iota about DMI. We're doing fine."

Don refused to feed into the negativity. He'd lived that existence for a long time and was free. He wasn't going back to the constant bickering, but Abigail's plea wouldn't be silenced. If she said DMI was in trouble, it was in trouble. "I'm not trying to resurrect our differences. This isn't about you or me. This is about retaining the company that our father started. I was asked to help, and I'm offering my support."

"Who asked you?" Joel said, surprisingly calm. "Your mother?"

"Actually, it was Abigail." A name Don was certain Joel didn't expect to hear. Her level of unwavering devotion to Joel had been difficult for Don, but time had created a scar of acceptance. Joel said nothing. "She believes I can help. So, here I am."

"Thanks for the offer, but I have DMI under control. You can keep all your focus on handling your business in South Africa and I'll take care of the U.S."

"Are you sure?" Don asked, refusing to give up so easily.

"One hundred percent."

"Then I guess that's that."

"I guess it is," Joel said, maintaining the same edge in his tone.

The good-bye was abrupt. Don held the receiver, not knowing what he'd expected to happen with the call. Of course Joel wasn't going to hand over the reins of DMI to someone who would come in and tell him what to do. No CEO would. Don got that. His involvement would face opposition. Joel had won the last round decisively. Don grappled with the request that had come from a woman who could have been his wife had Joel not stolen her affection and discarded it along his path of recklessness. Joel's pattern was consistent with women and with DMI, a company their father didn't deem Don worthy of inheriting although he was the oldest. He held a master's degree in business, and possessed ten years of experience at the time the decision was made. While Joel had barely completed college and had one or two fragmented years of experience.

Maybe the day had come for Don to face his demons and return to Detroit, to grapple with DMI, to face his brother, to take a stand in the place where he was being drawn by his bond with Abigail, to deal with the suppressed guilt about his mother's predicament, or his passive frustration with God. He wasn't certain what the most compelling factor was in this instance. Don returned the phone receiver to its base long enough to get his sister's number. Hopefully Abigail's miracle was on the other end of the call. Nothing less could move his sister, Tamara, to action. Getting her to agree to do the unthinkable and sign her stock ownership over to Don was impossible. If by some miracle she was on board, he could take control of the company and be empowered to get DMI back on track quickly so that he could regain his solitude. Attempting to work with Joel had failed. Going in by force united with Tamara and Mother was the next option but not his preference. Truth was, he wasn't up for an all-out battle. The notion trampled around in his thoughts, sparking an undesirable feeling. The voice that was directing him along this path better belong to God, otherwise Don might as well jab the dagger into his own gut and accelerate his demise.

chapter

2

Joel stood in his office, peering out the window. The conversation with Don two days ago wouldn't vanish. There was a time when getting a call from his big brother would have been a joy. So much animosity, too much time and rejection had mounted. Who did Don think he was calling to help fix DMI? It wasn't broken. Nobody had given Joel a fighting chance when he was named CEO. He hadn't robbed Don of the job. That was purely their father's choice. Once the decision was made, Joel dedicated his life to learning the business, obtaining wisdom, and mastering the CEO role. Realizing that his bachelor's degree in economics was insufficient, he aggressively pursued an array of executive management programs weekend after weekend, packing in the knowledge. People saw him as someone gaining wisdom overnight, unaware of how hard he worked to obtain it. He moved to the desk and pounded his knuckles lightly.

No one could deny that DMI had tripled in sales under his watch. It was him, not his father, who was finally taking the company international with the pending merger. Still, it wasn't sufficient to please the naysayers. He was the unrecognized child of Dave Mitchell, questioned from birth, and nothing he'd ever do could overshadow the stigma. Don's word left no lingering sting. Joel had perfected that technique from his childhood. His training came from growing up as the only child with half brothers and sisters who didn't acknowledge him. He'd spent his whole life living in the shadows of his father's other children, the ones deemed legitimate. He had value and he refused to let anything stop him from proving it. After he achieved his goal, there would be no one on earth who could deny his worth as a bona fide Mitchell, the deserving keeper of his father's legacy. Don was not an issue, but having Abigail speak ill of him stung. Making DMI a success was his main priority, and he needed her more now than ever. He went to her office determined to regain her trust.

Joel stood in Abigail's office, close enough for her to be sucked in by the scent of his distinctly bold cologne and the allure of his hypnotic words. "I got a call from Don."

"Really," she said, not sure how much he knew of her call to Don.

"I have to admit, I was quite surprised," he said placing his foot on the corner of her couch and resting his hand on his thigh. "He seems to think that you want his help in rescuing DMI from the merger and from me, too, I guess."

The road with Joel was rocky, but she didn't want to stir ill will with him. She chose her words carefully, separating emotion from business. "It's no secret where I stand."

"As the leader in this ministry, my first allegiance is to keeping the doors open for business and maintaining a vision," he said.

"You can't consider this a ministry anymore. The purpose of a ministry is to help others. The only person you seem to be helping is you. Where's your allegiance to the rest of us?"

"Where's your allegiance to me?" he pushed back.

She shot a piercing gaze at him that was sure to burn a hole in his retina if maintained too long. Commitment wasn't a subject she cared to address with him. There wasn't ample time in the year.

"What will it take for you to change your mind?" he asked. Like being in a trance, she had to shake free and keep focused. She realized it was a nearly impossible task as he continued. "I need you, Abigail, like I've never needed you before. I don't care what the rest of the executive team does, but you matter to me. I can't pull this merger off without your support." He took her hand. "We're a team, a good team, and you know it. Nothing or nobody can stop the two of us when we're united."

She snatched her hand back, refusing to be sucked in again as she'd so easily been throughout most of their partnership, relationship, or whatever the right term was for what they used to be. Maybe one day she'd be able to figure it out, sometime later, after it didn't hurt as much. "Let's be honest, you don't need me. Aren't you planning to get married?" He didn't respond. "Like I said, you don't need me." He'd betrayed her, but the four-letter word "hate" would never enter her heart when it came to Joel. With her reaching out for Don's help, Joel would probably chalk up her decision to join the opposing management team as betrayal or revenge, but she knew better. As the executive senior vice president, she had an obligation to protect the integrity of DMI. She'd been in denial too long. The company was headed in the wrong direction with Joel at the helm. It was time for action. Her mind spoke as her passion remained silent. "Your father founded DMI on religious principles. Those principles have always been our foundation. I can't support your decision to merge with a company that has different principles than ours."

"What's the big deal?" he said, leaping to his feet and pacing the room with his hands brushing across his head. Abigail noticed an elevation in his voice that she didn't typically hear from Joel. He was always calm and controlled. "Who cares what religion they practice? Our focus is on buying a stable company that happens to have an extensive base of international customers. We have to concentrate on the business, not some holy-rolly diversion."

She could see that the man standing in her office was Joel. The voice was recognizable, but that was the only familiar characteristic. His agitated tone and lackadaisical view about religion rendered him a stranger, making her argument easier to defend. "You're right, this isn't about religion. This is about maintaining a Godly foundation in this ministry, one that your father built," she said, feeling a tinge of frustration. "He sought God for direction and ran DMI accordingly. You did, too, at first. I don't know what's happened to you, Joel. You're scaring me."

"Why, because I'm willing to step out of the shadows of my father and run this company with leadership and my own vision? My father did okay, but you know DMI has never been as profitable and worth nearly as much until I took over. You have to give me that."

"Okay, fine. I agree with you. Your statement was true up until six months ago, but not now. We're losing customers." What Joel was losing was far worse and more important to her—his perspective.

"So what? We have so many customers that losing a few won't matter. Besides, once we merge with Harmonious Energy, we'll quadruple the few shortsighted customers that have left. If they don't want to be a part of an award-winning international team, so be it," he said, flailing his hand haphazardly into the air.

When Joel was first chosen to be CEO, he had had an unquenchable thirst for wisdom. From that time on, he was unstoppable and undeniably brilliant in the boardroom, with his ideas, people skills, vision, and way of motivating the team. DMI days were amazing back when Joel was spiritually grounded. After Joel excluded God from his way of life, morale had spiraled downward in the office.

"Joel, it's not too late to drop this merger. Tell Mr. Musar Bengali we've changed our minds. We can put this mistake behind us, rally together, and get this company back on track." There was a time not so long ago when the strength and uniqueness of their bond would have been adequate to sway this decision. The man standing before her was not that man, the one whose soul used to dance with hers daily, tiptoed jointly around pitfalls, and leaped over obstacles together. This dance he had to do alone. She wouldn't dishonor the memory of Dave Mitchell, her mentor and the closest image of a father she'd known, by collaborating with Joel on a doomed strategy. There wasn't much hope of changing Joel's mind since he was adamant about the deal, but she had to try one last time. "If you won't reconsider for me, think about your father. He dedicated his life to building this ministry. He instructed us to keep our spiritual convictions in the forefront of this ministry and, most important, he told you never to sell off pieces. If you merge with Harmonious Energy, you'll have to sell off the West Coast division, and you know your father would roll over in his grave."

Without hesitation he said, "I'm in charge, not my father. Like you said, he's in the grave. I'm the one running this place. I'm doing what's best for DMI."

"Same here. I'm going to do what's best for DMI, and for me, too, for a change. How about that?"

"And what does that mean? Is there something you're trying to tell me? Normally I wouldn't have to ask, but you and everybody else are acting weird lately," he said, stroking his chin a couple of times and staring past her. "I don't know who to trust around here. What's this emergency board meeting about anyway? Do you know?"

She shrugged her shoulders. "I'm as curious as you are." She couldn't tell him about the plan to vote him out and put Don in charge. It had to be a total surprise if the management team had any chance of being successful. Joel was smart and not easily defeated. Awkward as she felt, Abigail was resolute in supporting the coup against Joel and salvaging Dave Mitchell International, otherwise DMI didn't have a chance.

"Something is up. I'm sure of it. Madeline must have something up her sleeve. My dear old stepmother refuses to give up." Joel waved off the notion of her pulling off a strike against him. "She's the least of my problems, not a threat. Although I'm sure it will be entertaining, whatever it is she has planned."

His disposition lightened as he spoke of Madeline, clearly not concerned about an attack from her. Abigail wasn't sure his cavalier attitude was justified. Madeline was not one to be taken lightly. She hadn't gotten over the chain of events, and felt that her children had been slighted again with favoritism going to Dave's second wife, Sherry, and her only child. Madeline was determined to correct what she perceived to be a lapse in Dave's judgment. For Joel to discount her was a lapse in his.

"I have to run over to the library before the board meeting." He took the phone out of his suit coat pocket and waved it in the air. "Call me when you change your mind about the merger."

She waved her phone in the air. "Call me when you change your mind about the marriage."

He smirked as only Joel could do and waved the phone again. "I'll see you at the meeting."

chapter

3

Adrenaline surged through his veins, threatening to explode. Don was woozy standing in the lobby. When he had landed in South Africa three years ago, he was determined never to set foot in DMI again, maybe Detroit, but definitely not in the doors of his father's precious company. The twenty-two-hour flight to Detroit, with a brief stop in France, hadn't settled his nerves. He was humbled, reflecting on the renewed faith God had given him. The compelling mix of purpose, forgiveness, and unconditional love brewed a powerful but delicate concoction. Against every fiber in his body, he was standing in the lobby. Any tension would threaten to knock the concoction out of balance and cause an eruption, driving him back to the sanctum of home, away from here.

"Are you sure you're ready to do this?" he asked his sister.

"I'm not sure, but I'm willing to do this for you," she said, "so long as I don't have to see Mother. I'm definitely not ready for a family reunion."

"She'd love to see you, Tamara, you understand that."

"Maybe one day, but not today. If it's okay with you, I'd like to sign my stock over to you and jump on the first flight back to Monte Carlo. I'd like to be home tomorrow morning."

Don shook his head in affirmation but refused to accept a response of no. They embraced, regrouped, and approached the security desk. "Don Mitchell and Tamara Mitchell are here to see Attorney Ryan."

"Of course, Mr. Mitchell, it's good to see you," the guard said. "You don't have to sign in with us. Feel free to go right up."

"I don't want to go upstairs," Tamara said, frantically waving her hands. "I don't want to run into Mother. I can't." Don gently pulled her away from the desk and off to the side. "One look at me and she'll feel guilty about my rape. She'll want to yank me back to seventeen and relive those days to fix what's unfixable."

"You know Mother and how much she loves us. Sometimes she goes overboard, but she means well."

"I don't deny that, but I can't take the smothering. Those four years after the rape were the worst years of my life. I couldn't breathe with Mother hovering. If I'd stayed here, I would have died, too. That's why I'm on one continent and she's on another. That works best for my sanity," she said in rapid fire.

"How much more time do you think you'll need?"

"Don't know. I'm taking it a minute at a time. That's the most I can handle," she said, appearing to get agitated again. "Believe it or not, I live a full life over there. I'm pursuing my writing, my art, and my music. I'm a totally different person there, alive. In Michigan, I'm a dead bird waiting for the shameful vultures of the past to pick my bones. No thank you. I'm staying there."

Don appreciated her candor and resilience. She could have gotten lost in the darkness after being attacked in the safest place on earth, her home. He'd never forgotten waking up on Tamara's twenty-first birthday with a panicked call from his mother telling him Tamara was gone. A note was the only link she'd left between them and her. She deserved time and distance to rebuild, but fourteen years was a long time. It had only taken Don three years to rebuild his life, but he certainly wasn't going to stand in judgment because it was taking her much longer. Her reality wasn't his. "Okay, okay, it's all right," he assured her. Don stepped back over to the guard desk. "Can you please call Attorney Ryan and ask him to meet us in the lobby?"

"I'll let him know you're here."

"This is your last chance. You can take your stock and run back to Europe, and Mother won't ever know you were here," he told her, not really wanting her to take him up on the offer.

"I'm tempted, believe me, I'm very tempted, but, honestly, this isn't quite as awful as I was expecting." She initiated the hug this time, not as shaken as she was a minute ago.

"Excuse me, Mr. Mitchell, Attorney Ryan will be right down," the guard told them.

Don spun around the lobby in slow motion.

"And to think, you will be the new CEO before the day is over," Tamara said.

"Hopefully as soon as the board meeting is over, which is in about three hours," Don said, peering at his watch. "But as crazy as this family is, I'm not counting my chickens before they're hatched. This whole plan that Mother has concocted could fall apart at the last minute, like the countless other failed tactics she's tried ever since Father made Joel CEO. She refuses to let Joel have the company. With the questionable business decisions he's made recently, I guess she was right all along in questioning his ability to run the company."

"Quite frankly, I couldn't care less about DMI, or . . ." she said and stopped.

"Or the family, is what you were going to say." She winced. "It's okay," he said, placing his arms around her shoulders. "Like I said, this family is crazy. Our father definitely has to be put in that category. Why would he require you to physically be in this building in order to sign over your stock? I don't know what that's about." Don wouldn't dare raise the topic, but he knew Tamara's distance had been equally directed toward both parents. Mother seemed to get the brunt because she did more pushing. Dave Mitchell had an irritating way of accepting what he couldn't change and shifting his focus to what he could. A noble gesture in theory wasn't so great for those on the other end, which Don learned firsthand.

"Well, Dad may have gotten me here, but I'm not staying," she said, peering out the plate-glass windows and honning in on the cab waiting out front.

Having his sister within arm's reach was going to be short lived, but no less gratifying. "Mother is going to burst a blood vessel when she finds out you're home."

"I'm not home," Tamara said, shaking her index finger at him. "Monaco is home."

"Uh-huh, I said the exact same thing when I moved to South Africa and look where I am," he said, stretching his arms wide. "I'm not sure where my heart is, but this is where I am for now."

A couple of jovial people from the training team and one from the mailroom got off the elevator. Don immediately recognized them.

"We heard you were in the building. Welcome back, it's good to see you," they told Don, each offering their own greeting and vigorous handshake. Tamara had been gone so long that the employees didn't recognize her as Dave Mitchell's only daughter, but when the people swarmed, Don sensed her discomfort. In the midst of the well-wishes, Don heard his cell phone ring and extracted it from his pocket. "It's Mother," he told Tamara. A cloud of panic hovered over his sister, ready to erupt. He took her hand and answered the phone with the other.

"Where are you?" Mother asked. "I've been trying to get in touch with you for hours. You know the board meeting is in less than three hours? Please tell me that your plane has landed and that you're in Detroit."

As they talked, Attorney Ryan arrived in the lobby and extended greetings. "I have a room reserved upstairs. Please come with me."

"No!" Tamara belted out. Her hands were moving faster than her words. "I'd like to sign the papers right here if it's okay with you. I have a cab waiting and a plane to catch."

"This is too open. There are too many employees around."

Don juggled Madeline on the phone while staying engaged in the dialogue between Tamara and Attorney Ryan.

"It's right here or nowhere," she demanded.

"No problem," their father's estate attorney said, and commandeered a coffee table and small sitting area with the documents. He used the folder to cover 85 percent of the legal-sized paper. Not much more than the signature line was exposed.

They were within minutes of completing what had seemed like two impossible feats a month ago, having Tamara in the U.S. and assuming the CEO role. Don was both overwhelmed and woozy again.

"Who is that in the background?"

"Attorney Ryan and Tamara are signing the papers."

"Are you here in the building?" Madeline shouted with excitement impossible to contain.

"Yes, we are, Mother," he said, keeping an eye on Tamara.

"I'm on my way. Are you in one of the guest offices on the third floor?"

"No, we're in the lobby, but don't come down here."

"What do you mean don't come down there? My children are in the building. I haven't seen my daughter since she was twenty-one and you tell me not to come down there. Only death could keep me from lugging these bones down there, do you understand?"

Don knew any further discussion on the matter was a waste of time. Her mind was set, and deep down he understood but wasn't sure Tamara would be as accommodating. She was fragile and couldn't handle much more attention. He excused himself from the growing crowd of employees and found his way to Tamara. Maybe it was the look on his face or the lack of confidence that he expressed. Whatever the hint, Tamara figured out the gist of the conversation he'd had with Madeline.

"She's on her way down, isn't she?"

He wouldn't lie to his sister. At his request, she'd made the sacrifice of leaving her sanctuary, far from the strife of DMI, to help him. He owed her honesty and that's what she got. "Yes, she's on her way to the lobby."

Tamara's gaze scoured the document and then the floor. In a split second she leaped to her feet and bolted toward the door. "I have to go."

"Tamara, wait—I can stop Mother at the elevator." This close to easily becoming CEO without having to wage a war, how could he let her walk right out the door with his mission trapped in her fingertips? Yet he'd clamored back to sanity, purging the anger and rejection heaped onto him by his father and God. He could appreciate her need to be away from this situation, from these people, from the agony until her healing was realized. Half of him wanted to plead with her to stay and the other half was willing to let her fly away like a wounded sparrow seeking refuge.

chapter

4

Securing financing, a drop in sales, Abigail's betrayal, and Madeline's schemes. Joel was juggling a list of issues with no support, except from his mother. He left his car in the company's circular entrance. Approaching the entryway, he fixed his eyes on a woman fleeing the building. A natural hairstyle framed her caramel-colored face. She blazed past him in a whirlwind, but not before his gaze zoomed in on her beauty during a fleeting glance. A sense of familiarity overcame him but Joel shook it off. Between DMI and the exhaustive media attention he'd claimed over the past three years, there was no telling where he'd met the woman. He was prepared to squeak out a hello but she didn't allow a single second for socializing. In a swoop she was in the cab barreling away from the complex. Joel shrugged his shoulders, thankful for the brief distraction while equally intrigued about why she looked so familiar. Madeline came tearing out of the building and ran smack into Joel.

"Get out of my way," she told him, practically plowing him down. "Where is she?" she belted.

"Where is who?"

"Never mind," she said, appearing worked up, and went back inside.

Today wasn't making much sense for Joel. He walked through the revolving door and stopped. The lobby was filled with employees, but his gaze was drawn to Abigail, Attorney Ryan, and Don. That's when it clicked: the lady outside was Tamara, his half sister. His knees buckled, understanding the significance of her visit. She'd left Detroit when he was twelve. With the strain between his father's two sets of children, he didn't have much interaction with Madeline's four children, and it wasn't from lack of interest on his part. He remembered the fantasy of having a real relationship with his siblings. He recalled going so far as to create fictional events with them which never came true. Honestly, he didn't really know the two older brothers, Sam and Andre. They died when he was a young child. He knew Don best, but Tamara was pretty much in name only, except for a few family photos his father kept. In all these years, she'd never returned to Detroit, not to his knowledge, not for their father's funeral or for the reading of his will. Reflecting on the specific terms outlined by his father, there was only one reason for her to show up now, signing her stock ownership over to somebody. It didn't really matter who, if it wasn't him. Joel wanted to panic but beat down the notion. He needed answers. Business had to be handled first; he could deal with his fears in private later.

Don approached Joel and extended a hand. When he came for the reading of their father's will, Joel reached out in an effort to make amends. Don was cordial but not receptive about fostering too much brotherly love. Their attitudes were reversed. Joel wasn't in a friendly mood and didn't accept Don's handshake.

"What's going on here?" he asked Don.

"We have a board meeting."

"Come on, man, you can do better than that. I know we have a board meeting, but you haven't shown up since I've been CEO for any other meeting and suddenly I'm supposed to believe that you and Tamara just happen to be here on the same day for an emergency board meeting." Joel's blood was pumping fast, racing through his veins. His thoughts wanted to get ahead of his words, overcome by the massive number of possibilities threatening his position in the company. They were out to get him, to undermine his ability to lead. He knew it. He had to think quickly. He couldn't be discounted, otherwise they might get another chance to validate his illegitimacy. Who could he trust? The security guard was in on the sneak attack, he could tell. He panned the room, logging the face of each employee lining the lobby. They were to be watched, too. No one was going to blindly knock him out of the CEO position, not without a serious duel to the death. The job was his. He had been chosen for the role.

Joel pushed past Don and Madeline in search of Abigail. He found her and aggressively grabbed her arm. "What's going on here?"

"Joel," she cried out, startling him back into the moment. He let her arm go. For a bit, his thoughts had carried him far off into a state of confusion, a place he was frequenting more often.

"Are you turning on me?" he demanded.

"Joel, get ahold of yourself. This is a lobby full of your employees," she whispered. "Don't make a scene down here. This isn't like you." She pulled her jacket down on both sides.

Don flew into the conversation with Madeline in tow. The day was already a bust without having to deal with Madeline and her mouth, but there didn't seem to be an escape route.

"Joel, you need to back off of Abigail. If you have a concern, address it to me," Madeline said.

"What is this, you have to protect Abigail from me? Come on, you can't be serious."

"That's not what she meant to do, Joel," Abigail said.

"Everybody take a breath and let's go talk," Don butted in to say.

"Okay, big brother, since you're speaking for the entourage, you tell me what's going on, as if I don't already know."

"Let's step into the waiting room. Everybody out here doesn't need to know what we're discussing," Don said.

"Oh, and who are you, the new boss giving orders and taking charge?" Joel chuckled, having no other way to relieve the mounting sense of vulnerability.

"Come on, Joel, let's talk," Don offered again and pointed to the waiting room off to the side of the lobby.

"I don't need a private room to hear your lies," Joel told Don. Then he turned to Madeline and said, "I know this is your doing. You just won't give up. When are you going to get this in your head," he said, tapping his index finger on his temple. "I'm CEO, not you, not your son, not my father, me. Deal with it," he said and walked away.

"Mistakes can and will be corrected," Madeline said, pouring her rhetoric over Joel like molten lava. He was instantly yanked back into the heat. Before he could hurl a word, Don stepped between Joel and his mother.

"I said back off," Don said. "This is between you and me, leave my mother and Abigail out of this."

"Or what, big brother, what are you going to do? You've taken me on before and lost, each time," he said, stepping within breathing distance of Don. Joel didn't want to ignite a duel but he couldn't show any signs of weakness. If Tamara had signed her stock ownership to Don or Madeline, then that meant they had controlling interest with 55 percent and enough weight to oust him from the CEO role at the upcoming board meeting, not counting Abigail's 5 percent. His thoughts were jumbled, his emotions frantic, but they couldn't know.

"Joel, what's gotten into you? This is not you. Don't you see what's happening?" Abigail said in an emotional tone not easily hidden. "Ever since you started pursuing Harmonious Energy, you've become a different person. You have to see this," she persisted.

He didn't want to hear anything she had to say. She was in the other camp, a traitor. Joel stormed up the stairs two at a time, bypassing the elevators. He needed time and space to figure out how to stay the coup d'etat that was obviously brewing among these people masquerading as family and friends. Six flights up didn't allow adequate time, but it was a start.

chapter

5

"Well, that went well," Madeline said, tapping the toe of her spiked heels, arms folded, barely able to harness the unbridled anxiety stemming from not catching her daughter in time. "I can't believe Tamara is gone." She was unable to calm the escalating sense of not knowing what to do next. When it came to plowing down Joel or running the East Coast division of DMI, she was effective and resolute, needing help from no one. But reuniting with her daughter wasn't a task she'd mastered. "That's it. I'm going to the airport. I'm not letting Tamara leave Detroit without me seeing her. I'm not going to let that happen," she said and trotted to the door.

Don called out to her. "Stop, Mother, let her go."

"I can't," she said, refusing to break down. She needed to maintain composure and get to the airport. This could be her one and only chance to reach Tamara. If her daughter had come this close to home, there was a chance that Tamara was ready to reconcile. Madeline couldn't be deterred. Finally she had both of her last remaining children in town, a dream come true. Grief sneaked in as she pushed away the crippling demise of her two oldest sons. Tamara was her concern.

"She needs time to figure out her feelings," Don said.

"How much time does she need? None of us are going to live forever. I wish she'd give me a chance to be her mother again." Grief and anguish swooshed in. Rationally she knew Tamara's rape wasn't her fault, but as a parent she assumed the guilt. Madeline threw up the barricade on her soul and kept focus on Tamara.

"Mother, she has her reasons for wanting to keep a distance. I'm not going to judge her. You know I've been there."

"But you're here," Madeline said, clinging to Don. She heaved a deep sigh, acknowledging that there was hope. She released the grip, feeling slightly less anxious. "At least we accomplished one key goal, getting Tamara's stock signed over to you." She patted Don on his back, full of joy, finding the impossible act to be a pure miracle. Don tried to interject, but she didn't want to lose her train of thought. "Who would have thought that you would be standing here today, ready to assume the CEO role after your father foolishly appointed Joel? It really is a miracle." Don tried to interject again, but she was almost finished. "I guess God finally decided to have mercy on this old woman and let me have something in life, too, finally. Every other time He let me get close to something good, He would then let it disappear like a mirage. Finally the mirage has become reality. Finally my children have come out on top for a change. It's bittersweet, with Tamara leaving the way she did, but I'm thrilled for you. Now, what were you saying?"

He wouldn't make eye contact, which made her nervous.

"I don't have Tamara's stock."

"What do you mean?" Madeline said, feeling the anxiety zip up the chart to a nearly unbearable level.

"Tamara left as soon as she realized that you were coming to the lobby. We didn't get her signature on the papers."

"Don't tell me this," she said, wanting to pull the strands of hair from her head and let out a shrill scream that could probably be heard two continents away. Why was God always doing this to her? "How can we be this close," she said, pinching her thumb and index fingers together, "and lose again? I really don't think I can stand another loss. This is it. If we don't claim this ministry now, there will be nothing left in a few months, based on Joel's poor management. If this merger with Harmonious Energy goes through, we can kiss our churches and other religious-based clients goodbye. The sacrifice and years of service that I've poured into this ministry with your father will be down the drain. I can't let that happen. Your father was a fool for appointing that inexperienced child in the first place, but I'm not giving up on righting his wrong."

"Mother, there's no use. We need to let it be. You need to come to terms about the demise of DMI and move on. My company is doing well in South Africa. Say the word and I'll carve out a key role for you at LTI. You and Abigail should consider joining me there."

"Maybe you're right." The weight was heavy. She couldn't think clearly. Nothing seemed right. "Maybe DMI is doomed, but right now my primary concern is to see my daughter. I'm going to the airport. I'll be back, hopefully with your sister."

"Mother, I won't be here when you return. It's time for me to go home."

"This is your home," she said, pounding on his chest with each word, struggling with her full might to maintain composure. Neither of her children was making it easy. She wouldn't give up both children and the hope of regaining DMI all in a single day. Madeline had to keep Don in Detroit. They could regroup and work out a plan together. She desperately needed him near, more than he knew. "Four hours, give me four hours. Is that too much to ask? Please, don't leave until I return from the airport. I'm begging you," she said, clutching his hand and placing it against her chest, as close to her heart as she could get.

"I d-don't know," he stammered.

Abigail was waiting off to the side with the attorney. Madeline beckoned for her to come over. "Abigail, please talk with Don," she said, placing his hand on Abigail's. "Please convince him to stay for the afternoon until we work out a plan."

"What do you want me to say?"

"I don't know, whatever he needs to hear," Madeline said, reaching the revolving doors. "I can stall the board of directors for a few hours—that's not a problem. In the meantime, I'm going to find Tamara." Based on routine checks from her private investigator, Madeline knew that Tamara lived in the south of France somewhere around Monte Carlo or Nice. She'd kept her distance more than any reasonable parent would have. "Do you know which flight she's on?" Madeline asked Don.

He shook his head no.

Not that she expected him to reveal his sister's secret anyway. "Then I'll have to take my chances. It can't be that many international flights leaving Detroit headed for the south of France." Madeline turned around one more time to say, "Abigail, I'm counting on you to keep my son here, no matter what it takes. If anybody can keep him here, it's you. That much I'm sure of." She turned and rushed out the door.

chapter

6

A pound of elation had been crushed with a ton of familiar disappointment. Don was baffled as he tried putting pieces of the day together, to orchestrate a scenario that justified him leaving the comforts of home and willfully thrusting himself into the family feud again. He wasn't certain that God had led him to Detroit to assume the CEO role. His conviction wavered. "I must be crazy. What was I thinking coming back here?" he said to Abigail, the last remaining person in the lobby besides the security guards. The other employees and people with good sense had left, obviously better judges at recognizing when it was time to abandon a situation. It was discernment he didn't feel. "I should have stayed in Cape Town and left DMI to crash and burn on its own."

"You're being here right now is not a mistake. God has brought you here for a reason," Abigail said standing near him.

She was one of the few people Don trusted implicitly, besides Naledi and his mother. There was no question of Abigail's sincerity, yet he had to challenge her perspective on the botched takeover. Maybe the plan was purely a reflection of his exuberance or his desire to honor her cry for help. Whatever the motivation, it wasn't so clear that he should stay. "If this is God's plan, I could sure use some clarity. I was okay with coming here at first, but now I have no purpose here," he said. The confidence he had carried upon entering the building nearly two hours ago had left with Tamara. "I'm not interested in fighting Joel for DMI, and being here is a reminder of how quickly this environment can zap my inspiration. Somehow the struggle doesn't seem worth the effort."

Abigail drew close to him and placed her hand on his shoulder in an endearing, not romantic, way. Her conviction was not easily overlooked. He had to take notice.

"Don, some battles are destined to be fought. It can't be avoided."

He wasn't accustomed to seeing Abigail speak against Joel. The surprises of today were endless. "What happened to your loyalty to Joel or, I should say, your love for him?"

She removed her hand from Don's shoulder and let her gaze dip before regaining eye contact. "My mind is clear for the first time in several years, no more living in the clouds and hoping for a fairy tale. I'm being practical now. Joel has lost his mind and there's no need for DMI to be put at risk while he gets himself together."

"That's what you say today, but that's your hurt talking. You won't feel that way in a few weeks or maybe months." He slid his hands into his pants pocket but maintained eye contact. "Take it from me, I know. You're mad at Joel, but it's not over. My gut tells me you still want a life with him," he said, gently lifting her chin with his index finger.

She chuckled. "Not everything that I want is good for me and apparently Joel is on that list." Don didn't speak. "What?" Abigail asked. "What's with that look on your face?"

"What look?"

"The one that's saying, *Sure, I know you don't believe that I'm moving on without Joel.* Besides, I don't have a choice. He's already moved on. But it's different for you. You have a choice. You can choose to go back to South Africa, ignoring God's calling, or stay and fight this battle that you were probably created to win."

"Probably isn't exactly convincing."

"You know what I mean. I know the Lord, but I'm not prophetic. I can tell you what I feel in my heart and in my spirit, but you have to hear God on your own. That much I learned with Joel."

Don took a seat in one of the cozy sitting areas. "So I should stay, according to the great Ms. Abigail Gerard."

She followed him to the seats. "If you ask me, it's your destiny. I truly believe that you were destined to run DMI at this point in time. This is your season." She had to admit that some of her motivation was purely selfish. She'd busted her behind for this company, poured countless days and nights into OMI, and was not about to let her investment turn out to be worthless.

"What about Joel?" A continuous loop of images played—wanting his father's vintage Porsche that of course went to Joel, being passed over as CEO for Joel, getting fired by Joel, and getting kicked out of the family estate, the one his mother built and lived in before Sherry had moved in. He'd come to terms with a degree of the past, forgiven his father, God, and his half brother, or so he claimed, but the truth was undeniable. "God and my father chose him to run the company. Do you believe they were wrong?"

"No, I don't. Joel was appointed first, and I trust your father and God. So that was the right decision, at the time, but it's like anything in life. We have choices with every gift and blessing that comes our way. We either take care of it or we don't." Abigail scooted to the edge of the seat and rested her elbow on the chair's arm. "Joel messed up. He has everything and he's letting it slip away. Don't get me wrong; he has been an amazing leader until recently. Now it's like he's on another planet. I can't talk any sense into him, no one can, not even God. He's not listening to anybody and that terrifies me because that's not the Joel that I . . ." she said and looked away.

Don understood. "Go ahead and finish: it's not the Joel that you love."

Abigail returned her gaze to Don, gently wiping her finger across her eyelid and clearing her throat. "It's your time now to run this company. If there's any hope for DMI, we need you—I need you here."

He leaned forward in the chair. "You, my friend, are asking a lot. You really want me to give up the peace that I've finally found, to push my company and Naledi to the side, to put my life on hold and come here to fight Joel over a position that he legally inherited?"

"It sounds bad when you put it like that, but basically yes."

Abigail had an aura that boosted Don's enthusiasm. There wasn't anything in particular that she did, it was just her. The feelings he harbored for her years ago pricked below the surface but weren't strong enough to overpower his intent on making the right professional and spiritual decision. Besides, history reminded him that Abigail might not be with Joel physically, but her soul was married to him, eliminating her as a viable romantic option. Then again, being CEO of DMI hadn't appeared to be a viable option several years ago, either. What a difference time and circumstance made, turning the impossible into probable. "I don't know who is more determined to get me here, you or my mother."

Abigail reached across the tiny decorative table and patted his hand, which was situated on the armrest. "It doesn't matter so long as you stay."

Her argument was compelling. In spite of Abigail's appeal, Don couldn't emphatically bear witness in his spirit that he was meant to be in Detroit at DMI. It was satisfying having Abigail's encouragement and Madeline's unconditional support, but to sacrifice his hard-earned contentment residing on the other side of the world required a deeper cause, one that would give him the endurance to withstand the fireworks that were sure to come with his play on the CEO role. Despite his desire to avoid engaging in a new battle with Joel, his calling from God had to supersede his personal feelings and doubts. Perhaps Joel's unexpected and arguably unwarranted rise to power had to happen in order for Don to have searched his own heart, dealt with the demons that bound him to hate and contempt for his deceased father, and forced him to grow up and be ready to lead the company with wisdom, compassion, strength, and an ability to forgive. He might not have wisdom seemingly infused overnight, like Joel had early in his tenure, but he was willing to seek God and obey his call, something Joel was choosing to abandon. Don meditated on the idea a while longer before giving Abigail a controlled nod.

"Is that a yes?" she said, gripping his hand but not leaping for joy. He understood that this couldn't be easy for her, bittersweet to see the man she was in love with ousted from a company he was chosen to lead but had failed.

"Yes," he said, relaxing into the seat, anticipating that his moments of calm would soon be a distant memory.

chapter

7

Fearful wasn't a characteristic Madeline used to describe her personality—she believed in deciding what had to be done and getting on with doing it, regardless of how daunting it was. She was part of DMI from the beginning, standing by her husband's side the first day he'd stepped into the building. Leaving her for Sherry was old news that, for the most part, was gone with Dave, but restoring the fragments of her life was never ending. Tamara chose to separate from the family and, for the first time in a long time, Madeline's daughter was now within reach. Madeline was determined to see her child. Her first call en route to the airport was to have an emergency page placed for Tamara to call her mother. The next call was to have the board meeting delayed a few hours. Other business affairs were a distant priority for Madeline the mother, not the infamous executive.

Parking in the long- or short-term sections at the airport was instantly discounted. Madeline whipped the convertible Bentley up to the curb outside the departures section. The plan was to let the valet park her car—cost wasn't a concern. With one car waiting in front of her, Madeline blew off the valet and exited the car. She dashed through the doors in search of her daughter.

She wanted to stop and check the departure boards, but instead opted to head straight for security. There was a better chance of finding Tamara at one of the gates than in the unsecured ticket counter area. Racing thoughts and uninhibited energy zipped Madeline through the airport. She checked every face that passed while keeping her sights on security. She didn't know if Tamara's hair was long or short, straight or curled. Had she kept a thin physique or put on weight, not that it mattered. Was she fashionable or more of the casual dresser? She had absolutely no idea. Reaching the line of about twenty people, she hopped to the first-class ticket entry, where there was no one waiting.

Tamara took a few sips of her latte, finally calming down during the cab ride to the airport. Hearing her name repeatedly blasted over the intercom was more unnerving with each announcement. Maybe Don was trying to find her, but if she had to seriously guess, it was her mother. Out of nowhere, there she was—Tamara saw Madeline approaching the line on the other side of security. Heart pounding, nerves jittery, Tamara had to get out of town and back to her safety zone in France as fast as the airline could get her there. The six hundred dollar cost of changing her ticket was money she didn't have to spare. Modest living and casually working had enabled her to stretch the trust fund dollars year after year, but with each move, her nest egg had dwindled. Normally connections were a downer, although it was typically what she could afford. This time she wasn't resistant to a stopover or two if it meant getting out of town fast.

She shifted the weight of her purse, the only item she brought. Tamara took comfort in catching a glimpse of her mother and settled for distance. Madeline had never harmed her directly, but the family memories and degree of dysfunction were too crippling. Tamara wasn't ready to see her mother and rehash the sadness, the guilt, the shame, and the trauma of the past. She'd spent almost a decade and a half purging cancerous memories and developing a safe and stable spot in her soul.

Madeline never indicated that she blamed Tamara for the rape. As a matter of fact, her mother consistently assured her that the opposite was true. However, if Madeline was honest with her feelings, how could she not have some animosity or resentment toward Tamara? Being the center of the drama that resulted in her parents suffering the loss of two children in a single tragic stroke wasn't easy for anyone to overcome. Her oldest brother, Sam, committed suicide after killing their other brother, Andre, for raping her. There was no way she could stay with the family after that, so she left with one suitcase and the remains of her trust fund. Several times she considered returning and starting over, but her mother was too much of a reminder of what she'd tried to forget. She took a few deep breaths, dumped the latte, and devised an exit strategy. Since her flight didn't depart until early evening, hanging around the airport was too risky. She had to elude her mother in order to maintain sanity.

Madeline stepped to the security checkpoint podium.

"Boarding pass and ID, please," the Transportation Security Administration agent asked.

"I don't have a boarding pass," Madeline said, plopping her designer handbag on the podium.

"Then do you have a gate pass?" she asked.

They were wasting time. Tamara could be boarding the plane at this very second. "No, I don't have a pass or a ticket, but this is an emergency. I have to catch my daughter before her plane leaves," she said, grabbing her purse and stepping past the agent.

"Excuse me, ma'am, you can't go through security without a pass. You'll need to go back to the ticket counter and get a boarding pass or a courtesy gate pass."

"You don't understand, I don't have time to wait in a ticket line when I have to catch my daughter," she said, taking another step toward the baggage conveyor belt.

The agent stepped between her and the belt. "Ma'am, I'm calling the airport security and you'll be detained. I'm trying to give you a break."

"Hold on," Madeline said. "Don't touch me. Do you know who I am?"

"It really doesn't matter. I don't care if you're the president. Unless you have a pass, you can't get through this security checkpoint."

Madeline should have cared, and at any other time would have, but nobody and nothing was more important to her than reconciling with Tamara. Most likely her car had been towed by now, which was fine. Two or three hundred dollars was like a penny when it came to saving her children, two or three hundred million, for that matter.

"Get me your supervisor," Madeline demanded, tired of wasting time with an agent who was determined to follow directions by the book with her but probably let terrorists and other shady characters sneak arsenals through security, undetected. Madeline's agitation was reaching the boiling point.

"No problem. He should be here in about fifteen minutes."

"Fifteen minutes? I can walk home by then." Madeline trudged away. Getting arrested wasn't an option. It would delay her mission. Waiting for the supervisor wasn't an option, either. Fifteen minutes was like fifty years. Tamara's plane could be departing any second. Madeline didn't know which flight or airline carrier Tamara was on and Don offered no help, protecting his sister's privacy at the worst possible time. She picked the carrier with the shortest line—Air France, first class. "When is your next flight leaving for any city in the south of France?"

The agent tapped a few keys and glanced at the monitor. "We can get you on our seven p.m. flight to Nice with a stopover in Paris tonight."

No way was Tamara going to wait around for an evening flight. Madeline had to get past security and comb the terminal if she was going to find Tamara. "Actually, I'm trying to find my daughter. It's an emergency and she's on a flight departing today. Is there any way you can look up Tamara Mitchell for me?"

"No, ma'am, we can't divulge passenger information."

Madeline sighed. "This is very important. You have no idea how important."

"I wish I could help you, ma'am, but the policy is very strict."

Madeline's voice cracked. She cleared her throat and shoved away the despair. "Are you a mother? I hope you are, because then you'll understand why it's important for me to help my daughter," she said, drawing near to the agent and eliminating the chance of other travelers overhearing.

"I wish I could help you, ma'am, I really do, but I can't."

Madeline didn't want to accept defeat. That would equate to letting her daughter down again, an act too difficult to bear. "Give me a ticket on your next flight."

"The next flight to Nice?"

"Doesn't matter, anywhere."

"Round trip or one way?"

"Doesn't matter." She wasn't going to use the ticket. It was only to get through security, an expense she would gladly pay. Madeline wanted to reach over the counter and book the ticket faster. Her patience was short, unable to remember the last time she had to take a commercial flight. The DMI private jet was her mode of air transportation. She'd forgotten how chaotic the airport could be. "Please give me a one-way or round-trip ticket on any plane leaving today that will get me through security and to my daughter."

"No problem, but I'll warn you that transatlantic tickets purchased on the day of departure can be costly."

"Don't you worry about cost," Madeline said, plopping the ultra-elite American Express black Centurion card on the counter. "I'm not." Madeline was smart enough to know the odds of catching Tamara were slipping away, but she pressed on with the same zeal she had the day her daughter left the nest. She would press on relentlessly until her dying day.

chapter

8

The executive-size office was cramped, like the walls were closing in. Joel sat at his conference table twiddling the rings of
keys Abigail had tossed to him practically a month ago. His head
was throbbing, with no relief coming from applying pressure to
his temples. He needed a bigger fix for the tenuous situation he
was in. His hands stroked up and down his face repeatedly. Swirling in a state of confusion wasn't a familiar place for Joel. He
twiddled with the keys some more, wondering how Abigail could
turn on him. The knock on the door gave pause to the sea of frustration he was drowning in. Only a small group of people could
get past his administrative assistant and be able to knock on his
door. "Come in," he said, too tired to stand, hoping it was Abigail.
He needed her more today than he had when he took on the
daunting task of running the company. The two of them had
racked up hours upon hours, nights, weekends—whatever was
necessary to get the job done in exceptional fashion. They ate
most meals together. They were partners.

"Hello, son," Sherry said. Joel was upset that Abigail hadn't
come to talk, but his mother was a shot of support he'd gladly
take. "There's a buzz going on in the office. Do you know anything

about a group of employees gathering in the lobby for a big announcement?"

"How did you know?"

"I'm your press secretary. It's my job to know."

The throbbing in his head intensified. "Madeline is up to another one of her schemes, that's what I suspect."

Sherry plopped down in one of the chairs near Joel. "What is she doing now?" she said without a hint of surprise.

"I'm not sure," Joel said, popping to his feet and pacing. "I wish I knew."

"And I thought she'd finally given up."

"Never. Whatever she has planned, it's big." He leaned his elbows on the table. "Tamara and Don are in town."

Sherry gasped. "They are?" She was silent, probably processing the implication like he had a little while ago in the lobby. "You don't think Tamara signed her stock over to Madeline, do you?"

Of course that was what he thought. He had to act quickly to counter Madeline's ultimate power move. With Don's 15 percent, Madeline's 25, and Tamara's 15, his father's first family was in control. Joel and his mother would be kicked out into obscurity, leaving them scrounging for respect. There was no way Joel was going to allow it. He and Sherry were finally enjoying the satisfaction of being on top. He was a Mitchell, too, entitled to the same rights and privileges as the other children. He hadn't asked to be born. His father and God made that decision without his input. He was just living out the life he was handed.

"What are you going to do?" she asked, wringing her hands.

"Not sure yet, but trust me, this isn't over, not by a long shot," he said as he grabbed a folder from his desk.

"Where are you going?" she asked, hustling behind him.

"I'll be in the legal department if anyone is looking for me," he said, "especially Abigail." The best plan Joel could muster on short notice was to act quickly and keep moving.

"Excuse me, Mr. Mitchell," his administrative assistant said, catching him before the elevator doors closed. "The board meeting has been pushed back to three o'clock."

Delay equaled trouble for Joel and the merger, trouble he was determined to mitigate. "Why was the meeting delayed?" he asked. He let his body rest on the door, causing the buzzer to ring. The bewildered look on his assistant's face was appropriate, given his rhetorical question. As CEO, he was supposed to have answers, not more questions. "Thanks for the update. Please adjust my schedule so that I'm free for the three o'clock meeting. Thanks." Poised and being in control were the outward projections he gave, but internally he was fuming. He tapped button number two several times and bolted from the elevator as soon as the door opened.

Contracts for Harmonious Energy had been underway for two weeks. The legal team estimated the process would take four to six weeks to negotiate the terms and conduct the proper due diligence necessary for such a transaction. The problem was that Joel didn't have four to six weeks. He had a matter of hours to produce results before the board meeting. There was no sense in asking God for help. Harmonious Energy didn't serve a single god, and there wasn't time to seek spiritual or professional advice from anyone before the meeting. The only possibility that remotely came to mind was the older lady whom he'd met last year during a local church visit. The last time he'd gone to see her, she directed him to God but didn't give the kind of straight answer he was seeking. No sense wasting the trip. He had to create his own miracle. "Where's Jim?" he asked the junior attorney sitting immediately inside the double doors. The chief counsel had to get Harmonious Energy expedited today, no exceptions.

"I'm not sure, Mr. Mitchell."

"Who's working on the Harmonious Energy deal?"

The attorney fumbled around his desk. Joel didn't have the time or patience to haggle with a rookie. He needed the top dog to get the job done. "Tell Jim to get ahold of me as soon as he's back in the office. I need an immediate update."

"Yes, sir."

"Be sure to let him know this is urgent. Have my administrative assistant interrupt me if I'm in a meeting—got that?"

"Yes, yes, sir."

Joel walked into the stairwell, talking along the way, bent on not wasting a second. There was too much at stake. He wasn't about to be dethroned by a bunch of sore losers who couldn't or wouldn't embrace the future. Confident that he was acting in the best interest of the company and his family, Joel thrust his energy toward removing the primary stumbling block, which was to quickly and quietly secure the financing necessary to close the deal with Musar Bengali for Harmonious Energy. Joel stepped to the corner of the hallway, called DMI's lending institution, and got the company's private banker on the line. Raising the purchase price without the board's approval was going to be a challenge.

"Mr. Mitchell, how can I help you?"

"We're in the middle of a business deal that's going to require some additional funding, and I need to find out—how much and how fast can we secure funds from you?"

"We can wire funds into the DMI account within hours, Mr. Mitchell. DMI's entire two hundred and fifty million dollar credit line is at your disposal, and one million of that requires only your signature as CEO. Let us know when you're ready and we can complete the transaction to your satisfaction." Joel felt a tinge of worry release. He was pleased that his signature carried the kind of clout needed to hopefully close the Bengali deal. Between the bank and DMI cash reserves, he could comfortably complete the transaction quickly. Finally there was a ray of hope with the merger. After the series of today's events, he was overdue for good news. "We appreciate your business and, as always, we'll make ourselves available to you. I'll wait for the call from your chief financial officer."

"No," Joel immediately responded but caught the tone in his voice, careful not to sound anxious or clandestine—discretion was key. "I'll be working with you directly. This deal is highly sensitive and requires top level confidentiality."

"Understood. I'll wait for your instruction."

Joel heaved a gigantic sigh of relief as he exited the stairwell.

Having the credit line at his disposal alleviated a need to secure total funding in the open market, particularly with DMI taking a slight dip in sales. Searching for the full chunk of money would have delayed and possibly obliterated his chance of buying Harmonious Energy. Thank goodness only an abbreviated search was necessary.

chapter

9

The mood at the small conference table was somber. Madeline had returned from the airport unable to find Tamara. She sat with Abigail and Don, much more reserved than usual. It was almost unnerving to see a lioness as gentle as a lamb. Madeline was strong-minded but effective. Many were intimidated by her. Abigail found Madeline refreshing, reliable, and bold, the ingredients they were in dire need of unleashing if DMI was to survive. Abigail was pleased that she had been able to convince Don into staying, but she wasn't sure for how long. A plan had to be constructed quickly, before he changed his mind.

"Madeline, do you have any comments on the board meeting this afternoon? We don't have the votes to override Joel," Abigail said.

The words pierced Madeline like a laser, slicing to the core. Push the tinge of emotion aside and concentrate, she thought. Joel had made his decision with no regard for Abigail, and it was time she acted definitively and not merely with unconditional love masking as loyalty and friendship. Her head was in the room. Her heart had to wait outside. Madeline didn't respond as she toyed with one of her Mont Blanc pens.

"Madeline, did you hear me?"

"Huh . . . what?" Madeline asked, clearly flustered.

"She asked about our plan for the board meeting today. We don't have the votes to kick Joel out of the CEO spot. What are our other options?" Don asked.

Madeline didn't immediately respond, again toying with her pen.

"Mother!" Don raised his voice and clasped his hand on top of his pen. "Are you all right? You seem to be distracted."

Madeline looked away. Her voice faded as she said, "I couldn't find Tamara." She slid the chair away from the table and stood. "I can run the East Coast division of a billion-dollar company with my eyes closed, but I couldn't get past a little security guard at the airport to find my child. Tamara needs me and I let her down." She just stood in one spot, leaning on the top of the chair. It didn't appear that she was crying, at least not with tears, but was obviously bothered.

Don stood and went to her. "There's nothing you can do, nothing. She wasn't ready and we can't push her."

"I'm not pushing," Madeline said, lashing out at Don. "I'm sorry. I don't want to drive you away, too." A tear must have fallen or was getting ready to fall because Madeline took a quick swipe across her eyelid and gently pushed Don back. "Enough with the sulking, let's get busy," she said. "I should be crying over that four hundred and fifty dollar towing fee. They had the gall to charge me extra because my car required a special flatbed tow truck." She sighed. "Whatever . . . it's only money."

Just like that, Madeline was back to her normal self. Abigail was intrigued at how easily Madeline could conduct day-to-day operations while keeping her composure—except when it came to Sherry. Everyone familiar with the Mitchell family was quite clear about how Madeline felt. Her disdain seemed to lessen somewhat after Dave had died, but Madeline and Sherry weren't close to becoming friends. Joel, being Sherry's son, was an automatic target. However, today's doing was squarely a result of Joel's questionable management, and not solely Madeline's revenge.

Madeline's energy appeared to have returned as the three sat at the table.

"So, the question remains. What are we going to do about the board meeting?"

Madeline responded instantly. "We need time to pull our action plan together. All is not lost. I know we were counting on Tamara's stock." Her voice faded on Tamara's name, but finished strong. That was the Madeline that Abigail knew. "But that's not our only way to regain control of the company."

Abigail and Don listened intently, sure Madeline had a take-over idea—she always did. It wasn't always ethical or popular or effective, but she was never short on ideas. "Here's what we're going to do. Let's get Jim in here. He can give us an update on where we are with the Harmonious Energy contracts. He can also tell us what potential things could end up delaying the merger. At a minimum, we can try to stall the deal in legal proceedings, ideally for six months. I have to believe that any deal requiring us to surrender an entire division violates at least one of our core goals, but who knows with the way poor decisions have been addressed around here. Either way, Jim should be able to give us some insight."

Don grimaced. "If I'm going to do this, we have to maintain discretion. I'm not comfortable letting Jim know what we're planning."

"Me either," Abigail added. She was a part of the coup, but the fewer people that were aware, the less likely Joel would get rattled. He was a few weeks or months from diving into a mockery of a wedding to consummate the merger. She shouldn't care what he thought. Truth was, she did care, and it would take time not to.

"Okay, let's take another approach. One of us can stroll down to legal and have a nonchalant meeting with Jim, get the information we need, and have him none the wiser about our motives," Madeline suggested.

"Can't be me," Don said, "I'm not really here, remember." He pulled his phone out and returned it to his pocket.

"Not a problem, you know I don't mind going," Madeline said.

"No, let me go," Abigail chimed in, drawing glares from both Madeline and Don.

"Oh," Madeline said, coy. "You sure you want to jump into this pond? It's bound to get dirty. Joel will eventually find out that you're on the opposing team. Are you sure you're ready for the fallout?"

Abigail wasn't sure, but it wasn't a factor. "I'll get the impromptu update from Jim."

"All right, it's on you. Make sure you find out what the potential pitfalls are in the merger. Those are the areas where we want to launch our attack," Madeline said as she extended her hand toward the center of the table.

Don had his phone out again. "Excuse me. I have to take this call from Naledi."

"Everybody in?" The three stacked hands like high school kids before a big game, before Don stepped away. Must have been important, Abigail thought, noticing the way he hustled from the room. Her mind returned to Joel. She was on the opposing team, and he was alone. The decision wasn't so hard—any man who couldn't listen to reason couldn't be good for her, or for the company.

chapter

10

Jitters in Don's gut were flipping, compelling him to flee for South Africa and leave the turbulent DMI boardroom for those more resilient. He spoke a silent prayer asking for guidance, believing his request would be honored if he truly was destined to be CEO. How and when the transition of power occurred between the two brothers was God's challenge to handle. Being available and willing was Don's role, one he was trying to accept. He drew in a deep breath of confidence when he saw Abigail approach. He would need to become staunch and unmovable if this plan was to work.

"How did you make out with Jim?" he asked, glancing at his watch as others filed into the room, greeting him in the process. "We only have a few minutes. Let's step to the side," he told her. Joel approached and paused. No words were exchanged, but the piercing gaze he gave Abigail before passing by spoke clearly. "Don't worry about him," Don told her, certain she was feeling the impact of siding against Joel.

"Jim gave me some good information."

"I hope good news," Don said, just as Madeline was exiting the elevator. He beckoned for her to join the circle. "We're only a few minutes from showtime."

Abigail pursed her lips and subtly shook her head no.

Don was hoping for better news. "Go ahead, spill it."

"Apparently Joel is pushing to have the contract done today or tomorrow."

"What?" Madeline said, rearing back. "He can't cram this deal down our throats. He might be CEO for the meantime, but we have a voice in this company. I've been around a long time. I can still call a few shots," she said, letting her head jerk around with her signature *take charge if necessary* attitude.

"We need to slow this process down," Don said, wanting to remain level in his direction and not be influenced by emotion.

"You got that right. We have to bring this to a close," Madeline said.

Abigail didn't offer any suggestions. She listened. Don could imagine the internal struggle she was battling. He'd felt the same agony when Joel had claimed both DMI and Abigail, forcing Don to find another love and place to call home, which he had.

Don glanced at his watch, again confirming that there was only a few minutes left before meeting time. "All right, our strategy is to extend the merger time line and construct a sound plan of action." Both ladies nodded in affirmation. "Good," he said. "After you, Mother." He then turned to Abigail. "I'll catch up with you immediately after the board meeting." He couldn't believe she wasn't a board member yet. Joel had had the right idea when he'd promoted her to executive vice president. He just hadn't gone to the next level. Once Don was in charge, he would get Abigail on the board of directors and an office on the sixth floor with the rest of the executive team if she wanted. She'd proven her loyalty and vision for the company.

Don and Madeline entered the meeting. Protocol commenced and ended quickly. Several items filled the agenda. Don waited patiently as the topics were discussed. His mother wasn't as accommodating.

The disappointing news of key clients leaving must have fueled her fire. "We have to address a critical problem," she said, taking the floor after the quarterly sales report was read. "We're hemorrhaging clients and everyone in this room knows why." His mother pointed at Joel, who sat tall in his seat, appearing ready to take exception. Don could hear the battle cries; war was near. "This ludicrous notion of merging with an organization that doesn't share our core principles is increasing customer uncertainty and driving them out the door. This can't continue if we want to be around in five years," she said without taking a breath.

"How many times are we going to have this same discussion?" Joel jumped in to say. "This company is well overdue for an international market expansion. I didn't hear anyone complaining last quarter about my decisions when we paid out record bonuses." No one could refute Joel's claim. "DMI will be fine once we get the merger completed. This constant internal bickering is the problem. Simple as that."

Don was certain Joel and his mother were going to lock horns and tussle around the board meeting until someone passed out from exhaustion or was too bloody to proceed. There was another way to combat Joel. If Don was going to be involved, it had to be legal and ethical, not necessarily overt. "Clearly Joel is correct. He's responsible for unprecedented growth. On the other hand, Madeline is correct, too. We can't discount how many key customers have left due to your dealings with a questionable company." Don was striving to bring order into the discussion.

"There's nothing questionable about the company," Joel lashed out to say, clicking his keys.

"If our clients aren't on board with the merger, it's fiscal suicide." Nods of affirmation about Don's comment circled the table. "I suggest we take a step back and make sure this merger fits the long-term vision."

"This is a one-time deal. If we don't act quickly, Musar Bengali is going to take his company to the next highest bidder. I can't believe we're wasting time talking about this again. My father wanted to expand into international markets for forty years. He didn't. We can, end of story."

"Maybe you're correct, but why don't we take the time necessary to understand what we're undertaking?" Don added.

"We know what we're undertaking because we've been here for the past three years' worth of board meetings, unlike you, who was off in Africa somewhere running another company."

"He's a member of this board and that gives him the right to speak," Madeline said. The cease-fire between the two was over, and each was lobbing missiles across the room in words and stares. The sweet whisper of Naledi's voice and the South African warmth ushered in Don's oasis, although brief. The tension in the meeting thickened. Don had to regain control of the topic again, a never-ending battle with Joel and his mother.

"I'm tired of this debate. I'm calling for an end to the discussion followed by a vote," Joel said, agitated.

"Vote on what?" one of the board members asked.

"Funding approval. Like I said, we need to act quickly. I'm ready to close the deal. The contract will be ready no later than tomorrow at noon. Let's stop debating and get to action," Joel said, seeming to calm.

"There's no way you're getting my vote," Madeline said.

Don wasn't sure which stubborn person was going to require more work in managing, his relentless mother or his angry half brother. "I move that we suspend a final decision on the Harmonious Energy merger for six months, allowing sufficient time to have an independent counsel complete a thorough evaluation process. Simultaneously, we'll have an assessment done by our legal team." Don was hopeful that he'd get the necessary support. It was the only immediate way to slow Joel down. "Ideally, they'll end up with the same results."

Joel rose to his feet, shocking Don and drawing stares from members in the room. "I'm CEO, and I'm calling this deal done." The board members had entered into many heated discussions throughout the years, but none to the point of being unprofessional. Strong leaders, strong opinions were expected in the boardroom. Joel's outburst was an exception.

Technically Joel was the top-ranking official. Since the company was privately owned, he wasn't accountable to shareholders, not that it would have made a difference. He was listening to no one, except for a spiritual advisor every once in a while, according to Madeline. Guidance from the board of directors was valued by their father. Joel had another way of leading—his way only and to heck with anyone else, making it difficult for others to differentiate his wisdom from ignorance.

chapter

11

Joel couldn't allow his throbbing temples to hamper his ability to think. He plopped into the desk chair, recounting portions of the meeting, rubbing the keys frantically, growing angrier with each memory. This was his company. He was in charge. He was the reason DMI had soared in sales. A few bad quarters weren't driving them to bankruptcy. He knew what the company needed—an expanded presence. Before his father had died, the words he'd passed on to Joel burned in his consciousness—"Don't be afraid to make the tough decisions, the ones no one else can make." Joel was determined to proceed.

"Can you please get a copy of the most recent Harmonious Energy contract from legal?" Joel asked his assistant through his private line. "And I need this immediately."

Joel massaged his temples to no avail. Fifteen minutes later his assistant was knocking on the door to present him with the contract file. "Thank you," he said. "By the way, do you have any aspirin or Tylenol, anything for a headache?"

"I can get you some ibuprofen if that will help."

"Yes, please," he said. Opening the contract folder, the seven hundred million dollar purchase price soared from the page, intensifying the pounding in his head. "Please give me whatever you can find," Joel called out, in a low tone, to his assistant. A few seconds later she entered with a small cup of tablets and a crystal glass of water.

"I gave you four tablets, two for now and two for later, just in case you need more." Joel gulped down all four pills and chased them with the water, causing the assistant to raise her eyebrow. If two were good, four were better. "We should put some basic meds and first aid kind of items in the executive dining room," he told her.

"I'll take care of it, Mr. Mitchell," his assistant said on her way out.

"Please close the door behind you and hold my calls." She acknowledged leaving Joel to tackle the nearly impossible feat of raising seven hundred million without support from the board of directors. Had they given their endorsement, half would have come from company reserves coupled with the rest from the credit lines. He rubbed his temples repeatedly. Scrounging for that amount of money had never been a consideration. Wasn't impossible, maybe improbable, but the alternative of failing was definitely not an option.

The pills hadn't yet kicked in to reduce the suffering in his head, but he pressed on. He combed through the proposal, page by page. By the end of the document nothing had changed; he was at the short end of a daunting task. He snatched a sheet of lined paper from his portfolio and scratched out a few numbers. With an executive order, he could approve one hundred million from company funds and one hundred million from the bank's credit line without any other endorsements.

Every avenue had to be considered. This wasn't the time to grow timid and conservative. His bold strategies had worked before and he'd force them to work again. His antagonists would soon be groveling with apologies after the successful merger and recovery of DMI's small setback. The headache eased to a faint tingle. Five hundred million dollars more. A rough assessment of his personal belongings, cash, various liquid assets, and property holdings, which could be used as collateral on a personal loan, amounted to two hundred million, leaving a three hundred million dollar shortage. Joel tossed the pen into the air and let it crash to the desk, then rested his head on his index finger and thumb.

There had to be an answer. He needed guidance, like the early days, before he became Joel Mitchell, the man full of business acumen. Communication with God had become dormant. Joel hadn't intentionally set out to create distance, but his heavy schedule, focus on achievement, and finagling personal matters consumed his time and energy, leaving minimal time for spirituality and church. There was a time when both had framed his perspective and highly influenced his decisions. That wasn't the case with this merger. Joel wondered in what direction God would have led him with the merger had he inquired. He pondered the question but was unable to answer. He was better off sticking to his agenda and being unwilling to accept opposition from anyone.

He picked up the pen and jotted numbers again and again. Each scenario produced the same result: a three hundred million dollar shortage. Sherry popped in and right back out of the equation. He wasn't willing to jeopardize his mother's livelihood now that she finally had a taste of contentment and independence. Pushed to extreme means, he could think of only one person who could help him raise the funds—Sheba Warden. He liked that she didn't require a label on their one-year-old relationship. He vividly recalled the day she'd walked into his office, a stranger determined to make an eighteen million dollar donation toward his pet project, the construction of the Dave Mitchell Library. Something about her had captured his imagination, and it hadn't changed.

Joel bounced to his feet, feeling the heaviness shed. He dashed from the office, then dialed her number. God had briefly entered his thoughts again, but Joel was becoming an expert at pushing those out almost instantaneously.

chapter

12

Turbulence and mounting wind gusts shook the corporate jet en route to Chicago. Joel buckled in for the ride, unable to control the external forces attempting to derail his plans. After a tumultuous flight, the plane was on the ground, where the limousine awaited his arrival. The chaos of the day seemed to shift into order as the car door opened and Sheba's presence greeted him. Her power never diminished. She was the muse he needed.

"Well, Mr. Mitchell, I was surprised to get your call so soon after your last trip," she said with words so soft it tantalized his back and shoulders, shaking off the tension from earlier in the day. She was the drug he longed for.

"Am I overextending my welcome?" he said, engaging in their playful banter that happened every time they met, which was every chance they got. With him in Detroit and Sheba running her chain of boutiques in Chicago, rendezvousing was limited to about once or twice every other month.

Sheba gave him a teasing wink and stroked the back of his hand. "Never. Your invitation is open-ended," she said in the way that only Sheba could—sensual, alluring, natural. He loved her confidence. Mostly, he loved the way she understood him, his drive, his need to accomplish certain goals. That's why he was ready to meet her anytime, anywhere, for anything. She didn't crowd him with expectations or layers of judgment.

He sank back in the seat, prepared for the forty minute drive along the Edens Expressway that took them from the private northwestern suburban airstrip to her office downtown on Michigan Avenue. He let his eyes close for a second, glad to have a morsel of solitude.

Sheba scooted closer to the center of the backseat, closer to him. "Okay, what's going on? You seem tired."

"You don't know the half of it." He was overjoyed to finally have a chance to talk with someone he trusted. The image of Abigail standing side by side with Madeline and Don in the lobby earlier formed a sick feeling in the pit of his stomach. Loyalty is what he sought and that was what Sheba freely gave. "I'm trying to close the deal with Musar Bengali."

"That's right, how is the merger going? Have you been able to get your management team to buy in on the idea? They seemed pretty resistant several months ago."

"And they still are," he said, shifting his gaze to the cars passing by. "They just don't see the big picture. They can't envision a presence beyond U.S. borders. Maybe I need to fire all of them and bring in a team that can implement my vision." He peered out the window, repositioning his feet. "What I have right now is a bunch of closed-minded executives who've gotten too comfortable with their plush offices and bonus structure." He felt anxiety heating up. "They're stuck in the past and refuse to consider supporting any other vision except that of my father. Don't get me wrong. He was a good man, a good leader, and a great father, but he's not perfect and most importantly, he's not here. I don't know why the team can't see that. There is room to improve DMI beyond what my father envisioned. I should just go back to Detroit and kick everybody out."

"Including Abigail?"

He wanted to say yes, but the words didn't easily glide across his lips. She'd betrayed his trust by siding with the opposition, yet she was Abigail. They'd been in the trenches, working as a team, and he thought she understood what he had to do. He wasn't willing to accept the possibility that she was done with him. "Abigail hasn't changed her mind. She's not in favor of the merger."

"I told you that you should have married her already. You would have her vote if you had," she said, her voice sprinkled with humor.

He leaned his head on the headrest and let the humor soothe him. "Please don't start in with the Abigail conversation. We've had that talk too many times," he said, beginning to loosen up.

Sheba flashed him a gaze that routinely grabbed his attention and kept a grip on it. "I might not be able to predict the future, but good old-fashioned perception tells me that you and Abigail have engaged in a dance that neither of you seems to know how to end." Joel was about to respond when Sheba said something else. "You're a wise man, one of your many appealing characteristics, I might add. You know I'm telling the truth. You have my full support with buying Harmonious Energy, but you have to be certain about the arranged marriage piece of the deal. Do you really want to marry Musar's daughter? Is this deal worth sacrificing your personal life?"

"You don't have to worry," he quickly said. "Our friendship is not in jeopardy. Nothing will change with us—nothing." The marriage was an extreme means to an end but sacrificing his personal life was a small price for fulfilling his mission of taking the DMI philosophy to the world. His father wanted to spread godly principles. Joel wanted to spread the company's name, formulating an indelible legacy. Their motives were different but the end result was the same.

"I'm not concerned about us. I'm wondering if you've seriously considered how this will affect Abigail."

"She's not happy, obviously, but what can I do? I never made any romantic promises to her, never. She's like a sister to me."

"Trust me, she doesn't look at you like a brother, not based on what I saw when I spent those three weeks at DMI last year. You let her oversee the construction of your new house. She's not going to be happy when Musar's daughter moves in."

"Abigail will come around. She appreciates sacrificing for the company."

"This isn't about business. She's in love with you, plain and simple."

"Love doesn't trump vision."

"Look, I'll support whatever choice you make. Just don't discount Abigail so hastily. That might be a mistake."

Joel didn't want to think about Abigail. There was a strong chance that she'd change her mind and join him. In the meantime, he had to secure funding. The deal was about to slip away and he had to move mountains to make it happen. Failure was not an option. The limousine careened smoothly down the highway and deposited them into the Kennedy Expressway with the Chicago skyline in the distance. They chatted freely for twenty minutes more. His body fully relaxed. Sheba was his hope. "I need your help," he said.

"You have it," she said.

"But you don't know what I need."

"Doesn't matter, you have it."

He heaved a gigantic sigh. "You're amazing," he said, delicately touching her cheek this time. "My life changed the day you came to Detroit."

"The day I showed up with a check in one hand and a request for you to be my mentor in the other." She giggled. "I'm surprised you didn't kick me out. Instead, one day turned into three weeks."

"Like I said, my life changed the day you came to Detroit."

"For the better or for worse?" she asked.

This time he laid his smile on her, the one that often drew her into his magnetism. "Which one do you think?"

Their playful bantering intensified. "So, what did I just agree to do?" she asked.

His glance dipped briefly before returning to her. He was confident in their relationship and didn't have to hide anything from Sheba. "I need to borrow money. The board of directors is blocking the merger. Between the limited DMI funds that I have access to, my line of credit, and my own money, I've raised four hundred million. I'm short three, which I'm hoping to borrow from you."

Sheba's gaze dropped and Joel's assurance followed. "I don't have three hundred million, Joel."

"This is only a loan. I'll pay you back with interest. You set the terms and I'll honor them."

"I'm not concerned about you paying me back. I actually don't have the liquid funds. You know my expansion project is underway, thanks to your encouragement. You helped me to make it happen," she said with her voice dropping off at the end. "Unfortunately that expansion has burned through my cash reserves."

"It's okay, I understand." It really wasn't okay. Sheba was his last best hope, but it wasn't her fault. The timing didn't work out for him, but he was thrilled for her. This was his time to support her.

"Joel, I have one hundred million that you can have."

The limousine came to a stop in front of the John Hancock Center on North Michigan Avenue. Sheba told the driver that they needed a few more minutes.

"No, don't worry about the money. You're in the middle of a project. You might need the cash yourself. Hang on to it. I'll figure out something," he said, not sure what that meant.

"You're taking the money. Give me the information and we can go upstairs right now and have the money transferred into your account."

"But—" was the only word he could get out before she spoke.

"You're taking this money. I'm not taking no for an answer. If the situation were reversed, you'd do the same for me. Besides, I remember when you gave me a check for thirty-five million as an investment into my boutiques, with no strings attached." She rested her hand on his. "Consider this an investment into your vision."

"Thank you," he said, grateful to have Sheba in his life. He was still two hundred short but, thanks to her, the road left to trudge was shorter and the goal more obtainable. She would forever be in his inner circle, no matter who else was in his life.

chapter

13

Abigail and Don sat in the great room of his infrequently used condo. *Confusion is not from God.* Don repeated the paraphrased verse over and over, reassuring his conscience that the mound of chaos wasn't the end result. It never failed. If he was at DMI, there was going to be trouble. He could develop a complex if it wasn't for the success he'd achieved before Joel's reign and the substantial accomplishment he was currently realizing with his own company. Cape Town seemed far away; Naledi did, too. When he'd hired Naledi to be his assistant, there wasn't the slightest inclination that their rapport would evolve into a relationship of sorts. His thoughts were humming.

"Can I get you some more water?" he asked. "You know that's all I have here." He propped his feet on the ottoman. "I need to get rid of this place, but Mother won't hear of it. She's gone so far as to offer to pay the monthly maintenance fees."

"I don't blame her. As long as you have a home here, it feels like you're not really gone," said Abigail.

"I'm here, but I do have to run back home and take care of a few things. I left Naledi there with no idea of how long I'd be gone." Don noticed Abigail fidget when he mentioned Naledi's name. "What's wrong with you?" he asked.

"It's nothing."

He groaned without responding.

"If you leave, how do I know that you're coming back?" she asked.

"Trust me, I'm coming back. You're the main one who helped convince me that this chaos is my so-called destiny."

Abigail wasn't in her usual jovial mood. Don didn't press the issue. There would be time to figure out what was going on with her, outside of the obvious dejection stemming from Joel's recklessness. For now, Don had to set Detroit aside and take care of LTI. His own expansion plans into France and England were underway and required his leadership attention. God had to have a plan. It was the only way this confusion could make sense. He was stretching across two continents, two companies, two missions, and two endearing friendships, none of which he wanted to surrender.

The day-long flight to Cape Town was preempted with a stopover in France. Don hadn't spoken with Tamara since she'd run out of the building four days ago. He dialed her number again, at least the fiftieth time since she'd left. Worry threatened to consume him. He resisted, choosing to concentrate only on positive images. Tamara had suffered more than her share of trauma and grief. Don fervently prayed for his sister. In roughly twenty-five minutes, the driver he'd hired at the Nice airport was pulling up to her flat in Monaco. Don had never actually been to Tamara's home. She moved every two or three years. He'd convinced her last year to let him have her address in case of a major emergency. Reluctantly she shared the information, mostly afraid that he would give the address to their mother. He promised never to reveal her address and had kept the promise.

Don's French was weak, which was why Naledi was such a

blessing. She spoke several languages fluently, including French. Her image brought comfort to his jittery soul. Worry and anxiousness mixed in his spirit, hurrying him to the doorman. Don rattled off the two French phrases he knew, which translated into "Do you speak English?" and "please."

"*Oui*, monsieur, I speak a little English," the gentleman responded.

"I'm here to see Ms. Tamara Mitchell in flat number forty-three. I'm her brother, Don Mitchell, visiting from the States. Can you please let her know I'm here?"

"No, I can't, sir."

Don's mixture of worry and anxiousness turned to determination. "Why not? I'm her brother." Tamara deserved her privacy, and he'd honored her request for many years, but she had to understand that he was frantic to know that she was okay. When he was only sixteen and Tamara seventeen, he couldn't protect her from their brother, Andre. As a man now, Don was not leaving the building without seeing her. "I have to see my sister." The language barrier didn't prevent Don from making his intentions clear. He wasn't leaving. Prepared for a battle, the doorman extracted a card-sized envelope from the receptionist's desk and handed it to him. *Don Mitchell* was written across the front.

"I believe this is for you, monsieur."

Don stared at the envelope extended to him. He didn't want to take it. Notes weren't too cheerful for their family. Sam had left one when he'd committed suicide. Tamara left one before running off. Don stood in the lobby, unable to think or move. The doorman left him with the note.

Every man had a limit. He had to be close to his. He'd lost two siblings, a third if he remotely considered Joel. Tamara was the only one left. She couldn't be gone. There was no way he'd be able to comfort Madeline. Losing Tamara, really losing her, was certain death for his mother. He set the note down on the desk and buried his face into the palms of his hands and prayed silently: *Father God, I know that you have the power to make this right. I'm asking you in the name of Jesus to protect my sister. Lord, my family needs*

some grace, a lot of grace. I'm willing to do what you want me to do,
but I need your strength to deal with everything that's coming at me.

Don took a deep breath, ready to read his sister's fate. He slowly ripped the envelope open and removed the card, bracing for the worst. Skipping half the words in his haste to get to the end, the essence of Tamara's note told Don that she wasn't ready to be a part of the Mitchell family again. She apologized for letting him down and promised to contact him soon, when she was ready. Don buried his face in his palms again—this time in a moment of gratitude. "Thank you, Lord," he said in a whisper. He couldn't give Tamara a hug. He didn't know where in the world she was, but at least there was no indication that she was gone for good. If she could hang on to life and continue trying to navigate her way to stability, then he would continue moving forward, too. Don was committed to trying to save DMI and his family. What he couldn't figure out was why the road was so winding, painful, and full of struggles. He thanked the doorman, got in the car, and headed for the airport, unsure what calamity was in store.

The conference room was filled with local reporters. Joel hadn't shied away from the camera until his love affair with the media had begun souring. During his glory days, which had lasted for a few years, they'd treated him like a rock star, clinging to his every move, hoping to get the coveted scoop. Times had changed, and he had to ensure that his personal matters weren't exploited. Maintaining privacy was critical for his image. Joel removed his suit jacket and laid it across the chair in front of the podium. Abigail stood near the podium with Joel. Sherry stood off to the side. There were no signs of Madeline or Don, which pleased Joel.

"The conference begins in eight minutes," Abigail said, pulling him away from the microphones. "Remember, the purpose of this press conference is to ease concerns in the marketplace about the drop in sales, and to boost confidence."

"We need to talk," he told her, convinced that she'd change her mind and work with him to make the merger a reality.

She stepped farther away from the microphones, refusing to have her comments accidentally broadcasted around the room. "There is nothing else to say. Let's get the conference over with.

You can go back to what you're doing and so can I," she said in a snide tone that he had never experienced with her. She was visibly mad about the proposal to Musar's daughter. Their friendship wasn't easily discarded. That's what he chose to believe. Allowing her space was necessary if he was going to win her loyalty again. Right now the media had his attention and he knew how to court them.

Eight minutes flew by and, on cue, the cameras were rolling and the microphones turned on. "Mr. Mitchell, there are rumors swirling that DMI is experiencing an economic downturn and is near bankruptcy. Is there any truth to the rumor?" the first reporter asked.

They could come at him all day with questions about the solvency of DMI. Regardless of other traits Joel had, he was business savvy. "No, the rumor is not true," he said, relaxed, considering the circumstances. He adjusted the microphone upward for easier projection. "The company is solid. We haven't seen the same record growth in this past quarter, but that's to be expected given it took me two and a half years to double this company in size. We're here and we're not going anywhere. As a matter of fact, we have expansion plans underway that will catapult DMI into the international arena."

"Isn't the international expansion a source of concern for your client base, particularly those with a religious orientation?"

"Our customer base is sound." The adrenaline flowed, boosting his resolve like a drug, addictive, exhilarating. Today reminded him of times not that long ago when he was on camera and Abigail was nearby, cheering him on. He saw her in his peripheral vision, but she seemed disconnected.

"Mr. Mitchell, can you confirm or deny the rumor that you've recently gotten engaged? Who's the lucky woman?"

His legs wanted to buckle but he would stand firm. Abigail left the area, raising his suspicion that she had to be the one who'd leaked the information to the press. He'd only told three people in the U.S. about the arranged marriage, Abigail, Sheba, and Sherry. They were the only people he trusted in the world. His mother didn't tell and Sheba wasn't even a consideration. It had to be Abigail. The disheartening feeling lodged in the pit of his stomach was set aside until he could deal with the betrayal. He would wiggle around the topic until he was able to break free from the scrutinizing media. Confirming the allegation was premature. He couldn't spring news about the marriage in a televised venue. His customers had to be informed. Directly, in some cases.

"Engagement, my vacation plans, and my personal life aren't the topics of today's discussion."

Several remaining questions about stability were asked and answered. The conference ended with Joel determined to figure out what had happened. His mother left as Samantha Tate approached him.

"Mr. Joel Mitchell," she said, as coy and taunting as she'd been the first time she'd interviewed him for her show a year ago. He didn't mind, actually, today he welcomed the flattery. He was the master when it came to women, as Samantha had experienced firsthand. She was the refreshing dose of relief he needed. "Well, well, well," she said. "So, I hear that you're going to be off the market?"

"Come on, Ms. Tate, you can't believe everything you hear," he said, collecting his suit jacket without losing eye contact with her. She tried to maintain her flirtatious intensity. He knew she was no match and would cave to his finesse at his choosing.

She brushed against him. "Well, if you are getting married, let me take you to dinner. It could be like a good-bye dinner or a congratulations dinner or," she said, stepping closer, "dinner used to turn into breakfast with us."

"And if it's not true?" he asked.

"If it's not true, we can celebrate like old times anyway."

Joel had easily won Samantha over too many times in the past. Truth be told, Samantha was good company. She didn't give him the charge that Sheba did or the stability that Abigail provided, but Samantha was worth a dinner or two. "I have a full schedule over the next couple of weeks. We won't be able to turn this into a marathon this time. Dinner is all I have time for this week."

"We'll start with dinner and figure out the rest as we go," she teased.

That sounded like a plan he could entertain. He didn't expect much to change when it came to spending time with his lady friends after getting married. If the only sacrifice was his living arrangements, then he would gladly endure an arranged marriage for the sake of DMI. It was a price he would eagerly pay.

chapter

15

Sherry returned to her office to tweak the press release going out to the newspaper and magazines, curious why Madeline hadn't shown up to undermine Joel during the conference. Sherry had come to rely on Madeline's consistency. Deviations made her nervous.

About thirty minutes later Madeline walked into the office, interrupting and unapologetic.

"I was expecting a visit," Sherry said, taking off her reading glasses.

"I bet you were," Madeline said, taking a seat without waiting for an invitation.

After Dave's death, Sherry had been devastated, unable to see forward. Thanks to Joel's nurturing, Sherry was able to believe in a future, to believe that she had worth and could add value at DMI after being out of the workforce so long. After Joel was born, she'd chosen to terminate her administrative assistant role and become a stay-at-home mom, a decision she'd never regretted. However, there were times when she had agonized over Madeline and Dave working side by side, day after day. Madeline and Dave had divorced, but Sherry had long ago come to realize that there was an invisible link clinching the two together in some unexplainable way. She'd tried and tried to establish the chief wife title but didn't feel that it had ever been accomplished, despite Dave's reassurance of his commitment to the marriage. Taking the job as Joel's press secretary had been a huge boost to her self-esteem and worth. She was grateful to her son for rescuing her from her state of depression. If only she could keep Madeline out of her office and away from her son, depression would be obsolete. "Let's get this over with. What has Joel done now?"

"You mean besides driving my company into the ground?"

Sherry didn't bother responding. Madeline wasn't there to have a civil conversation. She came to do what she always did. The only difference between the office and the Mitchell estate was the address. It didn't matter to Madeline where she espoused her poison, so long as what she perceived as prey was within her grasp. The sun was shining and Sherry just didn't feel like being a victim today. "Joel knows what he's doing. Why don't you trust his decision for a change?"

Madeline burst into laughter, then stopped abruptly. "That will be the day when hell officially freezes over."

Sherry really didn't want to be bothered. She put her reading glasses on. The press release had to be finalized, and Madeline was hindering her ability to complete it and possibly spare Joel from having to answer questions from a slew of overzealous reporters looking to capitalize on fabricated information. Sherry returned to typing on the computer.

Ignoring Madeline didn't drive her away. "Why don't you talk to your son and convince him to make the right decision?"

"Which is what, exactly?" Sherry said, peering over her reading glasses.

"Resign, of course," Madeline said in her typically condescending way. Sherry was immune, and resumed her work.

"Don't you have any feedback?" Madeline asked.

Sherry shook her head no. She chose not to speak and further engage Madeline in a pointless conversation.

"You're a mother. I thought you'd be able to see what he's

doing and to help him think this through before he destroys his life and takes the rest of us down in this sinking boat with him." Madeline finally stood. Keeping quiet and letting the fire die out without fanning the flames worked best. The predictability gave Sherry comfort. Madeline was leaving without making a scene, a rare event when it came to these two ladies occupying the same space for more than a few minutes. Before exiting into the hallway, Madeline said, "When his little Lego world comes crashing down around the both of you, don't say that I didn't warn you, mother to mother."

Sherry wanted to jump in and offer a defense but there was no need. Madeline had gotten her dig in and retreated with no major damage. Sherry could live with it. She had for three decades. Dealing with Madeline's perpetual tirade for a few minutes was nothing. Madeline did manage to spark a nerve of concern. Joel was dealing with a huge decision, the biggest he'd made since becoming the boss. None of the other board members were in favor of the merger; even Sherry wasn't sure that this was a good idea. More important than trying to understand what was right or wrong businesswise, her job was to shield Joel from the media and from people like Madeline. That job she handled without fear.

chapter

16

Seventeen hours of travel between the south of France to Cape Town were a blur, not quite as long as the one to Michigan but equally draining. His prayers had to make a difference. Don's mind was flooded with an endless list of possibilities, most of which weren't heartwarming outcomes. He took solace in reflecting on Tamara's strength. She'd endured the unthinkable and survived on her terms. She would be okay. She had to be. Madeline was a different story. His heart pumped faster as he thought about telling his mother Tamara was gone. Madeline had always known Tamara's general whereabouts, but with the abrupt move, his sister was truly estranged. There was no easy way to break the news.

The twenty-five-minute ride from the airport landed him in his condo and on the phone to the States. Don stared at the wall clock, trying to decide if this was the best time. A seven hour time difference made it only four A.M. in Michigan. His mother was an early riser but not quite that early. He filled a cup of water, mulling over the decision. Don set the glass down on the counter and dialed the phone. Prolonging the inevitable wasn't going to make the news more desirable. A few rings and Madeline was on the phone.

"Don," she said, sounding wide awake, "I've been hoping to hear from you. Where are you? Is Tamara with you?" She fired off a few more questions. He was perfectly at ease with letting her talk and talk. The more she carried the conversation, the less he had to share. "Where are you?"

"I'm in Cape Town, Mother."

"Please tell me Tamara is with you."

"No, she's not." He concentrated on projecting the right tone, not too enthusiastic and giving false hope and not too pessimistic, confirming certain doom. The balance was razor thin, one he'd jockeyed with his mother many times in the past in an effort to protect her.

"I figured she went back to France. I guess I can be happy that she's safe there. I'm intentionally not calling it home, because you know I will always believe that home for you and Tamara is right here in Detroit with me."

There was another option. He could keep quiet and wait for Tamara to resurface. By the time Madeline found out she was gone, Tamara would already be found again. He had to decide if keeping his mother informed outweighed the hurt that was sure to follow. The answer didn't jump out at him, but finally the tug of truth prevailed. Like bad-tasting medicine, he blurted out, "Tamara is gone. By the time I got to her address in Monaco, the doorman said she'd moved. She left a note, that's it." After he finished, Don prepared for the hurricane.

"What do you mean she moved? Did you check inside her place? The doorman was probably lying because he doesn't know that Tamara has family members who care about her. He probably thought you were some strange man stalking their tenant. I'm taking the next flight to France and checking it out myself. No doorman, fireman, or any other man is going to turn me away. I can guarantee you that."

She was taking the news better than he'd hoped. Having Madeline fired up and ready for battle was always better than seeing her crumble into a ball of pity. Oddly, her streak of terror inflicted on others gave him comfort. "Mother, you shouldn't go to France."

"Oh, I'm going to France. Unless Tamara is sitting next to you in Africa, I'm going to France to see my child."

Calming her down was nearly impossible when it came to her children, but he had to try. Letting Madeline travel halfway around the world with pent-up anxiety wasn't a desirable scenario. He already had to worry about Tamara. Adding Madeline to the list wasn't feasible. He had to keep her in Detroit. "Mother, she will contact us. If you go after her, she'll run farther away. Is that what you want?"

"Of course not," she said, sounding slightly less resolute.

"Mother, it's obvious that she's coming around. Look at it from this perspective, at least she came to Detroit."

"And left before I could see her."

"But at least she came. We have to start somewhere," he said as his mother groaned. That's when he realized she was accepting his perspective. "I say we give her space and let her reach out to us."

"You can say that because you're not a parent. If you were, you'd know how difficult it is to let your child go, especially when there are unresolved issues involved."

"Have faith that God will work this out."

"Oh, please don't start preaching at me."

"I'll leave you alone if you leave her alone, deal?"

"Maybe I'll ease up, if you can tell me what we're going to do about Joel. We don't have the luxury of time if there's any hope of us taking over and finally getting that little brother of yours out."

"I don't have the answer."

"Well, we better get a plan, and quickly. We can only stall him for so long. He's already like a caged animal. He's dangerous. I don't trust him. I believe there's no limit to how far he'll go to keep the company." Don was amused, listening to his mother. Joel had no limit. Madeline didn't either, but she didn't see it that way and he'd never try to sway her perspective. "I still say that Tamara is our best bet. If we get her stock transferred to us, this game with Joel is over. We will have control of the company and end this charade. You can move back to Detroit, bring your company with you, and call it a day."

"You have the plan all worked out, I see, except for one tiny detail. Tamara is out of the picture for now."

"One call and my private investigator will get on her trail just like he has every other time she's moved."

"This time might be different. What if she doesn't want to be found?"

"Doesn't mean I'll stop trying."

"Mother, don't push, otherwise you'll drive her away for good."

"I didn't say that I would do it, just that I could. Besides, I've never violated her space. Knowing where she is and showing up on her doorstep are different."

Don could accept her need to know; as a mother, it was totally understandable. The rest of the conversation wasn't as clear. He didn't profess to have the answers. If the destiny theory was right, and he believed it probably was, he was going to rely on God to work the plan. No disrespect to his mother, but her barrage of plans consistently failed miserably. Certainty from a more reliable source was his preference.

He heaved a sigh of relief. Don picked up the phone prepared to call Naledi. Change of plan—he preferred seeing her in person as quickly as the twenty-minute distance to the office could be traveled. Being home felt good.

chapter
17

Don could relax, catch his breath, and let the day flow at its pace without the constant friction and finagling he was forced to do in Detroit. He entered LTI, chuckling. What could possibly cause him to give up what he had for a pipe dream? Settling for the sure thing had its merit. He hustled inside, making a direct path to Naledi. His passion intensified as his steps became brisker. Finally he reached her door and walked in. "Oops, I'm sorry, I should have knocked. Please forgive me," he said, halting once he crossed the threshold.

"It is no problem, please come in," she said with an electrifying brightness in her eyes. She stood and approached him, extending both of her hands.

He seamlessly reached out for hers and gently pulled her close, kissing one cheek and then the other, letting his grasp linger before stepping away. The brightness in her eyes remained, stirring his affection. It felt good having someone dedicated to him and him alone. There wasn't much else associated with the Mitchell family that could be put in the same category.

"I didn't know you would be in the office today, so soon after traveling."

"Why not? No need to be sitting at home. I know there's plenty to do here." Which was true, but while he could stand a day away from the office, a needless day away from Naledi was a different scenario. "It's short notice, but have you eaten lunch already?"

"I have not," she said, returning to her seat behind the desk and a mini mound of papers. "There is no time today."

"There's always time to eat," he said, reaching across the desk for her hand. She hesitated, looking baffled. "It's okay," he said, beckoning to her. "Come on, it's okay. I am the boss around here." He laughed. "At least some of the time, that is, when you're not running the place." He laughed more as her baffled look melted. She came toward him. "That's more like it. Let's get out of here and grab some lunch."

"The café downstairs is closed."

"I was thinking more like heading to the Cape for the afternoon."

Her eyes widened. "It's more than an hour's ride to the coast."

"And well worth it," he said, ushering her toward the door. There was no place on earth more refreshing than the Cape. The brisk air, scenic view from the rugged cliffs, and vastness of the Atlantic and Indian Oceans were hypnotic. He didn't know why the place had such a calming effect on him. Having a spot on earth that couldn't be explained, that just existed, helped him come to understand that not every detail or circumstance in life was explainable. Some things just were because they were. Being a Mitchell, there were a boatload of times when he preferred not trying to explain or rationalize the irrational. Tamara's running away, the struggle over DMI, his mother's plea, and Joel's irresponsibility swept in like the waves and brisk winds hitting the cliffs at the cape. He pushed away the burdens and concentrated on walking out with Naledi. Her presence reminded him of what was good. Nothing would rob him of this time. Today he would ease out the front door, leaving his burdens at the office. There was ample time to strap them on tomorrow and carry them around for several days afterward. "Let's go. You deserve a break, and I plan to make sure that you get one," he said, turning out the light behind him. By the time they took the scenic winding ride along the coast, grabbed a late lunch, and strolled along the shoreline, the day would be drawing to a close. There was plenty of work to be done and every bit of it would keep until later. Today belonged to him and Naledi.

chapter

18

Joel was handling DMI business, but he'd be lying if he said that being at odds with Abigail didn't affect him. Flat out, he needed her in his life, personally and professionally. He plucked the keys to his new house from the desk drawer. Every time he thought about the house, it was salted with the image of Abigail tossing the keys to him with an unforgettable expression of anger and dejection.

He opened the Harmonious Energy folder and pulled out his calculator. There were no apologies or requests of forgiveness that he could sincerely offer to Abigail. On the other hand, he was genuinely sorry for hurting her. But the choice between setting aside his goals for DMI or his personal feelings for Abigail wasn't a tough choice to make. Joel dropped the keys back into his drawer and stuffed his feelings for Abigail in the drawer, too.

The palm of his hand glided slowly down his face. Punching a series of keys on the calculator produced the same result each time, two hundred million dollars short. Where could he get that kind of money? His concentration was broken when his administrative assistant paged him on her direct line to his office. He answered the series of beeps by pushing the speakerphone and heard her say, "Mr. Bengali would like to speak with you."

Joel chuckled inside, not in a ha-ha way. He composed his answer, staring at the shortage of cash in front of him. "Tell him I'm tied up and I'll contact him as soon as I get a chance." Hopefully he could stall for a few more days and allow himself time to find the funds. Short of robbing a bank, he was open to ideas, conventional or otherwise. At that second his mind made the easy leap to Uncle Frank, the one man who had creative ways of raising funds. Embezzling money from DMI was proof of his diabolical acts, which is why Joel fired Uncle Frank his first day as CEO.

"I'm sorry, Mr. Mitchell, I wasn't clear." Joel didn't understand what the assistant meant. "Mr. Bengali is here."

Joel practically slipped out of his seat. "Give me a minute, please." He fumbled with the file in front, stuffing the papers inside, slamming the folder shut, and cramming it into his desk drawer. His anxiety soared, unsure why Musar would make an unannounced visit. Joel scrambled to clear his desk of any visible signs of his ill preparation. He straightened his tie, surveying the desk one last time, making sure there were no lingering documents revealing Joel's shortage. The deal would proceed as planned. He would get the funds regardless of the means. Once the evidence was hidden he told his assistant, "Please bring Mr. Bengali in." Joel approached the door to usher in his guest. "Musar," he said, extending his hand, "to what do I owe the pleasure?"

Musar entered, walking gingerly. Joel expected to see his twenty-three-year-old daughter, Zarah, follow several steps behind but she wasn't there this time.

"I'm here to finalize our deal."

Joel was stirred to concern without showing outward signs. "Please have a seat. I didn't realize we had an appointment today."

"We don't, but it's very important that I close this deal with you now," he said with the accented English that Joel had become familiar with and found no problem interpreting.

"Well, my legal team is reviewing the documents and completing the basic due diligence process. Our board of directors is very conservative when it comes to mergers," Joel had to say.

"The last time I was here, there seemed to be much concern from your leadership team about our religious beliefs. Does that remain a problem?"

Joel squirmed and choked through his words. "No, no, we're fine, just basic legal reviews. I expect us to be finished in another five to six weeks."

Musar laid his palm on the table. "We must complete this deal now. You see, my illness is progressing very quickly. My days are not many." He moved to the edge of his seat and put both hands on the table. "I must complete the deal for Harmonious Energy and the marriage for my only child. It is most important for me as a father to provide for her. It's my duty and my time is very little. I must be assured that you can come to India and finalize our arrangement this month."

Joel maintained a staunch disposition while the notion of two hundred million dollars trotted around the room, laughing at him. It was difficult keeping his gaze at eye level with Musar. "That's very quick. I'll need to check with my team."

"There are other suitors for my daughter in India. Perhaps I should go with one of them."

"No, no," Joel spoke up. "No need to pursue another company or another suitor. I will work out the details and, yes, I will definitely be in India by the end of month." Words were flying out of his mouth with truth set aside. They could fuse later, after Musar was convinced that DMI was the ideal home for Harmonious Energy.

Musar's body relaxed. "This is good news. I am very happy to know that my daughter will be provided for."

Joel reflected on Zarah. The first time they were introduced, he noted that her name was pronounced as "czar" with a short "a" on the end. There wasn't much else he recalled about his soon-to-be bride. He tried remembering the details of her face from their few encounters. The color of her eyes wasn't easily remembered. Were they soft brown and oval shaped like Abigail's or striking and hazel colored like Sheba's? He couldn't recall much about her except how quiet and timid she appeared with her father. Joel closed out the search for missing details. This was a business arrangement, not a love affair. Determined, he was ready to move forward. "I'll work out the details with you in the next few days."

Mr. Bengali stood and verbally thanked Joel, and followed with a handshake. The cautious steps Musar exhibited coming in were replaced with confident ones on the way out. This merger was as satisfying to Joel as it was to Musar, possibly more. Joel had something to prove to the world and Mr. Musar Bengali was his catalyst. Zarah came with the package.

His guest was gone. Joel remained standing, with one leg on the arm of a conference table chair. He could smell the sweet fragrance of victory, a scent for which his nostrils had grown familiar. The stench of failure was far in the distance. The gaping shortfall in funds broke up the premature celebration. He returned to his desk, finally sitting. There was work to do.

Joel dialed the bank, wondering if, by some miracle, more money was available to him with the credit line. A pseudomiracle, one that only required a few forged names on a contract, was just as good. The executive team could thank him next year when their bonus checks doubled.

The banker was on the line. "Mr. Mitchell, what can I do for you?"

"We're getting close to wrapping up this merger. We've already discussed the one hundred million dollar credit line available with my signature, but it looks like we'll need a little more cash to close the deal. What other funds do I have with you?" If the bank was not able to do another two hundred million, one hundred million would suffice. Joel could negotiate Musar down with the balance. He was feeling the wind in his sails—soaring high above the doubters and distracters.

The banker was gone for several minutes. When he returned, he said, "Mr. Mitchell, there's been a development with the DMI account that has been brought to my attention."

"What kind of development?" Joel asked, standing again.

"The one hundred million dollars is accessible to you, but a hold has been placed on the disbursement of any other funds without the approval of two executive team members, your CFO and one other authorized signer."

"What?" His thoughts were jumbled. "Who put the hold on the account?"

"I'm not sure, but I can find out."

"You do that, and let me know. I'm the CEO. Nobody has the authority to put a hold on anything without my knowledge."

"I assure you, Mr. Mitchell, that we received the proper paperwork, but I will definitely confirm that the standard procedures were followed."

The perception of stability was critical to maintaining positive ratings and value in the company. He couldn't appear to be out of control. This call was going nowhere as far as securing funds. Joel needed to rescue his image and conclude the conversation. The banker didn't have to tell him what he already knew. Madeline was behind the bank hold. She was determined to stop him, and he was determined not to be stopped. The concept of being blocked by her infuriated him. Cool and calm jumped out the window. The duel was heating up.

chapter

19

Madeline was the first to arrive at the status meeting in the boardroom. Abigail and George, the head of finance, weren't far behind. They took their seats.

"I wonder if Mr. CEO is going to be here," Madeline said. Abigail shrugged her shoulders. "He's missed so many meetings over the past three months. Between his media schedule and entourage of women, he's a busy man, awfully busy." The words were gone, too late to take back and spare Abigail the anguish. But the truth was the truth.

"Alleged entourage," Abigail said.

"Humph, if you say so," Madeline said, and left the conversation right there, with Abigail refusing to denounce a loser and Madeline wise enough to know better.

Joel's administrative assistant entered and dialed the conference room phone situated in the middle of the table. A few key punches and Barry, the senior vice president in Chicago, was on the line representing the Midwest, Connie from the Southern division, and Brian from the West Coast. Madeline wanted to yell out the absurd aspects of Joel's merger. If he had it his way, Brian and the West Coast were gone. The managers in the meeting were clueless about what was going on, except for Abigail, and that was preferred for now. Greetings ensued. "Where is Joel?" Madeline asked the assistant, expecting him to be the usual no-show.

"I'm right here," Joel said, entering on the heels of Madeline's question. He peered at his watch. "Right on time." Madeline stewed. She was prepared for him to be absent, which would give her more justification for ousting him. "Let's get started," Joel said smugly. Madeline took satisfaction in believing that his days were numbered, for real this time.

Abigail read the agenda, nothing unusual, the standard updates from the division managers followed by some comments from Joel. Madeline wondered if he would bring up the merger, the subject generating the most curiosity. Before they got to that debacle, the executive team had to deal with the most pressing issue—which amounted to staying in business.

"Connie, you're up first, followed by Barry," Abigail said.

"My numbers aren't as good as they normally are," Connie said, creating a clumsy moment of silence. "Sales in the Southern division are down twenty percent."

"Is that for the year?" Abigail asked.

"No, that's just for one quarter." Another awkward pause hovered. Madeline wanted to cut in but kept quiet, for now.

"I know it's hard to believe, but we've run the numbers several times, checked and double-checked. The numbers are down twenty percent," George said. He'd proven to be a strong chief financial officer. Madeline trusted his numbers. If he said the numbers were down, then the numbers were down.

Joel had to be as shocked as the rest of the executive team but he showed no visible reaction. As far as Madeline was concerned, he was in a dire situation either way. If the report was correct, he needed to get out of the head role. If it wasn't, his lack of concern was grounds to force him out. Either way was suitable for Madeline. The sooner he got out, the better, leaving more time for the rest of the team to stop the company's bleeding. DMI was on life support and if she could push Joel out in the next few days, resuscitation was theirs.

After the first report was read, more bad news about the Midwest was readily digested. Brian gave the West Coast update, which wasn't as bad, only a small setback. Apparently the West Coast clients hadn't gotten the wired news about DMI being held hostage by a narcissistic tyrant who'd sold a portion of the company and his soul to the first demigod willing to write the biggest check.

"What is that noise?" Connie asked over the speakerphone, shaking Madeline out of her trance. When she looked up, there was silence in the room and everyone was staring at her. The pen she held in her hand was tapping so frantically that it had put several nicks in her leather portfolio. Madeline tossed the pen down and brushed back her hair with her hand. Her fury burned, but scanning the room, she hated exposing her personal distaste publicly, especially when it came to Joel. The perception of one foolish, out-of-control Mitchell was plenty for the management team, possibly the world. She corralled her scattered thoughts and herded her mind back into the meeting. "What?" she said. "Go ahead."

"It's your turn, Madeline. We're on the East Coast update."

Madeline let her gold-rimmed reading glasses rest on the tip of her nose. She opened her portfolio and flipped to page two of her report, tapping her Mont Blanc pen lightly on the paper. "Does everyone have a copy?" Nods of affirmation and responses on the phone circled the room. "The East Coast is doing the same as the other divisions—poorly," she said and closed the report. "Let's quit playing this game." Abigail wore a perplexed expression, probably not sure what Madeline was going to say but fully aware of what she was capable of saying. Joel's expression didn't change. Madeline clasped her hands on top of the portfolio. "In the forty years that I've been in this company, which is from day one"—she removed her reading glasses, calmly set them on top of her portfolio next to her pen, and drew in a breath of air, determined to be calm despite her brooding frustration bottled deep within—"I've never seen such a dramatic drop in sales or accounts, especially our large accounts." Madeline knew she was right and didn't need a support team to speak the truth. She directed her gaze at Joel and pointed her folded reading glasses at him. "The swirling rumors of instability and immorality are taking a toll. You've taken this company from one of integrity and an impeccable reputation to some struggling backwoods company that is two accounts short of scrambling for rent money. You need to do the right thing and step down. It's the only reasonable reaction to these ridiculous sales reports," she said, tapping her index finger on the portfolio containing her report.

"What are you talking about?" Joel finally managed to get out. "I've taken this company to new levels, and you know it."

"And you'll have us out of business in another six months, so what's your point?"

Joel tossed his arms into the air. "I'm not about to get into this debate with you, Madeline. I am the CEO."

"For two years, eleven months, seventeen days, and thirty-nine seconds to be exact, but don't quote me. I might be off on the seconds," Madeline said.

Abigail would usually step in as the referee, but she must have been really mad with Joel this time because she stayed on the sidelines of the argument. Madeline took that as a cue to keep applying pressure.

Joel leaned up to the table and spewed, "Get over it. I'm running this company. If you're truly this opposed to my decisions, there's always the door." He leaned back in his seat.

If the pressure in her head raised one more notch, she was certain to blow the top off her head and probably the building, too. This little snot-nosed boy was playing with building blocks when her children were taking driving lessons. He had gall the size of the Grand Canyon and a degree of ignorance equally as big, which was the pitfall she was intent on exploiting.

"I'm not leaving," she said, chuckling. The mere concept was comical.

"Maybe not voluntarily, but I'm the one in charge." The rest of the meeting participants were nonexistent. This posturing was strictly between them—two pit bulls—and Madeline wasn't receptive to caving in.

"I'm tired of your divisive antics. You can either quit or get fired, that's your choice," Joel said. "This meeting is over."

Decorum between two top ranking executives had been checked at the door. The bloody fight to the death was assumed. Madeline did try to reserve a drop of professionalism and asked that the meeting be tabled. Those on the phone disconnected and the room cleared. Abigail reluctantly left at Madeline's request, after Madeline assured her they weren't going to literally draw blood.

"Listen here, Mr. CEO, I'm not going anywhere," Madeline said, standing and leaning on the edge of the table as soon as Abigail left. "I have more rights to this company than you will ever have. The terms of my divorce state that I can never be fired. That was a gift from Dave Mitchell." Madeline smirked. "If you don't believe me, go check the records, Mr. CEO." She strolled toward the door. Joel remained seated with his back to her. "You see, I'm a definite when it comes to DMI, and you, sir, are a big maybe." She finished and strode out of the room, having spoken the last word.

chapter

20

Sailing into her office on the tips of feathers, Madeline had hope. This time, she was close to actually fulfilling her dream of ousting Joel from a position he never should have inherited. No need to dwell on the past . . . the future was hers and Don's. She dialed with the speakerphone on, barely able to stay grounded. The restraint broke once her son was on the call. She skipped greetings and cut right to business. "You have to get back to Detroit, quickly. Today, if you can."

"Well, hello to you, too, Mother. What catastrophe is going on now? I'm sure that's what you've called to tell me."

Joel's luck had run out. He definitely didn't have backing from the executive team. More important, Joel didn't seem to have the favor he once had with God, the kind that made everything he touched golden. Madeline could duel, toe-to-toe, with any person in DMI, or outside for that matter, but God was different. He wasn't somebody she chose to challenge. She felt justified in being upset with Him periodically, but that's as far as she went. If Joel didn't have God in his corner, he was no match for her.

"We had the executive team meeting today and the sales are awful. We're down by twenty percent since last quarter." Madeline strolled around her desk with arms folded. She expected a drop in sales, not a landslide. She'd worked too hard for too many years, sacrificed a marriage and her livelihood for DMI. Joel wasn't going to ruin her life's work. "Clients are leaving left and right, which is no surprise given that we're founded on biblical principles. Eighty percent of our client base is churches and other religious entities." She stopped pacing near the side of her desk where the phone was and leaned against the desk. "Of course we were going to lose them as soon as word got out about the merger and the sale of a key division." She was in awe at Joel's brandish actions. "This is Joel's doing, completely." His arrogance and ignorance had finally collided and washed out his common sense. "I guess he lost his renowned wisdom," she said without an ounce of sincerity, "when he lost his spiritual edge. Good for me, makes him easier to take out. Now you see why I called. I can smell his downfall coming and you need to be here."

"I'm not panicking, Mother. We have a plan. The board has postponed the deal for six months. Joel can't make a move on the merger without our backing. We have time to let this play out."

"Don't you hear me? Sales dropped twenty percent. That has never happened. We can't wait. Time for games is over," she said, coming around the desk and taking a seat. "We need to act or there won't be a company left to take over."

"Like I said, I'm not panicking and acting hastily. It hasn't worked for you. Let's try another way," he said.

Madeline couldn't refute what he was saying, but sitting idle and waiting for progress wasn't her way. Action was what she believed in, right or wrong.

"Look, if God has called me to run DMI, then I'm going to trust His plan. If you want me to run DMI, you need to trust the plan that I'm following. I won't be pressured into something half baked, Mother. I love you dearly, but you have to step back and see the big picture. Take a breath and let me get back to work." She knew he was right. "Remember, I have a company to run here, too."

The idea clicked like a light switch. "Why don't you offer your services to our customers that have left?" She was charged, thinking about the possibilities. Madeline was so proud of the idea that she could have patted herself on the back. "Why didn't we think of this sooner? Never mind, it's on the table now. Isn't it a fantastic idea?" Most likely Don was going to say no. She knew he'd avoided churches and other religious entities when he'd started LTI, wanting to create distance from the religious-oriented DMI world and his new one.

"My client base is mostly corporate and educational institutions."

"So what? You know this business. You were the first division head to realize double-digit growth when you ran the East Coast. You have what it takes. This is too perfect." Madeline couldn't contain her glee. "We have to regain our lost customers. If we want to expand internationally, what better connection than Leadership Training International, run by none other than the oldest legitimate son of Dave Mitchell?" She spun around in her desk chair. "I'm so excited that I'm silly."

"You may be on to something this time, Mother. Let me give this some thought and lay out a few scenarios. I'll have Naledi do some market research to determine how the two companies could work together, but this is a good idea."

"You better believe it's a good idea. I'm your mother, and it's my job to get you home. If coming up with a good idea every now and then is what it takes, so be it." Madeline ended the call, soaked with a gush of victory. Finally the time was coming to reclaim what rightfully belonged to her children: integrity, and the top spot on Dave Mitchell's inheritance list.

chapter

21

Madeline meant well but was constantly driven by passion and retaliation. Don wanted to be methodical, definitive, and responsible. There was no rush. He mulled over the positives and negatives of expanding LTI into the religious sector, not quite sold. He'd call Abigail. She'd have solid insight. Since the recent visit to Detroit, the two of them stayed in frequent contact, three to four times a week. Their reconnection didn't require formal greetings. "Abigail, I'd like to bounce an idea around with you. My mother suggested that I pitch LTI to the customers who have left. I'm actually giving the idea serious consideration. You're on the front line and you know how much I value your professional opinion. What do you think?"

"It's a great idea," she said, talking fast. "You have the background and the market knowledge."

"You don't think it would be a conflict of interest?"

"No way, there's no conflict. The customers are gone, thanks to Joel," she said. "At least they wouldn't be totally lost to the entire Mitchell family if you took care of them. It's a great idea. Seriously, I'm not just saying that."

"I need to run the numbers on market share and determine the logistics since I'm based out of South Africa. If I did this, I'd have to get Naledi involved."

"I know she's important to LTI, but why would she need to be involved with your reaching out to DMI clients?"

"I would need her to run the business here while I spend time there meeting with clients."

"I thought you were going to be spending time here anyway?"

He detected her intensity. "I'm wrapping up some critical projects here before I come back to Detroit. I just told my mother earlier today that we have a six-month moratorium on the merger. Joel can't push forward before then." Don was returning to Michigan, but running back now at the expense of his own company's stability was counterproductive. Don had to figure out how to be a willing member of the Mitchell family without compromising his dreams and self-worth. Thirty-four years of life had already been plenty.

"You're not changing your mind about being CEO, are you?"

"No, not at all. I'm all in. When you or my mother tells me that Joel has resigned and the CEO role is ready, I'll be on the first plane."

Abigail was briefly amused. "We both know that won't happen. Joel would rather die than resign. Being in charge is his life. It's the only role he knows."

"We'll rely on the independent counsel and our legal team to find a way to remove Joel. Between the two teams, they have to uncover something useful." Revenge tried rearing itself in the decision. Don quickly shook off the notion. He'd come to terms with Joel and God before arriving in Detroit to assume the lead role. "I made it clear from the very beginning. I'm not sure how and when God is going to bring this plan to fruition. My job is to believe that He will and that I should be ready to step up when the time is right. In the meantime, I'm going to keep LTI profitable."

"Running two companies is a lot. Let me know how I can help."

"With you there and Naledi here, I'll be okay."

"That's right, Naledi. She's turned out to be quite a special partner. There was a time when the two of us were joined at the hip. Looks like I've been replaced," she said. Don assumed she was joking. With Joel so deeply rooted in her affections, she had to be.

chapter

22

Don was the master at splitting his energy, a skill forced upon him during his childhood. He had to juggle time and loyalty between two parents after Dave left Madeline for Sherry and started his new family. He remembered giving Madeline a lot more of his time and loyalty since she was the saddest most of the time, at least the first couple of years, when he was four or five. Now he was making his own mark, thanks in part to Naledi. Not a day had passed since he hired her that she hadn't managed to brighten his spirit. She was a godsend at a time when he needed to trust in someone, in something positive. Her presence had kept him sane during the early months. He owed her more than a paycheck.

"Did you get my note?" he asked, referring to a note he'd left in her office earlier.

Naledi entered the office and sat. They'd come so far as a team. Abigail was right. There was a time when Don and Abigail were a solid force, well suited, at least until she shifted her loyalty and love exclusively to Joel. The affection he had for Abigail wasn't the kind to easily vanish. Don wiped away the notion. Those days and feelings were done and life continued. Thank goodness for Naledi.

Don reflected on their initial meeting, not knowing whether it was more appropriate to shake her hand or bow or do nothing. The clumsiness had dissipated. The fact that Don and Naledi were born and raised continents apart, with different values and cultural perspectives, ultimately became secondary to the basic need of the human spirit to connect.

"Yes, Don, I did get the note, and I'm not sure of what to do."

He came from around the desk and took a seat near Naledi. "Remember when I told you that my mother and Abigail want me to run DMI?"

"Of course I do," she said with her eyebrows raised. "But you came back because it did not work as you planned."

"Right, right," he said, leaning forward and placing his elbows on his knees. "But I still have to go back, probably soon."

"In six months, yes?" she said, with each word tastefully seasoned by her accent—not annoying or untranslatable, rather soothing and mesmerizing.

"Probably sooner." Her eyelids widened. He detected her confusion. Touching her hand for reassurance was acceptable between them. Many dinner dates and walks along the harbor made it so. They hadn't gone beyond lighthearted courtship labeled as friendship, which helped eliminate awkwardness in the office. "I may need to go back as early as next week."

"I don't understand."

"There's an opportunity for me to expand LTI into the U.S. with clients that I've worked with in the past, but I have to act quickly."

"Is this important to you?"

He clasped his hands together and locked his gaze with hers. "Yes, I believe so."

"Then how can I help you?"

As simple as that; he voiced a desire and she was on board without opposition. She was the puzzle piece that enabled him to make South Africa home. He couldn't wipe away the dormant fretting associated with claiming the CEO role, but he was doing his best to let the details manifest. Naledi's grace for him helped smooth the rough edges internally. At this critical junction in his life, she was the only one on earth who could do what he needed.

"I'll be doing a great deal of traveling over the next couple of months, but I can't let LTI suffer in my absence. We've worked too hard and accomplished too much to put this company at risk. That's where I need you. I will feel comfortable if you're running the company for me while I'm shuffling back and forth. You're the only way that I can make this work." Naledi fidgeted in her seat, trying to speak, but only utterances came forward. He had only touched her hand temporarily at the onset of the conversation and found himself touching it again, hoping that he was providing reassurance. "I know you can do this. I've worked with you for nearly two years. I know what you're capable of doing. You can do this."

"I'm not sure that I can be in charge of this place alone."

He followed her wandering gaze with his, refusing to stop the search until his gaze was locked with hers. "You won't be alone. I may not physically be in this office, but you will have access to me any time. I promise you that you will not be alone."

Her disposition seemed to mellow. He continued with the reassurance. "I'll hire or promote any other resources that you need to feel comfortable." He felt her pulse slowing in the grip he had on her hand. "Besides, we're only talking about a few months at first. We'll work on the longer-term plan later." The radiance of her face was returning. "What do you say?"

"I will do it for you. I will do my best."

"Thank you," he said, standing. She stood, too. He shook her hand, deliberate and balanced with affection. She gave a slight bow in return. He yearned to share his passion with her and cast away any doubt, but opted to maintain a small semblance of professionalism. Time and purpose would take care of the rest between them. "Oh, I forgot," he said, slapping the heel of his palm on his forehead. "I'm giving you a raise."

"No, Don, that is not necessary. No, I am very pleased to do the work for you for no more money. I am quite satisfied with my salary."

Don raised his hand like a stop sign. "No argument, I'm doubling your salary. I honestly don't know how long you'll be in the role, but you'll keep the raise, no matter what."

"Please, no, Don."

"It's done." He faced her and said with sincerity from the depth of his existence, "I am grateful to have you working with me. You are so important to this company and to me." He extended his hand to her and when their fingers met their connection was solidified.

chapter

23

Rejection and compassion dueled in Abigail's soul. As one gained a slight edge in the battle, the other tussled more vehemently for control. Back and forth, constantly, until Abigail couldn't bear the torment any longer. She sprang to her feet, eager to reach Joel's office before rejection landed a final blow. "Is he in a meeting?" she asked his assistant with her hand on the doorknob but not quite ready to burst into the office improperly. Respect had its place, despite her mood.

"No, he's in there alone."

Before the assistant could formulate her next statement, Abigail opened the door, drawing a reaction from the assistant. Abigail had to burst in while her remaining shred of compassion for Joel existed. It was rapidly fading. Opening the door appeared to have startled Joel.

"Good, you are here," she said. He nodded without speaking. There had never been a time where the wall of tension was so high that she couldn't reach him. His silence hurt but she believed, wanted to believe, that the wall was only at knee level. With some minor effort she could step over their disagreement and erase the distance between them. She had to try. "You've been hard to find these days."

"I didn't know you were looking for me," he said, looking up briefly before dropping his gaze to the laptop situated on his desk.

She didn't know whether to sit or stand or what. Finally she approached the desk and eased into the seat closest to his desk but seemingly miles away. "I don't usually have to look for you. You're usually just there."

He shot a cutting glance at her and let it quickly break away. "I could say the same thing," he said, closing the laptop and peering at her, this time without looking away.

She shrugged her shoulders. "Maybe, but I'm not really okay with that." She was starting to relax. After all, Joel wasn't a stranger, not really. She might not recognize his recent actions or agree with his motives, but Abigail knew that Joel had a good heart. He was worth her effort. "We're friends, have been for years. Is this the end of that?"

Joel reared back in his chair. "You tell me. You're the one who changed the rules between us."

"What do you mean? I've been the same."

"Humph," he responded.

"I have. You know I have."

"Come on, Abigail, get real. At the time when I needed you the most, you abandoned me to side with Don and Madeline, of all people. You might as well drive a knife into my spine. The effect wouldn't be as harsh." He took a quick peek at the buzzing PDA on his desk.

"Aren't you going to get that?"

"I'll get back to her."

"Who is her?"

Joel raised his gaze. "Colleague."

In a hot second she was catapulted back to the days when Joel kept an active list of female companions, but they were set aside when he got serious about wanting to be the best that he could be. "That's what you're calling them nowadays."

"I'm sure it doesn't matter to you."

"Correct."

"Abigail, Abigail, when are we going to quit playing this game? You know we have a bond. Have and always will. Why try to fool yourself into believing otherwise?" he said, leaning closer to the desk, shortening the distance.

Perhaps he was right, but there wasn't much she could say except "You're engaged. That doesn't leave much bonding for us."

"Nothing has or will change between us. Why can't you understand that?"

"Why can't you understand that marriage is supposed to change you?"

"Not this kind."

"What am I supposed to be? Your friend? Your colleague?" she said, letting her words bite.

"Why does what we are require a label? What we've always been, we can still be. That doesn't have to change. I don't want it to change." He came around the desk and reached for her hand. She didn't respond.

"I've been with you from the beginning, pretty much from the moment Dave appointed you CEO. I've poured my time and energy into DMI and into you," she said.

"I didn't realize you considered our time together to be such a burden," Joel said and walked away.

"Stop it, Joel," she said, scooting to the edge of the seat, determined to keep focused on work and not their label-less relationship. He wasn't going to stir up her affection, leaving her distracted. "You know what I mean. I've been loyal to you, but you can't expect me to support something I don't agree with."

"Here we go with this conversation again," he said, letting his hands fly into the air. "We've already been down this path. I don't have time to rehash this." He looked away.

"So that's it, there's no middle ground—either I agree with you or we have no friendship?"

"You tell me, Abigail, what do you expect me to do? I need you and you're not there for me—bottom line." She couldn't think of anything to say that hadn't already been said. "Everything we've done in the past won't matter for DMI if I don't complete this next deal. This is my only priority. I can't let any other distractions, issues . . . or personal feelings cause me to lose sight of my mission. My father told me that there were decisions to be made that I'd have to make alone. I guess that time has come."

"You're being alone is by choice," she said, gaining strength to say what had to be said. Joel was in trouble whether he knew it or not. She was willing to forgo pride and reach out to him. She stood and leaned on the desk. "Let's regroup. Let's do what we used to do," she said, feeling invigorated, hopeful for the first time since the conversation started. "We can go to church on Sunday. Maybe we can visit Greater Faith Chapel with Mother Walker, remember the lady they called Big Mama, the one who gave you a prophetic word?" Much of what Big Mama had said in the past hadn't pleased Joel and his aspirations, especially the part about him being deceived and lured away from God. The old lady knew only one way, God's way. Joel didn't like the conviction of her words, but Abigail knew he respected the church mother. "Remember, you really liked her."

Joel cut Abigail off. "I don't have time to run to church every Sunday. Contrary to popular belief, I am the CEO, which means that I'm trying to run a company, with very little help, I might add."

Abigail's hope plummeted. There wasn't anything else to say. She retreated from the room in total silence.

chapter

24

Going around in circles wasn't familiar to Joel. He was motivated by directness and action. When he spoke, people moved to carry out his request. Why couldn't the company recognize that he knew what he was doing? He wasn't some random aloof guy making whacked out decisions without merit. He was Joel Mitchell, one of the primary heirs to the Mitchell dynasty. He was the one out of a long line of contenders who was left holding the keys to the chief executive office. He was the chosen one. Not Don and definitely not Madeline. Joel grabbed the phone from his desk. He scrolled past the missed calls from Samantha Tate without a second of consideration. The nostalgic moment deposited a sufficient boost of energy in his weary bones. Two rings and bypassing the receptionist got him where he wanted to be, on the line with his personal banker.

"Mr. Mitchell, I've been expecting your call. How can we assist you today?"

Joel didn't have the entire cash outlay situation figured out, but getting what he could from the bank was a huge help. He'd secure funds from the credit line and worry about the rest next. "I'm ready to complete the merger that we discussed previously. I'll need the entire credit line limit, and I'd like to discuss other options for securing the rest of the money that we need."

The banker didn't hesitate. "Based on the account hold, the only funds available to you are through the credit line, which can be accessed solely on your executive order. Other funding would require a new evaluation of DMI assets and approvals from two members of the executive team, as we've discussed."

Joel was clear about the other signatures stemming from the board's attempt to hold up the merger, but the evaluation was a surprise. "Why do you need to find out the worth? You have the most current value."

"Mr. Mitchell, there has been a perceived change in your company's value."

There was no way Madeline had gone this far with her cancerous lies. DMI hadn't shown growth last quarter, but the ten quarters prior would surely offset the dip. He wasn't going to be discounted, not when he was so close to realizing his dream on an international scale. "DMI is solid. You have balance sheets for nearly three years. I don't see the problem. Either you want our business or you don't."

"Absolutely we want your business. We've been working with you, or should I say the company, for more than thirty years. We value you as a key client."

"Then why are you giving me such a hard time when I'm trying to throw a significant chunk of business your way?"

"Well, the problem is that for the first time since the line of credit was established, the perceived DMI value has dropped sizably. As a result, the collateral has weakened and the eligible credit line is reduced to fifty million."

"You can't be serious. That's not nearly enough."

"Mr. Mitchell, I really am sorry. I wish there was some way to meet your business needs, but my hands are tied. I can't extend additional credit to you without a dramatic increase in the company's value. When you factor in the hold limiting your access to funds, we're left with a single source."

"Since we're at an impasse, we can consider this discussion to be over," Joel said, bitter.

"What about the fifty million? Should I wire that to an account?"

Joel hesitated. Fifty million was fifty million less that he had to scramble and find. On the other hand, his pride was worth more, at least another two hundred million more. "No, we prefer to do business with an institution that values a long-term relationship."

"Mr. Mitchell, I'm sorry you feel that way. Your business has been and continues to be very significant to us. I'm sure this is a temporary situation and will be resolved very quickly and we can continue our partnership."

"I don't think so." The banker tried wedging a pathetic line of empty rhetoric before Joel cut him off. "Have a good day," Joel concluded and ended the call. He held the receiver for a while until the dial tone hummed. The fury burned within. Nobody said no to Joel Mitchell, no one of significance, except Abigail. The bank was merely an inconvenience, not a showstopper. Abigail was a whole different perspective. Joel and Abigail shared a sense of purpose, vision, a desire to achieve what others hadn't. She was the fuel in his engine, vital yet subdued in the background. Having Abigail flip her loyalty was troubling, but not permanent. He brushed away the glaring reminder and put full force toward securing the funds.

An hour passed, and then another. Joel paced the room when he wasn't sitting at the desk scratching out financial scenarios. One from Sheba, one from DMI treasury, and two from borrowing against his personal assets only totaled four hundred million no matter how many ways he calculated. Balled up sheets of paper surrounded the trash can near his desk. There had to be an answer. If only he could pray for guidance. It was the one option he hadn't tried. Honestly, he wasn't prepared to hear "no" or, worse, hear nothing. He continued racking his brain for the additional money.

Although he'd privately solicited spiritual advice on a couple of occasions, Joel didn't feel compelled to do so again. He wasn't convinced they knew any more about the future than he did. He was about to take a break when Uncle Frank dropped into his mind. The rumors were plentiful about Uncle Frank and his shady dealings with those who didn't trade on Wall Street. Joel hadn't cared if the rumors were true in the past. It wasn't like his father's brother was a close family member. Uncle Frank was just a man with the same last name as his. Until now, the less contact Uncle Frank made the better.

Joel dug through his private papers in search of a number. He almost called his assistant and asked her to get it, but thought it best not to let anyone know he was talking with Uncle Frank. His uncle was bad news. He knew it and anyone else in the company would know it, too, if the word got out. Instead, Joel dug further through old financial documents until he found a number hand-written on top of a four-year-old income statement. Confident in his decision to pursue Harmonious Energy, Joel was content pursuing nontraditional loans. Besides, there would be an abundance of cash coming his way once the deal with Musar was final. The plan was to pay off the loan immediately, without anyone else knowing about the source.

Joel snatched one of the balled-up pieces off the floor, took several steps back, pretended to dribble the ball around his back, shot it into the trash can, and landed the awkward shot. His goal was finally within reach.

chapter

25

Joel didn't pay attention to the dialogue springing from his conscience. If he had, his Lamborghini wouldn't be sitting in the parking lot of an obscure diner sixty miles from Detroit. He was amused, thinking about his situation, not quite sure how he ended up in it. The same scenario acted out by anyone else would be perceived as desperate, but Joel and desperation were total opposites, never to exist in the same sentence. He killed the purring engine and peered around the tiny parking lot, looking for his uncle. Joel tapped the leather-bound wheel, wanting to fast forward through this creative financing meeting. His head swiveled every time a car passed. He checked his watch five times, beginning to wonder if Uncle Frank had duped him, when the Mercedes two-seater swung into the parking lot and whipped into the slot next to him. Joel gripped the handle to open the door and go into the diner with his uncle. Before the driver-side door could extend open, Uncle Frank was sitting in the passenger seat.

"Well, if it isn't my nephew, the same one who fired me."

Joel didn't want to stroll down memory lane with a man who stole from his own family. Uncle Frank made the last months of Dave Mitchell's life stressful. Joel was certain that if his father had been alive, he'd be outraged to see his son do business with Uncle Frank, the reputed crook. Unfortunately, the other financial vehicles were blocked thanks to the Mitchell family, the people who took great joy in watching Joel fail. He was bent on not letting them get the satisfaction. "Like I said on the phone, I have a business proposition that I think you'll be interested in. I'm not here to talk about what you did at DMI when my father was in charge. Honestly, I don't care. I'm here to handle business right now." Joel's voice was sharp, unflinching. "If you think that you're going to have a problem working with me and you don't want a cut of the money on the table, then step out of my car, so that I can get the heck out of here." Joel pushed the button to start the engine.

Uncle Frank laid his hand on Joel's wrist and pressed down lightly. "Take it easy, nephew. Family is family and business is business. I don't have any hang-ups with you so long as there's money on the table." He pressed Joel's wrist again. Joel killed the engine that time. Uncle Frank turned his body in an awkward way toward Joel, with his shoulder against the window. "You didn't share any information on the phone but you said this was urgent. What's this about?"

Greed glistened in Uncle Frank's eyes. He was fired up at the smell of money. Joel welcomed the pit-bull spirit. Uncle Frank was the person he needed to get the deal done. If there was cash on the streets anywhere, Uncle Frank could get it by any means. It was the main reason why Joel could never offer his uncle another job.

"I can't get into the details of the deal that I'm working on, but I can say that I need three hundred million dollars like that," Joel said, snapping his fingers. "This deal is hot and I don't have time to go through the red tape at the bank. This is a one-time opportunity. I have to act now." He pounded lightly on the steering wheel.

"Whoa, did you say three hundred million dollars, as in over a quarter of a billion?" Joel nodded yes. "That's not a small chunk of change. You're talking investment banker dollars. I can't help you with that kind of money." Uncle Frank reached for the door handle to leave. "I'll see you around."

This was the last hope. Without funding from Uncle Frank, the deal was as good as dead. Joel refused to play out the loser scenario. He'd played that role with Madeline and her children. He'd sacrificed his livelihood, his desires, and now his personal wealth to see DMI excel. Joel had finally built a name of success and there was no way he could let that be destroyed. Pride and integrity had to be silenced. "Do you know anybody who can loan me that kind of money right away?"

The door was open. Uncle Frank had one foot on the ground. "I'm not on Wall Street. I can't get you that kind of money. Come on, you must know that what you're asking is ridiculous." The second foot was about to land on the ground, too.

"Do you know anybody?" Joel yelled with such force that Uncle Frank froze.

He turned to Joel and responded without any snide comments, "Maybe I do."

Joel had his uncle's attention and wasn't going to let it drop again. "Then name your price."

"What are we talking?"

"I said, name your price. How much do you want off the top for arranging the deal?"

Both feet were instantly placed in the car and the door closed. Uncle Frank peered straight ahead, choosing not to look at Joel. "This is a huge undertaking. You practically need the approval of the president and Congress to get this kind of money in your hands."

"Look, cut the crap, Frank. Are you in or out?" Joel said, reaching for the start button again. He had no intention of moving the car without an agreement, but Uncle Frank didn't need to know that much.

"All right, all right," Uncle Frank said, tapping Joel's wrist once again. Joel was pleased. He'd shaken Uncle Frank into action. Acting angry was a risk, but in the end, Joel was positive Uncle Frank wasn't going to walk away from a large chunk of money under any circumstances. His dirty dealings weren't up for judgment as far as Joel was concerned, so long as he came through with the three hundred million. "You want me to name my price. Here it is—one percent consulting fee, nonrefundable, nonnegotiable, nontraceable, no contingencies. I mean none. Once you have a deal for the money, my fee is paid regardless of what happens afterward."

"I can live with your terms, but you're the one brokering this deal. You have to at least stay involved until I get my money."

"I'm not a broker, a banker, or a member of the chamber of commerce. I'm a simple businessman with simple terms. If you want this money you have to agree to my terms, period, nonnegotiable," he said as he reached for the door handle.

"Hang on, I can meet your terms. You just get the money."

"You'll hear from me in a few days."

"I only have a few days," Joel said, not playing around.

Uncle Frank must have detected the tone of seriousness and said, "You'll hear from me." He got out and turned to say, "This is just between us, and we can't talk about this on the phone."

"No problem, you let me know when and where." Joel was feeling a burst of confidence. Finally the situation was turning in his direction. Uncle Frank said something else before closing the door. "Nephew, I didn't check you for a wire."

"Why would you?"

"Exactly my point. I know you're a smart kid. I'm taking you at your word on this deal. Just so you know, you can't get funds like this from your local ATM. This is a huge undertaking. I assume that if you could get the funds any other way you wouldn't be here talking to me. So, like I said, I'm taking you seriously. That means you better take me seriously. The people who are willing to loan this kind of money won't take kindly to a wiretap, if you know what I mean." Uncle Frank leaned his head fully into the car. "Think long and hard about this transaction. This better be legitimate, because once I leave here, the deal is in motion and those aren't wheels that can easily be stopped. Are you sure about this?"

"Completely."

"So be it." Uncle Frank got out of the car. "Sit tight. You'll hear from me in a few days. Have my three million ready. Uncle Frank pulled a piece of paper from his pocket. "Hand me a pen." Joel scrambled to find one and handed it over. His uncle jotted down something and handed the paper to Joel. "This is to my account in the Cayman. The first five digits are missing. I'll give those to you when the time is right," he said and tapped the window frame. "See you later, nephew." Uncle Frank closed the door, jumped in his car, and left.

Joel tapped on the steering wheel, not wanting to get too over-confident. He was close this time, real close. His conscience tried reflecting on the means of getting the money. Joel refused to give in. He wiped away the thought of any shady dealings. Uncle Frank wasn't getting the money from Wall Street. That was evident. Then again, Wall Street wasn't the epitome of honest trading, either. He felt justified in pursuing his unconventional method of raising capital. He wasn't going to be denied. He pushed the start button and let the engine hum, sweet, just like his soon-to-be victory over those who tried to shut him down. He couldn't wait to see their faces when he announced closure on the merger. He put the car in reverse and savored satisfaction. Maybe Madeline would eventually quit, especially if she loathed the prospect of working with Harmonious Energy. Uncle Frank was a crook, but he was Joel's favorite relative for the day. The car eased onto the state highway and then Joel floored the gas pedal, leaving failure in the rearview mirror. He was where he wanted to be, in charge.

chapter

26

Don couldn't help but to think about Naledi being left behind. His heart warmed. The cab arrived at the office. He paid and went inside the DMI building. Two months ago he'd sold his BMW. At the time there was no reason to keep it. He was eight thousand miles away and glad about it. Time and purpose had changed. With the amount of trips planned for Detroit, he'd take time out to lease one in a day or two.

Upstairs he poked his head into Madeline's office. She practically ran to the door. "Ah." She wrapped her arms around him and clutched tightly, not letting go right away. He was so used to Madeline and her mothering. Secretly, he appreciated the doting. There were times when her coddling kept him going, kept him from feeling parentless or alone. Her devotion was unquestionable and overshadowed some of her other less endearing characteristics. "You should have called me. I could have picked you up from the airport," she said, releasing him slowly.

"I took a cab. It was no problem."

Madeline walked back to her desk, brushing down one side of her hair. Don tossed his carry-on luggage onto her tiny sofa.

"What's this about a cab? You can afford a private car, you know." She tugged gently at the bottom of her Chanel suit jacket.

Don chuckled. "So long as I get here, that's what matters, right, Mother?"

Madeline groaned. "You and that brother of yours have nothing in common except for Dave's DNA. Obviously Joel got the watered-down version."

"Don't start."

Madeline pretended to zip her lips. "I won't say a word about Mr. Joel. His actions are speaking much louder than I ever could. I prefer to spend my energy on something productive. Are you ready to get to work?"

"That's why I'm here. Where's Abigail?"

"Hang on," Madeline said, grabbing the phone receiver. Once Abigail was on the line, his mother said, "Come on up to my office when you get a chance. Our Don is here." Mother said a few more words and nodded several times during the conversation. Afterward Madeline said, "She's on her way up. She was very pleased to know that you're here, not nearly as thrilled as I am, though."

Less than five minutes passed before Abigail was knocking on the door. Her expression of glee sailed into the room, invigorating Don. He gave her a friendly greeting and each took a seat.

"When did you get in? I thought you were coming next week?"

"Thanks to Naledi, I was able to get here sooner." Abigail crossed her legs. "If I didn't have her in the picture, DMI wouldn't be a possibility for me." Abigail switched legs.

"You really seem to rely on her." Madeline nodded her head. "Is there something you're not telling me?"

"You know Don keeps us up-to-date," Abigail interrupted to say.

"Maybe not."

Hearing the two women talk as if he wasn't there was intriguing. He would remain invisible as long as possible, keeping quiet.

"Oh, he does. Trust me, there's nothing going on that he hasn't told us. Isn't that right, Don?" Abigail asked.

"Ignore me. This conversation is working well with just the two of you."

Madeline opened the leather portfolio on her desk and slid on her reading glasses. "Don't you get married over there in Africa without letting me know something."

"Don isn't getting married," Abigail said in a stern tone, placing both her feet on the floor.

"Is it so farfetched?" he asked, taken aback by Abigail firmly discounting the possibility.

Madeline peered over her reading glasses, thumbing over a few papers. Abigail didn't respond. Don opted to let the discussion drop to the floor. There were more important matters at hand. Speculation about his marriage would hold until later. "Where are we with the merger?"

Madeline continued flipping through her papers. Abigail opened her portfolio, too. Both women had seamlessly reverted to their serious mode. Speculation and jokes were set aside to handle DMI business. If they were going to save the company, time was running out. God had a plan—had to. That was the only spark of certainty Don could absorb.

Madeline stopped halfway through the report she was reading. She let her pen trace along the lines and then said, "According to the most recent report, both Harmonious Energy and Musar Bengali are solid." She flipped to the front page and scanned a few lines. "Yes, this is definitely the latest report." Abigail nodded in agreement. "The independent counsel hasn't found a shred of issues." The news didn't sit well with Don, as his mother continued, "Can you believe it? Joel makes a boatload of bad decisions, but the one we needed him to screw up, he didn't." Madeline raised the report and let it drop to the desk. She pulled the reading glasses off.

"Looks like we'll have to count on the DMI legal team for more favorable news," Don said. He'd hoped the review would net sound reasons to override Joel and ultimately negate the impending duel. Each day looked more and more like war was approaching. Don told himself he was ready, that he was prepared to seize the CEO role by whatever means was required. He believed he'd convinced himself that the pursuit of destiny was his purpose in life. His rationale had sounded plausible when there was likelihood that the lawyers would find flaws in Joel's plan and oust him. Instead, Don was on the front line in enemy territory. This wasn't Cape Town, this was Detroit, Joel's playground.

Abigail crossed her legs again and closed her portfolio. "I think this is good news."

"Y-you do," Madeline asked. "Why?"

"Because sales are down."

"And who can we thank for that?" Madeline said.

"DMI value is slumping, but Joel's decision isn't as bad as we thought." Don didn't get a chance to comment. Madeline dived in. "You must be kidding. Where have you been for the past three months, six really?" Madeline tapped her pen frantically on the portfolio. "You must see something in Joel that the rest of us don't see. That's the only justification you can have to make such a statement."

Joel had dumped Abigail to pursue his personal goals. Planning to marry another woman was extra. Don marveled at Abigail's undeniable tie with his half brother. Having someone's love, no matter how many failures were committed, was a desire he cherished. He'd pray that one day he would be blessed with such a woman.

"So, what are we going to do? Joel isn't going to quit, and we don't have the information necessary to bury him," Madeline commented.

"Let's stay on plan. The board approved a six-month evaluation period. Let's use it. We have five months left. An entire world can change in five months." Don knew that to be true. In less time, he'd been bypassed by his father for the CEO role, fired by his brother, driven to exile in South Africa, only to rush back to Detroit upon word that his father had passed. A grand total of six weeks captured the peak of turmoil in his life. That was then and today was now. "Let's take our time and let this unfold. We'll have to wait and see what happens."

"I'm not good at sitting around waiting for others to dictate my life," Madeline said.

"Sometimes you have no choice," Don said and relaxed as best he could.

chapter

27

Abigail longed for the good old days, the ones when her schedule was crammed with fourteen to sixteen hours of work, with at least two of those spent eating dinner with Joel. The past represented a simpler, more satisfying time. Today was a new day. The advice she'd given Joel about going back to the beginning was also true for her. She dialed the closest phone and wished for a friendly voice to answer. Three rings and her wish was fulfilled, hopefully the first of many. "Mr. Mitchell, you're going to church with me this morning, and I won't take no for an answer."

"Well, if you put it like that, I guess I am. Are you picking me up or am I coming to get you?"

"I'll come and get you for a change. You can give your new bimmer a rest. Be ready in one hour."

"Yes, ma'am."

"I'll call when I'm on my way."

"You got it," Don said.

Just before she disconnected, Abigail added, "And, Don, thanks."

"There's no need to thank me. I'm glad that you're getting me out of here. I need to be in church anyway, Lord knows I do. I should be thanking you."

"Thanks for always being my friend. It means a great deal to me." Especially now that Joel seemed lost to her.

Abigail dressed hurriedly and cut the forty minute drive to Don's place down to twenty minutes, calling him along the way. He was waiting in the lobby downstairs when she arrived and came right out.

"Wow, that was fast," Don said, getting into the car.

"I don't mess around when I have somewhere to be," she said, carefully easing into traffic. "Just so you know, I'm going to this church called Greater Faith Chapel. I've gone there before and there's a real sense of holiness in that church. There's a lady there named Mother Emma Walker, who spoke to me and Joel several years ago and she's amazing."

"Are you going to see her? Is that why we're going there?"

"No, not really. I'm just going because I need a boost of something that I can sink my teeth in. It's almost like I feel starved, spiritually malnourished." She whisked onto the highway, intent not to be late. "I don't know, kind of like God and I aren't as tight as we used to be."

"Trust me, I know that feeling. When I left Detroit, religion and my father were the last things I wanted to hear about, read about, or talk about. The two fathers in my life seemed to have let me down and I just cut them off. Done, no conversation."

"But you found your way back."

"Oh, don't be fooled. I'm working on it, but this is a day by day journey. This sparring with Joel and DMI is constantly challenging my faith and what I think I'm hearing from God."

"It is tough. Even with the best of intentions, we can end up following our own heart and desires as opposed to doing what we're intended to do," she said.

"Well, my problem is that I'm willing to do what God wants me to do, so long as I'm sure that I know what it is," Don responded.

"Like running the company, right?"

"We'll see."

"Oh no, don't even try it. There's no room for doubt. You've already tossed your name in the ring and you know your mother isn't going to let you get out. Me neither. God has called you to do this and you know it."

"Take it easy. I'm only teasing. I'm not quite as wishy-washy on the matter as I may appear. I told you before, I'm all in."

"Good, so long as you're only teasing," she said, letting the lightheartedness roll off her tongue. She wasn't telling Don anything God hadn't put in his heart. It was easy reassuring Don about the plans for his life, not nearly as straightforward when it came to hers. She pulled into the visitor parking slot at the church and turned off the engine. Engaging in a two-way conversation gave Abigail a jolt of renewed vigor, a simple pleasure she hadn't experienced in a long time. The late night and early morning conversations with Joel about DMI, life, and whatever else came up were resigned to another era. "We're here. Let's go. I don't want to miss a single song or a single scripture. This is a new day. I can feel it," she said, exiting the car. The smell of spring was in the air.

"Right behind you," Don said.

chapter

28

Inside, the church lobby was filling with worshippers. The last time Abigail had gone there with Joel, the crowd of people had flocked to him like a celebrity. The lobby buzzed with electricity.

Don entered the church without recognition, and tranquility replaced electricity. As Don helped Abigail remove her spring coat, a gentleman approached. "Good morning and welcome to Greater Faith Chapel, where God is in charge."

"Good morning to you," Abigail said, with Don chiming in.

"Here, let me take that coat for you," the gentleman said, handing it to another person. "You are a visitor, right?"

"Yes," Abigail said with hesitation. "We are visitors, but I've been here before."

"Welcome back, we're glad to have you with us again. Your coat will be in the hospitality lounge," the gentleman said. "Let us know when you're ready to leave and someone at the hospitality desk, right over there, will get it for you," he said, pointing to a table halfway down the hall. "Enjoy the service and please let us know if we can do anything for you."

Don thanked the man and was ready to enter the sanctuary when Abigail interjected. "There is one thing you can help me with. I met a lady here about a year ago named Mother Emma Walker. Is she here by any chance? I'd like to say hi and introduce her to my friend."

"Oh, you mean Big Mama. Of course she's here," the gentleman said, chuckling. "She's here when the pastor can't make it. Rain, snow, heat, doesn't matter." He chuckled some more. "Why don't you wait right here and let me find her. I'm sure she'll be glad to see you."

Abigail whispered to Don, "You have to meet this lady. There's something about her that's very special. I'm telling you seriously, she's special."

A few minutes of waiting and there she was, a tiny lady not more than five feet tall, grayish hair, simply dressed. "Mother Walker," Abigail said, approaching her and reaching to shake her hand.

Instead, Mother extended her arms. "We give hugs around here." The embrace was soothing, a shot of what Abigail needed, genuine love and warmth. She took an extra few seconds. "Sure is good to see you again, Ms. Gerard."

"Abigail. Please, call me Abigail."

Mother Walker nodded in acknowledgment. "And who do we have here?"

"Oh," Abigail said, latching onto Don's arm. "This is my friend Don Mitchell. He's the oldest son of Dave Mitchell."

"Okay, there are two sons. I met the other brother with you the last time."

Abigail hesitated. "Yes, that was Joel."

"How's he doing?" Mother Walker said, hugging Don. "He's dropped into my spirit a number of times since I last spoke with him. Usually that means that I need to pray for him. Don't always know why God have you pray for somebody, you just do it."

There wasn't ample time in the day, especially not in the remaining ten minutes before service began, to lay out Joel's challenges and why he needed prayer. Abigail took comfort in having a person like the church mother praying for him. Prayer was what he needed, and lots of it. Any extra wouldn't hurt her, either.

"We sure are glad to have you worship with us today," Mother Walker said to Abigail and Don while still holding his hand. "Oh, my goodness," she said, rubbing his right hand. "There's a peace about you."

"Excuse me?" Don said.

"There's a peace in your spirit. You've been through a journey but God has allowed you to come out on the other side." Abigail knew what was going on but Don appeared uncertain.

"I've had my share of challenges, that's for sure," Don said.

"But God done seen you through. Now it's time to pick up your cross and do the work He has created you to do."

"I don't understand?"

"You have a job to do, and you know what it is." Abigail knew and Don did, too.

"Are you talking about the CEO role in DMI?"

"I don't know nothing about a CEO role," the church mother said, amused. "Baking and cooking, now you're talking my language. Business I don't know a thing about, but what I do know is God is true and His word is true and His spirit is true. He's never going to call you to do a job without directing you or without equipping you. He might equip you with nothing but faith, or he might give you book smarts, whichever way it goes. However he's prepared you, it's time to step into your calling." She beckoned for him to bend down to her level. "You can't give in to fear and doubt and confusion. Those ain't from God. Some things you have to take by force with God's anointing. You understand me now."

Don didn't hesitate. "I do."

"The Lord will be in the fight with you and he never loses, thank you, Jesus." A small group had gathered and was crowding in, hanging on to each soft-spoken word as though they were meant for them. "I keep hearing the word 'destiny,' in my spirit. Does that mean anything to you?"

"Yes," Abigail blurted out. "See, I told you."

"You mighty feisty this morning, Ms. Abigail. I guess you're ready to serve the Lord. No need me holding you up. We might as well get on inside." Mother Walker clutched Don's arm. "You're going to be my guest today. I'm going to be like Elisha in the Bible today. With all that anointing hanging around you, I'm not letting you leave this church until I get a double portion."

"Big Mama, you already have enough anointing to cover this entire church. Leave some of that anointing for the rest of us," said the gentleman who had greeted them when they'd arrived. The small crowd was amused, and many laughed openly. Laughter was good. Abigail took Don's other arm, feeling renewed. If there was extra anointing hovering around Don, which equated to the out-pouring of God's favor, then Abigail wanted to be on the receiving end, too.

chapter

29

Papers, folders, and notepads carpeted the living room floor. Don preferred the open space instead of his office. The floor to ceiling windows framing the condo kept him grounded and rooted in the real world. With two laptops running, a handful of mechanical pencils, a few pens here and there, and a half-eaten Reuben sandwich, he was sure two new gray hairs had materialized since yesterday—no proof, merely a suspicion. Faith in a positive outcome was the motivation keeping his eyes open for sixteen or seventeen hours a day. LTI was bursting with new clients, most of which had canceled their contracts with DMI. The abundance was overwhelming, but he couldn't take satisfaction in Joel's brooding defeat. There wasn't time, interest, or a need.

He hammered through a stack of proposals. A smart CEO didn't turn down business, but looking at the stack of work remaining for the night and the next night and the next and on and on was choking. If new LTI business was consuming every free second, there wasn't time left to work on the DMI takeover plan. Don teetered toward fretting and each time it seemed to have a grasp of his peace, the voice of the little lady at the church rushed in. He could hear her voice like a tape recorder turned down low.

There's a peace in your spirit. You've been through a journey but God has allowed you to come out on the other side. Her words were crisp, the java boost he needed to keep going. He had to be patient and ready for the precise time to take action.

The moment of reflection ushered in calm to Don's spirit, but perusing the floor and sofa didn't help to maintain it. The ton of work and new business was undeniable. He remembered the early months in LTI, at a time when South Africa hadn't yet become home. It was more like a rest stop from his troubles, his life, and his Mitchell name. Over the months, Cape Town had sunk in to his soul and spread throughout his heart. It was where his life was balanced and comfortable. Too bad being comfortable and fulfilling a calling didn't appear to be coinciding. He let his head lean backward. He missed working with Naledi. She had been like an angel. She had entered his life at a time when both he and LTI were struggling for solvency. She'd been his constant source of friendship and companionship. He peered at his watch, using the few brain cells awake to do the time translation. Eight P.M. in Detroit was three in the morning for her.

"Man," he said, followed by a sigh. He let his head lean all the way back against the couch and feel the warm summer air of Cape Town, the sweet cinnamon-flavored malva pudding, and the melody in Naledi's voice. The smell of mountaintop air swooping down to meet the breeze of the bay ushered him away.

The phone rang, startling Don from his sleep. He didn't immediately gain composure, taking a few gazes around the room. He answered the cellular phone half expecting the caller to have disconnected already.

"Hello, are you there?" he heard Abigail ask.

"Yes, I'm here," he said, pulling the phone away to clear his throat.

"You sound like you've been sleeping. Come on, this early? It's only nine thirty."

Don snatched his arm, which was sprawled across the back of the couch, to confirm the time. He couldn't afford to have wasted an hour and a half, not with the amount of work remaining for tonight. The watch confirmed nine thirty. "I'm glad you called. I don't have time to be sleeping. I have a ton of U.S. proposals that are in the second round of negotiations and have to go out tomorrow."

"Anything I can do to help?"

"I wish, but no. This is LTI business and as a member of the executive team your knowledge or involvement would be seen as a conflict of interest."

"You're right," she said, sighing. "I really wish I could help you."

"Me, too. You have no idea how much I need the help. As a matter of fact, I wanted to call Naledi before I fell asleep." he said, pushing the paper on the couch toward the edge so he could have a small circumference of free space. The work wasn't gone but at least he could breathe freely for a minute.

"Do you want me to let you go so that you can call her?"

"No, it's too late or too early, depending on how you look at it."

"You sound disappointed. Don't you talk to her constantly about LTI?" Abigail asked in a weird tone.

"We do, quite often, but I'm drowning with this new flood of U.S. business. Plus, you know I haven't worked with churches in three years. I intentionally shied away from religious organizations after going through the situation with my father and God." Don and Abigail knew the details. The point was that he was out of touch with training churches.

"Leadership training is leadership training. You'll be back in the swing of things in no time."

"I guess, but it would be nice to have Naledi here. She was my rock during the early days at LTI. With this backlog staring at me, she's really the only one who can truly help me regain a piece of my sanity." Abigail was unusually quiet, so much so that Don asked, "Are you there?"

"I'm here," she said curtly.

"You're so quiet. I thought you'd fallen asleep this time."

"No, I'm here," she said in the same tone. "I didn't realize you relied on her so heavily."

"Are you kidding me? She has been amazing. I couldn't have found my way back to Detroit and to a place of forgiveness without her giving me someone to rely on."

"I didn't know you felt so friendless."

"That's a good way to put it, friendless. She was a friend and a savvy business partner when I needed one the most."

"Funny, that's what you used to call me, your savvy business partner."

"Hmmm," was all he offered in the form of a response. The rest wasn't necessary.

"Look, I know a lot happened while you were away. I clearly wasn't the best of friends, but now that you're here in Detroit. I am and will always be your friend. For the record, you aren't and never were friendless. I'm here for you. I might not be able to help with LTI business, but I can help you in other ways. You are not in this alone."

"I know that, but thanks."

chapter

30

The morning sunlight swept into the living room. Don glanced at the caller ID and caught a glimpse of an international sequence. The last time he recalled looking at his watch was around three A.M. before deciding to collapse on the couch for the night. Between the U.S. and existing clients in South Africa, Nigeria, and Europe, he couldn't begin to guess who was calling, but answered anyway.

Silence was on the line. "Hello, hello," he said, not sure if the connection was clear and his voice was heard on the other end. "Hello," he said one more time, ready to disconnect.

"It's me," the soft voice spoke.

He was overcome with both joy and fear. "Tamara," was the only coherent sound that could initially get through.

"Yes, it's me."

He let his heart slow to a trot and formed his words. A million thoughts were racing. "Where are you? Are you okay? Is there anything wrong?"

"Whoa, hold on, little brother. I'm just fine. I'm settled in a new place," she said.

"You have no idea how glad I am to hear from you," he said, eager to hear what she had to say, overjoyed that she was alive.

"Well, quite honestly, you've been on my mind, you, and Mother, and DMI."

"That's a first. You haven't had much interest in DMI. What's going on?"

"I really don't know why I've been thinking so heavily about Detroit and DMI. Who knows? What's important is that I want to give you my new information, only if you promise not to tell Mother."

Don had been through this scenario many times before. He knew the routine. "But you have to admit, this time is a little different."

"No, not really."

"You were actually in Detroit. Mother was so close to seeing you. She's our mother, and trust me, I know how overbearing she can be, but this is different. She's worried sick about you."

"It's not that I don't care, because I do. It might be hard to believe, but I do care."

"So, can I at least tell her what country you're in without giving up the other information?"

"No, you can only tell her the continent, that's it. I mean it, Don, you have to promise not to tell anything else and you know why. She'll have that pit bull of an investigator hounding me." Don was aware of Madeline's investigator but didn't realize Tamara was, too. Mother wasn't as discreet as she thought. "I'm finally settled and I really don't want to move again, that's becoming very tiring and expensive."

"Do you need money? I can wire whatever you need."

"No, I'm fine with what I have. I'll manage."

Having a connection with Tamara was important, even if it meant not telling Mother. "Okay, but let me know if you need help."

"Thanks for the offer. I'm in Bristol. It's out in the English countryside. Here's my address," she said, reciting her information.

"Is your phone number the one that came up on my caller ID?" he asked.

"Whoa, I'm glad you said that. I have to get that fixed immediately. I can't take any chances with Mother lurking out there."

Don chuckled.

"What's so funny?"

"No one would have ever imagined a girl from the big city of Detroit ending up in the English countryside trying to escape from her mother. It sounds like a tale right out of an international mystery novel." He chuckled some more. "Between you and Mother, I don't have a dull moment, truly, not a dull moment."

"Keep laughing, little brother. If I remember correctly, your address is in South Africa." He was amused. "I'm not the only one in this family driven to the outer edges of the earth in order to maintain sanity."

"Is it working?"

"What?"

"The sanity thing?" he asked.

"I'm definitely not sure, but I have a shot at it so long as you don't release Madeline on me."

They both laughed. Don hadn't felt so alive and hopeful about his family in years. His heart was warmed as he heard the joy radiating from his sister. God was still in the miracle-making seat, exactly the kind of power required if DMI was going to be wrestled from Joel's death grip.

chapter

31

Samantha Tate sat across from Joel, situated at a table near the front of the restaurant, visible but not easily accessible. Joel might as well pay rent for the table. He'd sat in the seat many times, with Abigail mostly. His thoughts were scattered. Joel took a few more bites from his prime rib.

"You must not be too hungry," Samantha said, clearly satisfied with the salmon she'd ordered, judging by the tiny piece remaining on the plate. Joel heard Samantha speak but didn't catch what she said. "Hello, over here," she said, letting her fork dance lightly in midair, trying to capture his attention.

"Oh, I'm sorry," he said, returning to the conversation. "I have a lot on my mind"—none that he could share with Samantha, not the problems with the merger, the distance between him and Abigail, the cash problem, or the restrictions from the board of directors. The list was long. She didn't have the expertise that Abigail possessed, the one that blended with his like hot chocolate and whipped cream. Joel pushed the plate away and leaned back in his seat, fingers crossed and thumbs tapping together.

"I must be losing my charm," she said, forking another bite of rice and asparagus. "I remember around this time six months ago, food wasn't your primary interest when I was around." She twirled the fork slowly in her mouth and tossed him a wink. He felt her foot inch up the outer side of his lower leg and didn't comment. "What is going on with you? Have you slipped into the married man role already? I thought you'd wait at least until the wedding, which is supposed to happen when?"

The headwaiter approached the table, saving Joel, who was very familiar with the Chop House staff. More important, they were familiar with Joel and his tastes. His list of upscale restaurants was long but in the midst of plenty, there was always a short list of favorites. "Mr. Mitchell, is there a problem with your meal?" the waiter said, extracting the plate from the table and wearing a distressed expression.

"No, Carl, no problem at all. As usual, the meal was perfect."

"Are you sure, sir?" the maitre d' said, beckoning for another waiter to come and get the plate.

"I'm sure," Joel said, placing the thick, folded linen napkin that was on his lap onto the table. The maitre d' removed it immediately.

Samantha continued eating, but much slower.

"Do you care for another selection, or dessert?"

Joel pinched his lips together and shook his head no.

"Can I interest you in a coffee or a dinner liqueur, complimentary, of course?"

"No, Carl, I'm perfectly fine," Joel said, resting his elbows on the armchair.

"Yes, sir, your entire service tonight will be on me," the maitre d' told Joel.

"That's not necessary. Ms. Tate enjoyed her meal."

"I most certainly did," she said, finally setting the fork down. The waiter left. "Should I order dessert here or do you have another choice in mind?" she said, letting her gaze wiggle around him. Any other time Samantha would have been a nice after-dinner mint. This evening she left him empty. She didn't have three hundred million dollars or the means to get it. The best she could do was to serve as a brief distraction from his impending doom. He glanced at his watch as his phone buzzed on the table. "Unknown Caller" displayed on the PDA screen. Fearing that it might be Musar, he didn't answer.

Samantha closed the dessert menu. Their private waiter rushed in to take her order. The phone buzzed again. "Unknown Caller" displayed again. Joel didn't want to hear the bad news that his time had run out, but he couldn't hide from the inevitable. As Samantha spoke with the waiter, Joel excused himself to take the call. He braced for the worst.

"The ducks are in line," the voice said on the other end.

Joel hustled to a quiet section down the back hallway leading to the men's lounge. "What?"

"I said the ducks are in line. You can pick them up any time."

"Are you serious?" Joel said, interpreting his uncle's statement to mean the deal was done. Three days since the roadside meeting. Joel expected Uncle Frank to take much longer, given the nature of his loan. "Are you saying—" was the most Joel could squeal out before Uncle Frank cut him off.

"I don't discuss confidential matters over the phone, and if you want to stay in that CEO position, you better learn discretion, too."

Joel wasn't the least bit frazzled by his uncle's reprimand. The only words that rang with substance were those confirming that the loan was approved. The deal was on and not a millisecond to waste. Musar would be calling at any minute. Joel held the phone in his left hand as he extended his right arm and leaned against the wall, letting his gaze slowly lower while talking. "How do I seal this deal?"

"It's a good thing I'm on a secure line with you. I don't think I'd fare well in a cramped cell. If you want to stay out of the limelight and the feds database, you better learn to speak in codes or not at all over the phone. Take that as free advice from your dear old uncle—no charge. As far as this deal goes, the one that you're so eager to make happen, well, the investor will be in contact with you within twenty-four hours. Stay tuned."

"You have my cell phone. You know how to reach me, but don't take too long."

"Like I said, the investor is eager to work with you."

Joel turned his back to the wall, speaking in low tones even though nobody was walking by. Samantha was probably wondering where he was but she'd be all right. Handling the deal was his sole priority. "You keep saying investor, and maybe that's because of the discretion factor, but I need you to be clear. I'm looking for a loan with straight terms—no investors."

Uncle Frank waited and then responded. "Let *me* be clear. You need funds and I've lined up an interested party for you. Based on my efforts, I can expect my consulting fee to be paid in full, one hundred percent, nonrefundable, nonnegotiable, nontraceable, no contingencies. That's our deal. I've done my part." He rattled off the missing five digits for the Cayman account. "Now do your part," his uncle said, drilling the words into the phone.

"What exactly does this pseudoinvestor want that a simple loan doesn't provide? I already told you that I'm willing to pay a hefty interest rate. I said that from the beginning."

"DMI is a very attractive company. Let's just say that opportunities to invest in a place like DMI don't happen every day for the kind of investor you're going to attract. For starters, they're asking for a ten percent return on their investment with the full amount due in ninety days."

"What happens if I don't make the ninety days?"

"You'll make the ninety days. If there is any reason that you think might cause you to miss the payoff date, then don't take the money. Walk away. Trust me, this isn't the group to be indebted to long term. Get the money in ninety days, eighty-eight if possible, just to be sure."

"But what if I don't make the deadline?"

"That's where the investment factor comes to bear. If you miss the payoff date you can forget about paying back the interest. Keep it, because you will be handing over ownership for one of your divisions instead."

Joel pulled the phone away momentarily. "That's not an option. We never discussed ownership in DMI. That was never on the table."

"You told me to find you three hundred million dollars and I did. You're a businessman. Nobody is going to give up those kinds of funds without asking for significant collateral."

"I don't know about this." The victory celebration was short-lived. Uncle Frank had him in a no-win situation. He could take the money with an unacceptable set of terms or pass on the money and accept failure as his fate. Joel heard the sound of Madeline's voice discounting his abilities. Her and Don were heckling him, with Abigail standing nearby. The image was able to sway his decision. He couldn't bear to fail. He felt the stamp of rejection and inadequacy glide across his forehead. He'd take the money regardless of the terms. Once the merger and the marriage were complete he'd have immediate access to hundreds of millions of dollars and saw no issue with repaying a measly three hundred million dollar loan.

Samantha found him in the hallway. He was surprised she hadn't come to find him sooner. He covered the phone with the palm of his hand and whispered to her, "I'm sorry, this is an important call. Have a glass of wine and I'll be back in a few minutes." He gave her a peck on the cheek, which seemed to work. She retreated like a starved pup waiting on a treat. The call with Uncle Frank was just about over, anyway. Joel was pleased that Samantha had waited. He was in the mood for dinner and dessert. "By the way, how do I get a secure line?" he asked Uncle Frank after Samantha left the area.

Uncle Frank chuckled into the receiver. "You get a disposable cell phone from the local electronics store." He chuckled some more. "Although your best bet is to stick with the traditional financial institutions. Not everyone has the stomach for my investment channels."

Joel had to agree with his uncle, being aware of his propensity for fraudulent activity, but desperation had converted a culprit into an ally. Joel didn't want to give recognition to the implications. Instead, he concentrated on the major accomplishment and headed to the dining room for an extended celebration with Samantha, the local media celebrity. When the time was right, he'd persuade Samantha into featuring him and the newest component within DMI, Harmonious Energy, on her TV show. He stepped into the dining room, a renewed man with the favor he used to be accustomed to and hadn't enjoyed in months.

chapter
32

The memory of being with Samantha last night was quickly overshadowed by the call of duty. Joel locked his hands behind his head and eased into the tranquil moment of victory. Who knew that Uncle Frank would one day be the source of Joel's renewed spirit, restoring his faith in making a deal go right. With the push of one button, his administrative assistant was on the direct line. "Please get Mr. Musar on the line for me."

"Is he in India this week?"

"I think so. His assistant will know where to reach him. Please let me know as soon as you have him." Joel wanted to spin around in the seat like a kid. He felt alive. The world was back where it belonged, in his hands. There were no limits to the success he could amass with continued hard work and a bit of good luck. Before tranquility could saturate the room, his assistant was buzzing in. "Yes," he answered.

"I have Mr. Bengali holding on line one."

"Great, please forward him to my office." Now that Joel had the cash and the stamina to close the deal, he cast doubt aside, homing in on the next steps, for better or for worse. "Musar," Joel greeted once the call was connected. "I have very good news: the funds are secure. There aren't any more delays." He had to get the legal papers finalized but those were a technicality. Raising funds was the biggest hurdle. Buy-in from the DMI management team was unlikely, endorsement from Abigail wasn't happening, and further delays due to a legal review wasn't a possibility, either. Nothing would stop the train he'd put in motion. Harmonious Energy would be under the DMI umbrella, and a few days would make the union legitimate.

"This is very good news," Musar said. "I am most pleased, and this is very good timing because my health is not as strong as it was when we last met. I am most eager to complete the wedding ceremony for my daughter. How soon can you come to India for the ceremony?"

"I don't know, maybe a week or two."

"I was hoping a bit sooner."

"What did you have in mind?" Joel asked.

"Four days."

Wow, four days was fast. Great for merging Harmonious Energy, no problem there, but the rapid rush to the altar did curb Joel's enthusiasm. He drew a few extra breaths and let the phone receiver twirl in his hand a few times. Hearing Musar call out his name a few times drew him back to the phone. "Yes, I'm here." He drew one more deep breath, reaffirming the goal. "Four days is fine. I should be able to handle that. I'll make the necessary reservations and get back to you with the travel details." He twirled the phone again, trying to make himself be okay with the impending arrangement. Abigail's image was lodged in his thoughts. Sheba flashed through, distantly trailed by Samantha in Detroit, and then there was the reporter he used to see on trips to L.A. There were plenty of others, whose names he couldn't recall. "Do you need my help with the wedding plans?" An event equivalent to the justice of the peace was suitable for Joel. He was pretty sure Musar and Zarah had grander ideas.

"No indeed, my family will make the arrangement for the wedding festivities. It is our custom."

Family wasn't a component Joel had given thought to. He figured it wouldn't be appropriate to attend his wedding without having someone to sit on his side of the church. Was the wedding in a church? Joel wondered. Most likely not. Bengali wasn't Christian and didn't have the same beliefs that Joel did. He wasn't deterred. Actually, Joel took pride in being more accepting of others and their cultures than the rest of the executive team. How was the company going to become a dominant player on the world stage if they didn't broaden their horizons and embrace differences? For him, entertaining various religions was as liberal as his view on beautiful women. There were plenty to go around. If one didn't work out, try another until the best match was found. Joel and Musar ended the call, both seemingly pleased with the final outcome. Joel got his assistant on the phone. "I need you to book me on a flight Thursday for India. You'll need to check with Musar's office again to coordinate the details and travel arrangements."

"Do you want to travel on the company's jet or a commercial flight?"

Joel didn't give two hoots about the board of directors, but why stir the pot of stewing disenchantment. He would leave the corporate jet grounded and trudge to India in a first-class seat on a commercial flight. The fewer who knew about his travel plans the better. Joel snatched up the Harmonious Energy folder and tore out of the office. He juggled putting on his suit jacket and keeping the folder intact. Nothing could be lost this close to the finish line, but he wasn't heartless.

Joel took the stairs two flights down to the fourth floor. He was standing at Abigail's office door, not sure why. He knocked and she let him enter.

"You're here," he said.

"Every day, all day," she said, not elaborating. She wasn't making it easy for him to say what he wanted to say, but, then, he hadn't extended her much grace when she'd reached out to him. "I know you're mad at me, but can we agree to disagree."

"You tell me, Mr. Mitchell."

"Wow, so it's Mr. Mitchell now." He entered the room but

didn't sit and she didn't offer. The distance between them wasn't ideal. "Our relationship has deteriorated to the point that we're not on a first-name basis anymore. That's tough," he said.

"I'm sure it doesn't matter much to you. You've made that perfectly clear, repeatedly."

She wouldn't believe him, but it did matter to him. He approached the desk and leaned on it but didn't crowd Abigail. "I want you to know that I never meant to hurt you. You're important to me."

"Funny way of showing it," she said, resting her chin on her clasped hands.

"I want you to forgive me, please. My life is complicated. It was from birth," he said.

"Humph."

"I'm not making an excuse. He leaned a little closer to her over the desk. "You know me. You do. You're mad at me and you're hurt, but you know me. From the beginning, I've made DMI my priority. I put everything else second, everything," he said, leaning away. "You of all people know that and never judged me." Abigail maintained the same stare without a comment. He wasn't sure if he was getting through but his conscience had to take a chance before boarding the plane to India. There was a time when his secrets were entrusted to Abigail, information he couldn't trust to anyone else. That Abigail was lost to him. He couldn't tell her about the trip to India or the impending merger status. Reminding her of the wedding wasn't a consideration. "We made a great team, you can't deny it."

"The operative word is 'made,' past tense."

"I'll accept that. I deserve it. What can I say except that I'm sorry for the way we ended. I can't apologize for my vision. Expanding this company into the international market is the way for us to go. You've trusted me before. Why can't you trust me now, when I tell you that this merger is right? I feel it in my core. It's my calling, my purpose for being alive, and it supersedes everything else in my life."

"Good luck with it. I hope it keeps you happy." The unusual

harshness in her response didn't offend Joel. It wasn't Abigail speaking. It was her hurt. He understood. "I hope you find what it is you're seeking."

He had. At that moment the spiritual connection he had suppressed with God pricked his consciousness, causing him to pause with his plans, but his need to fulfill his desires overrode and shoved him toward the door. "Good-bye, Abigail, you're special to me. That won't change," he said.

He stepped down the hallway to the elevator bank. God and Abigail tried to flood his thoughts with emotions, conviction. Joel discounted it all, no time for confusion.

A quick start in the Lamborghini, he zipped down a few roads, and bam, he was handing the valet keys to a parking lot attendant located next to a short building. The law firm had done other freelance work for DMI in the past, particularly when the workload at the office was too much for the in-house staff. Joel hustled inside and waited as the receptionist buzzed him into the office. He refused to let the legal department or the board members stall the review process. Joel planned to press the documents through the independent counsel. He had one day to get the documents finalized, possibly two if he waited until the last possible hour on Thursday before heading to the airport. A day here or there wasn't an issue. The firm would meet his deadline or he'd find another that would, repeat business being the motivating factor.

chapter
33

Joel cruised back to the office. The money had been wired, the legal documents would be ready in two days, and an airline ticket was reserved in his name. "Dial Sheba," he spoke into his hands-free mobile headset. The voice activation feature dialed as requested. With minimal effort, Sheba was there, a truth he'd grown to cherish. "Guess what—I have the money."

"Of course you have the money. I knew you'd work it out, never a doubt."

"When are you leaving Chicago and moving closer to me?" he asked, and she laughed. "I need you and that positive attitude of yours here with me. I can't tell you how much it means to have your faith in me. I don't see much of that around here," he said, exiting I-75 at Grand River, four city miles from the office, twenty minutes tops.

"My only regret is that I didn't have more to give you. If I had the entire three hundred million, it would have been yours."

"Your hundred was perfect. Trust me, every dollar made a difference," he said with no intention of sharing how far he'd gone to get the money. He didn't want the three women he cared most about to be subjected to his creative financing. As soon as the marriage was in effect and Musar expired, Uncle Frank's people would have their money and the ugly mess would be over like it had never existed. In the meantime, no one would know, not Sheba, Abigail, or his mother. "I couldn't have gotten this far without you."

"I'm flattered, Mr. Mitchell, but you didn't need me."

If only she knew. When he fell short on encouragement, she stepped in and offered the best of what she had. It was enough to get him recharged and back on the attack. She was irreplaceable. "This time next week I'll be the proud owner of Harmonious Energy."

"You'll be a husband, too. In spite of the conditions, there has to be a tiny amount of excitement that you're feeling?"

"Excitement" wasn't the right word. "Obligated" was far more appropriate. "I'm okay with what has to be done. Just so you know, nothing changes between us."

"It has to change."

"No," he said, bent on making sure. "We're solid. You've been with me during tough times. I can't abandon you, and I won't entertain the thought of you abandoning me."

"You'll have a wife, and of course there's always Abigail."

"Please, let's not go there. Like I said, DMI isn't lined with people that put trust in me. You and my mother are it."

"I'm in your corner, but I'll have to keep you honest when it comes to your marriage. I couldn't be considered a true friend if I didn't encourage you to do right by your new wife. It will be the godly thing to do," she said, submerged in humor.

"She doesn't believe in the God you're talking about. So His rules don't apply in my situation."

"Isn't this ironic? When I first met you, I wasn't convinced that God existed, but being around you, your faith was rich, like electricity," she said. Talking about religion made him squirm in his seat. "Remember that. I repented for my sins standing outside your boardroom, acknowledged Christ as the son of God, and accepted Him as my savior. That happened solely because of you. Let's face it, I haven't managed to incorporate church visits into my schedule, but I'm definitely a believer. That's why I said it's ironic, because you're the one who opened me up to spirituality. So what's happened with you since then? You seem tenser."

He didn't want the pressure, not even from Sheba. "Different discussion for a different time," he said, not interested in discussing religion any longer. He wanted to keep his visit free, uncomplicated, like every other time he had with Sheba. "My wife will adjust with no problem."

"No, she won't. She will be a stranger in a new country. I'll always want you, but she'll want you more. I'm sure of it."

"The marriage isn't what you think. It's purely an arrangement. I have to stay married three years and then we both go our separate ways," he said, turning into the corporate parking lot.

"That's what you think. Women see marriage differently than men. Indian, Asian, African, or American, doesn't make a difference. She's expecting a husband."

"We'll see." He pulled into the executive row and eased into the top spot. "I wish I could route the plane through Chicago to see you and then go on to India."

"Why can't you? I thought you ran the company?"

"I'm on a commercial flight this time. My perks don't work everywhere."

"Since you can't stop by, then let me wish you safe travel and may the Lord be with you."

He fidgeted, absorbing her comment. She didn't usually push religion on him. There was a time when her faith and hope were reduced to a box of crystals and stones. His influence on her spirituality had come full circle, becoming a source of torment for him. He let the comment sit without a response to the Lord portion. God was silent when he and his mother were being attacked relentlessly by Madeline. God hadn't shown up along the way and there was no reason to push the issue. Joel had worked hard without assistance. The victory was his, and his alone. "I'm at the office. I'm going to dash in and tell my mother the good news."

"I'm surprised you didn't tell her first."

"I keep telling you that you're high on my list." At that moment his mind was drowned with the flood of information he'd once shared with Abigail. She used to be his first to know. Those days were over. He wasn't going to dwell on her and let his spirit fall. He had to cast Abigail out of his mind—not forever, but definitely for this moment.

"Good-bye, Mr. Mitchell."

Joel killed the engine and got out of the car. "You mean see you later—never a good-bye from you." He was amused but she couldn't see the content look on his face.

"Let me know when you return. I'd like to get you a wedding gift."

Joel walked into the building and waved past the security desk. "That won't be necessary. My new house is completely furnished."

"Safe travels, my friend. We'll talk," she told him.

He couldn't stop thinking about the house. When he initially asked Abigail to oversee the construction, his intentions were sincere. He had no idea that a marriage to someone else would follow. Joel sighed, thinking about the anguish Abigail had felt when he'd told her. He wasn't heartless, having experienced loneliness and rejection from childhood companions. He knew what a broken heart felt like.

Joel ended the call and entered the elevator. He went to the executive floor and stopped two doors from his. He knocked on the door and heard the quiet voice on the other side.

"Come in."

He entered. "Mom, do you have a minute?"

"For you, I have a whole hour. Is everything okay?" she asked with a fearful expression.

"Better than good. Life is wonderful. DMI is wonderful, and—" he reached for her hands and gently letting her rise to her feet— "you're wonderful."

"Joel Mitchell, what's gotten into you?"

"Victory. There's nothing like the taste of sweet victory. We won."

"What did we win?"

"Harmonious Energy. I have the deal finished."

"Oh, son, that's great news. I'm happy for you," she said, holding him tightly. She wasn't a businesswoman with the level of experience that Madeline had, but his mother possessed class where Madeline fell short. His mother understood how important the merger was to him, and it gave him comfort in not being totally alone. "I had no idea you'd convinced the board of directors to change their minds and let you proceed."

He pushed from her hug. "I didn't exactly get their endorsement."

"What do you mean?" she asked, letting the fear frame her expression once more.

"I'm CEO. I can run this company. I already have, flawlessly. I'm not going to let a group of shortsighted busybodies cause me to lose the deal of a lifetime."

"What's going to happen when they find out?"

Joel ushered her to the phone situated on her desk. "We'll handle one crisis at a time. By the time they find out, it will be done. The first order of business for you is to get a ticket to India. My assistant can get you the information. We don't have any time to waste. We need to hop a plane in two days and get to India to close this deal."

"Two days, that's not nearly enough time for me to get through this stack of papers."

"Don't worry about the papers. The CEO is giving you several days off, mandatory to go to India with your son. He truly needs you there."

"All right, all right, I'm going but it's only because I love you," she said, lightening the mood substantially. Joel was ready to leave when he turned to say, "Be sure to bring a dress for the wedding ceremony."

"You're going through with the wedding," she said, taking a seat behind her desk. The enthusiasm fled and left a ring of seriousness. "Are you sure this is what you want to do?"

"Positive." Wanted to do, needed to do, had to do, it was the same. "No sacrifice is too great if it can keep DMI afloat." Finally he could make his family's legacy an actuality. His father would be proud of his youngest son, the one who made it happen in the face of staunch opposition. Not Don, the son who got to wear the label of legitimacy.

"Joel, your father is gone. You don't have to live out his vision." She stood and went to Joel. "You are the only child I have. You are fulfilling your father's legacy by living your best life. I want you to be happy. If that happens to mean marrying Mr. Bengali's daughter, so be it, but make sure you're doing it for the right reason. It's the only way you'll be able to survive. You can't live in bondage, locked in a marriage of convenience. You won't survive. As crazy as times got between your father, Madeline, and me, my love for your father was what enabled me to stay, otherwise the chaos would have driven me to suicide."

"Mom, don't worry," he said, lifting her hands and leading with a few dance steps. "I'm doing exactly what I want to do. This is happiness for me, truly I'm happy." She seemed convinced. For a second he felt convinced, too, before truth rushed in.

chapter

34

Thirty years. Every grueling minute of those years had been met with accusations, put-downs, and flat-out mean-spirit-edness mostly waged by Madeline. Loving Dave Mitchell was her joy in the beginning but realism had a way of stamping out the flame, leaving just a smoldering whiff of love between them. Sherry tidied her desk in preparation for the upcoming trip to India. Her support for Joel was unquestionable. The decision he was making for his personal life was very questionable. She was overcome with doubt. Sherry went downstairs to Abigail's office hoping for something, she was not sure what.

Abigail was finishing up a conference call but beckoned for Sherry to come in anyway. The wait was brief. "You were looking for me?" Abigail asked as she ended her call.

Sherry meandered to the windows located on one side of Abi-gail's office. "You know Joel is—" she said and caught herself. She remembered Joel telling her the board of directors didn't know about the trip to India, which probably meant Abigail didn't know, either. She needed to confide her concerns in someone but couldn't risk betraying Joel's confidence.

"I know Joel is what?"

The awful distress swirling inside threatened to overtake her hopes for Joel. She'd lived out a distressed marriage for what seemed to be the right reasons. Inhaling the air of independence and self-worth transformed her view of those years. She saw the marriage with Dave for what it was, awkward from the beginning and straight through until the end. There was more for her son and she wanted him to have it now, not wait until he was fifty-five years old to start living, as she had.

"If the merger ever goes through with that Indian company, you know he's going to marry the daughter." Abigail acknowledged Sherry's comment through eye contact but didn't respond. Maybe it was Abigail's heartache, or her confusion, or worse, her lack of interest in Joel. "Did you hear me?" Sherry said turning her body to face Abigail, but staying by the windows with her arms clasped. "He's going to marry another woman."

"And what do you want me to do about it?" Abigail asked. "Do you want me to go and plead for his love, hmm?" Sherry kept her arms locked and looked away into the sparsely cloudy sky. "Do you want me to wrestle him to the floor, or, better yet, how about this: what if I clobber him over the head and tow his limp body back to my cave and make him mine?"

"Of course I'm not suggesting you do anything remotely as dramatic, but you should do something."

Abigail gazed up to the ceiling, then back down to the desk.

"I know you love him," Sherry said, taking a few steps toward the desk. "You are what he needs—stability and genuine love. I'm not going to be here forever, and I'd like to know that he'll have someone in his tiny corner."

"Now who's being dramatic? You are the picture of health. You'll be around for a long time. That's not a concern."

"Perhaps, but whether I'm here one day or one hundred years, I want my son to experience happiness every day of his life. The prospect of him engaging in a marriage for business purposes is absolutely frightening to me. I know Joel. Nothing good can come from that kind of arrangement."

"Well," Abigail said, seemingly distracted, "maybe you're worrying prematurely."

"What do you mean?"

"If the board is effective, Joel won't have the backing to finalize the merger. They've blocked his funding, stalled his legal review, and turned down his request for approval. Unless he creates a miracle, the deal isn't happening."

Sherry wanted to share the truth with Abigail but couldn't risk it. "I know it looks hopeless, but my son is Dave Mitchell's child. Miracles aren't beyond them."

That got Abigail's attention. "No disrespect to you, Sherry, but Dave and Joel are very different leaders."

"As they should be."

"Well, Dave's miracles came from the favor he had with God. I can't begin to guess where Joel would find a miracle, but I'm pretty certain it's not from God. At least not the same God that Dave and I serve. Joel has his own way of doing things."

"I didn't come here to demonize my son. Maybe I was wrong coming to you. I believed he meant something to you."

"You're right, he did, but that's ancient history. I've accepted his choice. Perhaps it would be helpful to all of us if you did, too," Abigail said and pushed the power button on her laptop.

Sherry read the signal and departed gracefully, refusing to let her son be maligned by anyone. She shifted her energy to the India trip. There was much to be done for Joel, and such little time.

chapter
35

Abigail was mildly agitated with Sherry's implications. Joel had made his choice. Abigail had accepted it; Sherry needed to. Abigail went a few doors down the hall to Madeline's office and saw Don there. "I didn't know you were in the office," she told him.

"I dropped in for a short visit."

"You can do that when you're around the corner instead of being two continents and thousands of miles away," Madeline said, not attempting to hide her satisfaction in having Don in Detroit. She'd struggled to get him home. Abigail's original purpose for coming to Madeline's office seemed juvenile in the presence of Don. Venting about being plopped in the center of Joel's romantic rescue plan was pointless and embarrassing with Don sitting there. "Are you here to see me or Don?" Madeline asked.

"I had a small DMI question, but it's no big deal," Abigail said, joining the two. "I'd much rather sit here for a few minutes and catch up with Don." She patted his knee before sitting.

"Your timing is perfect. Don is flying to South Africa for a few days."

"Oh?" Abigail said. She was becoming accustomed to his juggling multiple companies across multiple continents. His frequent flyer miles could cover a nice exotic vacation to any corner of the earth he wanted to visit, first class.

"Now that I have you here, it's tough for me to let you go, even for a short visit," Madeline said.

"I can agree with you there," Abigail said, "but I'm okay with you leaving so long as you're committed to coming back. We need you here." She, especially, needed him close.

"Why don't you bring Naledi here for a visit instead of constantly traveling there to see her?" Madeline suggested.

"I'm not sure that she'd come to the States."

"Why not? We know how to treat visitors. Isn't that right, Abigail?"

Abigail couldn't pull her comments together. She was stuck on him running back and forth to South Africa for Naledi. Where did his affection for her come from? What had she missed?

"It's easier for me to hop flights than to ask her. Plus, she's already running LTI for me there while I'm here saving a ton of your disgruntled clients. I have a stack of contracts this high," Don said, raising his hand vertically above his head.

"And nobody appreciates what you're doing more than I do."

"You're really serious about her," Abigail said, attempting to join the conversation without revealing her bruised emotion. "She means a lot to you?"

"She has been my lifeline."

"Well, I'm grateful that you have someone there, but you're here now. Between me and Abigail, you're covered," Madeline told him.

Abigail processed Madeline's response in fragmented phrases. Abigail felt like her priorities were messed up. Timing was the problem. She'd just been reminded about Joel's engagement and did pretty well with not letting it derail her. Having her friendship with Don threatened wasn't digesting as smoothly. When had it happened, she wondered. When had Don moved to a level of seriousness with Naledi? She wasn't prepared to deal with another departure from her inner circle. First it was Dave, then Joel, and now Don.

"I say you need to bring the lovely lady here. She needs to see you on your home turf anyway. Bring her to Detroit. It's springtime, the weather is decent. This is the ideal time."

"Maybe you're right," he said.

"Isn't it a twenty-four-hour flight or something like that? She might not like flying that far. I wouldn't," Abigail said.

"Naledi doesn't mind flying. She's traveled back and forth between Cape Town, France, and England since we landed our major account with Unilever. Flying isn't a problem for her. As a matter of fact, it's easier for her because she speaks so many languages."

"Oh" was Abigail's response. Naledi couldn't possibly be that perfect, nobody was. Abigail was somewhat embarrassed by her reaction but couldn't shake the feeling of being replaced in Don's life. Abigail was sure Naledi was a wonderful woman, but couldn't she find another man to dote on her?

"Your entire face lights up when you talk about her. Are you seeing what I'm seeing, Abigail?" Madeline asked.

"Not really. You know how Don is. He's good about complimenting the women in his life. That's just how he is."

He grinned.

"No, there's a little more to it than his usual complimentary self. Am I right, Don?" Madeline said.

He grinned wider.

"As long as you're pleased, I'm pleased, especially if you're here. Plus, I like Naledi and, on top of it, she's beautiful."

"That's an understatement," Don added. That was it for Abigail. She'd stomached enough talk about Naledi. They made her sound like a flawless princess. Abigail had been through the grueling experience of being discounted while an unknown woman consumed her man's time. Sheba was it for Joel and now Naledi for Don. He wasn't Abigail's boyfriend, but Don was most definitely her close friend, which was the next best alternative. She had made a mistake with Joel, waiting idly by and letting him slip away. She'd learned her lesson and wasn't willing to make the same mistake. "Don, excuse me, can I please speak with you outside for a minute?"

"Everything okay?" Madeline asked.

"Everything's fine. I just need to talk off-line for a few minutes. Please excuse us," Abigail told Madeline.

Don followed Abigail into the hallway. They sat at the mini sitting area located outside Madeline's office.

"What's going on?" Don asked with an evident look of concern. Abigail didn't know where to start. "Are you okay?" he asked, dropping his gaze to catch hers as she stared at the coffee table. He grabbed her hand and lifted it slowly. Her gaze followed.

"I need to tell you something."

"What?" he said, enveloping her hand completely in his and drawing closer. "Are you sick?" he asked.

"No, it's nothing like that."

"Then what is it?" he said, fishing for her gaze to stay lifted long enough to maintain eye contact with his.

"I'm embarrassed to say this, but I feel slighted by your relationship with Naledi."

"What?"

"I know." She wanted to pull her hand away but Don didn't release it. "I can hardly believe my own reaction."

"I don't know what to say," Don stated.

This time she was able to rip her hand free. "I know it's the last thing you were expecting to hear. You are swamped with DMI contracts, the takeover, your LTI business, and, on top of that, I'm burdening you with my personal feelings. I'm sorry, how selfish of me."

"Don't look at it like that. I am surprised hearing this from you, but I'm glad you told me." He sat back in the seat.

"So, what exactly are you saying?" she asked.

"I don't know what I'm saying," he said. "You're important to me and we've always been honest with each other. I felt like I had to tell you about my feelings toward Naledi."

"After dealing with Joel and Sheba, the thought of watching

you and Naledi together doesn't sit well with me. I'm really sorry, because I really do want you to be happy. I really do."

"What about Joel? What are your feelings for him?"

"There's nothing left between us. Honestly, I don't think there ever was anything real."

"You understand how complicated a relationship between us could be. Joel is my brother, even though we're not brotherly."

"I know, and I'm not sure that I'm asking for a relationship," she responded.

"Then what are you asking for?"

"I don't know. What I do know is that Naledi makes me feel uncomfortable," she said, watching Don grin. "Why are you smiling like that?"

He hunched his shoulders. "I'm listening to you and wondering what I'm going to do with you. The time when I hoped to have this conversation with you, there didn't seem to be any romantic interest from you."

"I didn't realize how you felt then."

"Well, that's true. I wasn't exactly as forthcoming as I should have been, but the truth is that a great deal of hurt and circumstances and other people have reshaped our situation and our feelings."

"You're right. I'm sorry. I shouldn't have said anything."

"No," he said, getting close to her again. "You did the right thing. No matter what happens with DMI or with us, we need to protect our friendship. Let's start there and see where we go. What will be, will be. You're the one who told me that destiny is inescapable."

Don had once longed to hear the words of love and interest flow from Abigail's lips to his ears. Why had she waited so long? The situation was complicated. He wanted to be settled and build a family. It was his dream. Naledi was safe and totally committed to him. He wasn't sure about Abigail. Her heart was torn and in the process of being repaired. Naledi was whole and ready. What he valued most was her purity. She wasn't tainted by Joel. There wasn't a lingering stench of secondhand love. There was a price-less tag he placed on being first in a woman's heart.

chapter

36

The Jet Airways crew announced the approach into Jaipur, India. "Welcome to the Pink City," said the attendant who'd serviced first class since they'd left Mumbai.

"I don't mean to complain, but this has been an incredibly long flight, or I should say series of flights. I've been exhausted since the stopover in London," Sherry said, collecting her book and a few other items around her seating area.

"I didn't think it was too bad. First class seats definitely help." Joel shrugged. There was a person on the flight from London to Mumbai nagging at his memory. No words were exchanged, but the brief eye contact was sufficient to stir a notion of familiarity. Joel couldn't recall who the man was. His mother snapped him back into the conversation.

"I'm glad Zarah's family is handling the arrangements, because I'm pooped. I won't be of any help for at least a week. Thursday to Saturday, three days of travel is grueling for your old mother."

"I'm glad you're with me," he said. More than she realized.

"You need me. I'm here," she said.

He didn't need validation for his decision to purchase Harmonious Energy but a friendly face on foreign soil was difficult to refute. There was a time when his spiritual convictions surrounded him incessantly, giving Joel a sense of security. Since he'd opted to pursue his own path, being alone became an everyday truth.

"Did you figure out why the person looked so familiar to you on the flight from London?"

"I haven't yet, but it's irking me." Odds would have said that he wouldn't see anyone he knew from the U.S. His goal was to secure the deal, get married, and return to Detroit without anyone back there finding out until he was ready to spin the news in his favor. The person on the other plane was a loose end, one he wanted desperately to neutralize, after he could figure out who it was.

"I'm sure it will come to you," Sherry said, but it offered little comfort. "What did you decide to do about visiting the actual office?"

"That's another plane ride I'm too tired to consider. Since Musar has come up north to meet us, I don't see any reason to do the extra travel. I'm going to take care of the paperwork with Musar and jump right into the wedding. I expect to be on my way home by no later than Wednesday. Four days is plenty of time to turn my life upside down," he said.

"You know it's not too late. You don't have to do this," Sherry said.

"Mom, we've had this discussion several times. Nothing is going to change. We're here in India to complete the merger and the wedding ceremony."

The plane touched down on the runway with little fanfare.

"I want you to know how proud I am of you," she said, gripping his hand.

He nodded, glad for the reassurance.

They exited the plane, stepping under the brightly colored canopy into the warm, damp air.

"Musar told me to expect warm weather. I guess he was right," Joel said, laying his trench coat across his arm and carefully descending the stairs with his thin briefcase tightly held by one hand.

Sherry took her time descending the stairs ahead of Joel. Once she reached the walkway leading into the terminal, Sherry said, "This is my first trip to India, just for you."

They entered the terminal and made their way to the open area after a very short walk. A gentleman stood near the doorway holding a sign with MITCHELL scratched on it. Joel raised his hand quickly to get the man's attention and dropped it back down to his side.

"Good morning," the man said. "I have been sent by Mr. Bengali to give you a lift to the hotel." His accent was thicker than Musar's.

"We have luggage," his mother said.

"I shall collect the luggage for you. Please, come this way," the turban-wearing gentleman said with a timid disposition as he avoided eye contact.

"I was expecting Musar to meet us. Was he delayed?"

"Mr. Bengali is very ill. He did not feel strong enough to travel to the airport. He is waiting for your arrival at the hotel near his hometown. The ride is about an hour and thirty minutes from here. There is no problem. I will take very good care of you."

Joel wasn't concerned about getting to the hotel. Musar's illness did have him concerned. The hurdles Joel had to overcome in order to be standing in India weren't going to be wasted. In fifty miles his number one mission would be completed, despite unbelievable odds. Prayer could have given Joel the extra shot of certainty that he sought. He attempted to formulate the words but came up short on what to say.

The driver had the luggage secured in the trunk of the car and they were on their way.

"I expected to see elephants and cows roaming freely, but I wasn't expecting this much traffic so early in the morning," his mother said.

Bikes, scooters, and rickshaws packed the roads beyond capacity. Movement was very slow. Joel felt anxious. "You said Musar is at the hotel?"

"Yes, Mr. Bengali and many of his family members have traveled to the hotel in preparation for the wedding."

Joel was unprepared for general discussion about his wedding. It must have been common knowledge among Musar's circle. Joel couldn't figure the number of family members gathered for the wedding but it certainly outnumbered his. He didn't give much credence to the nuptials but would have felt awkward with no family presence.

"Does Mr. Bengali have a home in the area or is he just here for the wedding?" Sherry asked.

Joel was curious, too. He knew very little about the personal lives of the Bengali family. Too late to worry now, so he didn't.

"Yes," the driver said, paying attention to the swelling traffic. "He has quite a modest home here, and it's not large enough for his entire family coming for the wedding."

"I wouldn't figure him for a small house." Sherry said.

"This house is probably a getaway for weekends," Joel said.

"Yes, you are right, sir. Mr. Bengali has his primary home in the south and comes here on holiday."

"Does Zarah live there, too?"

"Yes, she lives near Bangalore, in the south with him, but it is customary to have the wedding ceremony in the family's hometown. There are many family members who will come. It is tradition."

"I see," Sherry said. It didn't matter to Joel. He couldn't get to the little town fast enough. Wherever Musar was with the contract was where he wanted to be.

chapter

37

Two and a half hours later, the car pulled into the modest-looking hotel. According to Joel's administrative assistant, it was labeled in the luxury category. At home, he only stayed in five-star accommodations. For this deal he willingly made the exception. Sherry was worn out and went straight to her room to take a nap. Joel wasn't going to nap, eat, or use the bathroom until the contracts were signed. At this very second, nothing else on earth took precedence. Joel pressed the attending staff for directions to Musar's room. He had the prime suite located on the top floor. Five floors wasn't exactly equivalent to the Ritz Carlton in Michigan, but Joel wasn't seeking a luxury retreat. He had business to handle. His briefcase hadn't left his sight since Detroit.

Finally he reached the suite with the attendant leading the way. A few raps on the door and they were inside. Musar sat on a short sofa in the front room. He was thin, bone thin. Musar had freely talked about his illness and how fast he was deteriorating but Joel wasn't prepared to see him quite so frail. He must have lost ten to fifteen pounds since his most recent trip to Detroit two weeks ago. Joel sighed quietly, relieved to have arrived in time. He was determined not to leave the room without a signed contract. Delaying for even a few hours was risky.

"Musar, it's good to see you once again," Joel said, approaching his business partner.

Musar nodded delicately, following with a weakened voice. "I am most pleased that you were able to travel. We welcome you." Joel sat next to Musar. Business was paramount, but watching Musar fade in his presence tapped a sensitive wire in Joel. Maybe it was rehashing the passing of his father or, worse, the memories of watching his father suffer.

Joel extracted the contract from his briefcase. Musar stood with help from Joel. The two gingerly walked to the small circular desklike table located in one corner of the room. Musar's attorney introduced himself as Kumar. Joel couldn't understand the last name.

"Do you have the necessary papers?" the attorney asked.

Joel plopped the stack of documents on the table. "Everything is here—the final contract, verification of funds, the letter of intent for the DMI West Coast division, and a few other minor documents." Joel slid the papers across the table to Musar. "Do you want to review the final contract?"

"I trust that you have made acceptable changes," Musar said and pushed the stack to the attorney. The small effort seemed to drain his energy.

"I spoke with Mr. Mitchell's lawyers earlier this week and we agreed on the changes. The contract is ready for you to sign, Musar," Kumar said.

"I will give the order to transfer the seven hundred million dollars in U.S. funds at the opening of business on Monday, which you won't have access to until Tuesday morning in your time zone. Is that okay?" Joel asked.

"Tuesday is no problem. It's very good timing for the wedding." Joel had forgotten about the marriage. "I'm not worried about your money. Most important for me is Zarah. It is my duty to secure her future before my life transitions, which will be very soon."

"I understand," Joel said. "Everything is there." He pointed to the stack that the attorney was reviewing. "I'm signing ownership of the West Coast division to Harmonious Energy, which will belong to Zarah after your transition." Joel found the concept of transitioning from one state of energy to another bizarre, but what he believed wasn't relevant. Concessions had to be made in every aspect of his life if it helped to seal the merger.

"Zarah is my only child. She will inherit my earthly possessions," Musar spoke barely louder than a whisper. "The value will be one and a half billion rupees."

"That's U.S. dollars," the attorney clarified.

Joel was speechless upon hearing the sum. He'd ball-parked the figure several times but hearing the confirmation rendered him numb. That money could get him out of debt and back on top. Wearing traditional Indian garb, eating a slice of wedding cake, and living as a married couple for several years was totally worth it. His thoughts swirled but he battled to stay grounded. He could celebrate alone in his room later.

"Now that you've brought up the wedding, I do want to point out the clause that we agreed to earlier in the week about family," Joel said.

The attorney flipped to the back of the contract where there were several addendums.

"What was it?" Musar said, sounding very tired. Joel wanted to put the pen in his hand and move it along for him.

"The clause about having children," Joel told Musar.

"Oh yes, as a father, I appreciate the importance of having children. I agreed to your term," Musar said, which were the final words that Joel needed to hear. He pulled out his pen, eager to sign.

"If there are no children born to the marriage within the first three years of your marriage, you are released from your marital obligation to Zarah. You will also be granted the option of buying the West Coast back at fair market value," the attorney paraphrased.

Joel felt a bit embarrassed at having the exception stated in front of a man who was practically using his dying breath to make marital arrangements for his only daughter. Joel felt badly but not to the point that he had a change of heart regarding the deal. He felt accomplished. Each man at the table had received what was most important to him. Joel shouldered no guilt.

Musar reached for the pen and began signing as his attorney flipped the pages and pointed out the signature spots on the two sets of documents. After Musar was finished, Joel whizzed through his signatures.

"We're done," the attorney said, handing Joel his set of contracts. "I can leave the papers here if you don't want to carry them during your stay."

"Oh no, that's not necessary," Joel said, taking possession of his papers. He could lose his luggage and his dignity, but those documents were headed to Detroit. He secured the papers in his briefcase, to be protected with his life. After all, his life was the collateral on both the loan with Uncle Frank and in the marriage to Zarah.

"Now that we've completed the merger, I'd like to complete the engagement this evening and move to the wedding phase tomorrow," Musar said.

"Are you sure you're feeling strong enough? I'm willing to wait until tomorrow," Joel said.

"We must proceed this evening. I cannot waste the time," Musar said firmly.

"Then this evening it is. Where would you like for us to meet?"

"If I were well, the announcement would take place at my house. We would expect a formal procession with you and your family to my house." Joel and his mother didn't make for a procession and no one else was coming. "With my strength fading, we will treat this venue as our home. My family has traveled here. Zarah will not be robbed of a fitting ceremony."

"Just let me know what you need me to do and I will accommodate," Joel said, subtly rubbing the briefcase.

"Very good, we shall see you in the dining room this evening at six o'clock."

Joel could appreciate Musar's passion for a cause where the threat of death wasn't a deterrent. Now that he was breathing easier, Joel was almost looking forward to the upcoming party. It was the closest he'd come to relaxation in months.

chapter

38

Sherry entered the dining room clutching Joel's arm. Vibrant colors and culture oozed from each corner of the room. "My goodness, I didn't expect this many people," Sherry whispered to Joel. His lack of enthusiasm about the marriage hadn't prepared her for the gravity of the event.

"I didn't know, either," Joel said.

Realization was setting in with Sherry. Joel's decision was big. She felt out of sorts among the crowd of foreigners with whom she shared little, starting with their clothing. Joel's suit was top of the line at home but appeared inappropriate at the Bengalis'. Sherry couldn't find a source of contentment. Releasing her son, his future, and their family's legacy to people she didn't know made Sherry light-headed.

A man approached Joel and took him to the side. Sherry stood idle, appearing to be gazing into her cosmetic mirror. Thank goodness Joel wasn't gone long. "What did he want?" Sherry asked.

"He gave me a quick overview of what's going to happen during the engagement process." Joel must have sensed her concern and stopped her before a word of warning was uttered. "Don't think about telling me to turn around," he said. "The deal is done. The contracts are signed. This is it, so let's go," he told her.

A woman approached as they entered the dining room, wearing a purple Indian garment heavily laced with gold accents and a lace veil hanging from head to waist. It didn't cover her face, causing the small decorative jewelry on her forehead to stand out. The woman ushered Sherry and Joel to a slightly raised platform where Mr. Bengali and his daughter were sitting. There were two seats next to Zarah, where they were instructed to sit. Joel sat next to Zarah after greeting Musar. Sherry sat on the other side of Joel. It felt like being in a fishbowl. If this was the engagement, she couldn't comprehend enduring three days of wedding festivities.

Sherry leaned toward Joel. "I have to admit, she is lovely. I saw her in Detroit that one time, but I didn't realize how gorgeous she is."

"Uh-hmm," he responded.

Sherry understood how limited he was in his ability to respond, sitting that close to Zarah. After a few words from Mr. Bengali and the official engagement proposal from Joel, dinner was served. Sherry wanted to close her eyes and wake up in Detroit, wishing she'd somehow gotten locked into an awkward dream. The evening was ending but she had a feeling Joel's troubles were only beginning. It was to be expected when marriages were done under the wrong set of circumstances, she thought from experience.

chapter

39

Madeline felt agitated and out of the loop pertaining to information about Joel's doings. The DMI attorneys were stretching out the process and getting nowhere with finding a way to permanently crush the merger. She wasn't about to stand around and wait while others let her company collapse under the weight of Joel's ill-advised decisions. Madeline took the short walk past several closed doors to Joel's office. "Is he in? I need to see him," Madeline told Kay, Joel's administrative assistant.

"No, Mrs. Mitchell, he's out for the week."

"How can he be out of the office for a week when we're in the middle of a sales crisis? I know he's not on vacation."

"I'm not at liberty to say where he is."

The possibilities of where he was and what he was doing bombarded Madeline's brain. He was up to something, she was certain. "But I'm an officer of this company. You can tell me."

Kay dropped her gaze and began fidgeting with the papers on her desk. "He gave me strict orders not to share any information."

Madeline didn't feel it necessary to grill the assistant. She was only doing her job, and doing it well. Too bad Kay couldn't teach her boss about integrity. "Okay, I understand, but trust me when I tell you that your boss will have a lot to explain if he gets us into a situation that we can't handle. This company is as good as gone," Madeline said, taking a few steps back toward the elevator. "So I'm probably your best hope of saving this company and your job. If you know anything, you should tell me before it's too late." Madeline didn't really expect the executive assistant to divulge her boss's confidential information. In a weird way, Madeline was pleased to know that the top-ranking official in DMI had a trustworthy advocate, because if Kay willingly shared information with one person, she could do it with another, perhaps somebody outside the walls of DMI.

The assistant was a bust, but the hunt wasn't over. Madeline strolled two doors down, to Sherry's office. She raised her fist to rap on the door and stopped. Did she really feel like dealing with Sherry today? The sun was shining, spring was handing the reins over to summer, and it was a festive time. Did she truly want to usher in storm clouds? What the heck, she might as well find out where Joel was. She knocked several times with no response. Madeline gazed at her watch. Eleven fifteen. Everybody working for DMI should be in the office by nine thirty. Where was she? Madeline wanted some kind of answer for her efforts—a nibble would suffice.

Slightly agitated but more curious, Madeline returned to the only source of information available. "Is Sherry out today?" she asked Kay.

"Yes, she's out for the week, too."

"Wait a minute. They're both out of the office for a week at the same time?" She didn't know what was going on, but the slicing feeling in the pit of her stomach said it wasn't good for her son's claim on the CEO position. Madeline didn't know whether to scream in torment or rally the troops in a show of strength. She did neither. Diplomacy would be the approach. "I have to speak with Joel or Sherry. We have a couple of serious issues brewing and we need the CEO to weigh in on the situation. I have to speak with him," Madeline said, calm as could be, carefully and methodically speaking each word. If Kay had an inkling of the rift between

Madeline, Sherry, and Joel, she'd know that Madeline would never ask for Joel's help unless her house was burning down and the stairs had collapsed and there were no sheets available for her to climb out the window. Even then, she'd consider other options, until her last breath, when her smoke-filled lungs collapsed. But a smile and a few soft words were the master at winning over people. It wasn't Madeline's way, but she wasn't so old and stuck in her mind-set that she couldn't try a new approach. None of her other approaches had worked.

"Why don't I take a message and get it to him," Kay offered.

"How quickly can you get it to him?"

The assistant pulled a handwritten index card from her top desk drawer. "This is my cheat sheet. I get so mixed up with the time differences." She traipsed her finger along the card for a few seconds, apparently doing some form of calculation. "It's around nine thirty at night there."

"Where?"

"Jaipur, India." Before Kay could realize what she'd done, Madeline was leaving. "Oh no," Kay said, covering her mouth with her hand, wearing a look of fright. "I probably shouldn't have said that."

"Don't worry, you haven't done anything wrong. He's the CEO, for goodness sake, and I'm an owner in this company. Any business he does that pertains to DMI is also my business."

"But this was a personal trip." *Personal*, Madeline wondered, but didn't speak. The instant arch in her eyebrow must have spoken loudly because Kay regained her level of fear. "I'm sorry. I didn't mean that."

Madeline came close to the desk. "It's okay, you haven't done anything wrong. Don't worry. You're all right."

"I hope Mr. Mitchell feels the same way. I need this job."

"Trust me, you're all right. You didn't really tell me anything, and you definitely didn't volunteer any information. As far as I'm concerned, he should be glad to have you on his staff." Kay appeared less terrified. "If Mr. Mitchell has a problem with you when he returns, you have a job with me."

"Thanks, Mrs. Mitchell, but I hope that's not necessary." The phone rang. "Excuse me, Mrs. Mitchell. I have to take this call." Madeline hung around in case more information was revealed. Hunting for Joel was like putting a puzzle together. She gathered the pieces wherever she could. "Hello, Ms. Tate," Kay spoke into the phone. "No, Mr. Mitchell is not in the office this week." There was a long pause, while the caller spoke. Kay sat up in her seat, getting that look of fear again. Madeline couldn't wait for the call to end and find out what was being said. "No, I can't confirm or deny that Mr. Mitchell is in India. I'll take a message that you called and forward it to Mr. Mitchell. Thank you for the call." Madeline could hear the caller still talking as Kay hung up.

"I guess I'm not the only one who knows about Joel's whereabouts."

"I have no idea how Samantha Tate found out."

"The TV reporter?"

"Yes, her."

Madeline flashed a sincere grin. "Like I said, you're okay with me. If you need a job with me, it's yours," she said, giving a tap on the desk and then walking away. It was bad enough that she knew where Joel was, but Samantha Tate, Ms. Media, was far worse, for Joel, that was. Madeline sensed the warmth of the air. All the answers weren't there, but a snippet of information was the hope she needed to keep pushing. DMI wasn't dead yet. As long as there was breath in her body and vitality in the company, she would fight until the bitter end.

chapter

40

There were instances when Madeline felt alone in the recovery effort. Abigail and Don were on board, but their plan of waiting until God showed them a sign wasn't her way. She felt called to action, not willing to wait for the elevator to carry her down the three floors. She descended the staircase as fast as her four-inch pumps would go without sending her sailing into the air. She wanted answers and was not in a mood for excuses and laziness. Someone was getting fired if the progress she expected wasn't done. Time for playing around with Joel's whim of a merger deal was over.

Madeline burst through the double doors leading into the legal department doors. "Where's Jim?" she asked the junior attorney sitting near the entry.

"I think he's in a meeting."

Madeline didn't wait to find out with whom and for what. They had to get their behinds rolling. The legal team was the last hope. The independent counsel had done their job, although the results weren't good. There was no conversation he could be having that was more important than saving the company from Joel's huge mistake. The merger was a death sentence to DMI, and she had to stop it. Joel couldn't win. With Joel and Sherry both in India, it was clear that time and options were short. She maneuvered through the small legal office and knocked on Jim's closed door. The secretary looked as if she wanted to interrupt but Madeline's counter look of *don't even try it* won out. After three knocks, Madeline opened the door. No one was inside. She turned to the secretary. "Where is Jim? I thought he was in a meeting."

The secretary fumbled around a few keys on the computer, clearly frazzled, accessing Jim's calendar. Madeline wanted to tell her to relax, but decided to leave it alone. Her goal wasn't to torment the staff, but she was determined not to let protocol or confidentiality hinder her from getting the results she had to have. Finally the secretary said, "He's in conference room two, meeting with one of our vendors.

"Thank you," Madeline said with as much sincerity as she could ooze out. "You've been very helpful." The situation wasn't the secretary's fault and she didn't want her to feel the brunt of discontent.

Madeline dashed to the conference room, knocked once, and opened the door in a single continuous motion. Jim and the two vendor representatives were startled. "Excuse me, Jim, I need to speak with you." She also asked the representatives to excuse her. No one objected. Jim gave his apologies and hustled into the hallway, closing the door behind him.

"I need answers about the merger," she said, "but I don't want to talk here. Let's go to your office."

He pointed to the conference room. "Can this wait until after this meeting is over?"

"No, it can't," she said, not blinking or moving an inch. "We've dragged our feet long enough. I need answers now."

"Okay, but let me tell the vendor that I'll be right back."

She waved him on as if to say "do what you have to do, but let's get to your office." Madeline walked ahead and Jim was less than a minute behind.

"Could you please get them some coffee or pastries or something?" Jim asked his secretary before entering his office.

Once inside, he closed the door. He extended his hand toward a seat.

"No thank you, I prefer to stand. I feel like we've been doing nothing but sitting on this issue for months."

"It's not quite a month yet."

"One month, two months, what's the difference? I need answers. Where are we with finding loopholes in the contract or anything that gives us an indication that this merger with Harmonious Energy is a bad deal for DMI? Having to surrender the West Coast division alone presents a hardship."

"But legally it's not a showstopper."

"You can't be serious?"

"Divestiture is a call that the board will need to make but legally there's no barrier."

"Then find something that is."

"We've combed the document and it's in order."

"That's not what I want to hear, Jim," Madeline said, fixing her hands on her hips.

"I don't know what to tell you. We've done a thorough and impartial review."

"And?" she asked expecting more.

"And we've come up with very little."

"You really mean that you've come up with nothing, four weeks, and you have nothing." Madeline paced for several steps. "Why didn't we get an update earlier, letting us know that you weren't getting anywhere?"

"You and the board asked for a thorough and impartial review and that's what we gave you. Just because the results didn't turn out the way you wanted doesn't discount me or my team's effort."

Madeline didn't mind pushback. Actually, she preferred members of the executive team standing up for their work and for their team. She could respect Jim for that, but the stakes were too high this time. They weren't at odds about a vendor refusing to give a 20 percent discount versus 15. This was about the livelihood of a company, her company. She didn't expect Jim or others to have the same energy about stopping the merger. Most of the workers could and would get jobs elsewhere. Losing DMI altogether was about far more than her job. It would kill two of her babies, the company she conceived with Dave forty years ago, and her son's ascension to the throne of DMI. It was his birthright, and as his mother, she was determined to help him get it. He was relying on God's, but she had a backup.

chapter

41

By day four of the wedding ceremony, Joel was exhausted. He'd wired money for the company yesterday as promised. He mustered a chivalrous disposition wearing the traditional long, dresslike garment. The ceremony was frivolous to Joel but knowing how significant it was to Musar, he had no problem conforming to their customs and traditions. One final set of activities and this would be over. He could go home and rebuild DMI, his first love.

A song blared into the doorway as Joel waited in his bare feet for his queue to enter the dining room that was converted into a temple setting. Several men had rehearsed the program order with him two or three times last night and again this morning. Joel hoped to remember as much as he could, although he didn't believe that a minor mishap here or there was going to change the outcome. He and Zarah would be married, and Harmonious Energy was his. When the song stopped, Joel knocked on the door with his sword before entering. He'd practiced the knocking several times earlier and found it kind of amusing. Joel was led to the small platform where he was greeted and showered with flowers by an entourage of women in Zarah and Musar's family. They were old, young, heavy, thin, light complexion, some dark, an assortment. Joel took his spot in front of the platform, facing the priest and Musar. Surprisingly Musar appeared invigorated with a burst of energy.

A swarm of younger woman, around twenty years old, like Zarah, rushed her to the platform. Joel had to admit, Zarah was stunning, with dark silky hair, bronze skin, and deep brown eyes. Her natural beauty was accented by at least thirty thin gold bracelets on both arms. This was the first time he'd truly looked at her entire face.

Joel stood with Zarah. They were handed garlands at the makeshift altar while the priest chanted some type of religious hymns. The two exchanged garlands signifying their acceptance of each other as a married couple. The priest rubbed oil on Joel's feet and hands to ward off evil spirits. If they could have gotten married in the States, a quick trip to the justice of the peace would have eliminated the ceremonial marathon, half of which Joel had no idea what it actually meant. He was certain God wasn't attending. Then again, he hadn't invited Him. Joel glanced over his shoulder at his mother, seated near the platform and dressed in her Indian sari.

Musar stepped forth and linked Joel and Zarah's hands. He wrapped a strip of silk material around their hands, tying a knot. Musar turned to face Joel with a small container of water. "I entrust my daughter to you. I pray that you always have food, that you live with good health and energy," he said, sprinkling salty water over the two of them as he continued. "That you live in happiness, that you have many children, that you have strong cows and good animals, and that all your seasons are plentiful. May you be successful and free from hindrances. May you be blessed with pure love."

Joel wanted to shout in victory. He'd survived the ordeal. He didn't remember every element of the program, but when they got to the part where Musar spoke his libations, the end was near. Joel couldn't be more thrilled.

"You are husband and wife," the priest said. Joel didn't have time to hold his new bride or whisper into her ear. The platform was overtaken by a group of women who rushed to the front and claimed her. Secretly he hoped they didn't step on his bare feet.

Sherry rushed to Joel and embraced him. "You did it, son. You're married. Congratulations, I think," she whispered.

"Mom, don't even think about it," he said.

She hugged him tighter. "I won't."

Joel shook Musar's hand and so did Sherry. They were family. In four days he'd enlarged his family beyond the two-person team he'd come to accept as his lineage. Joel rescued Zarah and followed the wedding crowd to the lobby. He didn't know if there was going to be a decorated car or horse or elephant, pretty much the same to him. A few laps around the immediate area and they could pack for the airport, once he put on a pair of shoes. Detroit and gratification were in sight.

chapter

42

A day after the wedding ceremony, Joel prepared to leave. The driver loaded the bags into the car. Zarah's family crowded the hotel lobby—a massive group of people squished into the tiny space. Some were crying, others gave gifts. From what he could tell, most of the gifts were thin gold bracelets or earrings, which was good since the luggage was already packed. Nothing large was going to fit. The crowd aggressively tried to get to Zarah, Musar's only child.

Joel stepped aside, grateful for a moment of pause. He had his shoes on this time and was secure in his comfort zone. The surge of energy resonating from finally having the deal done and being on the precipice of inheriting a large chunk of much needed capital recharged him. He could go another couple days, easily, but wasn't complaining about flying out today. Between the time zone and return flight, they'd be home tomorrow. They had a two-day trip, leave on Wednesday and arrive on Thursday. The time change made it seem like they were gaining a day, but actually it was the same long grueling trip it took to get them there. The original plan was for Musar to join them, but he was too weak for extensive travel. He'd conserved and expended his burst of strength for the wedding festivities. Joel was impressed at the extent to which Musar was willing to go for his daughter. He was reminded of his father and how much he missed having him around, a person he trusted. Of course his mother was with him, but he meant someone with a sharp business mind. Those affirmations and chunks of wisdom were no longer there now that Dave Mitchell was gone. Joel had to continue making success happen on his own, playing the cards from the deck he inherited.

Joel should have felt guilty for hopefully anticipating the receipt of Zarah's inheritance, but he didn't. Musar made it very clear that his death was a natural transition to the next phase of his existence. That was Musar's belief. Joel didn't know what he believed anymore. For now he was content in his ability to revive his own dreams with hard work, wisdom, and a shot of cash from Musar.

The driver approached Joel, appearing reluctant to speak and not consistently making eye contact. "Mr. Mitchell, it is time that we go, in order to make your flight."

No problem; the words were like music to his ears. He knew where Zarah was. By now, both of her arms were lined with at least twenty new bracelets each. The ones she wore at the wedding were packed. If the Indian airport was anything like the U.S., extra time was definitely required to get Zarah and her two armfuls of bracelets through security. He wasn't about to miss the flight. They had to go. He peered around the crowd in search of his mother and caught a glimpse of her near the registration desk. He beckoned for her while maneuvering through the crowd to get to his wife. The word didn't ring well so he wasn't likely to use the label.

Finally Joel had his family in the car and en route to the airport, leaving behind a tearful farewell at the hotel. Zarah was sobbing softly. Joel was going to comfort her, but Sherry was already in the process. He left it alone, suspecting that there would be plenty of opportunities for him in the upcoming months, especially with Musar being so ill.

Much to his surprise, the airport security was more relaxed. He didn't have to strip down to his undies. Zarah did have to shed the jewelry, which took ten minutes alone, delicately removing each bracelet one by one. Taking off his wedding ring was quick, so quick that within a second he'd picked it up and put it inside his jacket pocket for safekeeping.

Joel periodically gazed at people, expecting to run into someone he knew, like he had on the flight over. The memory of that guy on the plane haunted him. He was familiar but Joel couldn't quite place him. He had hours and hours of flying time to ponder.

A day and a half later, they were landing. The flight was long but tolerable, with a few intermittent tears from Zarah. He planned to get her home and get her settled. It would take a while for her to truly get settled, and he would do what he could to help, when he wasn't working. She wouldn't be alone, not completely. As they exited the plane, baggage claim, and customs, Zarah clung to his arm. Being flanked by a woman who radiated with beauty was commonplace. Dealing with the media was, too. As Joel, Zarah, and Sherry stepped from the secured area, with the skycap pulling the cart of luggage close behind, they were plagued by microphones shoved in their faces, camera lights flashing, and TV cameras descending on them. Zarah was nearly hysterical and latched onto Joel's arm so tightly his muscle quivered. Bam, just like that it came to him, who the guy was on the flight to India and why he looked so familiar. There he stood, Samantha Tate's cameraman. Joel already had Zarah close. He pulled Sherry close, too, and barreled around the circus. The skycap had to make his own way, unassisted.

Samantha Tate ran ahead and pushed the microphone toward Joel, but he didn't stop. "Mr. Mitchell, is it true? Is this your new bride?"

Joel hustled, keeping his head low like they were in a war zone dodging bullets. The media attack was rapid fire.

"What's her name? Are you officially off the market? Are the rumors true? What's the state of DMI?"

Joel drilled past everyone. Catching a glimpse of his driver, he barreled to refuge. He gently shoved the women into the car. "Please help the skycap with our luggage and get us out of here as quickly as you can," he said, handing the driver two one hundred dollar bills. "Give one to the skycap, and give him my apologies."

"Will do, sir."

Abigail had come home early, not feeling well. She drank a cup of soup and relaxed on a sofa in the den, reading, mixed with some TV and nods of sleeps. The breaking news flashed across the screen. JOEL MITCHELL (CEO OF DMI) AND HIS NEW BRIDE ARRIVE IN DETROIT scrolled across the bottom of the screen. Abigail fumbled with the remote, eager to get the mute taken off and hear what they were saying. The woman attached to Joel was wearing a deep red and gold-accented Indian dress. Abigail couldn't tell if it was Mr. Bengali's daughter or not. Her face was on the screen for a second and Abigail had only met her one time at DMI months ago. She listened for a few seconds and then put the TV on mute again. She took another sip of soup and resumed her reading. Joel and the woman dashed in and out of her thoughts like surges of electricity. Abigail was determined not to cry, not to fall apart, not to give Joel the satisfaction of crushing her again. Wounds healed and she was positive hers would, she thought, choking back the emotions.

When the phone rang, she was alarmed and relieved at the same time. It was Don. She was grateful for the much-needed friendly voice.

"Are you watching the news?" he asked.

"Yes," she responded.

"I'm sorry, this can't be easy for you."

"What can we say, Joel is on a track to hell and no one can rescue him except God."

"God can, but does Joel want to be rescued?"

"I don't know and I want to say that I don't care."

"But we both know that's not true," Don said.

"Not yet," she said. "But I'm definitely getting there."

"Do you want me to come over?"

"No, I'll be okay. Don't worry about me."

"Are you sure?"

"Positive."

"Well, I'll be here."

Abigail allowed herself to receive Don's consoling and felt an extra spark of warmth as a result.

chapter

43

The limousine pulled into the circular drive, stopping directly in front of the double doors. They'd already dropped off his mother. Joel was exhausted from the travel and peeved with the press bombarding him at the airport. By six thirty, every nightly news program within five hundred miles would be featuring the airport shots. Zarah didn't utter a word for the entire forty minute ride home, and he didn't encourage her to talk. Musar would have made the ride more comfortable, at least for his daughter.

Silence didn't bother Joel. Quiet was good. Frivolous chatter wasn't his way, but Abigail entered his thoughts as he looked at the house. A part of it was reserved for her but purpose took precedence. Feelings were worthless unless used to accomplish his goals. Nothing and no one would stop him from succeeding as CEO. It was what mattered most. Those who doubted his worth and his mother's would soon be permanently silenced. Casualties along the way had to be expected.

"Well, we're here. Are you ready to go in?" he asked Zarah, trying hard to be sensitive after witnessing a look of fear on her face. He let his index finger lift her chin, letting his eyes chase hers until their gazes locked. "We're home, let's go in." She stiffened. "You'll be fine," he whispered, not getting too close for fear of scaring her more. The driver opened Joel's door. "Wait a minute and I'll come around to open your door," he said and got out. He opened the door and took her hand. She hesitated but he continued reaching out until her hand was secure in his. A step at a time and they were standing at his front door. Carrying her over the threshold crossed his mind, but that was for the romantic weddings, not theirs. Finally inside, she stood by the door. The housekeeper, who was more like a house manager, met them.

"Welcome back, Mr. Mitchell and Mrs. Mitchell," the house-keeper said as the driver set the luggage inside. "Is there anything I can get you?"

"Not for me," Joel responded. "But Zarah needs help getting unpacked."

"Absolutely. Would you like to show her the master suite first while I have the driver bring the bags upstairs?"

"No, you go ahead and show her. Maybe you can give her a tour around the house, too."

"Oh, okay," the housekeeper responded.

Joel detected the uneasiness from everybody except him and the driver. "I'll help with the luggage while you give Zarah the grand tour and help her get comfortable," he said, fully aware that there was just a small amount of luggage since most of Zarah's belongings were being shipped. Joel's phone buzzed in his jacket. He extracted it and glimpsed at the screen. The ID showed UNKNOWN CALLER so he let it go to voice mail. The phone buzzed again—UNKNOWN CALLER. The persistence swayed him to answer the call.

"Mr. Mitchell, this is Kumar."

"How can I help you?" Joel didn't want to hear that somehow the contract process had gone awry and Harmonious Energy didn't truly belong to him. The deal was done, no backing out. Joel glanced at Zarah. He had made good on his portion of the agreement. Musar Bengali had to honor his. Joel had bills to pay, and he didn't believe Uncle Frank's investors were the keep-them-waiting kind. He prepared to protest intensely if they tried stiffing him for the West Coast division without adequately compensating him. "Is there a problem?"

"Yes, there is a problem," Kumar responded.

Joel hustled outside so he could berate the attorney freely. "Look, we have a deal. It's too late to back out."

"I'm calling about Musar."

"What about him?" Joel said, prepared to hear the word "transitioned" or whatever term Musar's religion allowed. Last time he saw Musar, his father-in-law was rapidly deteriorating. Joel walked down the driveway, away from the window, careful not to be seen or heard inside. Admittedly, the weight of paying back Uncle Frank's "investors" would be relieved if Musar passed away, but Joel wasn't orchestrating the predicament. Musar was already terminally ill the first time Joel met him. Joel wanted to be cavalier about the business transaction, but he couldn't help feeling badly for Musar and for Zarah.

"He's in the hospital," the attorney said, his English shrouded in a thick accent.

Joel wondered why Musar was at the hospital—he expected Musar to let death take him during his sleep with no resistance. Going to the hospital sounded like he was putting up a fight.

"He collapsed on the way to the temple. The driver took him to the hospital unaware of Musar's wish to be left alone when it was time for his transition. Now the hospital won't release him until his condition is stable."

"What, is he in a coma?" Joel asked, hoping he was wrong.

"He's very ill and believes his time is near. There isn't very much the hospital can do."

Joel couldn't figure out why they let Musar go to the temple, as frail as he'd become. It made no sense, but it was a question to be saved for another day. "Is he breathing on his own?"

"Yes, he is. His belief does not allow the hospital to help him breathe with a machine. It must be his breath."

Joel didn't know how to process the news. In order to be of the most value, Musar either needed to be alive and well or dead and gone. Flopping back and forth between the two worlds was the worst scenario for Joel. Musar had to commit.

Joel returned to the house, deciding on the best way to tell Zarah that her father, the only significant person in her life, was dead or dying. In his mind Joel had rehearsed the scene several times. When he finally got the word on Musar's transition, Joel would push for the estate settlement to be accelerated and hopefully have cash in hand within ten days. His back alley investors could be paid off in record time.

chapter

44

Joel entered the house and stood in the grand foyer. Zarah and the housekeeper weren't there. He went upstairs to the bedroom suite, which occupied the entire west wing and was segregated from the other rooms for total privacy. He found the two unpacking clothes in one of the four walk-in closets located throughout the suite. It was an Abigail touch. She'd modified the original floor plan to include a shoe closet, ladies' winter and summer clothes closets, and an oversized one for Joel.

"Excuse me," he said, interrupting the two. "I need to speak with Zarah for a moment."

"Sure, call me when you're ready," the housekeeper said and left the room.

Joel wasn't sure where to start or how to say it. It felt like yesterday when he lost his father. The wound was fresh. He decided to blurt it out. "Your father is ill, very ill." Joel waited for her reaction before saying more. Her eyes were silent. Unsure what to do, he embraced her delicately, reluctant to get too close. "He's in the hospital." She still didn't say anything. Joel wanted her to speak, to cry, to scream, to laugh, react somehow. "If you want to fly back to India, I will make the arrangements." She remained quiet. Joel couldn't tell if she heard him or what was going on. This marital arrangement was already showing signs of difficulty.

"No, I will stay here with you. I must be with my husband. My father is ready for his transition. He is ready," she said with tears welling in her eyes, although she didn't cry.

"Are you sure you don't want to fly home?"

"This is my home now. I must stay with you," she said, clinging to him.

Clinging was unpredicted. He was accustomed to having his space, but compassion rushed in. She was alone and her father was dying on the other side of the world. He had to give her support. He took her hand and led her through the suite and into the hallway, looking for the housekeeper. He found her sitting in one of the other rooms upstairs, located on the other side of the house. "We found out that Zarah's father is very sick in India."

"I'm sorry to hear that. How can I help?"

"Could you please help Zarah finish unpacking and get her something to eat? I have to make a few business calls," he told the housekeeper. Speaking directly to Zarah, he said, "Then I can spend the rest of the afternoon with you." Zarah put up zero resistance. "If you need me, I'll be in my office."

By the time he walked the short distance to the stairs, he'd shifted to DMI mode. He really didn't want Zarah to lose her father. He didn't want any child to go through the crushing pain of losing a parent, but Musar was the key to his deliverance.

Anxiously Joel dialed Uncle Frank. When his uncle was on the call, Joel said, "Looks like I'll be able to repay the loan sooner than agreed. I'd like to work a deal."

"Shoot. I'll listen to any offer, but that doesn't mean I'm committed."

"I know we agreed to a ninety-day repayment window, but looks like I'll have the money to pay the loan off in another week and reduce the interest."

"Really, what did you do, hit the lottery?"

"Not quite. I'm not a risk taker. I go for the sure wins."

"Whatever works for you, but as far as the loan goes, that's locked. Let's just say the interest and collateral are the most compelling components of the loan. That's where they make their money and wouldn't be eager to give it up. Take my advice, stick with the terms, pay on time, and generate goodwill for the next loan."

"I won't need a next loan. This is it for me. I don't like having someone else control my affairs. I'm done with your investors."

"If you say so. I've heard that line many times. We'll see, but in case you do need help down the road, know that your credit is good with me."

Joel was certain. Having one of the DMI divisions sitting as collateral on the loan didn't raise his comfort level. Temporarily forfeiting ownership of the West Coast division to Musar was already a bear. Giving up a second division to Uncle Frank's investors wasn't acceptable. Joel was clinging to the notion of recouping the West Coast and reassembling the pieces of DMI. He knew his reign as CEO would be permanently stained if he didn't restore the company.

All of a sudden grief dipped into his soul, threatening to mount a full attack. He recalled the time, right before his father died, when he sat at his father's bedside, listening intently as Dave Mitchell poured out nuggets of wisdom. "Don't let the ministry get sold or split under any circumstances," Dad commanded with the power in his voice he'd had before getting sick. "You have strength as a solid unit. Once you're broken into pieces, there's no recovery. I trust you, and I am holding you to this promise." Joel shrugged in shame, reflecting on his promise. The words haunted him, the very same ones that once served as a source of profound encouragement. He was letting his father down, the one who had believed in him when no one else had, other than his mother. Nobody expected the "questionable" heir of Dave Mitchell to amount to much. His parents' tainted marriage was supposed to be the stamp of failure on his life. That's why he had to get the West Coast back, right away. He shoved grief away and homed in on what had to be done to restore DMI.

There was compassion left but it had to get in line. Victory was within his grasp. He could practically reach out and grab it with the Harmonious Energy merger at the core. Now that Mr. Bengali would be passing away any day and leaving his money to Zarah, Joel was obligated to use the money to maintain their solvency. Joel claimed some dignity with the promise he'd made to Musar that Zarah would be well provided for. Joel intended to honor the agreement until the three-year, childless marriage came to an end. Three days down and two years, three hundred and sixty-two days left. He could endure. Envisioning the money being wired back to Uncle Frank was his motivation.

chapter

45

Madeline didn't catch the original story on the news last night. Since it was played repeatedly on every network, she had no choice but to witness Joel's mockery of a marriage and the merger early this morning before coming to the office. The child had lost his mind. Madeline went from one window to the other, thinking, forgetting, remembering. Joel had finally flooded the place with irreparable mismanagement. Beyond his nuptials, who was he to sell off a piece of her company? She tried to clear her mind and concentrate on where she'd gone wrong. Had there been missed opportunities to end this farce? Maybe she'd let up at times when she should have gone at him with no mercy. She continued pacing with her arms crossed.

She wanted him to go away, to vanish, poof, gone, but he wasn't budging, not now. He'd beaten the entire leadership team and secretly pulled off the merger with Harmonious Energy. Madeline cringed. She stopped at the middle window and braced her hands on her hips. He was too stupid to realize how devastated DMI was going to be as a result of his reckless actions. Her anger fumed as she thought about his selfish act of personal gratification. Joel couldn't care less about DMI. Reason and perhaps self-preservation shouted for her to pack up and get out. Her sense of entitlement shouted louder for her to stay and fight. This was her children's birthright, not the snot-nosed kid's. Madeline snatched her Mont Blanc pen and portfolio from the desk and headed to the boardroom. This wasn't over. She'd grab Abigail.

Two hours flat and Madeline had exercised her waning power. The group was gathered for an emergency board meeting, some in presence, others chattering on the phone. The key decision maker was absent, fortunately. He was off honeymooning or busy shoving the company off a cliff, at least the divisions he hadn't yet sold.

"Attention, attention," Madeline said, standing, bent on getting the meeting started. The room quieted and Madeline seized control. "I'm sure you've heard the news about Mr. Joel Mitchell."

"How could we not," one board member said. "The network and local news stations have shown the airport footage over and over."

Abigail was out of the office. She'd taken the last couple of days off. Don, too.

"This is a media nightmare. We know nothing about the new Mrs. Mitchell," one member said.

"His marriage is the least of our concerns. I'm worried about how we're going to deal with the divestiture of the West Coast division?" The chatter simmered. "What about the employees?" Madeline said, falling into one of the chairs.

"And the company's private information?" someone added.

This was a mess. Madeline didn't feel like cleaning up Joel's irresponsible waste, but the choice wasn't hers. When she stood with Dave Mitchell and opened the doors to the public for the first time, she was hooked for life.

"Will the name change?" someone asked.

"Depends on who bought whom. If DMI bought Harmonious Energy then probably not, but if it's the other way around, the name probably will change," someone said.

"Ha, I'd like to see Joel try that one," Madeline said.

"He's gone this far without our approval. What would stop him from changing the name?" someone said.

Madeline was too blinded by outrage to address the name

change issue. She opted to stay on the more important merger topic. "I can't fold any aspect of Harmonious Energy into the East Coast if I have any hopes of holding on to the remaining churches that we're servicing. I'm telling you, mixing different religious practices under the same roof isn't going to work, but we can't seem to talk sense into Joel." Madeline let her gaze rest on the table. She needed help but the group wasn't motivated to action. It was understandable. They might lose an advisory board title, but Madeline had much more at stake.

"What do you suggest we do?" someone asked.

"I'm going to light a match under the legal team to see if we can undo what Joel has done."

"Isn't it too late? The merger is done."

"It's never too late. We're approaching desperation. No alternatives will be discounted before proper consideration." When the words left her mouth, Tamara entered her conscience, the most logical solution. Nobody was going to push Madeline around without a bloody duel. She was recharged, no thanks to the other board members. Joel had to go, kicked out as soon as her foot could align with his backside. She pondered the notion, almost smirking. "I have to leave, excuse me," she said, hustling from the office and ignoring questions about whether she was returning.

She'd leave the easy stuff to the chatterers. Her time had to be spent on making a difference. Her legs weren't moving fast enough. She'd get back to her office and call Don. "No" wasn't a possibility. That word couldn't rest on his lips. Her son had to go and get Tamara, tying her up and lugging her to DMI if necessary. It was Tamara's legacy at risk, too. Maybe not right away, but one day she would have a family of her own and want the proceeds from her share of the estate. Madeline could keep it protected until that day came, determined to never let the hope of her daughter's return grow cold.

chapter

46

Don was finally able to get his mother off the phone. She was roused by Joel, understandably. He went behind the board and made a deal of his own. Joel was out of order. Don agreed with Madeline in theory, but not with her tactics.

She was adamant about him contacting Tamara. Ownership of her stock had always been the instant resolution to the DMI problem. The fight would be over with the stroke of a pen. Confusion tried to sneak in. The notion of scheming like his mother was nauseating. If God was in the plan, and this truly was his destiny, no plotting and posturing was necessary. He searched his spirit. The only question to answer was if he was comfortable calling Tamara. He dropped to his knees and prayed, more fervently than he had in months, for direction and clarity. When he finished, Tamara was still roaming around his thoughts, but there was a peace that followed. By faith he accepted it as a confirmation from God. If he was wrong, by faith, God would fix it for him since he was stepping out in sincerity. He dialed the number before giving doubt and confusion time to rush in. A series of rapid rings and his sister was on the phone. "Good, I'm glad that I got you."

"Hello, little brother, please tell me that Mother isn't with you?"

"She's not, but that is why I'm calling."

"Why, is she okay?" Tamara asked in an elevated pitch.

"You know how she is. Mother is Mother."

"But she's okay," Tamara said with her voice mellowing to her normal level.

"I'm glad to see that you're concerned. She'll be glad to hear that."

"Don't get her worked up because that will be a sure path to my having to move, again," she said, "and honestly, I'm tired of that. I'm thirty-five. I told you before, I want to be settled."

"Tamara, it doesn't matter how many times you move or where you go on this earth, you will never have peace until you come home and face your demons. I'm not telling you to do anything that I haven't done." The company was at the forefront of his appeal. "Plus, I need you at DMI with me. I need your stock, sis." Tamara didn't respond but he could hear her breathing. The request was huge, one that he had to ask despite her fears. "I wouldn't ask if it wasn't seriously important. I need your help. I need you here and you need to be here."

"Maybe you're right."

He wasn't prepared for her response. "Does that mean you're considering coming home?"

"Maybe, but there's only one way that I could even fathom the idea."

"What? Name it."

"I couldn't be there with Mother. She'd have to leave me alone."

He chuckled. "There's only one way that would happen—she'd have to be on the other side of the planet in a remote location with no airstrip or phone lines." He chuckled more.

"I mean it, she will have to leave."

"You can't be serious."

"If you want me back at DMI with my stock, Mother has to resign and give me a year to establish myself. Those are my terms."

"You really are Madeline Mitchell's child."

"I want to help you but I have to take care of me, too," she said.

"But she's never harmed you. Why do you want to punish her?"

"Being around her is a constant reminder of what it's taken me over a decade to forget. Instead of letting me exist on my terms, she will overwhelm me and I couldn't survive the smothering."

"Your terms are much more extreme than my original request." The company could be theirs with Tamara on his side. "I'll have to talk with Mother. This is no small feat. It will take some doing to get her to agree on this one. You understand the position you're putting me in, sis."

"Do you understand the situation you're putting me in? Those have to be my terms. It's the only way I'll set foot in Detroit again," she told him. He listened, not wanting to overcommit. "I'm willing to help you. I'm sure you don't know how much your random calls helped me get past many tough moments, little brother. I owe you, and I want to help, but you have to help me, too."

"Come on, sis, what you're asking is equivalent to parting the Red Sea."

"Perhaps, but that's what it's going to take."

Joel hadn't left too many alternatives. Don resigned himself to the fact that if this was to be, a power more substantial than his was required to keep Madeline on one side of the world and Tamara on the other. No other force on earth could.

chapter

47

Abigail sat in her office. News of Joel's nuptials hadn't settled, probably never would. She mentally replayed the footage of the couple being accosted at the airport. Joel had told her months ago about the marriage, but hearing him talk about the concept was a gigantic departure from actually saying "I do." Her hope of a relationship was finished; friendship, too. "Can you believe Joel really did it?" she asked Don.

Don sighed, sitting at the small conference table, peering into his laptop screen. "Joel's actions haven't startled me in quite a while."

"I guess you're right." Hours of pondering couldn't paint a rational picture of Joel's decisions. "I feel kind of sorry for him."

Don shifted his gaze from the laptop to her. "Why is that?"

Joel wasn't her love. He wasn't even a close friend any longer, but he was a decent guy who deserved her compassion. "He's jeopardizing so much because he doesn't want to take anyone's advice."

"He believes he has the answers. He had so much success early on," Don commented.

"That's when his morals mattered and his spirituality meant

something." Abigail knew God had been an important ingredient in Joel's success back when he willingly acknowledged a power greater than his own limited abilities. Joel was blinded by his own goals, and no one could influence him at this junction.

"Maybe you should talk to him. I mean, you were pretty close," he said, letting his gaze drop to the laptop. "You never know, he might listen to you."

"Been there, done that," she said, slapping the file onto her desk and pulling it around the perimeter as she scooted to her seat. "We were close at one time, or at least I thought so, but those days have passed." She plopped into her swivel, high-back chair. She opened the file. "Thank goodness our friendship wasn't damaged in this mess."

Don snickered. "Well," he said, closing the laptop, "you did toss me to the curb when I first left for South Africa."

"That's not true."

"It is, but it's cool. I understand. You and Joel were an item then," he reminded her.

At least she thought they were. "What can I say, I was wrong." It wasn't the first time she'd been mistaken. Her days were seasoned with a scoop of reality, unhindered by raw passion. Sharing the moment with Don was the affirmation of hope and redemption. She couldn't fix Joel's predicament and was no longer trying. Joel and his moral compass were resigned to dealing with the circus he had crafted. She was off the roller coaster with him and seeking a less risky, more stable ride. There was an easiness to being around Don, but he was also Joel's brother. Her feelings were scattered. Watching the brothers dueling over DMI was more than she wanted to see. She didn't have it in her to raise another element of tension between them. "Remember when we worked on the East Coast megaproject?"

"Of course I do," he said, relaxing. "You were so green six years ago. That was the first project where I let you take the lead."

Abigail was tickled that he hadn't forgotten her first big professional success. "I'm glad you're here," she told Don, fighting confusion and vulnerability. She would keep her feelings tightly guarded even though their connection hadn't diminished. "It's like you never left."

But he had left, and for good reason. Forgiveness and God healing his wounded soul had saved him. There was zero interest in returning to a state of romantic chaos and despair. His livelihood was in check because he'd gotten out of the toxic environment just in time. Naledi was an integral part of his refreshened perspective. His heart warmed as he thought of her. She gave him the audacity to dream again, to think about building a family, to both give love and to have it freely reciprocated. They hadn't spoken romantically, not directly, but there were sufficient feelings to consider the possibility. But he couldn't deny the tingling fragments of affection for Abigail. Those feelings were mostly buried alive in South Africa along with the grief, heartache, resentment, and disappointments that had so easily weighed him down. They weren't easily resurrected without carting along a weary spirit, a traveling buddy he wanted to forget.

chapter

48

At four thirty, Sherry poked her head in to Joel's office. "Why don't you and Zarah come to my house for dinner tonight? We haven't had a family meal together since we came home. We're overdue," she said. "Besides, I need to spend time with my daughter-in-law if I'm going to get to know her."

"Mom, I'm going to pass on the dinner offer." His mind was too clouded. He had to get the cash from Zarah's inheritance.

"All right, let's make it another time then. Very soon, though. I really want to reach out to Zarah. This must be difficult for her, adjusting to a new husband, a new house, a new country, and a new culture. Wow, that's a lot for anyone to handle, especially someone whose father is gravely ill." Joel listened. The swirling thoughts were too many to share with his mother. "Let her know that I'm here for her."

"Sure, I'll do that," Joel said, wanting to end the talk about Musar and push the uncertainty out. His mother left but Joel didn't. Too much idle time left him drained. The merger was done, no work left to do on it. Clients were leaving in droves, no work there. His time in the office was in a state of paralysis, little to do, less to charge toward. Folding the companies into one was a challenge without the board's backing, especially since DMI wouldn't gain majority ownership of Harmonious Energy until after Musar's death. Joel had managed to keep that detail hidden. Musar had to choose a side before Joel lost control.

Six thirty. Joel relaxed as best he could at the conference table in his office. The air of insecurity hovered like a blanket. A third straight night of working late in the office and it was only Thursday. He couldn't rally the energy to go home, but didn't want to stay in the building, where he would be constantly reminded of the dire situation, the cloud of failure. He had to get out of there, right now. A tank of gas and loads of time were waiting for him outside. He grabbed his suit jacket and left his office. He pushed the elevator button and waited for it to arrive. The door opened as he shifted the jacket on his shoulder. "Abigail," he said, seeing her standing inside when the door opened. It was the first time he'd seen her since returning from India.

"Joel," was the only word she said, and pushed past him.

"How have you been?" he asked as she came out of the elevator. She continued walking and he followed behind, more desperate for the fellowship than he wanted to admit.

"I'm just fine," she said, slowing down but not quite stopping.

Abigail reminded him of a point in time when he was in control, when he wasn't desperately waiting for something, anything to happen that would give him the edge, the one he'd clawed to earn. The one he deserved. A board of directors couldn't rob him of his worth, his rightful place.

"I've been meaning to catch up with you. It's been so long since we talked," he said, letting the statement hover.

She slid a folder under his mother's door without responding. Turning toward him she said, "How's your wife?"

Joel pulled away. "She's adjusting," he said, unprepared to discuss Zarah. Actually, he wanted a clear evening, away from the stress of Musar, Zarah, and DMI.

"Well, good for her," Abigail said, pushing past Joel again and heading back to the elevator.

"What are you doing for dinner?" he asked.

"I don't know," she said, pushing the button. "I'll see what Don's up to or I'll grab something on the way home." The elevator door opened. "Why? Are you inviting me over to meet your new wife?" She stepped into the elevator. Joel looked away. "That's what I thought," she said and let the door close.

He rubbed his palm across his forehead and braced the other hand on the wall next to the elevator. Alone. He could have gone to God, probably should have, but his anger blocked the desire. There was only one place he could go. He lifted his head, adjusted the suit jacket again, and tapped the elevator button. It was too late to reserve the corporate jet for the night. Chicago was four and a half hours if he drove with haste. There was a better idea. He dialed his phone, feeling relieved already. When she answered, he said, "Sheba, it's me, and I need to see you, desperately."

"Where and when?"

His renewed energy level was rising by the second. "I have a crazy request."

"Share it with me."

She was the one he needed. "I'm hopping on the road right now. I can be in Kalamazoo in about two hours. That's halfway between here and Chicago. Are you free this evening and can your driver get you there in a few hours?"

"Sounds important.

"It is."

"That's all you had to say. Are you bringing your new bride with you so I can meet her?"

He took a long sigh. "No, I'm coming alone. I need a friend."

"Then I'll see you in a few hours."

"Sheba, thank you, this means a lot to me."

"There's no need for thanks. See you soon."

Joel exited the building, feeling lighter, less downtrodden, more alive. Sheba had that way with him. He thanked his lucky stars for her. Without Sheba, he would have been forced to go to God.

chapter
49

Thirty days had come and gone, with no progress one way or the other. Musar's life was in limbo and with it floated the livelihood of DMI. Joel desperately wished there was a way to expedite the process but realized there wasn't. Musar had to recover or pass away without assistance.

After a few hours of sleep, Joel walked into the library, located on the first floor, lined with herringbone leather floors. Abigail's touch swirled around the house, in classy, but not overly obnoxious, ways. He missed their relationship. If times were different and his life had another purpose, they could have been great. No sense pining over fantasies. A path of disillusionment was his guide.

Zarah sat in the library under the midmorning light. She had been asleep when he got in the bed earlier. Apparently he was asleep when she got up. It had become their routine.

"Why don't you turn the lights on," he said as he entered the library.

"I don't want to be any trouble," she said in her slight Indian accent.

The tense air hovered. "I'm sorry for getting in so late last night or, should I say, so early this morning. He'd wanted to stay overnight but Sheba wouldn't let him. "You were asleep by the time I got home." Truth was, he found it increasingly difficult to rush home and have to spend time with a wife with whom he had little in common. The office was a circus. Home was tense. He had no solitude, except for his sporadic hops to Chicago and now Kalamazoo. Meeting midway worked well.

Looking at Zarah without frustration was difficult. She was a constant reminder of his precarious situation. Two lives, bound by grief. His gain was built on her loss. Without the passing of Musar, DMI was dead. If he didn't get the money soon, the investors were going to rush in like vultures and pick the bones of DMI, one division at a time. His resentment simmered. He'd upheld his end of the deal, forfeited the West Coast, and married Zarah. Now it was time for Musar to honor his end and let go, complete the transition. Thinking of his father softened his heart. The agony was suppressed pretty well, but there were times when it bubbled to the surface. The situation wasn't Zarah's fault. "Have you eaten already?"

"I have not."

Adjusting to American food was more of an ordeal than he planned. The cook was doing the best she could with making vegetarian Indian dishes. "If you want, we can go out to the Indian restaurant again. It's late for breakfast, but we could catch an early lunch." Her demeanor lit up.

"I would love to go." She closed the book and delicately repositioned the scarf over her shoulder. "Will you have time to stay with me today?"

Joel didn't mind going to the Indian restaurant again for the third time in a week. It wasn't his favorite cuisine, but he could endure the lunch. It was better than watching Zarah mope around the house as she had during the first two weeks, with her energy depleted from not being able to digest the kind of food he ate. Extending the time with her wasn't on his schedule. He rolled his stiff neck around while remaining in the doorway, attempting to loosen the tension that was settling in. Each day he got closer to the ninety-day loan repayment date, his neck got a little stiffer. At this pace, his neck would be permanently locked in two months, similar to his fate if he didn't get the investors' money. "I need to check on your father today." Her demeanor saddened. Thinking over his answer, he said, "Why don't I get you a ticket to India? You can spend time with your father. I'm sure that he'd love to see you now that he's out of the hospital." Joel could unwind while she was gone, too. It was a win-win for both. He wished he'd suggested it sooner, getting excited at the proposition.

"I can't go to India," she said, sullen.

"Why can't you?" he asked, determined to put her on a plane.

"A wife's place is with her husband."

"But your husband wants you to go. You can go with my blessing and stay as long as you like," he said, becoming optimistic again.

"I don't want to go unless you come with me."

Joel's burst of zeal evaporated and was instantly reinserted into his vat of despair, hopelessly struggling to break free. Partially accepting his situation, he acquiesced and said, "Let's spend the afternoon together."

He didn't have a single idea of what they could do. Other than the marriage night in India, they had barely slept in the same bed, let alone broached the concept of intimacy. Time and interest hadn't meshed. His energy was reserved for handling the last piece of DMI business, quickly paying off the investors.

His patience was thinning. The doctors had given Joel no indication of how long Musar would be in this frail state. No way to tell medically. Joel was perplexed at the turn of events. A month ago he was positioned to pay the loan off early. Thirty days later, he was clutching to hope, fully aware of the consequences associated with not paying on time.

chapter

50

Don pulled into the DMI parking lot, having met with the first client at 7:30 A.M. Two others followed. His routine was well established. At night he plowed through contracts and proposals and met with clients during the day. Like today, he'd pop into DMI for an hour to work with Abigail on the transition plan, although there was little movement with overthrowing Joel. Don kept trudging forward with the belief that he was in God's plan. Why God chose him—that he didn't know and didn't harbor a need to find out. When the door opened for him to take over, he would be prepared.

For a split second, loneliness stopped by. He was caught off guard, being surrounded by those that he cared about. As he reflected on his situation, truth sailed in, too. Naledi was on one continent, Abigail on another. His heart hovered in the middle. God had a plan for his life when it came to DMI and LTI. He was absolutely certain. There had to be one for his personal life, too. The church mother had given him confirmation. It was the only source of relief he found credible.

Don entered the building and made his way to Abigail's office. The door was wide open. "Knock, knock," he said.

"Come on in," Abigail said after swallowing a bite of her sandwich.

"That looks good," he said.

"Here, you want half?" she offered, sliding the sandwich toward the edge of the desk as he approached.

"No, you go ahead. I'll get something on the way to my next meeting."

"You better take this." She gave it one last push, as far as the sandwich would go without falling off the desk. "And don't say I've never given you anything," she said, giggling.

The gesture was a welcomed act of kindness. He was hungry and didn't really have time to grab anything else. The surge of LTI business required his full dedication and more. He was working at maximum throttle. In the ideal scenario, he could merge DMI and LTI and take on the role as CEO under one corporate umbrella instead of being split across two locations. With his natural strength almost gone, the strain couldn't last much longer. Don took the sandwich and a seat, shedding his stress.

"Hello," Abigail sang. "Earth to Don, where are you, because your mind is definitely not here."

"You know me pretty well," he said. "I was thinking about DMI and LTI."

"Must have been a lot of thinking, based on the expression on your face."

"And I was thinking about Naledi, too." Don took a huge bite.

Abigail opened her desk drawer abruptly and rummaged inside. "Oh, Naledi, how is she?" Abigail asked, sounding serious all of a sudden.

"Busy as ever. I have to give her a break. She's putting in crazy hours to keep LTI afloat while I'm pounding the pavement here."

"I'm glad she's so helpful to you," Abigail said with her voice softening to barely above a whisper.

"You have no idea." Naledi swirled around his thoughts, drawing him away from the conversation.

"Sounds like you really miss her," Abigail said without lifting her gaze toward him.

"Truthfully, I do. I'm going to see if she wants to come for a visit."

That caused Abigail to lift her gaze. "Really, it's that serious."

"Depends on what you call serious. Naledi has been with me almost from the beginning of LTI. She has been a pillar."

"I get that," Abigail snapped. "It's just that if she comes here, who's going to handle your business over there?"

"Good question, but having her come for a visit isn't strictly about business," Don said. Abigail raised her gaze again. "She's special to me, and I miss her."

"I thought I was special to you."

Don didn't know what to say. Yet at the core of his relationship, friendship, or kinship with Abigail was honesty. Keeping quiet had once lost him a shot at her affection. Now he was airing on the side of honesty, with compassion. Lording his interest in Naledi over Abigail wasn't his intention. He had to find the right balance between maintaining a high level of friendship and professionalism with Abigail to keep the business moving while letting life and love play out on its own terms. His phone rang. He answered, kind of glad for the interruption at a time when the relationship discussion was heating up.

"Hello, little brother, I bet you're surprised to hear from me so soon."

"Hang on," Don told Tamara without saying her name. "Excuse me," he told Abigail. He stepped into the hallway, holding the phone while he searched out an empty conference room. Once inside he resumed the conversation. "Two calls in one month, wonders never cease."

"Can you believe it, and it's not even your birthday," Tamara said.

"Obviously I'm glad to hear from you, but I have to ask, is everything okay?"

"I'm fine. I've been thinking about the conversation we had last month. I'm seriously considering coming back."

"That's fantastic news." Don sat on the edge of the table, overjoyed with the prospect of reuniting with his sister. It had been far too long. "You know Mother will be out of her mind with happiness."

"Well, that's why I'm calling. Did you present her with my proposal?"

Don had hoped Tamara wasn't serious about the proposal. "I didn't tell her yet. I wanted you to have time to think it over."

"There's nothing to think over. I am willing to come back to DMI with my stock. You can have it, no strings attached, but Mother has to give me space."

Don had no rebuttal. What Tamara was asking was equivalent to Joel stepping down without a fight which just wasn't going to happen. Madeline wasn't going to walk away from her children, or DMI, or Detroit. He would be wasting precious breath by asking, but he couldn't blatantly pass up the opportunity to close out the deal the easy way. "The U.S. is a big country. What if Mother took an extended vacation? Would that work?"

"How long and how far?"

"I don't know," he said, standing. "I'm not sure she'd agree to go, but I can ask."

"Well, I've given you my terms. They are nonnegotiable. I really want to help you without tossing myself into an unbearable environment. I'm making a huge sacrifice if I come back. I'm giving up my solitude."

Don could appreciate solitude. It was what he craved, what he had to have for survival when he first left DMI. "I'll talk with Mother and see what I can do."

"I don't want to be difficult, especially with you, but I have to be smart, too."

"I understand."

"Just so we're clear, I am willing to come back and take my rightful place in the company."

"What are you going to do with the money and the condo Dad left for you in California?"

"I'm not sure. If I'm coming home, I guess everything is on the table, the condo, my inheritance, everything."

"That's a surprise. You didn't seem interested before." Don had to wonder if perhaps Tamara's money had run out or was close to running out, prompting her to come back. He was suspicious but had already asked once if she needed money. She'd said no and he wouldn't bug her again.

"You really did get me thinking. After all, I am the oldest living child. I should show more leadership."

Don reflected on Tamara's request long after the call had terminated. He was encouraged by the progress in one area and plagued by setbacks in others. He sat for a while, no longer able to take the mounting sense of longing. He dialed Cape Town, hoping to catch Naledi. The phone rang and rang with no answer. It was just after five P.M. for her. He quickly dialed her mobile number without having to look it up. Two rings and her soothing voice was on the line with the hypnotic effect he was seeking.

"What's your schedule look like over the next week? Would you like to meet me here in Michigan?"

"I'd be honored to meet you. How soon would you like for me to travel?"

He heard the enthusiasm, which could easily be confused with passion. "Come as soon as you possibly can." He wished the super-fast Concorde was still in business. Anything more than two seconds was too long. He wanted her, no, needed her in town this very moment. The inspiration and dedication was the shot of energy he desired and would have as soon as the travel agency got the reservations confirmed. His muse was on her way and he couldn't be more content.

chapter

51

Joel sat in the library, surrounded by darkness. Three A.M. He wanted to sleep, longed to sleep, but it wasn't his to claim tonight or last night, or the night before. Zarah eased into the room. "What are you doing up?" he asked with a modest amount of concern mixed with a heavy dose of irritation.

"I came to be with you." She sat on the floor in front of him.

He had to be alone, to figure out his next move. The air in the room was being sucked out. Each thought of DMI collapsing required an extra breath or two. "Why don't you go on back to bed. There's no reason for both of us to stay up."

Her gaze dropped, followed by a few tears. He lifted her chin with his index finger. "Zarah, are you okay?" The wet streaks down her cheeks and around her mouth were his answer. "Please, sit here," he said, lifting her hand, and her body followed. He got up and let her sit in the chair he was in. He bent down next to her. "Tell me what's wrong." She was reluctant to speak and turned her head to wipe away the tears, which were flowing steadily now. Getting her to openly talk with him was a task he hadn't consistently mastered. Close to three months seemed long enough to form some type of rapport. The compassion in him said to keep trying. Her father was very ill. He'd gotten better but was not on a solid road to recovery. Joel didn't know whether to applaud or cry for Musar's current state. Joel's head pounded day after day, being forced to rely on someone else for his path to freedom. "You're going to be okay."

She thrust her arms around his neck, practically cutting off his air with her tight grip. "Please let me stay with you tonight. I don't want to be alone."

Intimacy didn't exist. Layering complication on top of problems was unwise, a road he opted not to travel. In the middle of this night, though, he'd noticed a couple of times how much she radiated. He hadn't studied the details of her face much before. The softness of her silky skin rested on him. The feeling wasn't easy to ignore. He'd been known to appreciate an eye-catching woman, but not one with the label of his wife. She moved her arms down to circle his shoulder and wouldn't let go. The affection was more than he had expected and definitely more than he could manage. He pushed her away, gently. Then she hung on to his biceps as if they were a lifeline.

"Please let me stay with you."

"Why don't you go back to bed?"

"Are you coming with me?"

"I will." He imagined that was how a parent felt trying to comfort a child in the middle of the night. He would do what his parents did for him when he was a child, put her to bed and stay there until she fell asleep. Tonight of all nights he had to use every minute to carve a way out of his situation. In twenty-one hours his ninety days were up. Payment to the investors was due. Practically every hour of the past had been spent brainstorming, figuring this or that, each scenario leading to a dead end when it came to raising the money. He never dreamed of being in this predicament. He was too wise for this. He had to get the funds. Forfeiting another division to Uncle Frank's shyster investors wasn't imaginable. Madeline and the board of directors would certainly oust him. If it happened—he was determined not to let it, but if it did—he'd probably step down on his own and save whatever dignity could be retained.

He tucked Zarah in and sat on the bed next to her. Gazing at her, he saw the lives of two children cemented in order to fulfill the legacies of their fathers. At that moment he felt a spark with her, one of mutual purpose. He stroked her hair. She deserved more, a man who could love and cherish her. Not one who had at least three other priorities before getting around to her. He didn't have time to coddle. A woman in his heart had to be self-sufficient. She had to be independent, challenging, and full of excitement and uniqueness. Zarah relaxed into the plush covers as her hand reached out for his. An hour later she was asleep as Joel crept from the room.

chapter

52

Streaks of sunlight met Joel on the master staircase, having overtaken the dark. The day was budding, not yet in full bloom. Joel had a finite set of hours to save his life and that of DMI. He hurried to his private office near the rear of the house on the first floor. Entering, he locked the door behind him. The housekeeper would have to watch Zarah today. He couldn't be disturbed by anyone for anything. This was the single most important day of his life.

He whipped out a sheet of paper and jotted down a series of numbers. "Six thirty," he rattled. If Musar died by six thirty, Joel would have access to the money needed to pay off the investors. The ten and a half hour time difference dictated the cutoff time. Joel glanced at the pendulum swinging in the clock on his desk. Four thirty. He closed his eyes and slapped his open palm across his forehead. How did he get here? A struggle waged in him. He had to get the money but wishing death on Musar slowed his blood flow. There had to be another way, but desperation and circumstance blocked his view. He called India.

"This is Joel Mitchell. I'm checking on Musar's condition," he told Kumar, the attorney managing Musar's estate.

"He had a very good day today, much stronger."

"Oh, all right," Joel responded. Spewing out words of insincerity wasn't his way. Actually, the uncertainty was great within him. He didn't know how he truly felt about Musar's miraculous comeback. The fatherless boy was cheering but the man who wanted to make his father proud wasn't overjoyed at the news. The boy and the man would have to keep tussling until a clear winner emerged. In the meantime, he'd let the man have an edge.

"Please share the good news with Zarah."

"Of course," he said and ended the call.

Countless times Joel had wanted to ask the attorney for a loan and decided against it. He'd picked up the phone no less than fifteen times over the past three days alone. The handful of millions Musar gave him at the wedding was the traditional dowry, payment in exchange for marrying his daughter. Receiving money for marrying Zarah didn't bother Joel. That was their culture. Five million plus another two possibly from Sheba was miles away from the three hundred million he owed. It didn't even cover the thirty million in interest. His personal funds were zapped in the merger. Tapping his mother's money wasn't a consideration. She was secure and he intended to keep her that way. He had to think. There was money out there, but where? He could smell defeat at the door. For now the lock could keep it at bay, but he wasn't delusional. Time was dashing away.

Alone. There was no one who could give him the advice he craved. He'd hounded Sheba excessively for comfort over the past three months. She deserved a break from his troubles. Reaching out to God now, in a time of crisis, didn't seem sincere. Besides, there was no guarantee with the timing. He needed a finite solution in a matter of hours. The notion of waiting forty days and forty nights for an answer wasn't remotely a possibility. Completely out of solutions, he set pride aside and made the dreaded call, formulating his sales pitch as the phone rang.

"This is Joel Mitchell again," he told Kumar, hesitant to proceed. After need punched out pride, he continued speaking, faster, attempting to get it out before pride recovered. "I'm having a slight delay in transitioning Harmonious Energy with my clients."

"Is there a problem?"

He gave pride another kick, to stay down. "I need to raise three hundred million dollars in a short-term loan. The board members won't release the company funds until they're sure the merger is in the best interest of DMI. We know that it is, but they want some kind of assurance. My job is to keep the company going during the transition."

"It's important to Mr. Bengali that this merger be successful. It is his inheritance for Zarah and for her future children."

"I know, and I'm committed to making this work. I've invested all of my time and personal funds, and now I need help. I've depleted the financial vehicles in the U.S. I'm calling to see if you have any suggestions for me." The attorney was silent so Joel boosted his appeal. "I'm committed to making this merger work for the sake of me, my wife, my family, and my future children." Exactly which wife and children was irrelevant.

"Let me speak with Mr. Bengali."

"No," Joel blurted before he could think. "He's weak. I don't want to bother him with this." He recalled how frail Dave Mitchell was during the last days. Those precious moments weren't to be wasted on worrying about money and business deals. He was desperate for the cash, but wouldn't resort to flat-out heartlessness. "I'll find another way."

"Let me speak to Mr. Bengali's team. I'll get back to you."

Joel felt a glimmer of hope. "What time is it there?" as if he didn't know the ten and a half hour time difference precisely.

"Three o'clock in the afternoon."

"Okay, that puts me in a tough situation."

"Why is it?"

"I need the money before the banks close in the States."

"We've completed other transactions in Europe and Australia very rapidly. Let me see what we can do," Kumar said.

Joel was feeling whimsical. The chains were falling off, a thousand pounds at a time. "Give me a line of credit, a loan, and I can repay it."

"I'm certain we can get the money for you today."

"Oh, you have no idea how important this is for the merger. Thank you," he said with an air of sincerity that resonated from his toes and traveled eagerly to the crown of his head. Vitality was returning. This was a new day. He might even spend the day with Zarah, kind of like a peace offering. Her family had saved his. It was only fitting for him to show gratitude in a way that mattered to Musar.

Five minutes after ending the call with India, the phone rang. "Joel Mitchell."

"Mr. Mitchell, I have good news for you," Musar's attorney said.

"So quickly?" Maybe his luck was changing.

"We work very closely with our bankers and other colleagues."

"Good, that's good to hear." Joel glanced at the clock, relieved that he had nearly an hour and a half to spare before running out of time.

"We have three colleagues in Asia who will back your loan."

"What do they get out of the deal?" Nobody gave away three hundred million without wanting something in return, at least not where Joel lived and did business.

"What would be reasonable?"

Joel didn't have any extra money. DMI was the only collateral he had left that hadn't already been hocked to close the original deal with Musar. "I can offer one of the divisions if the money isn't paid as agreed." It was like an out-of-body experience. He heard the words utter across his lips, and couldn't figure from where they came. That would put three out of four divisions at risk. There was nothing else to offer. He would have given his soul, but the value was less than the diminishing worth of DMI.

"We'll need a market value for the papers, but it won't matter to our colleagues. They are long-time colleagues of Musar and want to help."

Joel was too ashamed to guesstimate the worth of DMI. The

value was plummeting deeper daily. They'd realized a drop of fifteen cents on every dollar since the contract was signed. He thought quickly. The only way to make the company look attractive and avoid giving the impression that they weren't floundering to the degree that they were would be to value DMI in pieces. His skin cringed, remembering his father's plea to not let the company be broken into pieces. It was like cancer. He had to offer up a limb to save the rest of the body. Joel was grateful to have the loan originated in Asia, away from the watchful eye of the media and the scrutiny of the U.S. lending institutions. There was plenty of worry to be spread around his brain. Cameras, uptight bankers, and nit-picking board members weren't welcomed.

chapter

53

Joel was revived. The knock on his office door wasn't a distraction. "Excuse me, Mr. Mitchell. What would you like for lunch?" the housekeeper asked after Joel opened the door. Zarah stood near the housekeeper.

"Thank you for asking, but I won't need you to prepare lunch today," he said approaching the door. The housekeeper stepped aside and Joel took Zarah's hand. "I'm taking my lovely wife out for lunch." Her tiny hand clutched his. "Please get ready, and I'll meet you at the garage in fifteen minutes if that's okay with you."

She nodded in rapid succession like the little bobble-headed puppy in the back window. Her demeanor appeared bright for the first time in months.

Outside, the sun was sitting high in the sky. He didn't have a single complaint about taking Zarah out for the afternoon. It was actually a blessing to get out of the office. The money was on its way, according to Musar's attorney, just in time to divert a disaster. There was only a shred of concern until the wire confirmation actually hit his account.

He opened the car door of the Mercedes for her, choosing to

give the highly charged Lamborghini a rest. The four-door Mercedes was more appropriate for Zarah, reliable, classy, but conservative. He'd leave the Lamborghini for Sheba. "Let's eat and then we can find a park. It will give us a chance to talk, to get to know each other. How does that sound?"

"Very nice." Seeing her spirit lighten gave him a sense of joy, too. She wasn't the enemy, in spite of the arrangement.

He pulled off the grounds into the street, talking and letting his gaze wander her way. She was like a giddy schoolgirl, blushing from the attention. Something she got very infrequently from him. "Let's go to Greektown. You can try something different." The mood was breezy and the day was shaping into a positive experience. "By the way," he said, wanting to share the information without damping the mood, "I spoke with your father's attorney this morning." Zarah stiffened. Joel placed his hand on hers. "He's doing much better, getting stronger." Joel felt the tension loosen in her hand. "I'm offering to send you home to see your father if you want to go."

"No, I must stay with you. It's what my father would want."

"What do you want?" Joel appreciated and, if he admitted it, tended to gravitate to a woman who was outspoken. Unintentionally he was surrounded by them. The afternoon was off to a good start. He wanted to draw her out of the clingy subservient shell and get to the core of who this woman was.

"I want to stay with you."

Joel patted her hand and then stroked her face. "So be it," he said, easing onto the highway. "We'll be downtown in thirty-five minutes. I sure hope you're hungry."

She gave a fully formed smile, one he hadn't seen since knowing her. At least Zarah was eating better. The transition was going to take time, a commodity he didn't have in surplus. He could give her what he had when he had it. Requiring extra attention would be a problem.

The phone lying on the console between the seats buzzed. UNKNOWN CALLER flashed on the screen. It was probably India. He took the call, eager to hear the good news.

"This is your friendly reminder that today is the day. Pay up or put up."

"It's good to hear from you," Joel said without giving any indication of who was on the phone. Zarah didn't know Uncle Frank's involvement and never would. He switched the phone to his left ear, closest to the driver's side window and the farthest from Zarah. "We're on track as agreed."

"Good, because you don't want to deal with the consequences of missing the due date."

"I'm sure," Joel said, intentionally being cryptic.

"I'm sure I don't have to remind you that these aren't the kind of investors who slap you with a late charge and a poor mark on your credit rating. They go for the jugular, understood?"

"Totally." Joel was quite aware of the consequences of missing the payment, the loss of another division and his reputation, neither of which he could accept.

"Then I'll say, it's been nice doing business with you. I look forward to working with you next time."

"Oh, there won't be a next time."

"Sure, whatever you say," Uncle Frank said. "By the way, I guess congratulations are in order. You're a married man." Joel listened without responding. "I saw you on the news a few months ago. Boy, I'd love to know the terms of that deal," he said, chuckling, and then disconnected.

Once and done. There was no intention of returning to his uncle or the pseudoinvestors. The terms turned out to be higher than he could handle. The stress of the past three months coupled with Uncle Frank's taunting wasn't worth it.

The afternoon passed, lunch was enjoyable, and the ride home around three P.M. was uneventful. He pulled the Mercedes into garage bay number two, sandwiched between his prized Lamborghini and the Land Rover, the vehicle he rarely drove. Nothing wrong with keeping a spare for backup, it was his philosophy.

"Can I sit with you?" Zarah asked, clutching his arm.

The afternoon was satisfying, but he had work to do. The day was passing and the transaction had to be cleared, the investors paid, and Madeline silenced finally. "I have work to do."

"I can sit with you," Zarah said.

"Not this time. Please, let me do my work and then we can talk later." She walked away, wounded. He started to reach out and then decided to let her go. Two hours would pass like two minutes. "I'll see you in a few hours," he said as she left.

He locked the office door and got to work. Several keystrokes and he was into his account. For a second he wondered why he hadn't used an offshore account to help keep his business private. Too late, the transaction was in progress. He checked the account and didn't see a deposit. Instantly he was on the phone to Kumar. One thirty in the morning Indian time didn't stop the call. "Are you still on track with delivering the money?" Joel asked as soon as the connection was made.

"Yes, there was a bit of delay. There was a power outage earlier this evening."

Joel's renewed zeal was squashed. Worry crept in while defeat waited outside the door. Why hadn't anyone called to give him a status update? Did they understand how serious this was? "Is it fixed? Is the money on the way?"

"The money is on the way."

"That's great news," he said, feeling his racing heart beat begin to calm. "We have less than two hours before the banks close on the East Coast."

"I will check on the progress for you. If they can't get the wire completed tonight, they will do it right away in the morning."

"No, no," Joel shouted. "I have to get the money this evening. It's critical."

The attorney assured him the money was coming. The statement rang of legitimacy, but Joel wasn't convinced. The situation felt dismal. Despair wanted to kick in. Instead, he opted to relish the rich taste of the past. He grinned as he reflected on the early days of being CEO, when everything he touched found favor. Those times were ages ago. He spent the next two hours checking the account every minute, maybe more. Nothing, no money, no confirmation, no luck. Finally, at five thirty, he logged off the computer, opened the door, and let defeat wrap around his neck, prepared for a long night.

Zarah was waiting in the library. She ran to him as he approached. "Can we sit and talk?"

"Not tonight. I'm tired," he said, not able to concentrate on her disappointment. His concerns were grander, three hundred million dollars grander. She had to busy herself for the evening since he wasn't in the mood for entertaining. The garage was the only haven he could think of that made sense. Defeat led the way.

chapter

54

Joel had been sitting in the garage for four hours at last count. He couldn't go upstairs. Zarah was there. He couldn't lament in the library. She was there most of the time, too. He couldn't be sequestered in his office without fear of the mounting anguish overtaking him in the closed space. Eleven forty-five. He schlepped to the office one final time for the night. He was sure the money wasn't there. He'd check anyway, one last time before midnight, before the loan was officially considered late. Nothing was posted to his account since the last time he checked.

Done, that was it. He laid his head on the desk and drifted away, not into sleep, just away from the situation. The phone rang at 12:20 A.M. rousing him from a weird state of being half asleep and half awake.

"Did you complete the process?"

He didn't care to be cryptic. His company was virtually gone, no miracles tonight and no secret decoder conversation. "No, Uncle Frank, I didn't make the payment," he said with an intentional tone of agitation.

"I told you from the beginning, this is no small undertaking.

No need to be upset with me. You understood the terms from the beginning."

"Look, I have the money. There was a power outage earlier in India. That's fixed and the money is on its way as soon as the bank opens this morning."

"Whoa, hey, that's too much information. I don't want to know the details of your deal. It's better for you in the long run. Don't talk so freely on these calls. How many times do I have to tell you? The less I know the less I'd have to admit under oath," Uncle Frank said, chuckling.

"Funny" wasn't the word Joel had in mind for his dear uncle. "You'll get the money in the morning."

As they spoke, his computer chimed, the sound it made when a screen was being refreshed with new information. He blurred out Uncle Frank and tapped a few keys with the other hand. An email flashed. "We apologize again for the delay. The systems are working again. The transaction is ready for your approval."

"Are you there?" Uncle Frank asked.

"Yes," Joel said, distracted. He typed "yes" and immediately hit send. The money was on the way. A few minutes late wasn't going to be a problem. He took a long breath. "Yes, uncle, you can stop the scare tactics. I just received confirmation that the money is being wired as we speak. I can pay off my investors and never be bothered with them or you again."

"Not so fast, young lad. You had a deal that expired as of midnight tonight."

"Sure, but come on. It's barely after midnight, no big deal."

"Oh, it's a big deal. I made it clear that the most attractive component of this party was the interest and the collateral."

"So what are you saying, that your investors expect me to give up one of my divisions because I was twenty-five minutes late paying them back?'

"Bingo, now you're getting it."

"That's ridiculous. You know I can't let that happen."

"Oh, you will."

"They'll have to fight me for it."

"That's your choice. They tend to do well in the alley and in the courtroom. Let's just say they have friends who sit in high places and low ones, too. Trust me, you don't want a confrontation. I told you what would happen. If you wanted to borrow the money with an exception clause or a grace period, you should have gone to the banks and not to my guys. Pay up like a good boy and be done with this. Next time you might want to stick with Wall Street."

"They're crooks, too."

"There you go, you choose."

Joel had no choice. "Uncle Frank, I'm begging you to change their minds."

"I can't help you. This is out of my league," Uncle Frank said without an ounce of concern. Firing Uncle Frank had been the right decision for DMI. But, as fate would have it, firing him wasn't turning out to be the best seed for fostering grace with his uncle when it was most needed. "You should prepare to give up one of your divisions. Take the rest of the night and decide which one. And don't worry too much about it, they're not picky," he said, erupting in full-fledged laughter before hanging up.

chapter
55

Don stopped by the office midmorning to see Madeline. The long night and mound of work didn't damper his spirit, not today. He found his mother meandering outside her office on the executive floor.

"Aren't you supposed to be at the airport?" she asked.

"I'm on my way," Don said, taking a quick glance at the time. "Her flight doesn't arrive for another three hours."

"I see," Madeline said with a smirk.

"Don't start."

"What? I didn't say anything out of line."

"Mother, you know it's not only what you say. It's always been about how you say it."

"Not today. I'm going to be on my very best behavior for Ms. Naledi."

"We'll see about that," he said, igniting a spark of amusement in both of them.

Madeline beckoned for Don to follow her into the office. "I'm not the one you should be worried about," she said. He knew she was referring to Abigail.

"What do you mean?"

"I know what I see," she said, convinced there was underlying affection between him and Abigail. "Please close the door. You never know who's lurking around."

"I guess you're right, especially if I can come and go as I like, although technically I'm the competition."

"You have a right to be here," she said, leaning against the window sill. Don took a seat and crossed his leg. "If it wasn't for you, the doors of DMI would be closed. So you've earned the right to walk around here whenever doing whatever you want and nobody, I mean nobody, is going to say a word," she told him, letting her index finger bounce back and forth in rhythm with her words.

He propped his elbow on the armrest and rested his head in his hand. "Do you remember how hard I fought to get away from God and the church?"

Madeline nodded in affirmation. "And now your base in the U.S. is comprised of the churches and religious groups who have left DMI. I told you time and time again: you were born to run this company. We can't teach leadership as an organization unless we have a strong and sensible leader ourselves, and that's you." She rubbed the side of her head, flattening her hair. I'm not sure why God is taking us along the scenic route."

"It wasn't always scenic."

"I agree with you there, but your time is coming, and soon. I can feel it."

It was hard to believe his life had transformed to this place of running one company and being instrumental in saving the other, a place of romantic stability, at least there was the opportunity for it. He couldn't help but feel grateful. "I wonder, what would Dad think about what's going on now?"

"I can tell you that your father would be furious. He wouldn't have tolerated Joel's hypocrisy. That little man can't decide if he wants to target the religious sector, which should be the case, or if he prefers to go anywhere he can turn a buck."

"Actually, his merger with Harmonious Energy is based on religion."

"That's true," she said, turning, "but a slew of religions wasn't your father's vision. If nothing else, he built the foundation of this company on his spiritual convictions." She turned toward the window. "Your father worked his behind off to keep this ministry afloat during the lean years." The volume in her voice dropped.

He sensed her mood change. "After all this time, you miss him, don't you?"

Madeline spun the chair around and eased into her seat. "Your father was your father. He was my husband," she said, twirling her Mont Blanc pen on the desk. "He's the man I decided to build a family and a life with." Don didn't interrupt. She was well overdue for a cleansing. "He wasn't a perfect man, by no means. Trust me, he gave me problems. Leaving me for Sherry was ninety percent of it, but he wasn't a bad man. He made his mistakes, and Lord knows he paid for them. We paid for them."

"You think Dad paid for them?"

"Your father paid in the toughest way. He lost what mattered to him, the trust and respect of his children."

There were times when it didn't seem like Dave had suffered while the lives of everyone else around him crumbled. In spite of that, when Don elected to forgive Dave he also made the conscious choice of forgetting—deciding not to hang on to the hurt, the bitterness, the rejection, the emotional seeds that produced a harvest of hatred in his heart. He'd let go and was hoping his mother had or would, too. "I didn't get to tell him that I forgave him, but I did," he told her.

Madeline reached across her desk, toward Don, not able to extend the entire way. The desk was too large. Don stretched out to cover the rest of the distance and touched the tip of her hand. "He knew you and Tamara both loved him. He did. He told me so right before he . . ." she said and sealed her lips, drawing her hand away. "Well, before he passed."

Don shifted the conversation, trying to gauge where she was emotionally with his father. "Have you forgiven him?"

"Oh, heavens, yes," she said immediately, twirling the pen again. "I have a big bark."

"And some bite, too."

"Okay, fine, some bite, too, but your father understood me. He didn't get bent out of shape when I said what I had to say. That's what I loved about him. I could be strong and not overshadow him." Her gaze zeroed in on Don. "That's one of the main reasons I never got remarried. It isn't easy finding a man who can understand me without moping around because I unintentionally said or did something that bruised his ego. I'm too independent to coddle a grown man's ego."

"Speaking of finding someone," Don said, quickly glancing at his watch. "I better get going. I don't want to be late." He sprang to his feet.

"Look at you," she said. "Go on, get out of here."

"I'm going." He headed for the door, then turned to say, "You are a tough cookie. There's no doubt about that, but you are an amazing mother. Always have been."

"And always will be," she added.

This was probably an opportune time to share Tamara's proposal with his mother, given the candid mood she was in, but Don decided not. The situation had to be ideal, a day with perfect weather, perfect people, and perfect circumstances. Asking his mother to leave DMI for Tamara's return was a feat that only God could truly perform without reprisal. That was a decision for another time, perhaps another life.

He trotted from the office, content. The DMI struggle wasn't over but, then again, it wasn't his to fight. This was on God. Don would just serve as he was led. The elevator door opened and Don darted in, eager to get to the airport and to Naledi.

chapter

56

Abigail watched Joel pass by her office as she reviewed the quarterly sales report. He didn't poke his head in, and she didn't call out for him. They were officially strangers, two people sharing the same workspace and nothing more. Being the executive vice president didn't make avoidance easy. They had to interact on a professional basis. In an odd way, Joel had minimized the uneasiness. By driving so many clients away there was less business to discuss with him daily. Joel was on his own, at least for the moment, with folding in Harmonious Energy. It was his mess to fix.

Perusing the document, it appeared that losses for the East Coast division weren't as bad as the other units. Abigail was puzzled and aimed to go upstairs to Madeline's office for answers. While they were in takeover limbo, they had to continuously find ways to stay in business. Having Don inherit his father's bankrupt company was pointless. She could slap Joel's hand for being so reckless with their lives. Abigail entered the hallway and saw Joel standing near the elevator with a woman she didn't recognize. Curiosity drew her toward the elevators. She didn't look like the woman on the news with Joel, his new wife, but then again, Abigail had only seen her for a few seconds on TV, and briefly at the office last year with her father. What Abigail recalled was hardly enough to identify Joel's wife in public.

Abigail approached the two standing there. Joel didn't notice her standing behind him. The woman's smooth bronze complexion with a hint of olive looked as close to perfection as one could get. Her eyebrows were thick, and appeared to have a natural arch, one Abigail had to pay twenty-five dollars plus tip twice a month to maintain. It also looked like permanent eyeliner had been delicately and precisely drawn on her eyelids. Abigail smirked. She unconsciously brushed across her own cheeks, hoping they felt as smooth as this woman's appeared.

"I'm sure that we haven't met. I would definitely remember you," he said in his usual Joel kind of way. "What did you say your name was again?" he asked her. Abigail stepped into his view. His manner changed some but not much.

"Naledi Mophuti," she said as Joel extended his hand precisely at the moment that Don came out of the break room carrying a bottle of water.

"Joel," Don said, rushing to the circle and inserting his hand in lieu of Naledi's.

Abigail stood in between the brothers, invisible. The focus was clearly on Naledi, the new woman on the scene.

"Big brother," Joel said, clearly agitated by Don's interruption. "I was introducing myself to our visitor."

"She's not a visitor. This is Naledi, my right hand in South Africa. She's here with me," Don said, putting his arm across her shoulder and erasing the space between them. There was no room for Joel to squeeze in. He backed off.

The brothers were like lions establishing claim on the pride and their lioness. Joel pushed the elevator button, as if to say that Don was ruling the pride for now. The younger lion might have to find another home unless he was willing to change his ways. Time would tell.

Abigail wanted to vanish; worse was that no one would notice. She did the only dignified act that she could. "Hello, Naledi, I'm

Abigail. Welcome to DMI. I've heard many wonderful things about you."

Naledi nodded in slow motion, with her neck tilted slightly. "I, too, have been told many wonderful things of you," she said with an accent that sounded French mixed with something else.

It was hard to tell her nationality. Her skin tone, eyes, and hair texture didn't make it evident. To be honest, her nationality didn't matter much. The dazzle, high cheekbones, full but not fat lips, and almond-shaped eyes set her in the exotic category on at least six continents, with Antarctica being the only one in question. Abigail wanted to dislike her on the spot or have a valid reason to feel uneasy about her, but there was nothing. No bad feeling, no unexplained negative reaction, nothing. She wore a designer suit that was fitted around her curvaceous bottom half. "Hello, Don," Abigail said simply because she didn't know what else to say. She prayed her inner thoughts weren't evident in her words or disposition.

"Perfect timing," Don said. "We were coming to meet you."

Great, Abigail thought, just what she wanted—to make her day officially lousy.

chapter
57

Joel got in the elevator. His fury boiled although he fought to keep his anger concealed. Letting Don sense his vulnerability was instant death in the wild. He would maintain a controlled and in-charge disposition until his situation was rectified. This Harmonious Energy and investor business would pass as soon as Musar did. It wasn't going to be long now and life could return to normal—his normal, the one he controlled and not his brother.

What a joke, he couldn't help but think. Gradually, then abruptly, watching Abigail side with Don fed his fury. Don's accession to so called bliss was too rapid and hopefully short-lived. The elevator door opened on the executive floor. Despair was waiting as Joel exited. He slapped it around a few times with a final kick out of his way. It would return but for now he was winning by a thin thread. He shook off the burden of the day and schlepped to his office, casting the image of Don, and the botched loan repayment attempt, from his mind, determined to let neither crush him.

His phone buzzed. It was Uncle Frank. Joel wanted to ignore the call, but realized it wasn't close to being a viable choice. He answered, prepared to deal with his temporary despair.

"I've spoken to your investors and they're standing by the missed deadline."

"Only twenty-five minutes late? You can't be serious."

"I couldn't be more serious. This is a done deal. Pay up, transfer the Southern division as the late fee, and you're done. That's what they want."

"That's not doable," Joel told his uncle.

Uncle Frank snickered. "Are you kidding? This is not up for discussion. Don't you get it? You lost this round. Take the money and bow out gracefully while they're still nice about it. You don't want to form a bad relationship with your partners right off the bat," he said, roaring in laughter. "Show some diplomacy. Look, I have to go check on my retirement. Your father didn't leave me much money and you fired me, so I've been forced to fend for myself. So thank you for the contribution. I should be able to sustain a modest lifestyle until you present the next opportunity for me."

Joel wasn't amused. He was frustrated about allowing himself to be reduced to the source of Uncle Frank's jokes. "Sure you don't want me to come back as chief financial officer?" The question didn't deserve a response. "I'll take your silence as a no, for now anyway." His uncle stopped laughing long enough to say, "I've proven that I can get creative financing deals done under the most precarious circumstances."

"No doubt that's why you were fired."

"Touché, young nephew. I'd love to keep chatting with you but I have other business that requires my expertise. There are those who value me." Joel couldn't see him but could imagine his smirk.

"Uncle, before you go," Joel said, agonizing over the hit his pride was about to take. There was no choice. "Can you please ask your investors—"

Uncle Frank interrupted, "Let's be clear, they're not my investors. They're yours."

"Fine, whatever. I'll need ninety days before I can publicly announce the sale of the Southern division."

"You're asking a lot."

"Just do it, Frank," he said, tossing aside the smidgen of respect he'd reserved for his uncle. "I paid you three million dollars. Earn your money." Joel was not willing to be totally lamblasted by his uncle's antics. Doom crept in while he was on the phone and sat patiently waiting for him to terminate the call. Joel paid no attention. He was frantic to come up with a plan to save himself and DMI, a feat growing more difficult by the second.

chapter

58

Don didn't let Naledi out of his sight. Joel was lurking and couldn't be trusted with decorum when it came to a radiant woman, available or not. He couldn't stop Joel from going after Abigail. Naledi was off limits. "Do you have a few minutes?" Don asked Abigail after they'd chatted near the elevators. Joel had already left.

"Sure," she said, letting her gaze roam up and down Naledi's frame.

Don wasn't oblivious to the simmering tension Abigail had previously expressed toward Naledi, but there wasn't much to do about it. Abigail motioned for them to follow her into the office. Each person took a seat inside the office, Naledi near Don, and Abigail at her desk.

"It is a pleasure to meet you, Ms. Abigail," Naledi said. Don wanted to close his eyelids and listen to her speak, with her voice flowing like a song, tranquility he didn't always have but appreciated. Having her in Detroit was an added blessing, one he didn't take lightly. She inspired him to keep working hard.

"How long are you going to be in town?" Abigail asked.

"I have not yet decided," Naledi said, gazing at Don.

Abigail tried to keep her expressions plain. Don didn't have to know how she truly felt about having another woman visiting. She and Don weren't an item, but she still found it difficult to grapple with Naledi being on her turf. Between LTI and DMI, Don had plenty of work with no time for distractions.

"Don thinks very highly of you," Abigail said, and Naledi blushed.

"More than you know," he told Naledi.

Naledi shifted her gaze away from Don for a dot of a second and had it right back on him. His gaze didn't fluctuate much either. She seemed to have a legitimate eye for him. The friendship half of Abigail was thrilled for him. The rest wasn't. The two had to spar it out before she could declare a sole winner and then be able to react.

Sitting in her office among two starry-eyed gazers wasn't the most ideal way for Abigail to spend her spring afternoon, especially when one of the gazers was Don. But she would smile, and be courteous and accommodating.

"Excuse me for a minute. I have to make one call." Don turned to Naledi. "Will you be okay here for a few minutes? I'll go quickly and come right back. We can see my mother for a few minutes and then get you settled into the hotel."

Goodness, did he really need to secure her safety? Naledi was a grown woman. Surely she would be okay for a while without Don. Abigail wanted to jump in but opted to keep quiet, choking on the excessive doting.

Don left and Naledi stayed. Abigail didn't have much to say and kept letting her gaze shift away. She didn't need to be constantly reminded of Naledi's striking looks. She didn't know much about the woman other than what Don had told her. Basic courtesy spurred her to strike up a conversation and eat up the time. "How long will you be here with us?"

"I'm not certain, but I'm here for Don. I'll stay for as long as he needs me."

Abigail wanted to gag. "Sounds like you put a lot into LTI."

"I'm committed to LTI and to Don."

"So, you're not married?"

"Oh no, not yet."

"Excuse me for asking such a personal question, but the way your face lit up, there must be a special someone in your life."

"There is, that's why I'm here."

"Who, you mean Don?" Abigail shared a nervous laugh, not finding the discussion funny at all. "He's married to his work, never having time for romance."

"Maybe that was true in his past when he was here. It is not so true back home. He appreciates loyalty and it is what I am most freely willing to give him."

"You're right, he does value loyalty. That's probably why we've maintained a close relationship for so many years."

"Yes, he has shared with me that his past was quite turbulent and he looks forward to a new future with a new perspective. Hopefully that's what I provide, a fresh perspective."

Oh no, Abigail thought, Naledi wasn't trying to lay claim to Don. South Africa was a long ways for Naledi to come and get her feelings hurt. Abigail wanted to preserve Don in her corner, at least until she'd recovered from the heartbreak. Abigail needed her friend and he had to be free to think clearly with no distractions from the likes of Ms. Universe. Circumstances had claimed Joel, but it wasn't going to be able to pry Don away so easily. Her time with Don would come if it was meant to be. This time, there wouldn't be the pining and hoping. She'd learned a valuable lesson with Joel. If any man was interested in pursuing her, he had to make the investment in her, and her alone. She was no longer willing to carry the bulk of the relationship without equal input. Sharing was out. For now, her newly refined guidelines rendered Don a friend. But that didn't mean being around Naledi or hearing her name constantly flow from Don's lips was going to be well received. She could guarantee that it wasn't.

chapter
59

As long summer days approached, Joel wasn't able to hide from the sunlight blasting into the room so late in the day. Back at home, he was sequestered in the library, tucked away in the corner chair, away from the primary line of sight into the hallway in case anyone walked by. He longed for a break, a piece of quiet, not to be surrounded by the constant chattering of people wanting this and that, telling him no, hounding his every move. Tired, he leaned his head against the high back on the chair. Sleep wasn't his intent, but he wouldn't turn it away.

The quagmire of being lodged between rest and weary wasn't a place he had visited in the past, not when he was on top with his mounds of wealth, women, and wisdom. The race to victory was faltering. The image of Don, Abigail, and Naledi hounded him, relentlessly nipping at his heels. They wouldn't leave him alone, serving as a constant reminder of how much Don was succeeding at the expense of Joel's despair. Losing was bad enough, but worse, to somebody like Don, a person he'd already knocked out in an earlier round. His struggle couldn't slip any further into the abyss for fear of being unrecoverable.

"Excuse me, sir, are you joining us for dinner?" the new cook asked.

Joel slowly opened his eyelids and said no. "Tell Zarah to go ahead without me."

"Yes, sir, would you like for me to wrap up a plate for you and set it in the refrigerator before I leave?"

"No, I'm not hungry. But you could do me a favor?"

"What's that?"

"Could you please join Zarah for dinner again tonight?"

"Sure, it will be my pleasure. I have a few more hours left anyway. Thank you for the offer."

"No," Joel said, sitting up. "I'm the one who should be thanking you. I'll make sure there's a little something extra in your pay."

"That won't be necessary. You explained to me when I started earlier this week that my job is to prepare dinner each night and to make myself available to Mrs. Mitchell in your absence."

"I know but I want to thank you," he told the cook as she left. He claimed a sense of satisfaction in knowing there was at least one decision he'd made that was working as planned. Zarah had a companion, some of the best money he'd ever spent. Joel returned to his position in the chair, head leaning back and eyelids closed. Peace was not his. He understood that and didn't search for it. Instead, he retreated to the place where his strength was never questioned. Sheba was his single source of pure companionship and unadulterated passion. She had a way about her that sparked his juices. Every time he left Sheba, Joel was recharged, ready to take on the world. She was what he yearned for, especially now, a boost to the one area reserved for his unquestioned success and charisma.

Feeling alive for the first time in days, Joel sprang to his feet, preparing to make the flight plans for a quick Chicago trip. Zarah met him at the doorway.

"I would like to eat dinner with you."

"I'm not hungry," he said, squeezing past her.

"I can wait," she said, trailing him.

"No, don't do that. I have to go out of town for a quick trip."

"Can I go?"

"No." He and Sheba didn't need any company. "The cook is going to have dinner with you." He approached his office.

"Yes, but I have not had dinner with you this week. I miss my family," she said, erupting into uncontrolled sobs.

He considered comforting her but was afraid the gesture would give the wrong impression and delay his chance to catch the last flight out to Chicago. "That's why I've offered to send you home for a few weeks or a month to be with your father and to see your family," he said, entering the office and hustling to the desk.

"I will honor my father's wish."

She'd said that repeatedly, and he'd heard it, but there wasn't any harm in asking again and again. Optimism wasn't totally lost.

Forget about her father, he thought. Joel had kept his end of the bargain down to the last detail. Musar made a bunch of promises and showered a ton of false hope only to be hanging on with a selfish shred of life. After forfeiting the Southern division to Uncle Frank's boys, Joel didn't want to hear or need to hear much about Musar. The deed was done and Musar was the clear winner, getting everything he wanted—the merger, the West Coast division, and probably, most important to him, a husband for his daughter. Well, she might have a husband but the marriage wasn't going to have him. Musar wasn't going to have a clean sweep.

Zarah's sobs continued. It wasn't easy to listen to her but his escape routes were limited. He went to her, laid his arms around her shoulders for a hot second, and released. A couple of nights he'd considered performing his marital duties, but there was nothing for him, no spark, no passion, not even a dab of satisfaction. They were exactly what the contract stated, an arrangement. Joel grabbed his PDA and scrolled feverishly down the list, looking for the number to reserve the corporate jet. Zarah remained at the door sobbing. There wasn't much time. He had to reserve the plane, and if it wasn't available the next option was to book a flight from Detroit Metro. Either way, he was getting to Sheba tonight. Worst case, he'd hit the road and see if she could meet him in Kalamazoo again. He wanted, no, *had* to have the reassurance she provided, the gumption that said he was still the man who could woo women like bees to a garden of pollen-filled roses.

chapter

60

Joel traipsed to the boardroom having little to no interest in dealing with Madeline today. Maybe another quick junket to Chicago was the medicine he craved. It had been two weeks since the last trip, and his shot had worn off. The pain of sitting in a meeting with a bunch of sniveling whiners who didn't have the vision required to resurrect DMI was draining. Joel entered the room and they were there, sitting, not thinking, just taking up space and eating away his time like a disease. The chatter died down as he approached the conference table. "I see you're all here."

"As always, we're here. It's you that's usually missing."

"Good to see you, too, Madeline," he said, not willing to let her disrupt the smidgen of tranquility he was clutching. She smirked and tapped that same pen, the one that drove him crazy. He was sure she knew it. That's probably why she did it. "Let's get started," he said, directing his gaze onto Abigail. The tension between them had lessened, not from any changes he'd made. Basically she avoided him. Except for extremely important matters, she didn't seek him out for day-to-day conversations. Joel reflected on his situation, too disturbed to laugh it off and too proud to let it show. He was a man who couldn't go home and couldn't stay at work.

Abigail passed around the monthly report.

Madeline picked it up and let it sail to the table like a sheet of paper flying in the air. "Awfully thin," she said. Joel would let her continue needling and nagging. He wasn't going to lose composure this time. She wasn't going to win. "Oh, that's right," she said, "the report is one division short. Is your wife or Mr. Bengali going to present the West Coast update?"

"Neither," Joel said and let the sarcasm pass.

"Is Brian on the call?" Abigail asked, checking off names as she scanned the room.

He chimed in as Joel spoke. "As I've stated at the last two meetings, the West Coast will continue operating in its current structure and with the same management team until otherwise decided."

"That makes no sense," Madeline said. "It's owned by another party."

"That's right," Joel responded. "There will be one difference. The division will have its own profit and loss statement. It will be treated as a subsidiary under the DMI umbrella. George is breaking out the financial reporting structure as we speak and it should be ready before our next meeting." Madeline balked. It didn't bother him. The room of people didn't have to know that he was really depending on Musar's death to reclaim ownership of the West Coast division very soon, and that changes wouldn't be required at least for that division. He continued, hopeful. "In the meantime, it is business as usual for the West Coast."

"Now that's a problem," Madeline said, "because we're short on business around here." The room of attendees stirred. "Barry, are you on the call?" Madeline said, leaning forward, closer to the tabletop intercom phone. "You better speak up before your Midwest division gets sold, too."

Madeline couldn't find out prematurely about the Southern division already being lost. If he had a choice, he would have given Uncle Frank's goons the East Coast instead of the South. He could have gotten rid of Madeline with the stroke of a pen, but her division was the strongest performer. So, there she sat, Madeline. "What do we have here?" Joel said, opening the report which was stapled in the corner. "I'm not accustomed to seeing the reports like this."

"Like what?" Abigail asked in a seemingly defensive tone.

"Stapled like this," he said, fanning the papers apart.

"We can't waste money on fancy bound reports," Abigail responded.

"We have to cut costs somewhere," Madeline interjected. "We should consider bringing a few flashlights in to have around the office, in case it gets dark around here," she said, letting her voice trail off into a low tone.

"Let's hear the East Coast update." He'd rather die a brutal death than tell Madeline that he admired her business prowess. If there was going to be good news in the numbers it would be from her division.

"I should have brought an extinguisher, because this report is hot." Madeline tossed her gaze toward Joel. "Don't you think it's time to call it a day and step down? You have a wife and other matters that demand your attention."

Ignoring her might work. Nothing else had come close.

"My division had a slight drop in revenue and a few major accounts opted out of renewing their contracts, but at least we didn't totally lose them. They're in good hands," Madeline said.

"What do you mean" Joel asked. He'd heard rumors about business flopping to a competitor but didn't have time to hire a consulting group and get to the bottom of what was going on. He'd find out in due time. For now, he wanted to rebuild quickly, stop the massive client exodus, and establish a new base.

"I guess everyone that's running away is already gone. We'll just limp along with this handful of clients." She tapped that pen. "I was joking about the flashlight earlier but we might run out of working capital soon."

"That's an exaggeration," Joel said.

"Actually, she's not far from the truth." Abigail searched through the small report. She stopped about halfway in and laid the page open in front of him, keeping her hand on it. "We budgeted fifteen million dollars for expenditures in the second quarter. Based on this," she said, pointing to a number highlighted in red ink. "We're short about five million without going into the reserves."

"In forty years we've never had to use reserves to pay the bills," Madeline stated.

"Whatever we do is temporary," Joel lashed out. "This bumpy road is going to pass. We need to rally together and get DMI back to its rightful position in the marketplace."

"Huh?" Madeline gasped. "Are you serious? Where have you been? Your definition of temporary has turned into catastrophic and heading toward unrecoverable. If I wasn't an original owner, I would have left months ago and joined LTI. Now that's a company that has vision and cash."

"Nobody is holding you here, believe me, you can leave any time. Please do me and everyone else a favor, go."

"We've had this discussion too many times. Let's move on, because both of us know I'm not going anywhere as long as the *M* in DMI stands for Mitchell," she told him.

He was tired of Madeline's negativity. She wasn't going to change.

"In light of the budget, we have no choice in this mess. We have to consider laying off employees," Madeline said.

Abigail added, "We could start with a voluntary separation package and see how close we get to the budget."

"No one is getting laid off," Joel shouted, rising to his feet. "We have the money. Just do your jobs and figure out how we can rally together to get this company back in the black." He would get a line of credit based on Harmonious Energy's value. That could keep them afloat for months to come. He was in charge. Not Madeline. He fixed his gaze at her. "I'm only interested in positive feedback from this group. You're my management team. We have to show a united front. If it looks like we're falling apart, the other employees will think we are, which would be bad for morale, too."

Abigail was in agreement. He knew her and could tell even though she didn't make eye contact with him. The glimmer of support boosted his confidence and tenacity. Periodically glancing at Abigail, there was hope for more.

chapter

61

Finally the meeting trudged to a close. The discussion wasn't pretty, but Joel wasn't bothered. According to Madeline, they were on the brink of collapse at any second. Joel had long gotten past the point of letting her ranting cloud his judgment. He thought or maybe wanted to believe that conditions would improve. He would single-handedly revive the company if necessary.

The PDA buzzed in his pocket again. He'd noticed it about three or four times during the meeting and discounted it once he got the rush of control. It felt good, thanks in large part to Abigail. He pulled the phone out and saw a series of missed calls as Abigail prepared to leave. "Abigail, can I speak with you for a moment?" he asked. The last person had left and the conference call line was disconnected.

"Sure, what's up?" she said in a stoic, totally unattached, tone.

He wasn't deterred. The confidence was back and soaring high. "I want to thank you for your support."

"What are you talking about?" she asked with eyelids squinted and lips pursed.

He fumbled with the phone, half distracted for a moment. Abigail prepared to walk out as he grabbed her arm. "Wait a minute."

"I can see that you're busy. I'm not going to stand here and wait patiently while you answer your messages. I have a life, too, you know."

"Of course I know that, and I'm sorry for making you feel disrespected," he said, setting the phone down. "See, there, done." He didn't want to start an argument with her, far from it. Today was the first sign of rekindling their relationship. He longed for restoration. He moved his hand from the light grip on her arm to her hand. "I know you, Abigail."

"Oh, really?"

"Yes, I do, and you know it. You were giving me the endorsement that I desperately needed in there. We make a great team. I need you in my camp." Abigail's gaze dropped. He could tell she was slipping from the conversation and pressed to regain her attention. "The two of us can bring this company around and get to where we always dreamed, running an international company. What more can we ask?"

"I don't know, Joel."

He took her other hand, too, sensing the wall of separation between them cracking. "Come on, Abigail, we can do this. I rely on you. I always have and apparently always will."

She retracted her hands and said, "Is that supposed to sway me? Don't you get it? I'm not the same long-suffering Abigail who was willing to work with you until the bitter end despite your lapses in judgment. Those days have long passed," she said, walking away. "Plus, you're not the same Joel, anyway."

"I haven't changed."

"Well then, maybe that's the problem." She left the room, leaving Joel alone with his thoughts.

He took a seat. His assistant walked in right afterward.

"Excuse me, Mr. Mitchell, you have an urgent call from India regarding Mr. Bengali."

Three months ago Joel would have bolted into the hallway, dashed to his office, and taken the call with the exhilaration of a kid on Christmas. After a string of false alarms and late payments, the call wasn't so urgent. "Please forward it to my phone in here, thanks," he told her, waving the PDA lightly in the air. "And could you please close the door for me, thanks."

"Yes, sir," she said.

A minute later his phone was ringing. "Joel Mitchell here."

"It's Kumar. Mr. Bengali has completed his transition."

Joel sat tall in the seat. "Are you saying that he's passed away?"

"Yes, he has transitioned to the next phase of his life."

Joel didn't know how to respond. He was overwhelmed yet complacent. The news was vital months ago, hadn't come, and now it was surreal. "You have my condolences."

With Musar's religion, Joel wasn't quite sure if condolences were appropriate, especially after Musar described death as passing into a state of contentment. Appropriate or not, there was bound to be a reaction from Zarah. He had sympathy for her impending grief. Within the week, he'd hire a personal assistant just for Zarah. After all, money was not a concern, not now, not after they inherited Musar's estate.

"Zarah and I will come to India right away. We'll be there Friday."

"We must perform the ceremony and cremation tomorrow."

There wasn't much Joel could do to get around the two days of travel from Detroit to the Jaipur, India, area. "Can you wait another day for us to arrive?"

"His soul must be quickly eased along its journey," the attorney told him.

"So, what should we do, travel there or not?" Joel didn't try to figure out the rituals of Musar's religion. It was too complicated for him, enshrined with gods, and transitions, and journeys, and chanting. He preferred the simplicity of death in his family—die, funeralize, and let the soul return to God.

"You and Zarah can travel here to collect Mr. Bengali's belongings when it's convenient for you, and she can sign the documents to close the estate."

"I will let you know our travel plans, and thank you, Kumar, for your help. I'm sure Zarah is grateful to you for your loyalty to her father."

"'Thank you' is not necessary. It is my duty."

The call ended. Joel breathed easy for the first time in almost a year. He reflected on the surge of cash that would open many opportunities, like regaining the Southern division, ideally before the announcement that it had been lost to investors. Regardless, the great news was that ownership of the West Coast now belonged to Zarah, his wife, his household, his family again. He eased back in the seat, feeling pretty good for a man that was wrestling with the futile outcome of his decisions a matter of days ago. He'd returned to the driver's seat of his journey and to the CEO position of DMI. Changes were coming hard and swift, the way he liked it.

chapter

62

Don paced in his mother's office. Naledi's stay was much too short. The visit was several weeks ago, but it seemed like a year ago. He had to admit, when she was in town, most of their time was spent working. Breaks were rare. He was stretched pretty wide across three continents when he factored in Europe, requiring him to pray constantly for endurance and wisdom.

There was a time when he might have complained, but his faith was increasing daily as he witnessed the puzzle pieces slowly falling into place. Every time Joel made a new play on the stability of the company, though, doubt crept in. The waiting and hoping was grueling for Don, even with God in the midst of the plan. Don reflected on the easiest and fastest way to get this over by using Tamara's stock position. A five second signature would save him the back-and-forth agony of waiting and wondering. He'd gotten past the question of if; when was the source of his unrest.

Madeline charged into her office. He could tell the meeting hadn't gone well. "Okay, what happened?" he said as his mother kept going until she reached the windows. She clinched her teeth while sipping in air and gripping her head with her hand.

"That boy is going to drive me crazy. Seriously, he is," she said, letting out a horrific sigh. "I just can't seem to be able to get rid of him. He is the thorn in—" she said, slapping her behind.

Don chuckled. "Come on, Mother, I can't believe Joel is getting to you after all these years. Usually he's the one that leaves the meeting in disarray." He chuckled some more. "Don't tell me the great Madeline Mitchell is getting soft in her old age."

"Who's old, first of all?" she said as he watched her countenance lighten. Her arms were folded as she leaned against the windows. "I know this shouldn't bother me at this point, but every now and then he does something so outrageous that I wonder if the boy has mental issues."

"Come on, Mother. Joel might have poor judgment and he might even be narcissistic—"

"Might be?" his mother interjected to say. "He is the most self-absorbed egotistical person in this building, heck, I might as well say in this country. Nobody's image of themselves is bigger than Joel Mitchell's. Trust me on that one," she said, turning so that her shoulder was leaning against the window.

"All right, Joel is self-absorbed, but he doesn't have mental issues."

"I'm not so sure."

"Come on, Mother. We can't lose our grip on the big picture." She peered out the window, but Don knew his mother was listening to every word. "We have to concentrate on gaining control of the company."

"Perhaps sound judgment would indicate that it's time to throw in the towel, but not me. I refuse to give up."

"Berating Joel isn't going to help us."

"When did you join the Joel cheerleaders' squad? I thought that was Abigail and Sherry's role . . . oh yes, and his new wife. We can't forget her," she said curtly. "They don't need you, too. You need to stay on my team." She tapped her index finger in the center of her chest.

"Nothing has changed. We're on the same team. It's just that I don't want to expend energy on tearing Joel down." Tamara wouldn't leave his thoughts. It seemed that Mother was in a receptive mood. This might be the time to tell her. Days were going to continue clicking by with Tamara wanting an answer. He had to act. "Joel isn't my primary concern right now, somebody else is."

"Who?" she said, leaning against the window while turning her gaze to him.

"Tamara."

"Why?" Madeline said, rushing to the desk and leaning across. "What's wrong with her? Have you spoken to her?" The questions were rapid fire, leaving him no time to respond. His mother's concern meter was ramping into overdrive and headed for an explosion if he didn't jump in.

"I have spoken to her several times."

"Is she all right?"

"Tamara is fine," he said, trying to decide if this was the best time. He could see his mother's worry level lower as she slowly took her seat at the desk and pulled it in close. Leaders had to lead. There was never going to be a perfect time. Now was it, but he would be as gentle as he could in breaking the news. "She wants to come home."

"What?" Madeline said, rearing the seat back so far that she nearly caused it to tip over. "Are you serious, my daughter wants to come home?" Madeline sandwiched her face between her hands and turned from side to side. His heart didn't want to crush her moment of bliss. He'd let her have a few more seconds before interjecting the "but." "Finally, she's coming home. Thank God, really, I thank Him," she said as tears formed on her eyelids. "What does she need? Where is she? She can't have much money left. I can wire her funds right now. I can have a mover pack her belongings and ship everything here. She can get on a plane today. I'll take care of everything." Madeline spun around once in her chair. "My baby is coming home."

Don felt awful. He'd waited one second too long. Her celebratory surge was overflowing. The letdown was going to be equally intense. "She wants to come home under one condition."

"Name it, no matter what it is, she can come home."

"She wants you to leave."

"Leave where?"

"DMI and Detroit."

"And go where?" she asked as her expression changed instantly.

"I don't know, but she was absolutely clear that she wants to come home and you have to be gone."

Madeline smirked. "I don't believe this. First I have to deal with Joel and now my own child. I knew this was too good to be true. You can't be in favor of this," she said, grabbing her favorite pen and tapping it in rapid succession on the desk.

"I told her that you're not going to leave."

"You can bet your last dollar I'm not leaving. If it wasn't for me spending my life and my time in this place, DMI would have gone under a long time ago, even before your father passed away. I've dedicated my life to this place. I'm not leaving. I don't know who's been trying to turn my child against me, but when I find out, it won't be a happy day for them. I can guarantee you that."

The top of her head hadn't blown off with fury. Don was stoic. The revelation had gone better than he'd hoped and with the outcome he'd anticipated. With no other obvious alternatives, Don refused to accept that he'd totally misread God's direction. He refused to let the series of unfortunate circumstances with Joel, Harmonious Energy, and Tamara sway his strategy. At that moment, when the realization of assuming the CEO role at DMI looked grim, Don resigned himself to the belief that he was standing on faith based on what he felt God had prepared him to do. God's word didn't change because of circumstances. Circumstances changed because of God's word. He was absolutely convinced of it. He took comfort in believing that DMI wasn't his fight. This was between God and Joel. Reassurance blanketed him knowing that his God had never lost a battle.

chapter
63

Joel went straight home to tell Zarah the news in person. He remembered his mother calling right after his father had died. His father had been sick months before dying but Joel wasn't prepared to hear the actual words coming from his mother: "Your father is gone." The ache in his heart that careened throughout his body was faint now, but never truly gone. He wasn't sure how Zarah would handle the news. Their cultures and religious beliefs were so different, but Joel suspected that death was loss, no matter who you were or where you were from. He entered the house and quickly found Zarah in the library. It had become her favorite room in the house, probably because that was where he spent much of his time when he was home. He went to her and took her hand, kneeling on one knee in front of her.

"Zarah, I have something to tell you."

Her expression lightened as she anticipated what he had to say. She seemed so excited. He wished there was better news. Best to say it straight out and deal with the fallout. He tightened the hold on her hand. "Your father is gone. I got a call from Kumar earlier." There was no initial reaction from Zarah. Joel felt helpless. "They can't wait for us to arrive. They plan to have the ceremony tomorrow, but we can go to India anyway, if you want." He wanted to draw her close and provide a shoulder for her tears. To his dismay, there was no outrageous crying, only light tears and a few sobs. There was no doubt that she loved her father. Joel couldn't figure the reaction. Once again, he felt the distance between their lives and beliefs. "Can I do anything for you?"

"This is a time of celebration for my family. My father has continued on his journey. I must pray to the gods for his safe passage," she said, beginning to chant. Joel stayed on one knee, not quite sure if he felt comfortable sitting in a compromised position with her prayers, unfamiliar with her native tongue. Since he wasn't actively practicing his own religion, he wasn't receptive to anything else, either.

After a day of preparation and two days of flight time, Zarah and Joel were in India. They were each scheduled to meet separately with the attorney. The marathon flights didn't seem long this time. There was nothing Joel could do about Musar's death. Like Zarah said, it was a time of celebration for her family. He could accept that, although it wasn't a normal reaction. Joel had to admit, getting the estate transferred and upping his account balance was going to be a long overdue reality. His enthusiasm was soaring. Today was a new day for him and for DMI. Distribution of Musar's assets wouldn't be a circus, like it had been when Dave Mitchell had died and split his life between two families. Zarah was it, the only child, the sole heir.

The surge of unbridled satisfaction was fleeting as Joel listened to the attorney. Kumar relayed the terms of Zarah's inheritance. To Joel's chagrin, funds were locked with a modest two million dollars available immediately and an additional million each year until year five, when the entire estate transferred to Zarah. The only exception was divorce. If her husband left her, she'd immediately assume ownership of the entire estate. Joel didn't plan to wait out the five years for her inheritance. That was her money, her legacy. The only thing she had that he desperately wanted was his division back.

"What about the West Coast division of DMI?"

"Sole ownership has been transferred to Zarah." Joel was relieved until he heard the stipulation. "As Musar promised, she can sell it to you if you have no children and choose to divorce after three years. But she can sell it to anyone else at any time before the three years expires."

"What, are you saying that someone could buy my division before I get the chance to buy it back?"

"Yes, she can sell it to someone now, but not to her husband."

"Why?" Joel asked, unwilling to accept this strike of betrayal from Musar.

"Musar wanted to make sure Zarah's husband did not leave her alone. He wanted her to be secure in the marriage," the attorney said.

Joel couldn't figure out if he'd angered the God of his father or the gods of Zarah's father. There was no way to keep DMI afloat for five years with the drop in revenue and mounting bills. Now that he'd have control of the entire company, he'd secure a credit line with Harmonious Energy as collateral. It would help, but taking on more debt wouldn't be the saving grace. Uncle Frank's comment about Joel borrowing more money resonated with him. There was no way he'd let that happen, if for no other reason than to not give Uncle Frank the pleasure of gawking. Joel wrung his hands, unable to tell the attorney and Zarah how he really felt. He had to get away and think. They'd take a flight back to Detroit today if possible, but definitely no later than tomorrow. His problems weren't less in Detroit, but at least he was on familiar soil.

His disposition was accommodating on the outside and outraged on the inside. Nothing had gone right in a year. He'd get close to a victory, real miracles, and then, bam, the deal would fall through, or the money wouldn't come, or death sat on its behind long enough to cause problems, instead of swooping in and taking over Musar like it had with his father. If Joel believed in being cursed, that would explain the happenings surrounding him. He opted not to go that far. Despite the circumstances, he preferred to believe that the power to change his future rested in him. He had to find a way out of the quagmire. Then he remembered the silver of good news. At least the West Coast was in his hands again, maybe not quite his hands, but Zarah's was close enough. He made a mental note to spend more time with her, or at least try.

chapter
64

Joel had been consistently unpredictable in recent months. Abigail couldn't guess what the emergency was today. She'd have to wait and find out like everyone else, no longer having the inside track with Joel. She suppressed her concern, wanting DMI to survive. The original vision, which was to train the religious leaders so they could be empowered to help the people, was sound. They couldn't be going out of business; today couldn't be that day. There wasn't time to get a debriefing. Abigail braced for the news and entered the boardroom already filled with Joel, Don, Madeline, and the other six board members. Sherry entered behind Abigail—surprised that they were both summoned. Abigail's concern grew. Joel either had fabulous news or really bad news, nothing in the middle would warrant a DMI gathering of this elite magnitude, one comprised of members from the executive team and the board of directors.

"Can we take our seats, please? I want to get started on time," Joel said, talking over the pockets of conversation and then taking a seat.

Abigail sat next to Don. Madeline sat next to him on the other side. "Do you know what this is about?" Abigail asked him.

"No idea, but we'll soon find out."

"I guess we will." Abigail waited for Madeline to comment since Sherry wasn't a board member or a key executive. About a minute had passed while people took their seats and Madeline said nothing.

"The matters discussed in this meeting are proprietary, which is why I have Sherry Mitchell, my personal assistant, here, who has also doubled as my press secretary for several years. She will take notes and craft a press release afterward." Madeline fidgeted in her seat. Don's elbow rested on the arm of his chair. "Everyone here knows that we're in the middle of tight times with the U.S. divisions."

"You got that right," Madeline said.

Joel continued. "The great news is that our international client base is strong, thanks to the merger with Harmonious Energy. I'm confident that the U.S. business will recover. Our strategy is strong and our leadership team is top notch. We can and will turn this around."

"How?" Madeline asked.

"The climb back to our place on top of the leaderboard will be frustrating at times and may require tremendous sacrifices, but no matter what happens in the process, we have to remember the end goal," Joel said.

"Joel, we don't need a pep talk. What we need is for you to tell us why you've summoned us to an emergency meeting in the middle of the day when we're busy trying to keep the doors open. You tell me that," Madeline said.

"Fine, let's get to the heart of this discussion."

"Now we're getting somewhere," Madeline said. Abigail didn't know if Madeline would ever like Joel, by the sound of her curt attitude.

"You're aware of the West Coast division's transfer of ownership from DMI to Harmonious Energy." The shock continued to resonate with Abigail. Not letting that happen was Dave's number one request. She couldn't imagine how Madeline felt. "I can proudly inform you that we have the West Coast division back in the DMI family."

"DMI owns all four divisions again?" Don asked.

"Not exactly."

"Here we go," Madeline said, pushing the seat away from the table and crossing her legs. "What have you done now?"

"Ownership of the West Coast transferred to my wife's trust once her father died late last week."

"Does it belong to you or to her?" Don asked.

Joel let his gaze fall. "It belongs to her technically, but she is my wife."

"That's all well and good, but the bottom line is that your wife's name is listed as the sole owner. That's what you're tap dancing around and trying not to say. Let's just call it like it is. You don't own the West Coast division, unless this meeting is the grand announcement that your wife is signing it over to you."

"Look here, team, the bottom line is that we have the West Coast under our umbrella again and under my control, regardless of whose actual name is on the statement of ownership."

"I'm amazed at how uninformed you think we are," Madeline told him. Abigail sat stunned but chose to listen to his explanation, then render her opinion. "A binding legal document declares the owner," Madeline said, drawing close to the table, fixing the palm of her hands on the edge and piercing her gaze into Joel. "That's the bottom line, and not what you want to believe in that concocted world of yours. This is a joke. I'm out of here."

"There's one more announcement."

Madeline walked toward the door. "What's left to give away? My division," she said, cackling.

"No, the Southern division."

Madeline stopped in midstep. A momentary hush fell over the room before babble dashed in and took over. Joel struggled to regain control.

"Is the Southern division gone?" Abigail asked, afraid to hear the answer.

"Yes, but—" was the most Joel could eke out before he was bombarded with questions, stares, and innuendos from more than Madeline.

"What happened?" Don asked with a bite in his tone—after all, a part of his DNA came from Madeline.

"I made an executive decision to save this company."

"You made a decision, without the decency of coming to the board or the executive team again. Who do you think you are?" Madeline said, holding each word a complete second. By then she'd come up to the table, still standing, and squeezed in between two of the other members.

"We needed operating capital. Madeline, you said yourself in last week's meeting that we had to keep the lights on, and we will."

She laughed openly. "Are you trying to tell us that you had to pay the electric bill so you hocked the Southern division? That's too funny," she said, letting the laughter come to an abrupt halt, "and too ridiculous for you to sit there wasting our time with this garbage. You owe us the decency of coming clean, stepping down, and letting us figure out what to do first. For once in your little life, do the right thing. Stop thinking only about yourself." Madeline's words were too controlled for comfort, Abigail thought.

"Wait a minute," Sherry chimed in. Madeline shot her a piercing stare that said *Don't even attempt to rescue him unless you're willing to drown, too.*

"Look, I don't have time to get into the full details but suffice to say that we forfeited the Southern division in an effort to save the rest of DMI," Joel said. "When a person has an infected limb, it's better to cut it off and save the body than to keep everything intact and die as a result."

"I'm not in a medical class. This is a board meeting. I can't believe you sold a division. You don't have the authority to sell it. We want it back!" Madeline belted. Joel ignored her. "Did you hear me? We want it back. Who did you sell it to anyway and for how much?"

"A private investor bought it."

"They won't be private much longer once the press release is issued," Abigail said. The man sitting at the helm wasn't Joel Mitchell, not the man she'd once loved and respected. This had to be an impostor, and not a very good one. Joel couldn't be serious. He was nothing like his father. Staring at him, she couldn't help but feel that he was a waste of talent and favor. Don had to rescue the company now or forever live with the rapidly approaching demise. Sadness gripped her. Joel was lost to her. Hopefully he wasn't completely lost to God but the indicators didn't look good.

chapter
65

Don and Abigail followed Madeline into her office, with silence leading the way. Don was the last inside and closed the door behind him. The three gathered around the small meeting table off to the side and took seats.

"Just when I didn't think Joel could sink us any further, he announces this craziness," Madeline said with her hands flailing in the air.

"I simply can't put my head around what Joel is doing. He's wiser than this. I've worked side by side with him," Abigail said.

"You wouldn't know it," Madeline commented.

Don wasn't out of sorts. He prayed silently as Abigail and his mother vented. Panicking wasn't going to help resolve the deep trouble DMI and his family were experiencing. He remained calm so the wisdom could flow freely, unblocked by outrage and judgment. His mother and Abigail had different approaches. Abigail was gentler, too accommodating. Madeline was the opposite, direct and lacking grace.

"We have finally come to the end. There is nothing else we can do," his mother said.

"I don't believe God would let DMI fail. I just don't believe it," Abigail said, turning her head from side to side.

"You're talking to the wrong person to say that. I wouldn't have believed that my marriage would fail, or that I would fail as a parent, but here I am."

Abigail gave a slight nod of affirmation.

"We can't blame God," Don said. "He gives us free will. My father, and Joel, and me, and you—we're all given an opportunity to do the right thing. God didn't make Dad leave you. That was his choice," Don told his mother as she looked away. "God didn't tell Joel to recklessly mismanage this company. Both Dad and Joel were set up for success under the leading of the Lord. They chose to step out of that grace and do their own thing, and the consequences are what they are."

"Don't tell me that everyone who suffers brings it on themselves."

"Of course not, some do and some don't." Don gained conviction with each word, resting in the revelation he'd learned through personal experience. "I believe some challenges are meant to develop our character and perseverance. Others are purely consequences."

"What's the difference? Suffering is suffering," Madeline said.

"One is for your personal growth and the other one not so much. The only way you can tell the difference is how much peace you feel in the midst of the challenge," Don told her.

Madeline returned her gaze to the circle and spoke slowly. "Maybe you're right."

"I know I'm right. We want to take credit for the good and blame God for the bad—doesn't work that way."

"Okay, okay, Reverend Don, I get the point," his mother said with opened palms extended toward him and then quickly retracted. The softening disposition iced with a slight grin was the confirmation he sought. She understood.

"So, what are we going to do?" Abigail asked. "I've been praying and praying and praying, hoping God will intervene."

"There is hope," Don said.

"Really, where?"

"I've been thinking, maybe I can make a power play and try to buy the Southern division under LTI. With the operating capital struggling at DMI, Joel should be strapped for cash," Don said.

"Which means he can't keep it," Madeline added.

"That's a great idea," Abigail said. "But Joel said it was a private investor."

"We'd have to do some digging, but we can do that, gladly," his mother said, getting excited.

"If we can buy the Southern region back, that leaves the West Coast out there. That also leaves Joel in charge. I have to ask, what do we do about getting Joel out of the CEO position?" Abigail asked.

"With our pitiful legal team, we can't count on them to run a gnat out of here, let alone a sanctioned CEO. They're totally worthless. We have to do this on our own, although I can't imagine how."

Don knew the time was right. He didn't know how the pieces would come together, but there was an opportunity they had to explore. He took another few seconds to be sure and to formulate the words. Ready, set, go. "There is a long shot that has its own challenges."

"Tell us."

"There is the option of taking ownership of Tamara's stock."

He watched his mother's excitement evaporate. Hurting her was the last thing he wanted to do. She had suffered her share of pain, but destiny and calling were forces too strong for him to ignore. Even when he wanted to shy away from God's leading, the pull was too intense to withdraw.

"I'm not leaving this company or this city. That's not going to happen."

"What are you talking about?" Abigail asked.

"Tamara has agreed to come back if I leave DMI and Detroit."

"Why?"

"I have no idea. I've done everything in my power to protect my children and this is my reward," she said, driven to tears. "If I understood why she won't let me back into her life, then, perhaps I could move forward."

Don remembered his mother crying many nights when he was a child. As the years passed and her heart hardened, he hadn't seen her cry much, except when it came to her children. His mother was good. He understood Tamara's need for distance. Don continued praying. There had to be a reason for the calamity. Good had to prevail, otherwise the torment and agony of separation and loss would win and that wasn't God's way. Don's faith was firm, and so would be his boldness.

"Do you think I should go?" she asked Don, pushing back the sobs by clearing her throat.

"Excuse me, I'm going to leave and let the two of you talk," Abigail said.

"I'll catch up with you later," Don told her and thanked her, too. His soul was crying out to comfort Madeline. "Mother, I can't tell you what to do. You have to decide. I can tell you that I've been at my own crossroads," he said leaning forward and resting his elbows on his thighs. "When I went to South Africa I was mad and bitter. I was really running away, or at least that's what I thought, but God met me there. He allowed me to step away from the tension and to get a better perspective. The distance from Detroit saved my life, physically and spiritually," he said, sitting up.

"Are you suggesting that I go on a pilgrimage and find myself, when I'm not lost?"

"I'm telling you what I had to do to get free from the burden of this place." She didn't respond. He took her hand. "Mother, you've taken care of your children. You've been the best mother I could ask for." She pulled her hand away. "No, I mean it, you have. Not many women could have endured what you did, and you're tough as nails as a result."

"Not everybody sees that as a positive."

"I do. You're tough, but you're also human. You've never taken the time to grieve the divorce, or Dad's death, or to properly deal with Andre raping Tamara, or Sam killing him in retaliation and then committing suicide."

"Yes, I have!" she shouted.

"No, you haven't. Instead, you pressed the trauma deep inside and lashed out at those nearby. You've barricaded yourself inside your pain and nothing except me and maybe Tamara are allowed an entry pass into your heart. Not even God Almighty gets in."

His mother stared at their hands and held her response. There wasn't tension in the room. No anger. No bitterness. For that sweet moment, there was raw vulnerability from his mother, a response he'd never seen from her. He let the moment penetrate.

"I am a founder of this company, that's no doubt. In a way, DMI is my baby." Don nodded in affirmation without interrupting. "Tamara is my child, a child that I love with all my heart. I would give my life for her," she said, struggling to hold the tears. "And for you, too."

"I know that, Mother."

"Here I am, having to choose between saving DMI and bringing my child home. Why does there have to be a choice? Why can't we have both? Is that so wrong of me to want both? I've given up so much already. Without them both, I'm nothing."

Don appreciated her dilemma. He'd had a taste and the sourness wasn't pleasant, but it was survivable. After thinking more about it, the request was unreasonable and as impossible as he initially believed. There had to be another way.

"Tell her I'll think about it and let you know soon."

"Mother, you don't have to do this."

"Maybe, maybe not, but I'm your mother and Tamara's. Maybe this fulfills my purpose. By walking away I can give both of my children what they deserve and what I've dreamed of you having for so many years. You could finally complete your father's life work and your sister could finally come home. If I can make both of those happen by leaving, then so be it."

The resolution in her tone screamed. She was seriously considering the possibility. Her mere consideration was a major miracle. There was hope, and he'd cling to the notion.

chapter

66

By late afternoon, Don couldn't believe his mother was seriously considering the proposal. The bittersweet taste consumed him. For him to become CEO, his mother had to pay the ultimate price. Fate was inescapable and so was the associated fallout he was quickly coming to learn. Tamara had to be told before it got too late in Bristol. He placed the call. A few rings and she was on the line. "Big sis, I hope it's not too late."

"Not at all. Actually, I'm glad to hear from you. I can't get DMI and Detroit out of my head now, thanks to you," she said punctuated with a giggle.

"Well, that's why I'm calling."

"I know, you don't have to tell me. Mother said no way to my proposal. She's not leaving DMI for anyone or anything, especially for her prodigal child."

"That's not true. I have to admit, at first she said absolutely not."

"I knew it."

"Wait, that was at first, and to be honest, I can understand her reaction. She was shocked and happy and upset all at the same time. When I spoke with her again, she'd moved to the middle. She hasn't said yes and she hasn't said no."

"Wow, I'm surprised."

"You shouldn't be. Our mother loves us. She's worked her entire adult life for us."

"I told you, my walking away from the family and Mother doesn't have anything to do with love. I needed space and time to heal."

"Look, sis, I'm not attacking you. Please don't feel that way. But I hope you understand my predicament. I'm in the middle. You can't blame me for wanting it all, DMI and you and Mother together in Detroit."

"That's not going to happen."

"Why? There has to be a way for the three of us to reunite in the same place. It's time."

"No," she belted out and then softened to say, "not at first, but I'm open to changing my mind later."

Don laughed. There was no other reaction worth exhibiting.

"What's so funny?"

"You might not want to hear this, but you are Madeline's child without a doubt. I'm so glad she only had one daughter, because it would be impossible to handle two little Madelines running around." His humor caught on and Tamara joined the laughter. Don didn't know what was going to happen next. He would just be prepared.

chapter
67

Joel inched the car along the route home, not really wanting to go there. He didn't want to see anyone or explain anything to anybody. He was tired of being questioned by a pack of whining pessimists whom he'd made extra wealthy with DMI profits during his tenure. He wasn't a loser, it wasn't in his Mitchell DNA. He'd prove it and shut up the growing list of people nipping at his heels. Joel entered through the garage door, keeping quiet, practically tiptoeing with a stack of mail and documents his administrative assistant had handed to him on the way out. It was early in the evening and he expected Zarah to be wide awake and craving attention, attention he didn't have the energy or the interest to give. Joel got as far as the casual dining room situated off the kitchen before Zarah swooped in like a watchful hawk seeking prey. No door was safe. She was going to sniff him out if he was in the house.

"I'm pleased that you're home today. The daytime hasn't gone."

"I know. I came home a little earlier so that I could get a jump on work in my office," he said, passing through the mud room, laundry, small den, and into the back hallway leading across to his office. Zarah was in close pursuit. He wanted to turn around and tell her to back off, to go away, to leave him alone, to let him breathe, but was determined to maintain civility.

"We can eat dinner together?" she asked.

"I'm not hungry," he said, entering his office and setting the stack of mail and documents on the corner of his desk. "I ate lunch earlier."

The hopeful expression drained from Zarah. She was overcome with a look of anguish. Joel's instinct, which he silenced, was to console her. She was a hungry kitten. If he fed her now, she'd be back for more and more, depleting his small ration of compassion. His pity would be interpreted as love and there wasn't enough in his heart left to share. From his birth, his parents were the only people requiring his love. There had never been a need to produce extra love in his soul to be rationed out to others. His half sister and brothers didn't require it. As a matter of fact, they flat out didn't want it. He had grown up alone in this life except for his parents. Zarah would have to get in line if she wanted more. His soul was bare, and what little he did have was already committed to Sheba.

Zarah sobbed. He took several steps toward her, torn about how far to go.

"There's no need for that," he said, standing in the middle of his office, wanting to vanish. "You don't have to eat alone. The cook and your personal assistant are here."

"But they always eat with me," she said, reaching for his arm.

"That's their job. That's what I pay them to do. Let them do their job," he said, raising his voice and retracting his arm from her reach. Zarah's tears flowed but her whimpers were contained. Joel felt his control slipping away. She was a distraction at a time when he had to give 100 percent to reviving his leadership position. "I'm sorry," he said, violating his rule and pulling her into his embrace. Her shoulders relaxed as she locked her arms around his back and held on. A minute passed and he tried wiggling free. Her clutch was not easily broken but he had to break free.

"My father expects me to have children."

Musar was gone and didn't have a single thing to say about what happened in Joel's household. He'd already done plenty of damage before his so-called transition to the next phase. Joel was agitated. As far as he was concerned, Musar was dead and followed the same path that the others before him had taken in death, leaving a trail of complications for others to untangle.

"This isn't a good time for us to have children." It wasn't like he could talk to her about the details of work. She didn't understand business. "I have a lot of work that has to be done. It is very busy at the office," he said and left it at that, going to his desk. He flipped through the stack of mail, stopping abruptly at the *People* magazine cover. The airport shot of him and Zarah were in a small box on the top right side of the corner. The wording burned his ego: MOST ELIGIBLE BACHELOR covered by a big red X. Joel's fury was percolating. Consciously, Joel processed that his predicament wasn't Zarah's fault. If he was about to die, perhaps he'd go the exact same route as Musar had to provide for his only child, especially a daughter. His rational thinking didn't blame her, but his emotions did. The cover enraged him. He'd lost both the West Coast and Southern division, his reputation as the wisest CEO, and now his most coveted title of eligible bachelor was gone. He had little left, including dignity. Joel desperately had to be alone.

Zarah stood there waiting for whatever was coming next. Joel was disgusted with himself for getting in such a situation of despair. He'd have to go to bed extra late tonight. Maybe he'd sleep in his office or a guest room to avoid Zarah's pleas. They'd consummated the marriage once, and Joel didn't see the number changing in three years.

The night had passed and Zarah was alone again. There was no husband lying next to her. Maybe she wasn't pretty enough, she thought. Maybe she wasn't intelligent enough. Maybe she was cursed for a deed her father had done years earlier. Zarah was desperate for Joel's affection. Pleasing him was her sole reason for living. She dressed hurriedly in her clothes from home and hustled downstairs to meet her personal assistant Ana. "I want to go to my husband's job. Can you take me, please?"

"Gladly," Ana said, arranging for a driver.

Zarah was antsy along the ride to Joel. She was pleased that Joel had gotten her an Indian assistant who grew up not far from her town. They were the same age, twenty-three, and had much to discuss, but the assistant wasn't Joel. The name "Ana" meant "wanted"—something Zarah longed for, to be by her husband.

"We're here," Ana said.

The short ride was over. Zarah was too nervous to exit the car immediately. "Please, may I have a minute? I'm not ready," she said, second-guessing her decision. What if Joel was displeased with her for coming there? What if she saw him but wasn't able to say words that made sense? Her palms sweated.

She was overcome with doubt when Ana said, "We can go in and you can sit in the lobby until you're ready."

That seemed to make sense, so Zarah got out. As she entered the building for the first time as a wife, the aura overtook her. Perhaps it was from being in the building again without her father, or for coming to see her husband for the first time at work, or from simply being outside of the house without Joel. Whatever the reason, she stumbled.

"Here, let's take a seat," Ana said.

"No," Zarah belted out. "I'm fine." She had to stand on her own in order to show Joel her strength. There was something she was doing wrong in his presence. She'd made every attempt to please him going forward. This was her first brave attempt and it wouldn't be ruined with a misstep.

"Then let's go upstairs to your husband's office."

"I'd like to go myself," she said, determined to be brave. Ana stayed downstairs as Zarah got clearance from the guard's desk and entered the elevator. It was a slow ride up the six floors. When the elevator door opened, Zarah's feet wouldn't move. She lunged off the elevator, gaining momentum and anxiety at the same time. Remembering her husband's assistant last year from the visit to DMI with her father, Zarah approached her desk.

"Hello, Mrs. Mitchell. I'm Kay, Mr. Mitchell's assistant. It's good to finally get a chance to meet you again and to say congratulations."

"Thank you." Zarah kept a contained smile and nodded. "I'm here to see Mr. Mitchell."

"He's at an off-site meeting."

"Sorry, I don't understand."

"He's meeting with someone at another location this morning."

"Then I shall wait for him to return."

"It could be a long wait. I believe he's taking the corporate jet to Chicago right after the meeting ends at noon and will return to Detroit around seven this evening." Zarah attempted to cover her feelings. "I can have him call you on the way to the airport."

"Yes, please." Zarah thanked Kay and turned to leave, mustering the energy required to take one step at a time. Halfway to the elevator, Joel's mother came from her office and met Zarah.

"What are you doing here?" Mrs. Mitchell asked. "And how's the newlywed?" Zarah had managed to retain her emotions, but the rejection and shame overtook her, setting off a tsunami of tears. "Wait a minute," Mrs. Mitchell said, pulling Zarah into her office as another lady slowly walked by, a person Zarah vaguely remembered meeting before. When they were inside the office, Mrs. Mitchell asked, "What is going on here? Why are you so upset?"

Zarah was filled with shame. In her culture, a wife was lower than a dog if she couldn't fulfill her husband and honor him with children. "There's something wrong with me," she wailed. The shame intensified. She was taught from birth to control her emotions in both pain and joy. Life was intended to complete one's purpose. Her family would cast her away and her father would be disappointed if they saw her in this state, but she didn't know what else to do.

Mrs. Mitchell handed Zarah a stack of tissues and went to the door. "Please get me a glass of water," she asked someone outside and then returned.

chapter
68

Madeline stood near Kay, filled with curiosity. "What is going on here," Madeline asked as Kay got the glass of water for Sherry.

"I don't know, but it must be something serious."

"Do you know what has Joel's wife so upset?"

"How did you know she was his wife?"

"Are you kidding?" Madeline answered. "There aren't a great number of Indian women dressed in their elegant native garb walking around the streets of Detroit or within DMI," she said, amused.

"You have a good point."

"Let's get back to his wife. What's her first name again?" Madeline asked, not sure if she'd forgotten it or had never known.

"Zarah."

Madeline said, leaning in, "And you don't know why she's so upset?"

"No, I told Mrs. Mitchell that Joel was at a meeting and that he was flying to Chicago for the afternoon. That was it. I hope I didn't say or do anything to offend her," she said, getting the water.

Madeline was too deep in thought to answer rationally. Most likely Zarah found out about Sheba and was beginning to realize that she wasn't the only woman in her husband's life. That would warrant a few tears, at least the first time. The tears were guaranteed to dry up over time, but Zarah was too young to have that knowledge. Madeline felt genuine empathy for Zarah. She had to give Joel his accolades. He didn't just destroy lives locally, he went internationally. No family with money and a daughter were safe from his reach and egotistical pursuit of control.

As Madeline returned to her office, the opened door to Sherry's office was too tempting to simply bypass without getting an earful of the drama brewing inside. Kay had returned to her desk. "Could you do me a favor and go get the money management workshop folder from Abigail's office?" Madeline asked. "It's a red labeled folder. I must have left it down there yesterday."

"No problem," Kay said, taking a moment to forward her calls to another administrative assistant for backup.

As soon as she was near the elevators, Madeline pretended to be reviewing a file near Sherry's doorway, out of the line of sight but within the hearing-clearly zone. Madeline wasn't worried about Kay returning right away. It would take some time to realize that the file wasn't there since it didn't exist.

"He doesn't want me as his wife," Madeline heard Zarah say.

"That's not true," she heard Sherry respond. Madeline's mind was in overdrive. Maybe there was one last plan in her, a good one this time, a surefire win. The giddy thought of pulling off her idea made her legs weaken.

"He doesn't. I know he doesn't. He won't let me have children. He doesn't want to be with me!" she cried out.

"Well, he's busy running this company, and your father's, too, now. That's a lot of work to handle."

"But I never see him. I eat my meals with the cook and Ana, the assistant that he has for me. He won't come to the bed unless I'm asleep," she said, crying. "What must I do? I am so ashamed."

"I had no idea this was happening. I'll speak to him for you."

"No, you must not tell him that I spoke with you."

"Zarah, he's my son and you're my daughter-in-law. The two of you are my family. I must help."

chapter
69

Madeline parked her hearing on Sherry and Zarah's discussion as her gaze kept watch on the elevators. As the conversation quieted, Madeline eased from the door and tiptoed to the elevator. She stood off to the side, in the break room, waiting. It wasn't long before Joel's wife approached the elevator alone, just as Madeline hoped. She zoomed in like a cat stalking its prey. There was no getting away. Madeline pushed the button hastily and reserved her conversation until they were safely on the elevator. "Mrs. Mitchell, do you remember me from the meeting that you and your father attended here last year?" Madeline asked Zarah. The awkward look said *yes* or *maybe*. "I'm also Mrs. Mitchell. I'm on the board of directors. Welcome to Michigan and welcome to DMI," Madeline said. The elevator ride ended in the lobby. "Do you have a few minutes?" Madeline asked. "I'd like to speak with you while you're here."

There was a little glow in Zarah's demeanor. "Me? You want to speak with me?"

"Yes, you," Madeline said and gave a faint nod.

"Yes, I'd be honored."

Madeline quickly pushed the elevator button, desperate to

avoid Sherry. Talking with Joel's wife was a risky move, but one Madeline was willing to make. The door closed and carried them upstairs. Madeline hustled to her office. By now Kay should have given up the futile search although Madeline didn't see her from a quick glance down the hallway.

Madeline's assistant stopped her. "No one can find the file that you wanted."

"Oh, don't worry about it, I'm sure it will show up," Madeline said, hustling Zarah into her office. She wasn't about to make the same mistake Sherry had. Madeline closed the door as they entered. "Have a seat," she said, pulling out a chair at the meeting table. "How's the U.S. treating you?"

"It is good."

"How about marriage?" Madeline asked, opting not to squander the time with small talk. Zarah's eyes filled, which was awful to Madeline. Based on the crying she'd heard coming from Sherry's office a few minutes ago, she didn't believe there could be any tears left. "Can I get you some water?"

"No, I'm fine."

"You're clearly not fine." Zarah was getting to Madeline. She tried to console Zarah while delicately remembering her reason for calling her into the office in the first place. "Perhaps I can help you." She had Zarah's complete attention. "Once upon a time, I lost my husband's affection."

"Were you able to get it back?" Zarah seemed to become livelier.

That was a dicey question to answer, requiring more hours than there were in a year. "Yes, in many ways, but what I went through, you don't have to. There's a better way for you."

"Tell me, what can I do?" Zarah said, wiggling to the edge of her seat, sitting like an elegant Indian princess. If charming looks were an indicator of contentment in a marriage, Zarah would have no problems.

"Your husband is stressed over the company's situation. It's not doing that great."

"I don't know much about his business or my father's."

"I know, but that's where I can help you, because I do. I'm one of the founders of this company." Madeline was focused. She had Zarah captivated and wasn't going to let up. This was the break she needed and was probably the only chance she had of staying at DMI. She pulled out every roadblock in her mind that said *don't go too far*. "I'm also Joel's stepmother. I know him very well and what will make him happy." Madeline knew she was a likely candidate to be struck down by lighting at the very second for telling such a bald-faced lie. She'd worry about the consequences later. The fish was dangling on the hook now and required action if it wasn't going to get away.

"Tell me, please, what should I do for my husband?"

"You own the West Coast division of DMI, right? Well, sell it to my son."

"I don't understand," Zarah said, her enthusiasm slightly fading, but not by much. The poor woman was so desperate to save her marriage, it appeared that she was willing to try anything.

"If you sell the division, Joel can have the cash that he needs to save the rest of the company."

"I'm not sure," Zarah said, fidgeting constantly now.

Madeline wasn't going to let her off the hook. She was too close. If she could get Zarah to sell the West Coast to Don under LTI and if Don could get the Southern division from Joel's investors, that would be it. Joel would be finished. He'd be forced to resign in total shame and bankruptcy, titles he'd rightfully earned.

"Your husband is struggling. He has no one else to help him but you. If he can get rid of the pressures at work, he will have more time and energy at home. Do you follow what I'm saying?" Madeline said.

"I think so, but do you think this will help him, truly?"

"Yes, and yes, a thousand times yes. This would change his life, and that's for sure." Madeline should have felt guilty for deceiving Zarah, and she did, but not enough to retract the offer. Joel could have stepped down on his own terms months ago, but he hadn't. He was the one who elected to play the game to the death, and Madeline was gladly obliging. Zarah wasn't getting out of the office without an agreement. "So what do you say? Are you willing to sacrifice for your husband's happiness and for your family's honor?" Madeline wasn't sure honor mattered but had a pretty good feeling that would carry extra weight in Zarah's decision.

"Yes, I will do as you say."

Madeline wanted to scream out in joy but couldn't get too excited. She'd been let down countless times before. This time she'd leave emotion outside the door, even her empathy for Zarah, and let her business sense drive. "Zarah, one last thing that's very important: you can't let Joel know about this until it's done."

"Do you think that's wise?"

"Absolutely. Like I said, he's overwhelmed and couldn't dare take on another project. Let my son Don and I handle this. Let's keep this from Joel until it's done. Then you can make the announcement, give him the cash, and watch his reaction. I'd love to be there for that special moment," Madeline said, sincerely wanting to be there when Mr. Joel found out that his reign of terror was over with the knockout punch coming from his timid wife. The thought alone gave Madeline zeal.

"You will have to work with my father's attorney."

"No problem, we will work with whomever you tell us. This will happen very quickly and hopefully you'll be able to share the news with your beloved husband by the weekend. Wouldn't that be special," Madeline said.

"Yes, indeed it would."

"Remember," Madeline said, placing her index finger on her lips, "not a word to anyone, not Joel, or his mother, or the people at your house until it's over."

Madeline couldn't wait to get Zarah on her way and to tell Don the unbelievable news. The transaction had to be quick, before Zarah changed her mind. Working with Mr. Bengali's attorney might be a problem, especially since she didn't want Joel to know, but that was a chance she was more than willing to take. Madeline ushered Zarah to the elevator and sashayed back to her office. Inside she closed the door, paused, heaved a sigh, and pumped her fists into the air screaming silently. Victory was hers.

chapter
70

Zarah bounced around the estate, pleased that she could help her husband. She found Joel in his office after eight P.M. "I've waited for you. Can we please eat dinner together tonight?"

"Not hungry," he said. "You shouldn't have waited around for me."

"I wanted to wait. It is my pleasure to wait for you."

"Well, don't do that, don't wait. I'm very busy and you never know how late I'll get home, if at all. You have an assistant who should be eating dinner with you every night if she wants to keep her job."

"Ana does eat with me and I'm very grateful to have her here. She gives me someone to talk to so I'm not alone here." She longed to have him look at her, see her standing in the room. Soon, once she could give him the money from selling the company, it would be better for her and her husband. He could be proud of her. She anxiously awaited the news from her father's attorney.

"I'm going to be very busy the rest of the evening. I'm going to ask you to leave me alone for a while so I can get started," she heard him say.

Zarah was saddened and left as asked. Soon the marriage

would change. He would find pleasure in her if she tried harder to be a good wife.

Joel messed around his office for hours, using the room as a safe haven from his obligations. He couldn't hide out indefinitely, so settling for a few scattered hours were sufficient.

Around ten P.M. the phone startled Joel as he laid his head on the desk. It took several rings before he was alert and ready to answer the call. Musar's attorney was on the line. "Kumar, how can I help you?"

"Zarah called today. I wanted to speak with you about selling the West Coast division of DMI. I know she has her heart set on selling it, but I wanted to make sure this is truly her desire."

Joel heard Kumar speaking but couldn't make sense of the conversation. There had to be a mistake. "What did you say about Zarah?"

"She rang me earlier to ask about selling the West Coast to someone at DMI."

Joel was completely awake, but remained baffled. "You said Zarah called you?"

"Yes, Zarah."

"Why would she call you, I mean, who is she trying to sell the division to? Why?"

"I don't have the name, but I wanted to speak with you and her to confirm everything before I prepared the papers. It's no problem with the request. As sole owner, it is your decision."

Joel wished it was his decision, but he realized Kumar meant that it was Zarah's, and hers alone. His hostility burned as he was reminded of her hold over him and DMI. The more he reflected on the news, the more his hostility boiled. How could she sell off his West Coast division behind his back? Her betrayal was crippling, maybe because he never saw it coming from someone like her. He'd let his guard down around her, totally vulnerable.

"Please, tell her to ring me again."

After the call concluded, Joel sat stiff, unable to move or process the conversation with Kumar. He finally mustered the energy to confront Zarah and sought her out in the master suite. He burst in, searching from room to room until he found her sitting in the small reading room near the rear of the five-room suite. Simple courtesies were discounted. "Zarah," he said, calling out to her. She jumped to her feet and approached him. He put his hand up like a stop sign. "I just got a call from Kumar about the West Coast division." Her gaze dipped. "You're trying to sell the West Coast division?" She didn't respond, slightly trembling. "Did you hear me?" Still no response. "Zarah, talk to me. What's going on with the West Coast?"

She mumbled. "I want to be a good wife." He let her continue. "Mrs. Mitchell told me that I could help you with money."

"My mother had no business telling you that!"

Zarah's gaze stayed on the floor. "Not your mother."

"What other Mrs. Mitchell is there?" he said and had a deep chill shiver his body as the answer popped into his mind—Madeline. "Are you talking about Madeline Mitchell?"

"Yes."

"What were you thinking?" he yelled, driving her to tremble frantically. Joel was beyond furious, not sure if Zarah or Madeline should bear the brunt of his contempt. There was plenty to share. How dare Madeline approach his wife and convince her to betray him! Didn't Zarah understand that the West Coast and his financial recovery were the only factors keeping him in the marriage? If she faltered on either, the marriage was as good as over for him. He didn't have to serve the total three-year sentence. He could break free at any time. As mad as he was, sooner sounded better. "What kind of a wife betrays her husband? The West Coast rightfully belongs to my family. You're only holding it temporarily. I know you can't sell it to me yet," he said, unable to regulate the escalating volume in his voice. "If you sell it to anyone else, then I will consider it the most severe act of betrayal and will want nothing to do with you," he told her and meant it. Zarah wept.

Joel was consumed with fury, realizing he'd gotten the worst end of a bad deal. Most of his money was tied up in purchasing Harmonious Energy. His livelihood was saddled with the burden of a wife that couldn't or wouldn't fend for herself but was naive enough to sell a portion of his company off to the highest bidder. The anger continued blazing as he thought of Madeline, Zarah, and what they'd done. A divorce was the logical reaction but abandoning the marriage this early into the arrangement would nullify any claim he had on restoring his money and the company.

Joel didn't care what time of day or night it was. Madeline had crossed him for the last time. He was going to scour the streets of Michigan until he found her. She wasn't about to get away with attempting to underhandedly steal his division without retaliation.

His Lamborghini swerved around cars, although there wasn't much traffic after eleven o'clock in the evening. Didn't matter. He had to show his ability to take charge and maintain the lead, falling second to no one in traffic, in life, or in the boardroom.

The route to Madeline's house wasn't fresh in his memory. There had been rare opportunities to go there, a few times as a child with his father and none as an adult. The car crept along roads in Rochester Hills looking for the address he'd pulled from his executive directory. Convinced he was in the right area, Joel peered into the dark of night looking for the wrought-iron gates lining her estate. Suddenly, there it was, the sprawling residence taking up the length and width of a square block. He pulled up to the gates, which were closed with no guard. Joel wasn't giving in this easily. He'd scale the fence to get in if necessary. Madeline had willfully crossed the line time after time. It was his turn to return the favor. He first opted to buzz the entry button and did with no response. He buzzed again and again, laying on the button and contemplating his next move. The rage he'd strapped on at home hadn't diminished. If anything, it had gained momentum.

"Yes, who's there?" he heard the voice say, barely audible coming over the intercom.

"Me, Joel, let me in."

"What do you want?" she blasted.

"We need to talk, right now." He could have taken the calmer approach. After all, it was nearing midnight and his tone might scare her off. Then again, it was Madeline. She wasn't easily frightened. As a matter of fact, she was probably waiting on his visit and had already prepared the estate for an attack.

There was a buzzing sound followed by the twelve-foot double gates opening slowly. It took nearly a minute before they were fully open. He dropped the car into gear and skidded along the extended driveway until he hit the bend where it began to curve around and approach the house. He came to a screeching halt near the front of the mansion, not bothering to use a parking spot. Joel whizzed to the door and rang the buzzer incessantly.

chapter

71

Madeline quickly changed into a pair of street clothes as she fumbled with the phone, trying to simultaneously call Don. Claiming a small victory, she had him on the line. "Son, you probably need to get over here."

"Why?" Don asked, sounding mostly awake.

"Your brother has gone ballistic. I just let him in the gate."

"Why did you do that if he's ballistic?"

Joel was out of control and crazy, too, when it came to running DMI, but he wasn't stupid. He wasn't about to show up at her estate with the intent of doing anything except spew off a little steam. That was the most power he held, as he would soon find out. She was eager for the party to get started. "I better get downstairs before he breaks my doorbell," she said, fired up and eager for the fight.

Don sighed. "I'm on my way. I'll be there in ten minutes."

"Take your time," she said, laughing. Madeline heard the doorbell repeatedly buzzing. She was dressed but chose to take her time descending the stairs and getting to the door. It wasn't because she was waiting on backup. The thrill of making Joel wait and further dangling control on a string in front of him was too tempting to pass up. Perhaps she'd get a cup of chamomile tea before opening the door. Then the banging began after about five minutes. She bolted to the door and snatched it open. "Boy, have you lost your mind, banging on my door? This is genuine hand-crafted solid wood," she said.

Joel pushed by her and entered the foyer. "I couldn't care less about the door or you."

"My, my, aren't we in a tizzy. How can I help you?"

"You know why I'm here," he said, spitting and sputtering with his index finger pointing at her.

"What's the problem now? You have so many that I can't honestly keep them straight. Can you?" she asked, enjoying her position, not frightened in the least.

He stepped closer. That took her by surprise, but nothing near panic mode. This was the nature of hand-to-hand combat. There were bound to be bruises in the process of determining the champion. "You tried to buy the West Coast division from Zarah."

"You mean your wife," Madeline said, reserving her amusement.

"You know who I'm talking about. You tried to swipe the division right out from under me," Joel said, taking another step closer.

Madeline stood her ground. "That's funny. I didn't realize you owned the division. Sounds to me like your wife is running your household and your business. What's she doing letting you out so late? Don't you have a curfew, young man?"

"Stop calling me young man, and boy, and this and that," he shouted. "I'm a grown man."

"Oh," she said, smirking.

Don burst into the front door. "What's going on here?" he said, immediately coming to her side and gripping her shoulders.

"Your mother and probably you, too, tried to steal the West Coast division from me. That's not happening."

"What are you talking about, stealing? Unlike you, we're offering a fair price in a fair deal," Madeline chimed in.

"You didn't come to me."

"You're right, I went to the owner, or have you forgotten your handcrafted predicament?" Madeline said, gaining greater confidence with Don by her side.

"Doesn't matter," he said with his head bobbing. "It's not for sale. My wife," he said with a scowl, "is retracting the offer. You lose this round."

Madeline wasn't totally shocked that Joel had found out about the transaction before it was finalized. The offer was a long shot from the beginning. She had lost the round, but watching Joel lose stability and toss that smug look of arrogance and the-world-rotates-around-me attitude aside was worth the effort.

"It's time for you to leave," Don told Joel.

"No problem," he said, appearing to intentionally brush against Don, "I've said what I came to say. This discussion is over, just like your run at the company is."

Madeline had more to level, but Don waved her off as Joel left.

"Mother, there's no reason to get yourself into situations like this with Joel. What if I wasn't here?"

"Oh," she said, "he's harmless, all bark and absolutely no bite."

"You don't know that."

"Well, he's gone and so is our run on the company." The confidence she exhibited in front of Joel left with him. "That was it, my last attempt to get the company for you. I'm tired of trying a slew of botched plans. Let God know that I'm done. I'm going to leave Him and his chosen son alone."

"Mother, you never give up. I'm used to seeing you fight to the finish."

"Well, wisdom says there's a time to call it quits. I'm older but I'm no fool. It's time for me to accept the way it is. This run is over."

"I want to be CEO."

"Do you truly mean that?" she asked, needing to be absolutely sure.

"Absolutely certain."

"Then I'm going to help you."

"How?"

"By taking the only option left to me, stepping down and getting out." She heard the words and couldn't allow them to recycle in her soul for fear of not being able to carry it out.

"What are you talking about?"

"Tamara's offer. I will step down from my position in DMI and leave Michigan."

"That's not what I want from you."

She laid her palm on his cheek. "I know, but it's done. I want my daughter home and my son at the head of this company. I'm the only one on earth who has the power to make it happen."

"I'm not asking you to do this."

"I know you're not. I'm volunteering," she said, gently patting his face.

"God has a plan."

"Can you tell me with absolute certainty that my leaving isn't a part of His plan?" Don's eyelids shut as he heaved a sigh. "No, of course you can't. The truth is that God has always been in charge, not Dave, not Joel, and definitely not me. I've put up a good fight, but I must tip my hat to the Master. He's the winner."

"But you make it sound like God has engaged in this master game with you."

She slowly pulled her hand away from his face.

"No, not at all. What I'm saying is that it's finally hit me: God hasn't changed. Whatever His plan was, it still is. The problem has been me trying to work my plan and insert it on top of His and it hasn't worked." She giggled.

"Now that's true. You have had some pretty lame schemes."

She let her grin widen, feeling the burden oozing away. "But some were pretty good, like the Chicago scheme with the two ladies submitting the same proposal for the DMI internship." It didn't work, but Madeline enjoyed the chaos it created for Joel at the time.

"I have no idea what to do with you except love you."

"With my faults and all." She drew in a deep breath, determined to stay on top of her feelings. They were trying to creep to the surface. "It's time that I make the ultimate sacrifice for the two most important people on earth, you and your sister. I've always told you that I would give my life for you."

"Mother—" Don tried to speak, but Madeline had to speak now or forever give up the opportunity to muster this level of courage again. It had to be now.

"It's done. Call your sister and let her know the answer is yes, with no strings or tricks attached." Her voice choked up and Don grabbed her. "Please tell your sister how much I love her and that there's nothing in this world I wouldn't do for her. Please tell her," she said, giving in to her pain and letting the manifestation of love flow freely down her cheeks.

chapter

72

Morning came slowly. Zarah was deeply wounded and alone. The disgrace she felt resonated. Layer upon layer of rejection pressed her further into the ground. She was useless. Her husband didn't find her desirable. He wouldn't allow her to bear his children. Her family would cast her away. There was no reason to get out of bed. Maybe if she wanted it badly enough, her transition could come swiftly and carry her to the next phase of life. There was nothing left in this phase for her. She lay on the bed, no longer wanting food, water, sleep, or comfort unless it was coming from her husband.

Afternoon shoved the morning out, and then evening took over. Day and night were the same to Zarah and both had come two or three times. She wasn't sure. Zarah hadn't moved from the bed. She longed to see her husband one last time, but he didn't come to the room. Her energy and desire to go on had completely faded. She began slipping in and out, sensing that her transition was close. Faintly she heard a voice in her sleep.

* * *

Joel rushed into the master suite. "Why didn't you tell me yesterday or last night that she was sick? What were you waiting on, the coroner?" he asked Ana.

"Mr. Mitchell, I sat with her. She didn't start to get sick until today."

Joel was fuming. "She didn't have any water, let alone food. Come on," he said, "you don't need a medical degree to see that there was a problem." He went to Zarah's bedside. "Zarah. Wake up, Zarah," he said, holding a glass of water to her lips. He wasn't sure if she could hear him, but he desperately kept trying to wake her.

Zarah showed movement. He was glad, choosing not to think the worst. "Zarah, drink this water," Joel said. This was proof that there was no end to his suffering. The favor he once possessed from Almighty God had vanished with no return in the foreseeable future. His plans and goals and dreams had crashed miserably. None of his recent maneuvering and positioning had progressed DMI, not like it had when God was a viable leader in DMI. He contemplated where he might have veered off course. A flood of scenarios rushed in. The possibilities were endless. Conversations he had with his father began pouring in, too. Without resistance, Joel uttered a silent prayer that she would recover, not sure what to expect.

Zarah sipped the water, helpless as a wilted rose. She deserved better treatment, he knew it. It wasn't her fault that she was born an only child, a girl, and had to rely on her father's vision and provisions to dictate her future. They had that in common. She wiggled a little, showing more signs of life. He set the glass of water on the table and stroked her hair, which had retained some of its silky sheen. He'd forgotten how striking she was at the wedding and was reminded as he caught glimpses of her laying on the bed, worn. Bronze-toned skin dipped in milk, pale looking, covered her petite frame.

Ana knocked on the suite door. "Yes," Joel said in a low tone, intentionally not yelling in Zarah's ear.

"Can I get anything for you or for Zarah?"

"No, you can go home early. I'm going to stay with her." Zarah reached out for him, weak. His phone buzzed in his pocket. He pulled it out and saw Sheba's number. He started to answer the call, and then gazed at Zarah. He'd have to call Sheba later, after Zarah was stable, strong, settled. He owed her that much, at least for the next two years and eleven months, or until she was able to take care of herself.

chapter

73

Abigail bopped up to the sixth floor again with a report in hand, looking for Joel. This was her second trip. "Is he in?" she asked Kay.

"Yes, he got in around two o'clock."

"Great, I need to see him."

"Why don't you go in and wait a few minutes? He stepped away but should be right back."

Abigail took the suggestion and went inside to wait. Her adrenaline was soaring. She replayed the events of the past year, unable to determine the precise incident or moment when Joel changed the outcome of his future. The golden path of wisdom and wealth had collapsed on him thanks in part to his string of women. He didn't think Abigail knew, but she did. She grieved for his situation while celebrating Don's long-suffering victory. For now, her immediate goal was to speak with Joel before Madeline and the board got to him.

Three minutes later he walked in. "To what do I owe the pleasure of this visit?" he asked in his typical Joel voice, but void of the seductive, flirtatious way that he mastered effortlessly.

Her shield was intact and working, at least so far. Constraining her affection for him wasn't as difficult as it used to be. After watching him deteriorate for six months, passion had transformed into pity. She set a copy of the report on his desk. "Take a look at this," she said with no further explanation required. The numbers spoke clearly.

Joel stared at the report, speechless, like she'd been earlier in the morning. "Have you confirmed this with George?"

"Yes, finance has confirmed the numbers. I've been working with him most of the morning. It's true. For the first time in the history of the company, DMI expenses have exceeded income for two consecutive quarters. We are officially in the red," she said, never having imagined uttering such a phrase and DMI in the same sentence. The news was surreal. "One of the main problems is that we've lost two divisions, which cuts sales on our books, but we're carrying the overhead costs on top of the dramatic drop in sales with the other two divisions."

"What you're saying is that we're covering the cost of those two divisions but not counting the income? That doesn't make sense."

"You're absolutely right. None of this makes sense. DMI can't sustain its own weight, and I can't figure out why these deals were structured like this. This makes no fiscal or operational sense."

Joel didn't defend his decision. Instead, he continued staring at the report as if he was drilling through to another world. "What should we do?" he asked, without raising his gaze from the lock he had on the report.

"You're asking me? You're the CEO," she said, meaning it. He was in charge, had been in charge, and wanted to be in charge. This was the critical time when a leader had to rise up, take control, and set the direction for the rest to follow. She wasn't convinced Joel had the gumption to do it. He was a stranger to her heart, generating a faintly familiar feeling. Staring at Joel, she was reminded of her treatment of Don: she'd cast his friendship aside as a second priority when it came to her devotion for Joel. Abigail was forced to question her judgment when it came to relationships. No time for that discussion. DMI was at the forefront.

"Who else has seen the reports?" he asked.

"Madeline probably has by now, which means Don, too. I've been trying to find you all morning to tell you." She paused, then said, "More like to prepare you. When Madeline sees this, she's coming after you. That's for sure."

"You're probably right," he said with no fight in him, which frightened her. "Abigail, I know that your trust in me is gone, and don't bother trying to deny it." She didn't try. "I'd like to know why you went out of your way to warn me, as opposed to blind-siding me with the other camp."

She had no explanation for the unsolicited courtesy other than Joel was truly in a bad situation this time. He wasn't going to easily get out of this one. His finesse was meaningless unless he could convert it to profit. She found no pleasure in beating a wounded dog, preferring to help the crippled animal to safety before the hunters got to him first. She didn't have to be in love with him to show mercy for someone who once held the key to her heart. She cared. That much was true and would most likely forever be.

"Where were you all day anyway?"

He shirked. "I had to take care of some personal business at home."

And personal it was. DMI business it wasn't. "You better take this time to figure out what you want to do. At any minute Madeline will be bursting through your door and you'd better be ready." She grabbed her folder and prepared to leave. "If I were you, I'd start with laying off a portion of the workforce."

"DMI has never had to do that," he said with a semblance of authority, but quickly tapered off.

"I know," she said, almost unable to contain her frustration, "but there's a lot DMI has never done, thanks to you." She did not mean it the way it came out. It didn't matter now. The hound dogs would have a sniff of the report very soon and would be hunting him down, out for blood. The time bomb was ticking. If he had an ounce of wisdom left, he'd pack up and go home.

"You think this is my fault, don't you?" he asked, catching her before she reached the door. She chose not to respond. "I thought so," he said in an unusually weak tone. "What do you think I should do?"

"I don't know."

"What would you do, honestly, what would you do in my position?" he asked. She absorbed his sincerity.

She turned and her gaze zoomed in to connect with his. "Honestly, if I were in your position, I would resign. I would count my successes and move on, but then that's me."

"Yes, that's you," he whispered and she left.

chapter
74

Sherry sat in the library with Zarah while Joel stood in the doorway, leaning against the frame. "You're looking much stronger," Sherry told Zarah. "We have to keep you eating."

"And drinking plenty of water," Joel said, generating a stir and expression of glee on Zarah's face.

I told you so would never roll across Sherry's lips. She knew, from the beginning, the marriage was a very bad decision. How bad, she had no idea until Zarah's bout with dehydration and depression. It was barely three months into the marriage and Zarah was suicidal.

"I'm feeling much better, much stronger today."

"Mom, I have to run back out for a while. Would you mind staying with Zarah a little while longer? I don't feel comfortable leaving her alone."

"I don't want to be a burden," Zarah said, appearing to become tense.

"Nonsense," Sherry said. "You're not a burden, you're family. Isn't that right, Joel?"

"Right," Joel said, saying very little.

Sherry knew Zarah had to hear the endorsement from her

husband, anyone else was a substitute. The clinging aura was recognizable, reminiscent of the time when she and Dave were together. Their beginning was blissful, dreamlike during the courting stage. From the moment he divorced Madeline and pledged his vows to Sherry, their romance changed, never to be fully recaptured again. Controversy had a way of choking the life out of euphoria and bringing a marriage to the depths of despair without warning. Sherry thought it even more likely to happen when the marriage was built on a shaky foundation, like hers with Dave, like Joel's now was with Zarah. She swallowed a sip of sorrow. The cycle of living in a distressed marriage of obligation had been passed from one generation to the next.

"Mom, can I see you in my office for a minute?"

"Certainly," she said, half afraid to leave Zarah for even a few minutes. Once a person willed themselves to death, they had to be taken seriously.

"Are you going to be okay for a few minutes?" Joel asked.

"Yes."

Joel didn't seem overly concerned about leaving Zarah for the few minutes or at least he concealed it well, so Sherry followed him down the hallway and into his office.

"Close the door behind you, please," he said, taking a seat.

The somberness in his voice wasn't typical of her son. She'd never heard him so monotone, so unenthusiastic. "What's going on? Is Zarah really okay?"

"Yes," he said, drawing in a long breath, eyelids closed, and letting his head lean back. "She'll be okay. As for me, that's a different story."

Sherry stood at the desk, near him, letting worry grow. "What's wrong?"

"I'm done."

Worry was rising . . . faster, stronger. "Done with what?"

"DMI is over."

Sherry dropped into the seat. "Why do you say that? We have endured a few tough quarters but I have faith in you."

"You're the only one. I'm even questioning my faith in me."

She didn't want to hear his despair speak this loudly. Defeat wasn't the core of Joel Mitchell. "Don't worry about Zarah. I'll take care of her. I'm sure that's weighing on your mind and keeping you distracted. I can stay here with her for as long as you want. Don't worry about her. Go to the office and take care of our company," she said, wanting to sound confident so that he would hopefully be inspired. He didn't need to know how frightened she was.

"She's only a tiny piece of my challenges at the moment." He opened his eyelids. "I wish that was my only problem." He grabbed a small rubber stress ball and squished it periodically in his palm. "Women, I can handle," he said as she squinted at him. "Well, excuse me, Mom, present company excluded," he said, grinning. She hoped there was more to come. He'd become her rock of support. Keeping him upbeat yielded an automatic benefit for her. "Seriously, I'm tired. I've played my last hand. I'm ready to fold in the deck and call it quits."

"You can't be serious. You've had tougher fights and never once were you interested in quitting. Madeline has tried and tried to drive you out of the company and you've beaten her every time. You're much smarter and wiser than she and the others who have tried to make your life miserable."

"Not this time, Mom. I didn't win." He extracted the report Abigail had given to him earlier. His mother didn't have to be a chief financial officer to understand the dire scenario the company was in. "See that," he said, pointing to the bottom line, "twenty million dollars short this month."

"It's not a lot. I can write you a check for that much."

"And what about next month, and the month after that? Are you willing to write a check each time? because I'm not."

"I don't mind investing into DMI if you need my help. That's not a problem."

"Mom, you don't get it. The money is only a small part of the problem."

"Then tell me what's wrong so I can help."

"The company is in a free fall. I've lost two of our four divisions. That's fifty percent of the company. They belong to some-body other than Joel Mitchell." He was too disgusted, remembering his father's admonishment. The words seemed fresh, yet he hadn't adhered to the warning and the results were final. His father was wiser than he'd given him credit for. DMI was no longer. His reign as the leader was coming to an end. "I don't have the ability to get this turned around in time."

"You don't have to give up. I won't stand for it. You deserve your father's company. He couldn't give you a sense of legitimacy growing up, but he entrusted you with his legacy. Sure, you're going through tough times right now, but that's no reason to quit."

He was shocked at how firm and resolute she was in wanting him to continue, but it wasn't in him. The Southern division was gone. The West Coast division belonged to Zarah, and in her frail state, he wasn't going to jeopardize her physical and psychological stability for business. "This has been a good ride," he said, stand-ing and tapping on the desk before walking toward the door. "Thank you for the vote of confidence. You're the only one who was with me from the beginning and never wavered." He scooped her up into his arms, grateful to have Sherry as his mother. His ex-istence had been livable during the early years, crammed with re-jection from others, because of her nurturing.

"Where are you going?"

"To prepare my resignation letter."

"No, Joel, no, at least wait until the morning. You might feel differently."

"I can wait, but my mind is made up. I'm tired." Saying the words gave him a surge of relief. The war was over. He'd lost to the seasoned warrior. Tonight he would collect his thoughts. Tomor-row he'd call Don. "God help me," he began uttering after Sherry left, intent on completing a full prayer for the first time in many months, longer than he could precisely recall.

chapter

75

Joel decided not to call ahead. He pulled into the valet parking, intending to run in and out. The valet approached his car. "I'm here to see Don Mitchell, my brother."

"Oh, I-I didn't know. I mean I haven't met you before," the valet said.

It was no wonder. Joel and Don weren't brothers, not really. "Do you mind if I leave my car here? I don't let too many people drive it." Actually, he didn't let anyone drive his car. The Lamborghini was his and his alone, one of the few things on earth that was.

"No problem, you can leave it here."

"You sure? Because I can move it to the side."

"No problem, here is good. If we need to move your car, we'll buzz Mr. Mitchell's unit."

Joel went inside to the front desk. He hadn't been to Don's condo in such a long time. He didn't remember the number. "Excuse me, I'm here to see Don Mitchell."

"And your name?"

"Joel," he said, questioning his conviction about being there. "Joel Mitchell."

"Mr. Mitchell, is Mr. Mitchell expecting you?" the security guard asked, then chuckled.

Joel chuckled, too. "I know, there's two of us, and no, he's not expecting me," he said, pacifying his urge to bolt from the building without Don knowing he was ever there. His rational thoughts said *no, stay.*

The security guard made the call and Don must have given the clearance because the guard beckoned for the lobby attendant. "Mr. Don Mitchell is waiting for you on the thirty-fourth floor. He's in unit eight. Will you need assistance in the elevator?"

"I can make it, but thanks." Joel wanted to dart in, handle his business, and hit the road. He entered the elevator, and when the doors opened Joel forced his feet to move. There was no changing his mind. This conversation was long overdue. Joel wasn't going to leave until Don heard from him. There he stood, in front of door number eight. He paused, collecting his thoughts and reinforcing his tenacity. He wasn't a loser. He was a man who understood opportunity and wasn't afraid to capitalize on it. He rapped on the door.

Don opened almost immediately and stood there, appearing dumbfounded.

"Your face says it all, big brother. You're totally surprised to see me here."

Don leaned on the door, nodding yes. "Let's just say my condo isn't on your list of frequently visited places."

"Haven't been here in at least what, six or seven years?"

"Something like that," Don said, firming his grip on the door.

"Well, this won't take long. I'm here to tell you that it's yours."

"What's mine?" Don said, planting both feet in the doorway and crossing his arms tight across his chest.

"DMI, it's yours."

"What is this, some kind of joke?" Don said, leaning on the door again.

"Trust me, this is no joke." Joel felt helpless in the hallway but wasn't about to ask to come in. There wasn't much else to discuss. It wasn't like they were going to share a cup of espresso and pass the time talking about current events. That was too farfetched for him and his brother to have that kind of relationship. He didn't dare dream of such a scenario. He let his concentration return to the moment.

"Then what is this about?" Don asked, not yet inviting Joel inside.

"I'm resigning, effective immediately."

Don burst out in laughter. "I know this is a joke now. What gives, little brother?" he said, zipping the laughter in a single breath.

"I have to step down." He didn't want to get into details about Zarah or her attempted suicide or his money woes. If he could resign and get out of there with a fraction of his dignity intact, then today could be redeemed and become something other than a complete disaster.

Don beckoned for him to come in. Joel hesitated and then accepted the offer, set on leaving quickly.

"Can I get you anything?" Don walked further into the condo. Joel remained by the door. "You want to take a seat?"

"No, I'm good. I've done what I came to do."

"Just like that, you're out, after the years of feuding with me and my mother for control of DMI, you're stepping down just like that?"

"Just like that," Joel said slowly, clearing his throat.

"You have to admit, this is hard to believe, at least for me it is," Don said.

"For me, too," Joel hesitated and then went on to say, "this wasn't how I saw this playing out, but circumstances happen, big brother. Life happens." The helpless sensation hadn't subsided much from being inside the condo. Joel was ready to go.

"Don leaned against the foyer wall. "Have you told the board yet?"

"Just you, you're the only one that I've told—and Don, I'd like to make the transition quickly."

"Like how quickly?"

"Today, if you can get the board members together today. I want out."

"I don't know if today will work." He could tell Don was contemplating the timing, but today was it.

"That's my offer. I don't know where my head will be on this tomorrow. If you want the CEO position, this is it, your shot, today. Do you want it or not?"

"Yes, yes, I want it. I'll get the members together. Don't you worry."

"Worries are something I have plenty of," he said, finding a shred of humor and spreading it throughout his crushed soul. "So, it's done," Joel said, turning to leave.

"I have to ask you, little brother, why are you handing over the company? I'll gladly receive it, but this doesn't make a whole lot of sense, knowing how attached you are to DMI."

There was plenty to say, to explain, to rationalize, none of which mattered. He opted to take the condensed response, the one that reflected the source of his agony and disappointment. "It's not the same DMI that I was chosen to run by our father. It's a different place with a different vision," he said. Joel had to get out of there. The space was closing in on him.

"That's a good point. What about Harmonious Energy? That doesn't fit in with the strategic direction of DMI."

"You can divest Harmonious Energy. That company belonged to my wife's father," he said, letting his gaze plummet to the floor.

"Are you all right?" Don asked.

Joel waved him off. "It's part of her father's legacy. I wouldn't ask her to give it up. Let's find a way to divest it from DMI."

"What about the West Coast division? Harmonious Energy owns it."

"My wife actually owns it outright. I can convince her to sell it to DMI if you want." It was becoming difficult to stay composed. He had to go and reached for the doorknob.

"I do want it back. What about the Southern division? How can I get that?"

The longer he stayed the more of his integrity melted. "Uncle Frank can help you with that one. All I can say is good luck."

"Uncle Frank? what does he have to do with this?"

"You don't want to know. Call him, if you want the Southern division. You might have a shot at it." He twisted the knob until it clicked and then opened the door. "My luck wasn't so good but, then again, you have a pretty important partner on your side."

"Who, Abigail?"

Joel pointed up to the ceiling. "I remember those days," he said, stepping into the hallway.

"God's love for you hasn't changed. He's right where you left Him." Don told him.

"Maybe so," Joel said and took the slow walk down the hallway. "I guess I'll have to see."

"Joel," Don called out. "Thank you. Seriously, thank you."

Joel pinched his lips together and kept heading toward the elevators. There was nothing left to say or do. It was done.

chapter
76

Don closed the door in a fog of doubt equally matched with certainty. Joel's visit left him pondering. Elation wasn't automatic. He was bombarded with questions, emotions, and reflections. Don tried to calm his mind, with no success. Anxiety and restlessness paralyzed him. Better to take a seat. Let his mind quiet so he could hear God clearly. The idea of Joel stepping down was too unimaginable. Don drew in the longest breath he could take and held it. If it were real, according to Joel he had to act without delay. If it was cruel trickery that Joel was pulling, Don didn't know what he'd do. He bolstered faith in the unimaginable by God's grace, grabbed his keys, phone, and exited the condo, setting out to claim his fate. He called Naledi, as soon as the valet retrieved his car from the resident parking garage, eager to share the news with her.

Ten thirty. Don rolled into the DMI parking lot letting his car creep down the first row, reserved for the executive team and handicaps. He stopped at the empty CEO spot and sat there. No one was behind him. He didn't want to use the spot yet. It was out in the open. He considered taking the CEO spot in the covered garage around back, but decided against it until he told Madeline and

Abigail the news in person. His victory was theirs also, especially his mother's. Today she'd planned to be in the office long enough to pack a few of her belongings. He couldn't guess how many boxes would be required to pack forty years of memories. She was adamant about leaving but unwilling to completely surrender her office. He understood, but none of that was necessary. The storm had passed and he was finally the one steering the ship. The precise position he wanted and had been destined to assume.

He walked in with an air of confidence, sure of his position, tough, when the gravity of the moment rushed him from the weak side and mentally tackled him to the floor. His body was standing while crumbling internally. He spoke to the people at the receptionist desk, made contacts with the small few in the lobby, and pushed the elevator button, appearing that business as usual was in order. His heart was pounding into his rib cage, blood rushing through his veins. He had to sit, quickly. Perhaps the realization of wanting something so intensely for so long and then constantly being denied it day after day had forced him to develop a protective shield. Pushing, scheming, planning, praying, hoping, and only recently preparing for this point in time, when he could claim the role of CEO.

His legs miraculously carried him to his mother's office without incident. Inside, he closed the door and leaned against it. "What's wrong with you?" Madeline asked, delicately placing a framed photo in a covered box.

"Joel stopped by my condo a little over an hour ago."

"That's a shock. What did he want? Did he threaten you?"

"Just the opposite," he said, standing in the same place and leaning against the door. "Joel has offered to resign."

Madeline stopped packing and said, "Quit being so mean, Mr. Mitchell. You see that I'm packing. I can't leave any faster. You and that sister of yours will have to wait a few more hours before you send in the buzzards to pick my bones," she said, wrapped in a dash of humor.

"Mother," he said taking his first step toward her, "I mean it.

This is no joke. Joel came to my place a little while ago to let me know that he's resigning."

She plopped into her chair. It was like watching the air deflating rapidly from a balloon. She should have been screaming with satisfaction, but none of that happened. The shock was too powerful, as it had been for him. He knew God was able to deliver, but Don wasn't looking for Joel to surrender.

"This is too much to wrap my brain around. Give me a minute," she said, grabbing her pen and tapping frantically. "Did he say why?"

"Nothing other than that he had to step down."

"Yes!" his mother belted out. "Finally, we drove him out." Madeline spun around in her seat, probably taking in the moment like he had.

"But we can't celebrate, not yet. I don't want to get too far ahead of myself until we have the board meeting."

Madeline glanced at her watch. "It's going on eleven." She seemed concerned.

"We have to act quickly."

"You're right, before Joel regains his senses, or do I mean before he loses them again? Oh, I don't know."

"Let's just say before he changes his mind again," Don said.

"That's it, exactly."

"Do you think we can get an emergency meeting together on such short notice? You seem to have the special touch when it comes to getting people here when they hadn't planned on coming," he said, taking a seat and relaxing a bit.

"Don't you worry, I'll take care of it. We'll have the board here for a three o'clock vote, no later than four." She picked up the phone's handset. "By the close of business today, you will be CEO." Her voice dipped. He was sure her euphoria was taking over. She waved him out. "Go, go get Abigail up to speed," she said, setting the handset down temporarily. She set the half-packed box in the corner of the room. He would have gotten it for her, but she didn't give him time. "Go, I have to pull a meeting together, the most important meeting of my life and of yours," she said, wearing a well-formed grin. "Don," she said as he reached the door. "Congratulations, son, on becoming CEO of your father's company. Better late than never."

He mouthed the words "thank you" and left. Abigail was next. Don walked past a few offices as Sherry met him in the hallway. She handed him an envelope. "What's this?"

"I came in to give you my resignation. I know Joel has resigned and I'm saving you and Madeline the trouble of firing me. I'll be out by this afternoon."

Don had forgiven his father for the actions of the past and had chosen to forget the pain and rejection that resulted throughout much of his life. The trip to Robben Island came to him. He wouldn't soon forget the stories about how Nelson Mandela was tortured in prison and forced to live in subhuman conditions. It was enough to spur a lifetime of bitterness. Yet Don vividly recalled the tour guide emphasizing how Mandela had forgiven his perpetrators and encouraged others to do the same. Don didn't profess to have the same conviction or calling as Mandela, but he understood the healing power of forgiveness. It was the only way to build a future. Don was willing to give Sherry the same grace. "I'm not accepting your resignation."

"What are you talking about? Take this. I'm leaving. I couldn't bear the thought of you firing me," she said with tears forming in her eyes.

He'd been fired by Joel and remembered how it felt. There was no need to force that gloom on her. "I have two questions. Do you want DMI to succeed, and do you feel like you have skills to contribute to the company?"

"Why, yes," she said without hesitation.

"Do you want to stay on board? That's the bottom line."

"I'm not sure. Joel needs my help with Zarah, and I don't know what I need."

"Then you decide. If it turns out that this is where you want to be, the job is yours."

Her gaze dropped. "Thank you for the offer. I honestly believe you're sincere, but I can guarantee you that with Joel gone, Madeline will make it open season on me. I don't have the stomach to keep fighting with your mother. Frankly, I'm tired. I did it for Joel, but I don't have to worry about that anymore."

"Like I said, the job is yours," he said, handing her the envelope and briefly letting his hand rest on hers. "Don't you worry about my mother. As CEO, my job is to protect the vision, the company, and each employee that God has allowed to work here, and that includes you."

Sherry let her eyelids close. The trickle of water glided down her cheek. "Thank you. I'll see how much Joel needs me, and who knows, maybe I'll be back."

"Do what you have to do. We'll be here." Don held her hand tight, and then, without reservation, hugged her. She relaxed her body and he could feel the tears through his shirt.

chapter

77

It wasn't official yet, but Don felt like the CEO-elect. Certainty showered him. Confidence poured into his spirit and he stepped firm, eager to tell Abigail. She'd weathered the DMI storm with him and deserved to know that the clouds had passed. He found her on the fourth floor in her office. "Knock, knock," he said, seeing her door opened.

"Come on in. Take a seat, Mr. Mitchell," she said, typing on her laptop and peering up at him a few times. "Are you here for a meeting?"

"I am," he said, not wanting to spill the news yet. "It's an emergency board meeting."

"Really," she said with curiosity piqued, evidenced by the giddiness in her demeanor. "I didn't realize there was a meeting."

"Well, there isn't yet, but there will be."

"What are you talking about?" she asked with her cheeks expanding as her countenance perked up.

"In order for me to assume the CEO role, we need a board meeting, don't we?"

"Don, what are you talking about?" she asked again with her

face contorted. He'd dangled the news long enough. It was time to tell her. Besides, he couldn't contain the excitement any longer.

"Joel came to see me a few hours ago to let me know that he's resigning."

Abigail sucked in unfiltered air as her mouth opened wide, then shut. Her hands ran up and down her face, rapidly, frantically. "Are you serious?"

"Very."

"I can't believe it. I wonder what happened. We've begged him to step down and he wouldn't hear of it."

She vividly remembered talking to him privately yesterday about the sales report. She'd strongly suggested that he step down in light of DMI being in the worst financial position the company had ever experienced. Maybe he heard her and was attempting to honor her appeal. There were any number of reasons why he'd left as abruptly as he had. She was relieved that he was no longer in a position to harm the company. At the same time, she was sad knowing he was most definitely wounded.

"It gets back to what you said in the beginning, that this is my destiny."

"And I know that it is."

"Me too. Months ago, I resolved in my spirit that if God wanted me in this position, then I'd make myself available, but the job of securing the position was on Him."

"That's funny you say that, because I was just thinking that only God could have changed Joel's heart so dramatically and so quickly. There's no other explanation for it."

"It goes to show that no matter how smart we are, or how we think a situation should turn out, God moves in His timing and in His way to fulfill His master plan. Our primary decision is do we want to play along or follow our own destructive path."

"I have to say," she said, leaning back and stretching her forearms and hands out along the chair arms, "when God works a plan, He works a plan."

She stood and went to him with arms opened wide, absorbing

the gravity of today's event. Neither rushed to break the connection. Don was relaxed talking to Abigail. She'd help calm him. He was ready for the meeting now. Nothing could go wrong.

Abigail couldn't move from her seat, stunned. Joel had actually resigned. Her questions were too plentiful to list. She reflected on the heartfelt times where they were inseparable, running the company with solid leadership, wrapped in vision, and secured with God's influence. Her soul saddened, remembering. Those days were never to be again. She ached for his predicament while reveling in the excitement of seeing Don finally succeed. He deserved the position. As a matter of fact, not only was he suited to run DMI, there was no one else with the integrity, relationship with God, and leadership skills that he possessed. The company was fortunate to get him. Abigail thanked God silently for Don as she twirled the chair around and stared out the windows.

What was next for her? Joel had a wife. Don had a lady friend. He wasn't married, but Abigail wasn't convinced that he was free. Her feelings were rampant. Maybe this was the time for her to make a change, start fresh, and broaden her horizons beyond the Mitchell compound. Before she let her mind career too far into the future or dip too far into the past, she had to complete a basic courtesy.

Abigail dialed Joel's number. She didn't know his home number since he'd moved into the new house, which wasn't an issue. She dialed his mobile phone, a number engraved in her mind from dialing it countless times during his better days. On the fourth ring she was ready to disconnect when he answered. At first she was at a loss of words. She was caught between wanting to reach him while not wanting to seem overly concerned. Abigail let the words find a way to the surface. "Don told us about your decision." Joel was quiet, which forced her to say something else. "I just wanted to tell you that I'm sorry things turned out this way. I really am sorry."

"I appreciate your call. I'm sorry, too."

Silence languished. Finally she sliced the quiet. "That's all I wanted to say. Take care of yourself." Before she disconnected, he called out to her. "Yes," she responded.

"I'm very sorry that our relationship was a casualty of this mess. Believe it or not, you have been and will continue to be someone very important to me."

She inhaled his words but didn't swallow. It didn't ring of truth to her. Joel was a wise man, or had been at one time. If she had truly been that important to him, he wouldn't be married or ousted from the company. When she thought about it, her feelings were of no consequence. Joel was defeated. There was nothing else she could do about his situation other than lift up a prayer for him every now and then. The rest was between him and God.

chapter

78

Madeline had pulled off the impossible once again. Less than three hours and she had gathered the other six board members, refusing to accept a single excuse. This meeting was too important. Her son was close to inheriting his birthright. She would have gone to pick up the members and hauled them to DMI if necessary. Gratefully, she didn't have to resort to extreme measures. They were there. She and Don made the count eight. Joel would make nine, but he wasn't present. Maybe he would show up, maybe he wouldn't. Regardless, the count would proceed without his presence just like it had when he was voted CEO based on a recommendation from his father. Although she acknowledged that it would be easier if Joel resigned openly in the meeting, instead of relying on an absentee letter. Then they wouldn't be forced to validate the authenticity of the resignation. Stalling the process gave Joel time to change his mind. She definitely wanted to bolt the revolving-door concept shut.

"Let's call the meeting to order," Madeline said.

"Should we wait for Joel?" one member said.

"No, we should proceed," Madeline responded immediately.

She was afraid to wait. What if he changed his mind or something jinxed Don's appointment, an outcome she couldn't bear.

Kay was taking roll when the door opened.

Madeline's nervous meter jumped into the red zone as Joel stood there.

"Joel," Don greeted. Joel eased into his chair. His demeanor didn't give any indication of what he was thinking.

Madeline wanted to proceed and get this over with. Either he was serious about stepping down and this would be an easy vote, or he wasn't serious and this meeting would be short. They would soon see.

"This meeting has been called because Joel has decided to resign," Don said.

"Is that true?" Madeline asked him directly, wanting it on the record.

"It is." He nodded, laying his PDA on the table along with his sunglasses. "I've decided to step down and recommend Don for the CEO role." Rumblings simmered briefly. "If it's okay with everyone here, I'd like to suspend the rules and go directly to the vote."

"Why are you resigning?" someone asked.

"I have personal obligations that will consume my attention for the immediate future. I can't give DMI the time required to get us back on track."

"Should you be stepping down when the company is in such a state of flux?" someone else asked.

Madeline didn't want them to bombard Joel. He'd made his decision and she wasn't going to let a series of congressional questioners derail the process. "Joel has made his decision. Let's honor his request."

"I agree," Don said. "He's already resigned. Let's respect his decision and proceed."

The first vote was taken to accept Joel's resignation. Seven votes in favor, one opposed, and Joel was an abstention. Simple as that, Joel was out. Months of scheming and plotting yielded no results. According to Don and Abigail, when God was ready for Don to take the lead, the door opened without opposition. Sitting in the boardroom watching the order of events unfold made Madeline a renewed believer.

"This next vote is to fill the position of CEO."

"Wait a minute," a board member interrupted. "We understand that Don is a Mitchell, but why should we vote him in as CEO? What's going to happen with his other company, LTI?"

"Don has already assumed fifty percent of our client base. There's not much left to claim. We should be so fortunate as to have him work with us," Madeline said, carefully articulating each word to be sure that they got the message. The top spot belonged to a Mitchell, period.

"Your questions are valid. LTI has assumed a significant number of clients who have left DMI," Don told them, much calmer and poised than she would have been. Joel sold the company in chunks out the back door and didn't get asked the tough questions. Don was working hard to save the company, and suddenly the leadership was awake and wanted to grill the rescuer. There was much Madeline could and wanted to say but she decided to stay out of Don's limelight. He was the CEO and could easily handle this bunch. "I have a management team in place to run LTI in Africa and Europe. Domestically I will be involved. My first order of business is to stabilize DMI by paying off the debt, spurring sales, and invoking confidence in the customer base. My longer term goal is to merge DMI and LTI into one international company once DMI is stable. Harmonious Energy will be divested, and we will attempt to regain both the West Coast and Southern divisions," Don said. The room quieted. His commanding and organized thoughts were well received. "Like I said, we have our work cut out for us, but this isn't impossible. We have the manpower and the vision to turn this company around, to turn it back into something more like a ministry focused on healing people. As CEO, I'm ready to take on the challenge, head-on."

"I've heard plenty," Madeline said, and others agreed.

The vote was taken, eight in favor, zero opposed, and one abstention. That was it. Don was the new CEO of DMI. He sat unresponsive. Joel scooped up his sunglasses and keys and headed for the door.

"Joel, thank you," Don called out. Joel didn't rush from the room. It was like he moved in slow motion. Once he had the knob turned, he left without a speech or good-bye or jab against Madeline. She was disappointed. The two had been in a constant battle, dueling at each opportunity. Watching her adversary crawl from the room chipped at her compassion. Joel had issues, but he wasn't a bad person. She really did hope he'd land on his feet. Kicking a wounded opponent didn't bring satisfaction, so she didn't. If Joel Mitchell was a wise man with strong genes, this wasn't over. He'd be back after regrouping. She was betting on it, actually counting on it. Of course he wasn't going to win, but Joel was engaging. No reason for him to know she was secretly rooting for him to recover, outside the doors of DMI, on another continent somewhere. So long as he stayed out of her son's way, Madeline had no issue with him.

The board members scattered, leaving Don alone. Three years and look at where he was, standing in the CEO position of DMI. There was much work to do. Joel had sold off half the company, squandered his funds, and Don had to restore DMI under the LTI umbrella. At least funding wasn't a problem. He'd amassed a mound of capital with the surge of business both domestically and internationally. Despair wanted to lay claim to his victory, reminding him of how poorly Joel had managed the company and what an awful state it was in. Why couldn't he have received it in the same condition that Joel had?

Don refused to let his victory be overtaken by vengeance. He reflected on how God's will hadn't change. The road map to destiny was lined with mistakes, successes, failed decisions, consequences, and so on. God had all the pieces when he crafted the path from start to finish. Just as Don wasn't intended to have DMI initially—Joel was the one chosen, and it was for a reason. Don acknowledged that Joel must have always been a critical part of the plan even when he couldn't see it. Adversity, too. God prepared him to lead, to embrace forgiveness, to exercise compassion, and to be steadfast in his beliefs. The adversity he'd endured was as much of a learning tool as the days he'd spent getting his MBA years ago.

His turmoil was settling down. After DMI and LTI were rolling along, Don planned to start a family. He couldn't help but to think about Naledi. She was perfect, attractive, smart, devoted, and secure. He didn't need to ask for more in a mate, but he couldn't discount Abigail. One day he'd take a bride, and confusion would not be a factor. Just like DMI, when it was time, God would direct the path for him to follow. He'd done it in business and God would do it with love. Don was sure of it and took comfort in not having to worry about selecting a mate. She'd be revealed in due season, just like the CEO role.

chapter 79

Madeline poked her head into the room. "What are you doing here?" she asked Don, who hadn't left the room although the meeting had ended over an hour ago.

He'd walked in faith for months. Witnessing an improbable feat humbled him. "I decided to spend some time alone with God." Don needed time to reflect, to unwind, to soak in the realization.

"I can't tell you how pleased I am," she said, giving him a quick tap on his back. "Our day has finally come." She took a seat next to him. "How does it feel?"

The feeling was indescribable. To want something so passionately for so long, despite the odds and challenges, and to finally see it come to fruition rendered him speechless.

"Don't try to explain it. Your face says it all," she said, beaming. He was excited about being the CEO, and the added bonus was seeing his mother finally get the best of the deal.

She patted his shoulder. "This is our day. No more Joel, no more Sherry, no more craziness." Her gaze eased down to the table. "We've won, hallelujah, we did it," she said, trying to contain a smile that refused to be suppressed.

"Actually, Sherry offered me her resignation letter earlier."

"Great."

"But I didn't accept it."

"Why not?" his mother asked, rearing back in her seat.

"There's no reason for her to leave." Don cast his gaze on his mother. He wanted to be sure she understood what he was saying. "We've been at war with Joel and Sherry most of my life. I'm tired and you should be, too. This is a time of healing for our family." Madeline tried to speak but Don wouldn't let her. "No exceptions, Mother. Let's concentrate on getting the company stabilized. I need all hands on deck to fix this situation, especially you and Abigail. I need you both now more than ever. There's a lot of work to be done and quickly."

"Well, I need to talk to you about that."

"Why, what's going on?" He didn't like the way she sounded.

"I'm leaving, just like we discussed."

"But you don't have to go now. Joel has resigned, and I'm in charge. You can stay put."

"No, I can't, not as long as I have another child out there who wants to come home," she said, sounding strong but appearing weakened by the notion of leaving DMI.

"You don't have to go. This is more your company than anyone else alive."

"You know I love DMI, but I love you and your sister more. If she wants to come home and I can help her, I'm going to do it."

"Where will you go?"

"I'm not sure. It's a big world out there, and it's high time that I explore it. Maybe I'll start somewhere along the Mediterranean. I could deal with some beach and sun for a while," she said, giggling. "But it really doesn't matter where I go. What matters is that Tamara comes back. That's my dream, to have both of my children working side by side, running the company that me and your father built. Now, that's your birthright, destiny, legacy, or whatever you want to call it. This is where you belong and this is where she belongs. I won't stand in the way."

Don appreciated his mother's consistent attempts to rescue her children, but he wasn't willing to let her go on the eve of his victory. He had to convince her to stay. "Like I said, it's time for this family to heal. We've had years of separation and that's behind us now. This is a new day, a time of forgiveness and reconciliation."

"If you say so, Reverend Don."

"I'm serious." Don glanced at his watch. "What are you doing this evening?"

"Packing. Why? Do you want to go to dinner before I leave?" she said in a chipper mood.

"Not dinner, England. You're hopping the plane with me tonight, and we're going to Bristol, England."

"What's in Bristol?"

"Tamara."

"Oh, she doesn't want to see me. Once you tell her that I'm on my way, she'll be packed and moved before we arrive." Mother patted his cheek. "Thanks for the suggestion, but that would be a wasted trip."

"You're absolutely right, which is why I'm not telling her."

"I don't know about that. Do you think that's wise? She might not be able to handle seeing me without advance notice."

"Mother, go home and pack a few items. We need to be on a plane by eight P.M."

"I don't know about this, Don."

"I do. Now go—that's an order. You know I am CEO now."

"But I am still your mother. So, what does that make me?"

"Loved," he said, not needing to say any more. They were going to be all right, each one of them—his mother, Tamara, even Sherry and Joel. He didn't know what the future held, but Naledi and Abigail would be all right, too. He stood, helped his mother stand, and left the room, turning the lights out behind him. His anxiety had been quieted and faith elevated, each fueled by the simple act of forgiveness. Every piece of the puzzle, including the inspiration coming from Nelson Mandela's incredible ability to forgive, was set in motion for this time. Nothing, not a single action or set of circumstances, was random. There was a God—he knew it. No one else could have crafted such a journey for his life, no one.

chapter

80

———————·———————

Don wasn't able to gauge his mother's emotional state. She took a nap during the seven-hour flight, talked sporadically, and ate a little. His mother was feisty, aggressive, and he appreciated the way she was. Witnessing the meek Madeline seemed too weird.

The flight landed safely as the morning light ushered them in. The line of traditional black British cabs lined the curb. "There's no need to wait for a private car," Don said.

"If you say so."

They grabbed a cab and settled in for the hour ride into the English countryside. Twenty minutes into the ride, Don asked, "Mother, are you okay? You're awfully quiet. I can't believe I'm saying this, but you're too quiet."

She giggled softly. "This is a major trip for me," she said, patting the back of his hand as it rested on his leg. "Thank you for doing this."

"I benefit, too. Having my mother and sister talking again takes the pressure off me."

"It's more than that and you know it." She patted his hand again. "You are an amazing man, not because you're my son." She gazed out the window as the car rolled along the countryside. "We're this close," she said, pinching her thumb and index finger together, "yet this far away," she added, spreading her arms farther apart. "I can't get my hopes up only to be crushed when Tamara runs away again."

"We have to have faith. God is able to work miracles, right?" he reminded her, not having recovered yet from his CEO appointment. "I have a good feeling about this. She'll be there, watch." Yesterday was the beginning of a new era for the Mitchell family. It had taken decades to dismantle the family. An enormous dose of forgiveness and grace saturated with time would be the building blocks to their healing.

The taxi pulled up to a very modest, almost dilapidated-looking building. The other four-story buildings on either side didn't look much better.

"Not exactly what I was expecting," Madeline said, and left it at that.

Don settled the bill and asked the driver to wait for their return. Secretly, he hoped to come back and tell the driver to go on without them. He and his mother would be visiting with his sister for the rest of the day. He hoped, prayed silently, and believed it possible. Madeline didn't jump out of the car. She remained seated. "Come on, Mother," he said extending his hand to her. "We're here. This is what you've wanted for a very long time. Don't freeze on me now. Let's go," he said, taking her hand and gently giving a tug.

"All right, all right, don't pull for goodness sakes. I'm getting out."

Don chuckled. "You have brutally raked Joel over the coals for years, but you get within a hundred feet of your daughter and can't move."

"Oh, funny, funny. Let's go, I'm ready, one way or the other. I have to get this over with. Either Tamara is going to see me or she's not. You're right, I'm not going to stand out here pining. Let's go. Which unit is it?"

"Twelve," he said, squinting at the tiny piece of paper extracted from his pocket.

Madeline went first. They calmly walked to flat number twelve. Madeline raised her hand to knock and then drew it back. She beckoned for Don to knock instead as she stepped to the side.

A few knocks and the door opened.

"Don, what are you doing here?" Tamara shouted with a glimmer of enthusiasm.

"I had to come see you."

"Come on in," she offered.

"I brought someone with me." He reached for his mother. "It's been long enough," he said as Madeline stepped into view, "don't you think?"

Tamara didn't move, Madeline either. They stared at each other in silence. Don had lit the flame. Keeping it burning required their effort.

"Hello, Tamara," Mother said, more guarded than Don had ever dreamed possible.

"Mother," Tamara responded. They continued standing, neither budging nor attempting to close the divide. "I've been expecting you."

"You have?"

"I have from the moment I left Detroit. One day I knew you would find me."

"You haven't made it easy."

"But one day I knew you would."

"Did you want me to find you?"

"I think everybody wants to believe there is someone in the world that cares enough to never give up on them."

"Sweetheart, I've never given up on you," Madeline said, taking two steps toward Tamara. "I've never stopped loving you, never," she said, taking the third step, slowly erasing the gap.

Madeline did away with courtesies and grabbed Tamara as she crossed the threshold, holding on for a while before it was reciprocated. Don was content watching them. He squeezed past them,

unwilling to disrupt what had taken fourteen years to form. The flight back to Detroit and the road to total family restoration were long and possibly filled with turbulent times, but so long as God was navigating the course, Don was willing to hop aboard. Life was good and getting better. He'd tell the cab driver to go on. It looked like they would be staying for a while.

Reading Group Guide

MAKES YOU GO *HMMM!*

Now that you have read *Destined,* consider the following discussion questions.

1. Do you believe that Don's feelings for Naledi are genuine or more of a rebound situation? Is it fair for Don to pursue Naledi if he has unresolved feelings for Abigail? Who is most likely to end up with Don? Why? Do you think Naledi will let Don go without a fight?

2. Joel went on a roller-coaster ride from being obscure to a highly popular and successful businessman to one of failure and disgrace. What did he learn? What could he change?

3. Will Madeline ever accept Sherry? Is she justified in her bitterness toward Sherry? Did Madeline still love Dave? If so, is it realistic for her to maintain feelings for an

ex-husband after so many years, in spite of their public disagreements and failings? Will either woman remarry?

4. Tamara mentioned that she was the oldest child. What are the pluses and minuses associated with her return to town? What role in DMI does she deserve? Is she coming back purely for financial reasons? When she returns, do you think she'll help Don keep the peace or create new problems?

5. Do you see Joel fostering a legitimate relationship with his wife? Will he stay and have children or divorce in three years? What about Sheba: do you see Joel giving her up? For biblical drama, read about the Queen of Sheba's visit to see King Solomon. (1 Kings, chapter 10)

6. Do you want Madeline to stay and help Don stabilize the company or leave so that Tamara can have the space she requested?

7. Does Don have to worry about a comeback from Joel? What would it take for Joel to be back on top? Was Uncle Frank correct: will Joel be back for more money from the "private investors"? What about Zarah—can she be strong enough to take control of her part of the business and become a threat to DMI?

8. What is Abigail going to do now?

9. What is Madeline's best and least favorite attribute? What is Joel's?

10. King David was a mighty warrior who defeated the giant (Goliath) as a young boy. He was honorable but also a man plagued by horrific challenges and sin that fell upon his family. Yet David is not remembered for

his shortcomings. He's revered as "the man after God's own heart." Why isn't he framed by his mistakes? Does forgiveness always, sometimes, or never erase consequences? (Question also posed in *Chosen* study guide.)

11. Dave Mitchell created horrific chaos in his family. Do you believe he suffered to the same degree as his family?

12. What was Big Mama's (the church mother) message to Don? Why wasn't Joel interested in her advice?

13. Abigail was hurt by Joel's rejection and marriage to Zarah. What do you think about Joel moving another woman into the house that Abigail designed? Will Abigail ever be freed from Joel emotionally? What do you think about a woman harboring feelings for two brothers? Does their being half brothers and/or estranged brothers affect your answer?

14. Forgiveness is liberating, as evidenced by Don and Nelson Mandela. How about you—is there anyone you need to forgive in order to move forward? What's the difference between forgiving and forgetting? (Hint: One acknowledges the decision and the other represents the actual act of making it happen.)

Acknowledgments

I extend a heartfelt thank you to my readers. I pray this novel will inspire you to use your talents, discover your purpose, and embrace forgiveness.

In addition to my Haley, Glass, Tennin, and Moorman family, I'm blessed to have a long list of supporters. Thank you for the constant encouragement. Big thanks to the ones who consistently cheer me on while I'm writing, editing, and promoting. They include my best friend and devoted husband Jeffrey Glass, our beautiful daughter, my family Rev. Fred Haley, Gloria, Freddy Deon, Daisy, Frances, Deacon Rome, Deacon Bob, Emira, Leroy, Dee, Toby, Robert, Rena, Roscoe, Pat, Eddie, Regina, Dr. Leslie, Eldridge, Susan, Larry, Jeraldine, Kenny, Tasha, Lori, Coleman, Leslie, Audrey, and my advanced editors: Emma, Laurel, Dorothy, Tammy, K.D., and Renee. Special thanks to my agent, to the Simon & Schuster team, to David Almack, Shirley Brockenburough, Beulah Grove, Milwaukee Alumnae-DST, New Orleans Alumnae-DST, to many book clubs, and booksellers.

While I was editing *Destined*, my mother (Fannie) was diagnosed with a brain tumor. I couldn't have finished this book without the support of so many who helped us through that time.

That includes my family, friends, New Covenant Church, Delta Sigma Theta Sorority sisters (especially my own chapter—Valley Forge Alumnae), readers, literary colleagues, and fellow believers. Words can't express my appreciation to those who prayed, called, visited, and gave so much support. I couldn't possibly list you individually, but you know who you are. I do, however, have to personally thank the 'A' team (my family) who volunteered to drive hundreds of miles each way to get my mother home since she was out of town when this happened. Thank you to Uncle Ben, Aunt Ada, Michele, Nic, Liz Glenn, and Katie Jordan. Your act of love was overwhelming. Thanks to the Lord, my mother had immediate surgery and a miraculous full recovery with no long term affects.

I will always honor the memories of my father, 'Luck', and brother, Erick, in my writings.

P.S. Happy 80th birthday to Uncle Cliff Tennin and 75th to John Foots, Sr. Congratulations Dana Reed, Brittany O'Neal, Kayo Bakare, my niece Ashley Tolbert, and goddaughters Rochelle Burks, and Nicole Prothro on their graduations. Much continued happiness to Donald and Mary Bartel on celebrating over sixty years of marriage and to Uncle Charlie and Aunt Mary Lou for fifty years. Life is grand and God is good.

Acknowledgments

———◆———

I extend a heartfelt thank you to my readers. I pray this novel will inspire you to use your talents, discover your purpose, and embrace forgiveness.

In addition to my Haley, Glass, Tennin, and Moorman family, I'm blessed to have a long list of supporters. Thank you for the constant encouragement. Big thanks to the ones who consistently cheer me on while I'm writing, editing, and promoting. They include my best friend and devoted husband Jeffrey Glass, our beautiful daughter, my family Rev. Fred Haley, Gloria, Freddy Deon, Daisy, Frances, Deacon Rome, Deacon Bob, Emira, Leroy, Dee, Toby, Robert, Rena, Roscoe, Pat, Eddie, Regina, Dr. Leslie, Eldridge, Susan, Larry, Jeraldine, Kenny, Tasha, Lori, Coleman, Leslie, Audrey, and my advanced editors: Emma, Laurel, Dorothy, Tammy, K.D., and Renee. Special thanks to my agent, to the Simon & Schuster team, to David Almack, Shirley Brockenburough, Beulah Grove, Milwaukee Alumnae-DST, New Orleans Alumnae-DST, to many book clubs, and booksellers.

While I was editing *Destined*, my mother (Fannie) was diagnosed with a brain tumor. I couldn't have finished this book without the support of so many who helped us through that time.

That includes my family, friends, New Covenant Church, Delta Sigma Theta Sorority sisters (especially my own chapter—Valley Forge Alumnae), readers, literary colleagues, and fellow believers. Words can't express my appreciation to those who prayed, called, visited, and gave so much support. I couldn't possibly list you individually, but you know who you are. I do, however, have to personally thank the 'A' team (my family) who volunteered to drive hundreds of miles each way to get my mother home since she was out of town when this happened. Thank you to Uncle Ben, Aunt Ada, Michele, Nic, Liz Glenn, and Katie Jordan. Your act of love was overwhelming. Thanks to the Lord, my mother had immediate surgery and a miraculous full recovery with no long term affects.

I will always honor the memories of my father, 'Luck', and brother, Erick, in my writings.

P.S. Happy 80th birthday to Uncle Cliff Tennin and 75th to John Foots, Sr. Congratulations Dana Reed, Brittany O'Neal, Kayo Bakare, my niece Ashley Tolbert, and goddaughters Rochelle Burks, and Nicole Prothro on their graduations. Much continued happiness to Donald and Mary Bartel on celebrating over sixty years of marriage and to Uncle Charlie and Aunt Mary Lou for fifty years. Life is grand and God is good.